GUMSHOE
IN THE DARK

Also By Rob Leininger

The Mortimer Angel Series
Gumshoe Rock
Gumshoe on the Loose
Gumshoe for Two
Gumshoe

Other Novels
Richter Ten
Sunspot
Killing Suki Flood
Maxwell's Demon
January Cold Kill
Olongapo Liberty

GUMSHOE IN THE DARK

A MORTIMER ANGEL NOVEL

ROB LEININGER

OCEANVIEW PUBLISHING
SARASOTA, FLORIDA

ISBN 978-1-60809-433-2

Published in the United States of America by Oceanview Publishing

Sarasota, Florida

www.oceanviewpub.com

10 9 8 7 6 5 4 3 2 1

PRINTED IN THE UNITED STATES OF AMERICA

For Pat, as always.

ACKOWLEDGMENTS

Thanks to everyone at Oceanview Publishing for taking on another "Gumshoe." You guys make dreams come true. And a big thanks to author John Lescroart for his encouragement, friendship, and for acting as a sounding board and wailing wall as needed. You rock, John.

CHAPTER ONE

ONCE UPON A time, on a day that had its ups and downs, I found the decapitated head of Reno's mayor in the trunk of my ex-wife's Mercedes. Mayor Jonnie Sjorgen had been missing for ten days and his disappearance had made national news. He was a shithead, but that in no way detracted from the fact that finding him was a major coup and a real feather in my cap—a promising beginning for a private eye not yet four full hours into his new career.

But that was old news, *and* the myriad body parts of other missing people I'd found in the two years since. Now it was Sunday, 9:05 p.m., and I was on Highway 6 out of Tonopah, Nevada, twenty-odd miles east of Warm Springs, moseying along in a rental Chevy Z71 short-cab pickup, no room behind the seat for anything more than a jack and a jack handle, trying to locate one Elrood Wintergarden for the law firm of Brady and . . . okay, just the one guy in the cluttered and cramped law office of Stanley Brady, PLLC, a fifty-something alcoholic barrister, the unlikely executor of the estate of Mildred Castle, 79, who had died of smoke inhalation in the form of unfiltered Camels. Unbeknownst to clueless great-nephew Elrood, 25, he had inherited $680,000, or would if he could be located within four weeks of Mildred's death—a caveat in her will that indicated she understood Elrood better than he understood himself. If he couldn't be found within four weeks, the money would default to half a dozen no-kill animal shelters in Nevada, Idaho, and Montana. Having learned something about Elrood, I figured some of that fortune would go up in a cloud of marijuana smoke or up his nose in the form of expensive white powder—*if* I could find him within twenty-five days. The clock was ticking.

Elrood.

Parents with a *Star Wars* fetish and a sense of humor?

Not that I have room to talk. My name is Mortimer Angel. *Mortimer*, of all things. My mom must've come up with that before she'd fully recovered from the stress and pain of childbirth. It could also have been payback for the trauma since I was born cesarean.

So I was on the road, headed for Ely, Nevada, Elrood's last known or semi-probable location. I had a recent photo of the guy, which showed a thin handsome face with a fair bit of bad-boy punk in it, pierced eyebrows, dark hair, dark eyes, hair uncombed in a bad-boy, devil-may-care way. He was six-one, a hundred sixty-five pounds, basic high school education, no college, no trade school, responsible to no one but himself and not doing a bang-up job of it. The last girl I'd spoken to said he was a charmer, that she could talk with him for hours—which actually meant he was a good listener. Bad boy was going to get almost seven hundred thousand dollars. This is how life laughs at the rest of us.

I had no motel reservation and no timetable. Just the way I liked it. When life gets planned down to the second, there's no room for surprise. Might as well watch *Gilligan's Island* reruns. No surprises there either.

Just be careful what you wish for.

* * *

Dusk. Faint pink glow lingering on central Nevada's mountaintops far to the south, heavy blue-gray brooding clouds headed my way from the north, lit from within by an occasional crackle of lightning, wind kicking up. A cool mid-August misty rain had been falling for the past half hour with the promise of more to come.

As I topped Black Rock Summit, 6,257 feet, I glanced in the rearview mirror. Behind me, the two-lane highway I'd just traveled was empty for eight or ten miles. Ahead, the road was empty for as far as I could see. This was one of the loneliest regions in Nevada—nothing but high desert scrub and brown mountains all the way to a horizon of yet more mountains and desert scrub. The temperature was 61 degrees outside and dropping fast.

I jerked my foot off the gas as a jackrabbit sprinted across the road in front of me, missing the right front tire by less than a foot as it made it across. Barely.

When I looked up, I saw someone at the side of the road a hundred yards ahead. Looked as if they might have a thumb out, but it was too far to see much in the drizzle and failing light. I didn't see a vehicle anywhere around. It didn't look like a breakdown, unless they had abandoned their ride and were hoofing it.

"Bad news," I muttered, leaning forward to peer past the wipers flicking across the windshield.

When I got within fifty yards, I determined it was a girl in a short skirt, *very* damn short, and a skimpy top. And, yes, her thumb was out.

I smiled wryly. Couldn't help it.

I'd thought that old post-IRS karma was defunct now that I'd married Lucy, a one-in-a-million girl, but evidently I was wrong—not that I was about to stop and unwrap this gift. Not that it *was* a gift, either. What do I know about karma? But from my first day as a private eye, a modern-day Sam Spade, pretty girls had flocked to me like pigeons to a statue. No kidding.

That pigeons thing wasn't my fault, not that I minded it. Best I could determine, it was my reward for discovering I had a soul after working sixteen years for the IRS as a field thug, then telling the bloodsuckers to take the job and shove it, as the song goes. Shortly after my forty-first birthday, I started a new career as a private investigator—a gumshoe—at my nephew's PI firm and never gave the IRS a backward glance other than to thank a constellation of lucky stars that I was no longer in that game.

So, lonely road at twilight, cold rain falling, a girl in marginal clothing with her thumb out. I had a momentary flash that she might have something to do with a couple of teenage girls who'd been missing in Reno since Friday, but I shook it off. Reno was two hundred miles away, this girl appeared to be alone, and my impression in the uncertain light was of a female somewhat older than a teen, though first impressions are often wrong.

I ran the passenger window down a few inches in case she wanted to yell at me, which I thought was likely.

One way to avoid trouble is to avoid trouble—which was a Zen proverb or something I'd gotten from a fortune cookie. I slowed the truck to thirty, gave the girl a closer look as I blew on by.

"Hey," she yelped.

I glanced in the rearview, hit the gas.

"Hey! Hey, you . . . *fuck*!" Her voice faded as I put distance between us. She watched me, one hand on a hip. The other might have been holding up a single finger, but that observation, done in a mirror through a rainy window, wouldn't hold up in a court of law.

I smiled, ran the passenger window up again and kept going, but retained the half-second retinal image I'd gotten as I went by.

Anywhere from sixteen to thirty years old—hard to tell at that speed and in that light. It was possible she was one of the two missing girls. She wore what might have been a running outfit. She had on sneakers or jogging shoes. In that fleeting glimpse I got the impression she was less than five-six and under a hundred thirty pounds.

"Beautiful," I breathed.

Not the girl. The situation.

Whatever it was.

*   *   *

If she was one of the two missing girls, I was about to make national news again. In fact, there seemed to be a lot of missing people in Nevada right then. Nevada's attorney general had also been missing the past three or four days. The stories were competing for headline space, but the two girls, being young and innocent, were in the lead locally. Nationally, our attorney general was ahead by a nose.

The girl on the road was too young to be the A.G., so I didn't have to worry about finding another famous missing person. Chances were she was nothing more than a girl in a bad place, bad situation, needing a ride.

I was on a long sloping downhill run that angled north half a mile or so beyond the girl. I could see for miles. No lights headed this way. No lights of any description in the wilderness. I pulled off the road and stopped, dug a pair of binoculars out of a duffel bag on the passenger seat. The binos were one of my private-eye tools. The .357 revolver in the bag was another. The rain kicked up a notch as I was scanning the gloom ahead. Miles of empty road stretched out ahead, not a light anywhere.

"Girl," I said to myself. "You are in deep shit."

Or would be, if not for me.

I did a three-point turn and headed back.

She was staring my way as I drew near. I slowed, went thirty yards past her, hung another U-turn and came back. I stopped on the two-lane road, left the engine running, and ran the passenger window down.

"Good evening," I said genially. Up close, I pegged her at twenty-five, give or take. She wasn't one of the missing teens. Too bad, actually. Finding one of them alive would have been terrific.

This one was exceptionally pretty, a green-eyed beauty with short butter-blond hair, slender, small-breasted. Her skirt was the shortest I had seen in forever. Her tank top was soaked, hugging her body like a second skin. Water dripped off her hair into her eyes.

She stalked to the window with a blue purse slung over one shoulder, lips tight, eyes narrow. "You just went on by," accusation heavy in her voice.

"Yes, I did. Then I came back."

She stared at me. "Why?"

"Thought you might want a lift."

"I mean, why'd you go by in the *first* goddamn place? I was just . . . I'm all alone out here and it's getting dark and it's *raining*."

"Uh-huh. Allow me to repeat—do you want a lift?"

"What do you *think*?"

"Dunno. Give me a moment to work it out."

I sat there, seeing what she'd do. Put a little stress on a person and they'll show you who they are. I took in her tank top—wet, tight, no protection at all in this weather.

"Oh, for *heaven's* sake," she said. "I don't *believe* this." She dug a nasty-looking little matte-black automatic out of her bag and aimed it at me through the window. It looked like a .38 or a 9mm. It might as well have been a cannon. "Get out," she snarled.

So *that's* who she was. Great. Just my luck.

"Hey there, girlie," I said.

"Don't 'hey girlie' me. Leave the engine running and get out. I am *so* not in the mood for this shit."

"Oh, c'mon. You can't—"

"Last chance. Get *out*. I'm not gonna ask again."

Okay, time to do as she asked. She might not want to shoot me, but with strangers you never know. I grabbed my bag from the passenger seat and slid out.

"Jesus," she said, looking at me over the top of the truck. "You're . . . huge. How tall *are* you, anyway?"

"Six four."

"Wow." She wagged the gun to her left. "Go around the back of the truck and *stay* there."

I did, as she went around the front through the glare of the headlights. The rain increased, coming down pretty hard. The temperature had dropped another five degrees in the past ten minutes. A jagged flash of lightning struck the earth, briefly lighting up black clouds to the north. Five or six seconds later the boom of thunder reached me.

Shit.

She was going to leave me there, thirty miles from the nearest town of any description, but I had two ways to stop her. I picked the milder of the two. As she got behind the wheel and banged the door shut, I got a folding knife with a serrated blade out of my pocket, crouched by the right rear tire and sawed through the valve stem, taking it clean off. Air whistled out.

"Sorry about this," she yelled as the passenger-side window slid up.

Well, good. At least she was sorry I was getting soaked in jeans and a thin cotton shirt.

She put the truck in gear and took off, air blasting out of the tire. I picked up my duffel bag and trailed along at a good clip, anticipating that she wouldn't get as far as she thought she would. As I went, I dug the revolver out of the bag and held it out of sight by my right leg.

The truck picked up speed, faltered, slowed, came to a stop in the middle of the road eighty yards away. Cut off a valve stem and tires go flat in a hurry.

The girl left the headlights on and got out. "What the *fuck*!" she yelled, not at me, presumably. More likely at the vagaries of the world.

She circled the truck, checking tires, then crouched by the flat right rear as I came up behind her.

"Trouble?" I asked, aiming the revolver somewhere to her right, finger outside the trigger guard.

She stood up, unarmed. She was somewhat smaller than I'd thought when I first drove by. Five four, maybe a hundred ten pounds. The word *petite* was made for her.

"You cut the . . . the tire thing?" she said. Then she noticed the gun in my hand. "Oh, shit."

"Yeah. We need to talk, kiddo."

* * *

But, first things first. Her clothes couldn't hide a pair of nail clippers much less a gun, so her automatic had to be in the cab. I backed her off fifteen feet into the desert and kept an eye on her while I opened the passenger door. I left the engine running. The dome light was on. Her pistol, a Beretta Nano, was on the passenger seat where she could reach it from where she'd been sitting behind the wheel. It was a 9-millimeter, not my favorite caliber but big enough.

Lightning flared again, bright on chromed surfaces. The boom of thunder came four seconds later, telling me the lightning was closing in on us.

I popped the magazine, racked the slide to eject the round still in the chamber, then tossed the gun to her. She caught it one-handed. Deft. I picked up the bullet I had ejected and thumbed the rest out of the magazine, put the magazine in a pocket of my jeans, bullets in another.

"Now what, mister?" the girl said, walking tentatively toward me. She stopped out of my reach. With hair rain-plastered to her head she looked and sounded a lot more polite than she had a minute or two ago.

"Like I said, you and I need to talk." I gave her a look. "*Without* guns. No one is going to get hurt here. Not me, not you." I swung the cylinder out of my Ruger and made a show of dumping the bullets out into my hand, made sure I got them all, then swung the cylinder back in. I shoved the bullets in a pocket, kept the gun in one hand.

"Get in," I said, indicating the passenger side.

Her skirt was blue with a black hem on the bottom edge. As she climbed up into the cab, I caught a glimpse of panties—a lighter shade of blue than the skirt. I shut the door, went around to the driver's side and got in, banged the door shut. The dome light went out so I reached up and turned it back on. I put the Ruger in the door's side pocket, out of her reach, wiped water out of my eyes. She sat there, holding her gun in her lap, turning it over in her hands.

"Might want to put that in your purse, bag, whatever that is," I said. It was made of canvas, not very big.

She looked at me, sighed, stashed the gun as another flash of lightning lit the interior of the truck. She jumped when it hit, hunched her shoulders as thunder rolled over us. In a small voice she said, "You said no one was going to get hurt, mister."

"And no one will. What's your name?"

She hesitated, then, "Harper."

Unlikely.

"Harper what?"

"Leeman."

She shivered. Goose bumps stood out on her thighs. I kicked the fan up another notch. The truck was canted awkwardly to the right. We were in the middle of the road, lights on, engine going. I activated the emergency flashers to keep anyone from slamming into us in the dark.

"How about you show me a driver's license, Harper?" I would call her Harper until I got her real name.

She frowned at me. "Seriously?"

"Yes, seriously."

"You . . . you're not a bad guy, are you?"

"Last I checked, no. But if I were, would I admit it? So why bother asking?"

She sighed again, opened her purse, dug out a wallet, pulled out a license and gave it to me. She hugged herself, still cold.

Harper Ann Leeman, street address in Vegas, age 28.

I gave the license back. So, okay, Harper it was. "Says here you're old enough to know better than to aim a gun at anyone, Harper."

"I know. I'm sorry. Really. For . . . well, you know."

I smiled because her voice was so much softer than before. She was trying to play nice, so I would do the same. Unnecessary confrontation is pointless. "Why do you have a gun?" I asked gently.

"Just . . . protection. My mother insisted. I've had a concealed carry permit for four years."

"Huh. You should brush up on the basics."

She looked away, then back at me. "Um, what's your name?" she asked shyly. "Since you know mine."

"Mort. Short for Mortimer."

"Kind of an odd one, huh? Different, like mine."

"My mother had a wicked sense of humor. Still does. I haven't forgiven her yet."

She smiled. "Did you have a hard time with that name in high school?"

Strange question. Felt like she was trying to get on my good side. Okay by me. "Not too much. As a sophomore I was six-two and on the varsity football team."

"Lucky you. A few girls called me Harpy. There's not much good about that—a shrew, a leech, a nasty creature in Greek mythology."

"They were probably jealous."

That comment got me a cautious look. She took a deep breath. "Okay. So *now* what, Mort?"

"Now I have to change a tire in the rain. *Cold* rain, with lightning getting closer. So thank you."

"I said I'm sorry."

"Want to change the tire? If you're really sorry, that would be a friendly gesture."

"I don't know how. I've never changed a tire before."

"Which means you've got Triple-A, right?"

"Well, yes. But I've never had a flat tire before either. So, you know, the situation never came up. The only thing Triple-A ever did for me was when I had a dead battery."

I had all the bullets in my pockets and the magazine from her pistol. That might be safe, but she could have a spare mag in her purse, not that it would do her any good. This truck was staying right here until I changed the tire.

She didn't resist as I took her purse from her, but she looked worried. She sat as far from me as she could get. No spare magazine in the purse so I gave it back to her.

"What were you looking for?"

"Another magazine for your gun."

"I . . . I wouldn't do that. Now. Really. I've never done anything like that before." She looked at me, then looked away and shivered.

"We can talk about it later. How about you stay put, keep out of the rain and be a good girl while I get wet, cold, and dirty with nothing but the light of a cell phone to work by now that it's almost pitch-black outside."

She gave me a hopeful smile. "Really playing this up, aren't you?"

"It's all I've got, Harper. I use what I've got."

"Anyway, I really *am* sorry. I was just . . . *so* angry, that's all. It wasn't you."

"Uh-huh. To show how sorry you are, how about we say you owe me a dinner, my choice of restaurant."

She smiled and looked happier. "Okay, yes. Deal."

I switched off the engine to keep from getting gassed out by the exhaust. I cut the headlights, left the emergency flashers on, then opened the door and got out.

The jack was behind the driver's seat in the cab, and the spare tire, of course, was tucked beneath the truck in the most inconvenient place ever devised by man to keep a spare. I got on my back on the asphalt and worked my way under the truck, set the phone on my chest for light and tried to turn the wing nut holding the spare underneath.

By the way, when you have a flat, the truck gets lower to the ground, so muscling the spare out from under the truck is *harder than it needs to be*. Tell the guys at Chevy. And, yes, I *knew* I could jack the truck up to give myself a bit more room, but I'm the kind of guy who thinks about how it would feel if the jack slipped. The wing nut fought for a while since it had rusted some, and when I finally got the tire down and onto the road, it was dead flat. Beautiful.

Right then the heavens opened and what had been too much rain turned into a freakin' deluge, laced with hail. A fork of lightning hit less than a quarter mile away. I had a hand on the tailgate when it hit and I felt the truck jump.

"Sonofabitch!" I growled.

The truck was a rental, not yet two years old. Wasn't checking the condition of the spare before vehicles left the yard on the to-do list, or was that too hard since the spare is almost inaccessible *under the sonofabitchin' truck*?

I got back in the cab and turned on my cell phone.

"I already tried," Harper said. "There's no coverage out here." She had to raise her voice to be heard over the rain hammering the roof inches above our heads. And *hail*.

Of course there wasn't, but I gave it a try anyway. "Guess what?" I said while my S10 searched hungrily and futilely for a cell tower.

"What?"

No signal appeared on my phone.

"Don't ask," I said.

"*You're* the one who asked."

"Did I? Okay, then, guess what? The spare is flat."

She stared at me. "So . . . what? We're *stuck* out here?"

I looked out the windshield at the night and gave that some thought. We had three good tires on a truck that typically ran on four. We were roughly thirty miles east of Warm Springs and about that far west of the next so-called town, Grange. So-called because calling Grange a town was a stretch. I'd been through there a time or two in the past twenty years and it was a general store and a sad-looking 76 gas station sporting a single pump built around 1935. The U.S. Postal Service didn't waste a zip code on it. I don't know why anyone bothered to give the place a name, but it's possible someone at the 76 station could change a valve stem or patch a leak.

"Now," I said, "you get to hold a light while I get that right rear tire off."

"What for? I mean, if the spare is flat."

"Trust me. I'm not in the mood to explain right now."

"It's raining like crazy out there. And *hailing*, Mort."

She probably said my name to get on my better side so she wouldn't have to get out. Which wasn't gonna work.

"Really?" I said. "Rain and hail? I hadn't noticed. Get out. Please."

I got out, came around and opened her door since she was still inside. "Let's go, girl. Time's a-wasting."

She wasn't happy about it, but she got out. It took five seconds for her to get about as soaked as if she'd just come out of a swimming pool. Me too. Good thing the hail was only quarter-inch bits, but they stung all the same.

"Give me some light," I said. I crouched by the right rear tire with the lug wrench as she shined her cell phone on it. Two minutes and a few cuss words later, the lug nuts were off. I bent down and positioned the jack, racked it up enough to start taking weight off the tire, then told Harper to get back in the truck.

"Gladly," she spluttered, spitting water.

I jacked the truck up far enough to get the tire off, then put it in the back of the pickup, far left side, as far forward as it would go. A nearby flash of lightning dazzled me as I set the spare on top of the other tire. Thunder was like a cannon going off right by my head. Perfect. I quickly jacked the truck down. And down, and down as the truck canted farther and farther to the right.

Shit. It wasn't going to stabilize on three tires.

I opened Harper's door. "Out. I need you to hold the light again."

In fact, I could've done this last part without light, or I could've held the light myself, but why *shouldn't* she be as cold and wet as I was?

"What for?" she said.

"Out."

"That lightning is getting awfully *close*, Mort."

"I hadn't noticed. Out, please."

She got out and followed me around to the left front tire. She held the light as I took the cap off the valve stem and began to let air out.

"Seriously?" she said. "We've only got three tires and you're letting the air out of one of them?"

"Patience, girl."

"Anyway, all you're doing is pushing in the air thingie, so why can't I go back inside?"

"I have to know when this tire's down far enough." A bogus explanation, but I wanted her cold and wet, too, so we could share and treasure this moment together.

"Far enough for *what*?"

"Patience."

I screwed the cap back on the stem when the tire felt slightly squishy, maybe twelve or fifteen psi left in it.

"Okay, get back inside," I told her.

"*Gladly.*"

She went. Around back, I lowered the jack some more. The truck still tilted down toward the right rear wheel, but it felt like the balance was close. I took hold of the wheel well and lifted. It took fifty or sixty pounds to rotate the truck until it sat level.

"Gettin' there," I breathed with rain and hail coursing under my collar and down my back.

I opened her door. "Go sit on the driver's side, Harp."

She smiled. "You called me Harp."

"Yes, I did."

"My friends call me Harp."

"Consider me a friend, now scoot over."

She clambered across the center console. I averted my gaze as she went. Man, that was a hell of a short skirt.

I lifted the wheel well again. With Harper behind the wheel the truck was almost evenly balanced on two tires, the right front and the left rear. I could rock the truck from side to side without much trouble. Lifting slightly harder, I could rotate it onto that squishy left front tire.

"Might work," I muttered to the night.

I opened the driver's-side door and put the jack and the lug wrench back behind the seat. "Scoot over, friend."

The truck tilted to the right as she moved over. I put a foot on the floor of the cab and the truck rolled back to the left. We were right at the point of balance.

I weigh two-ten. Harper probably weighed somewhere around one-ten soaking wet, which she was, which made it more than a little obvious she wasn't wearing a bra under her tank top—not that I notice things like that—though I *did* see *Billa-Bong* written across the front.

When she was in the passenger seat and I was behind the wheel, the balance felt loose, sloppy, but I thought I could make it work. I'd put the right rear tire in the back of the truck to get that thirty-five pounds as far to the left as I could. We were still damn close to tipping to the right. If we did, we would land on the tireless right rear wheel and the somewhat-deflated left front tire would lift off the road and the steering would probably go to hell. Which was bitchin', but there wasn't anything to do now but give it a try and give God a laugh.

CHAPTER TWO

I FIRED UP the engine, put it in drive, took off slowly. It didn't take long to discover that acceleration would lift the front of the truck, tilting us to the right. Hitting the brakes tilted us to the left, which was good, but brakes weren't going to get us out of the hills and down to Grange. I took it out of gear, eased off the brake and, engine idling, let the truck roll downhill under the force of gravity. That got us going too fast, so I rode the brake a little.

"Why'd you let air out of that tire?" Harper asked.

"I'm trying to get the truck to tilt to the left, away from that missing tire in back."

"Super. So we're running on three tires."

"Two and a half, actually. Don't breathe."

"Okay, this is kinda scary."

"Scary? We're not going eight miles an hour. I could slam into a moose and it wouldn't hurt us a bit."

She smiled. "You know what I mean."

Yup. Rainwater leaked out of my hair into my eyes. I wiped it away as I squinted into the night. The headlights lit the road ahead for fifty feet, then it was all flying water and black emptiness.

I almost lost it when the road began to angle left. The truck tilted to the right and I hit the brakes, steered to the right which I really didn't want to do, got the truck stopped half off the road.

"What happened?" Harper asked anxiously.

"I can't turn left without the truck tipping to the right. If it does, I'll probably lose the steering."

"That's so wonderful."

I knew what might fix this, of course, but Harper was still an unknown. I didn't know how she would take it.

"Harp," I said, probably too softly.

She looked at me. "Oh, no. What?"

"I've never driven downhill in the dark in a rainstorm on two good tires and a squishy third tire before. I'll have to try something different, but I think it'll work."

"You think?"

"Not sure. Only way to find out is to give it a try."

"Okay. Whatever it is, do it."

"The thing is, you're not gonna like it."

"Don't tell me I have to get out and *push*. There's no way I'm going to do that."

"No, and that wouldn't help anyway. But the way I see it, you've got three choices."

"Me? *I've* got choices? Not you?"

"That's right. Given the circumstances."

She stared at me. "The way you said it, I don't think I'll like any of them, but . . . what are they?"

"One, because we're right on the edge of balance and your weight is helping tip the truck to the right, you get out and walk. When I get to the next town I'll get someone to come back for you. *If* I make it."

"Wow, that is *so* not happening, Mort."

"Thought so. Two, you get out and lie on the hood or hang onto the left front bumper to put more weight on the left side. I should be able to turn left that way, slowly."

"You're kidding, right? No way I'm gonna do that."

"Two down. Third choice is you can . . . okay, I need to explain something that I hope makes sense to you. We're balanced on two tires, the right front and the left rear, but it's damn close so we're tippy. To explain this, I want you to imagine a straight line drawn between those two tires."

She looked fore and aft between the two tires. "Okay. Not sure why, but okay."

"Where does that line pass through the cab here?"

"Well, between us, about through this center console thing. Actually, a little closer to me, I think."

"That's right. The weight of everything on *your* side of that line wants to tip the truck onto that missing tire. The weight of everything on *my* side of that line is helping to keep the truck upright on our two good tires—and the left front."

Lightning flashed, illuminating her face for a fraction of a second. Thunder boomed. "What you're suggesting is, I'm on the wrong side," she said after the noise passed.

"Not just suggesting, Harp."

"Which is why you wanted me outside on the hood in the rain on the left side with lightning all over—which, just so you know, still isn't happening."

"That's right. Which brings us to . . ." I paused.

"That third choice," she said, as I knew she would. I wanted her invested in this.

"Right," I said. "But you're not gonna like it."

She sighed. "What is it?"

"Don't freak out, but if you were to sit on my lap with your back against the door, your weight would be over here on the left side of that tipping axis."

"Sit on your lap?"

I shrugged. "That's right."

"Are you *kidding*?" She stared at me in the dim light of the dashboard. "You're not, are you?"

"Wish I were, because you look kinda hefty. But, no. This isn't some sort of an idiotic come-on, Harp. I'm very much married to an incredible girl, a *wonderful* girl. We're still newlyweds, actually. We got hitched last November."

"So this isn't . . . isn't . . . a sneaky ploy so you can, you know, like cop a feel or something?"

"Nope. I don't cop feels, although that's a nice use of 1950s vernacular. This is basic physics. If you move four feet to your left, we'll get a few hundred more foot-pounds of torque in the proper direction, which might keep us upright and get us out of these hills. There is one last-ditch, Hail-Mary option, though."

"What?"

"You won't like it."

"I'm sure I won't, if it's last-ditch. What is it?"

"You drive, I'll sit on your lap. I could get a few inches farther to the left. Our weight distribution would be better that way—if you could drive this thing with me on your lap, that is. Right now, we're riding a seesaw."

She shook her head. "Guess what isn't gonna happen because one of us weighs about as much as a grizzly."

"Back to the girl on the lap scenario, then."

Harper pressed her lips together, thinking as we sat unmoving in the dark, rain hammering on the roof. Finally, she said, "What's her name? Your wife."

"Lucy."

"And she's incredible and wonderful?"

"More than I can say. She's my entire life. Nothing at all will happen if you sit on my lap, I promise."

Harper was quiet for a moment. "What I'm wearing is all I've got with me, Mort."

I smiled. "I'm in the same boat."

"And this wet top is kind of—you know."

"No, I don't. I don't notice things like that and I have no idea what you're implying."

"I'm sure." She smiled, then bit her lower lip. "No other way to do this, huh? I mean, it's not like I'm totally against it since I'm pretty much a normal girl, but it's, I don't know . . . unexpected?"

"Life is like that. And, no, I can't think of another way to get us going since you're unwilling to cling to the hood—which is a pretty bull-headed stance if you ask me, not that I haven't had my share of trouble with women in the past. The last and final option is that we sit here listening to the rain and hope some friendly person comes along."

"Which means we could be here all night."

"That's possible. We've got enough gas to stay warm, so it's a viable option. Someone could come along in the next ten minutes, or not until sometime tomorrow."

"Got any food with you?"

"No. You?"

"Nope."

We didn't say anything for almost a minute. I let her work this out. Finally, she said, "I have the feeling you're a nice guy, Mort."

"Thanks."

"What I mean is, nice enough for me to sit on your lap without it getting too . . . too . . . you know."

"I know, and thanks again."

"And you . . . well, you're kinda good looking."

"Don't make me blush. I hate it when that happens."

She laughed. "Maybe I shouldn't have said that since this is what it is. But it's true, and it helps that you . . . oh *hell*, now I'm sounding kinda batty. Okay, let's give it a try. Just don't laugh at me or anything."

"I'll try to hold it in. Before you do this, I have to ask if that short skirt's gonna be a problem. Sorry, but I thought I better ask now, not later."

"It's not a *skirt* skirt. It's a sports skirt."

"Huh. What's the difference?"

"It's for women's sports. Mostly running, but you'd see them at the U.S. Open. That's tennis. It has a built-in liner, which is about the same as panties except it doesn't come out. Hope that's okay."

"It'll have to be, won't it? Although I'm not sure I get the difference."

"There isn't a lot, except you couldn't find a skirt this short in a typical women's store, like Everlane, Uniqlo, or Zara. Also, this liner is flirty. It was *meant* to be seen. If it bothers you, don't look. That's the best I can do."

Intentionally flirty. Okay, then.

She removed her shoes, knelt on the seat and turned around, scooted across the console and onto my thighs. Warm, solid, wet female butt pressed against me. I caught a scent of girl as she looped her right arm around my neck, lifted herself and snugged closer to the door, wedging her body between me and the steering wheel.

There was some grunting, not mine. After a while she said, "This isn't actually working all that well, so hold on while I get myself packed in here better."

Hold on to what? Maybe she meant "wait." I could get into trouble holding onto any part of her since so much of her was bare skin.

She pressed against my left shoulder, twisted her body a little, then put her left foot flat on the seat and worked her toes beneath my right thigh, up fairly high.

"Sorry about my foot," she said. "I don't know where else to put it. I hope this is okay."

"I'll live."

She smiled. "I thought you might."

Her left leg was bent almost double, which flipped her skirt up. Her panties, liner, whatever it was, was visible in the glow of the dash lights. Her left knee was as high as my chest, right leg across the center console. She was cold, still shivering, left arm across my chest, half hugging me. The only place for my left arm was behind her back and around her waist. The fingers of my left hand couldn't reach the steering wheel so I would have to steer with my right hand. All in all, it was hard to imagine the two of us getting much closer than we were.

"Omigod," she said. "This is so . . . I don't know."

"Surreal?" I offered. "Necessary?"

"Both of those, especially that second one—not that this isn't surreal. Can you drive with me like this?"

"I think so. If not, we'll stay here and sing show tunes until someone comes along."

"Ha ha. See if you can get us going now."

The truck was still angled to the right half off the road. I made a wide left turn with the truck feeling wobbly and unstable, got us back on the highway, headed downhill.

I eased us up to eight miles an hour. After a while I got us up to ten or twelve whenever the road ran straight or banked to the right, less than five when it ran left.

At that rate, Grange was at least three hours away.

Lot of time to get the feel of this girl.

I came close to laughing out loud at the thought, but I managed to hold it in.

CHAPTER THREE

Rain, rain, and more rain.

Heater going. Emergency flashers blinking to keep anyone from plowing into us, windshield wipers beating a tired rhythm, wet female rump on my left thigh.

The only thing missing was conversation.

"Harper," I said.

"What?"

"The name. Where'd it come from?"

"From the novel *To Kill a Mockingbird*, of course."

"Of course."

She smiled. "A woman named Harper Lee wrote it. You should know that."

"I do now, so there, smartie."

"When I was in the eighth grade, I checked a book that had something like twenty thousand baby names. Harper wasn't in it. My mother wanted to call me Ashley, but my grandmother was still teaching high school English when I was born and my last name is Leeman. Evidently Harper Leeman was too good an opportunity to pass up since it was so close to Harper Lee. My grandmother's always had a way of getting her way, so Harper it was."

"It's a perfectly good name. Different. I like it."

"Thanks. So is Mort. A little offbeat, which suits you. Anyway, I grew up with Harper so I'm used to it. That and Harp, like you've called me a few times."

"Which means I'm a friend."

"You *better* be, driving around with me like this." She wiped a damp lock of hair off my forehead. "Speaking of which, could I lean against you a little harder? It's not easy, trying to sit up like this and not press against you too much, but I'm getting kind of a cramp in my side."

"Sure. But before you do, let me say something."

"I think I know what, but go ahead."

"Maybe not. I'm happy to have you lean against me, but I want you to know there's no way in hell it will lead to anything. Sorry if that implies too much, but it needed to be said. I don't want there to be any misunderstandings here. I'm happily and thoroughly married. But the tricky part of this commentary and the reason I'm saying all this is that I *also* don't want you to think I don't find you quite attractive, because I do. It's just that I'm not tempted to let that run wild, though I *am* glad you don't have a beer gut, whiskers, and your name isn't Bubba, because if any part of *that* were true, you'd either be on the hood or we could park this truck right here until Christmas. I hope all of that makes sense and isn't too far out of line."

"It does. It isn't. It means you like women, but you're one of the good guys. I should be so lucky—which I haven't been, yet. I got divorced four years ago and things haven't been going all that great since. It's like all the good guys have been taken already. So, can I lean on you now?"

"Be my guest."

She tucked herself against me and settled in. I had a fairly small, firm, damp breast making itself noticeable and comfortable against my left side. Her right arm was draped around my neck, left hand resting on my chest. Her skirt was made of filmy material, flipped up in front by her leg. I got a glimpse of pale blue panties in the dash lights every time I glanced at the speedometer—couldn't help it, but it wasn't a problem since I have the self-control of an anvil.

We rode in silence for a minute or two, then she said, almost in my ear, "This is still fairly surreal, Mort."

"Yes, it is. An hour ago I was driving along minding my own business, thinking I'd be in Ely in two hours, get a motel room, a shower, and a hot meal."

She chuckled ruefully. "Sorry about this, really."

"Yup. Not sure I am."

"Oh?" She smiled. "Why not?"

"This'll give me something to tell at Lions meetings. It'll also be a terrific story for my grandkids when they get old enough to appreciate it."

"You're a member of Lions Club?"

"No, but I might join so I can tell this story and maybe get free drinks. We should take a selfie as proof."

She laughed. "You're a little bit wild, Mort. But I like that. You're not all . . . tight."

"So tell me how you ended up at the side of one of the loneliest roads in the country at dusk with rain coming."

"I got dumped. Well, not *dumped*, exactly. What I did was, I hitched a ride with this older guy after there was a bang under the hood of my car and my radiator sprang a leak about half a mile south of Goldfield on Highway 95 and steam blew all over the windshield."

"Very few people have radiators."

She thought about that, then hit my chest. "My *car's* radiator, fool."

"Ah, that explains it."

"Anyway, Goldfield's a sucky place to have your car break down."

"Gotcha. I've been through there lots of times." With Lucy, in fact, when we met at McGinty's Café in Tonopah a year ago. I'd known her less than an hour when we passed through Goldfield on the way to Vegas. Hell of a ride, that was. It changed my life. And Lucy's.

"It was going to take two days to get a new radiator in for a 2008 Corolla," Harper said. "Older car, I know, but it's nice not to have payments and it still runs great."

"Except when the radiator blew."

"Uh-huh. That was so weird. The guy said it might take him a day to install the new radiator when it got there since he was backed up with cars needing repairs. This older guy, Frank, was there when I walked up. He heard what happened after my car was towed in, told me he was headed up to Tonopah then over to Ely if I wanted a ride. I couldn't pass that up since he'd heard me tell the repair guy I was going to Ely to visit my aunt Ellen and she was expecting me. The mechanic told me Goldfield didn't have any car rental places. And who the *hell* would want to stay three days in Goldfield? So of course I said yes to Frank.

"Anyway, I was dressed like this because, well, I *like* it, and it was 106 degrees when I left Vegas. I was gonna drive all the way to Ely by myself, so what did it matter what I wore? It was still a hundred in Goldfield when my car conked out. Frank looked about as old as my grandfather so I figured it would be safe. I'm dressed okay, or thought I was considering how hot it is, or *was*. A lot of girls wear skirts like this running ten-Ks and marathons."

She looked at me. "I didn't expect to get this cold, or this top to get *soaked*, which is one reason I'm not wearing anything under it— which might be kind of obvious."

"I wouldn't know."

She smiled. "Aren't you nice?"

"Not expecting to get soaked was one reason," I said. "What's another, since we're talking about tops?"

"Well, I'm kinda small on top. I don't really need a bra so I don't usually wear one, as in about never. The only two I've got are back in Vegas. I hope that's not too much, you know . . ."

"Information?"

"Yes."

"Don't worry about it. Lucy doesn't wear bras either. Same reason. The two of you could be twins. But you didn't bring more clothes for the trip?"

"I did, but Frank *stole* them—sort of. He acted nice all the way to Tonopah and past Warm Springs, but then he started to look at me differently, kind of checking me out. Finally, he reached out and put his hand on my bare thigh, so I pulled out my little Beretta and made him stop the car and let me out."

"You got good use of that gun today, huh?"

She patted my chest. "I'm *still* sorry about that. After you stopped, I saw you looking at what I was wearing. I was tired. And cold. I thought I'd got rid of one lecher only to run into another. I'll want the magazine back for my gun, and the bullets, but I'm pretty sure I don't need them right now."

"Only pretty sure?"

She laughed. "I'm *sure* sure, Mort. Anyway, I've never had to pull a gun on anyone before in my life. I guess it shook me up. I wasn't thinking clearly. I should've ordered *him* out of the car, but I wanted to get the hell away from him. I got out and was about to get my travel bag out of the back seat when he gunned the engine and took off with all my clothes and stuff."

"Bastard." I put a fair amount of irony in the word.

"Well, he *was*." She fell silent. After a minute she said, "I'm not too heavy, am I?"

"Not sure. What do you weigh? One eighty?"

She slugged my chest, not too hard. "*Not* a question a gentleman asks a lady. And I'm either kinda heavy on you or I'm not, so you could've just answered the question." She pursed her lips, then said, "One twelve."

"That would be soaking wet, right? Which you are."

"Omigod, you're a *treacherous* brute, aren't you?"

"It's part of my charm. At a hundred twelve pounds you're not the most effective counterweight I could wish for. Steering is still iffy. Can you sit heavier?"

"Don't know how to do that. Would you like it better if I weighed two twelve?"

I looked at her. "Don't think so, Bubba."

She grinned. "Thought so."

"Do you work?" I asked, changing the subject.

"Sure. I teach high school in Vegas. English. I finished my fifth year at Palo Verde in June. And I coach girls' cross country and track. Sprints, long jump, pole vault. I coach boys' pole vault, too, because the other coaches don't know how. I vaulted in college. I had an athletic scholarship."

Figures. She was a little smaller than Lucy, but she had a solid all-girl feel, not an ounce of fat on her.

"Cross country, huh? You run with the team?"

She laughed. "Thirty miles or more a week. Closer to fifty in the off-season, which this is since school is out. I've run eight marathons. I ran Boston last year and two years before that. My PR is three hours, seven minutes."

"Just my luck."

"Why's that?"

"I couldn't outrun you if I wanted to."

She smiled at me. "Do you want to, Mort?"

"Not sure yet, but I wouldn't want to make a fool of myself." Her arms were slender, hard with muscle. In fact, she was slim and solid all over. "Let me take a wild guess—you pole vault with the team, too."

"Of course, showing the kids how to do it. It's amazing exercise. I've cleared thirteen feet eight inches."

"Wow. School record?"

"No. The coach doesn't get the record. And the girls' high school pole vault record in the U.S. is eight inches higher than my college best, so I'm just the coach."

I couldn't think of any major muscle groups that were left out in the pole vault. She and Lucy would get along great. Put them in bikinis and they would stop traffic.

I glanced at her. "Just so you know, I'll tell Lucy about all of this."

"Me on your lap, you mean?"

"That's right."

"No secrets from the wife?"

"None at all."

"That mean you'll tell her I pulled a gun on you?"

"Yes, but she'll like you anyway since you didn't pull the trigger. I know Lucy. You're two of a kind. And you teach English so it's likely you're both grammar Nazis."

"That sounds promising. What I mean is, you think she and I will meet sometime? Where *is* she, anyway? Why isn't she here with you?"

"She's in San Francisco visiting her mother. And I'm not willy-nilly driving around. This is a business trip."

I didn't tell her the reason for Lucy's visit, that her mother, Val, was scheduled for her first colonoscopy on Wednesday. Under the circumstances, that would've been TMI. And isn't *that* a perfect time to visit someone—when the visitee is having the time of their life in the bathroom?

Lucy's father, Ed, was out of town, *way* out of town, somewhere in Indonesia. Lucy was going to drive Valerie home after her procedure. Lucy was supposed to return to Reno on Friday, five days from now. It was possible this thing with Harper and the gimpy truck could affect that, but Val needed moral support and a ride, so I hoped it wouldn't. This was Sunday. I didn't want Lucy to cut her visit short if it wasn't absolutely necessary.

Harper's face was six inches from mine. "You think I might be a grammar Nazi?" she asked.

"You teach English, so it's possible. Lucy is."

"How old is she?"

Right then I ran over a four-inch rock in the road that lifted the half-flat right front tire and dropped it again. The truck veered left and tried to tip to the right. I yanked the wheel and hit the brakes.

We stopped in the middle of the road, angled a bit to the right.

"Wow," Harper said. "Close one, huh?"

"Very. We almost crashed at six miles an hour."

She pursed her lips. "Okay, not so close. It was kinda scary anyway."

I got us going again. The rain had eased off some, but the wipers were still on full to keep up with it. I stared into the watery night, feeling half blind. Good thing we hadn't been going sixty miles an hour. Six felt pretty slow, though, so I eased it back up to ten.

"So," Harper said. "Lucy? How old is she?"

"She turned thirty-two in April."

"How old are you, if you don't mind my asking?"

"I'll be twenty-two in October. Lucy's a cradle robber."

She smacked my chest again. "Have you turned forty yet?"

"Been there, done that. I'm forty-three and what's it to you?"

"You look good for forty-three, Mort. Scars and all."

"What scars?"

She laughed. "As if you don't know." With a finger she traced a thin scar that ran across the bridge of my nose and across my left cheek. "This. And I noticed you're missing a little bit off the top of your right ear."

"Really?"

"*Yes*, really. But don't worry. It suits you, gives you a rugged manly lumberjack kind of look."

I didn't know what to say to that. We rode in silence except for the drumming of rain overhead, then she said, "We've been talking a lot about me—too much. I want to know more about you since I'm on your lap."

"What about me?"

"Everything. Where you live, what you do for work. And here you are, driving around in the middle of nowhere and you don't have a change of clothes with you. I have an excuse for that, but why don't you?"

"This wasn't supposed to be an overnight trip."

"Yeah? What was it? I mean, here we are, tearing along at, what? Ten miles an hour? We've got time to swap stories. How much farther is it to Grange, anyway?"

"Best guess, about twenty miles."

"Lots of time. So, this wasn't an overnight trip—and then it was. How'd that happen?"

"It was work. I'm a private investigator."

She leaned away and tilted her head, gave me a look. "Are you serious? Like Magnum PI?"

I smiled. "*Exactly* like Magnum, except that I've had more women drop into my professional life than he ever did. Like with you, now. It's a long, sad story."

She made a face at me. "Not *too* damn sad, I hope. Right now, I mean."

"Could be a whole lot worse, Bubba."

She smiled. "You're awful."

"A basic part of my M.O."

"I'm sure. So, what're you detecting, way out here?"

"I'm hunting down Elrood, nominally speaking. So far not so good, I have to say, but I'm a persistent cuss."

"What's an Elrood?"

"Near as I can tell, it's a twenty-five-year-old shithead who borrows money from women under false pretenses then splits, last seen driving a white 2006 Pontiac Vibe—and about to inherit over six hundred thousand dollars, if I can find him—but I'm not absolutely certain he's a full-on unrepentant shithead so I reserve the right to retract that impression without prejudice."

She smiled. "You are . . . something else, Mort."

"So I've been told. Okay, without any editorializing the story is that Elrood inherited a whole lot of money. The executor of the estate hired us, my partner and me, to find him and let him know."

"You have a partner?"

"Maude Clary. We call her Ma. She's sixty-three and crusty."

"Unlike you."

"That's right. She's female, I'm not."

"Uh-huh. I noticed that about you right away."

"Means you're fast on the uptake. Ma is training me."

"Really? You're in training?"

"Still. Forever. Among other requirements it takes ten thousand hours of training under the mentorship of a licensed PI to get a license in this state. It's like a form of institutionalized nepotism. I've got just over five thousand hours left to go."

"So you're not a real PI?"

"Hush, child. Last location anyone had for Elrood was in one of Reno's older neighborhoods. By *anyone*, I mean a woman about thirty years old who'd given him a thousand dollars and let him borrow her Pontiac Vibe. That was with the understanding that the thousand was just a loan. He was gone by the time I got there. Missed him by three days, so I did the private eye thing and a neighbor girl seventeen years old gave me an address around Sparks High School. She wouldn't tell me how she got it, and I don't want to know. That got me to a cannabis-enhanced goof in his late twenties who told me Elrood owed him a hundred bucks but Elrood needed another hundred for gas because he had to get, now, *two* hundred from some chick in Tonopah who owed him five hundred—but he would be back later that evening. That was a little over two days ago. He was last seen driving that Vibe. According to Judy Alcott, the gal who let him borrow it, it had bald tires."

Harper laughed. "The cannabis guy and Elrood sound like winners. *And* Judy, if she let him borrow her car."

"Do, don't they? Judy has a second, better car, but I think she lost a thousand bucks. Anyway, the stoner found me a Tonopah address for the girl, said he'd split whatever money with me that I got from Elrood. I asked him why he didn't go to Tonopah and pound the money out of Elrood himself, and he said, 'Dude, it'd cost me like a hundred bucks to go get a hundred,' at which point this hundred-thirty-pound scrawny twerp rolled his eyes like *I* was the one smokin' ganj. But when you're right you're right, so I didn't put him in the hospital."

"I can't imagine you putting anyone in the hospital."

Little did she know. I've put people in the hospital, *and* in the ground. One in particular that only three other people in the world know about. We hoped no one else ever would, but that's an investigation that would be active forever, unless they catch the perpetrators—me, Ma, and a gorgeous girl named Sarah, whom I first knew as Holiday Breeze of all the unlikely names. The FBI could still turn over a rock we hadn't considered and catch up with us, but it's been almost two years since that event, so the three of us are sleeping better these days. The only other person who knows the whole story is Lucy.

"I try not to," I told her, "but sometimes it's hard. The Tonopah address got me to a pimply girl of nineteen who could stand to lose thirty pounds. Elrood had bought her dinner—a hamburger and fries—spent the night with her in an old thirty-foot, single-wide trailer, taken her for four hundred bucks and moved on, not that she appeared to be aware that he'd moved on. He phoned her from Ely and pleaded with her to send him another two hundred, which he didn't get. He called her on a cell phone registered to a person named Zola, presumably female, but these days you never know."

"Zola? No last name?"

"I'm trying to keep this confidential and professional, but if I end up needing your help, I'll deputize you, pin a star on your tank top, and name names."

She smiled. "Really? *You* will pin it?"

"It appears that I misspoke. You will self-pin the star while I micromanage the operation verbally."

"Uh-huh. Anyway, you might need my help? For real, or are you just making noise?"

"As if I ever just make noise."

"Yeah, right. I think I'm getting you figured out."

"You're visiting your aunt in Ely so you might end up with free time and get bored. You also have a gun and you show spunk, two fine traits in an unpaid assistant."

"Spunk, wow. Now there's a word I haven't heard in a while. Like almost forever."

"My partner, Ma, came up with an address for Zola using the number that appeared on the shithead's call to Tonopah. There I was in Tonopah, no point in going all the way back to Reno in order to drive to Ely, so here I am."

"In a truck going ten miles an hour. I'm sorry."

"Which you've said four or five times now, so you can shut that down since I've finally got the gist."

She laughed. "Okay. And, hey! It occurred to me that after all this time I *still* don't know your last name—Mort, private eye."

Uh-oh. No telling how this would go. "Angel," I said.

"Angel?" She backed away a little. "Mortimer *Angel*?" For several seconds she stared at my face in the dim light of the dash. "Omigod. You *are*."

"Hey, whatever you might've heard, ninety percent of it is wrong, and the rest isn't my fault."

"You . . . you're famous. Here in Nevada, anyway. I mean, you're the guy who, who, who—"

"Don't say it."

"Who found those *heads*, Reno's mayor and DA. And that politician guy's hand."

"I said don't say it. And like I said, none of it was my fault. I'm a patsy, a shill for the gods. I've been in the wrong place at the wrong time over and over, that's all. No idea why, unless it's punishment for being an IRS thug for sixteen interminable years."

"Wow." She sank back against me. "An IRS thug. That sounds nasty."

Little did she know. I once audited a guy who pointed out that pallets of taxpayer money was given to Iran who used it to sponsor terrorism. I told him the government is actually a collection of inept, bumbling clowns smoking exploding cigars and getting rich on corruption, but you'll have to pay up anyway since you're a no-body, not a corrupt politician. Now *that's* nasty.

"The Internal Revenue Service," I said to Harper, "is a 'service' like a mortuary is a theme park. I tried to keep my thuggery to a minimum, but it wasn't easy because it was a condition of my employment."

"And now you find missing people who—"

"Don't say it."

I didn't think running through my entire curriculum vitae was a splendid idea since it included finding a dead stinky rapper in a garage and the skull of an IRS goon, stripped by harvester ants. And killing two birds with one stone. Well, two guys with one rock. A big-ass rock.

"This is just too, too freaky, Mort."

"I'm harmless. Really."

"I believe you, but that's not what I meant."

"Oh? What did you mean?"

"Running into you like this. *You* of all people." She backed away a few inches, gazed into my eyes. "My *mother* is missing. She's been gone for four days, Mort."

Four days. Oh, Christ, no. Harper *Leeman*. Suddenly that last name jumped out at me. Not *again* . . .

"Nevada's attorney general," Harper said. "Annette Leeman? No one's seen her since sometime Wednesday. It's been in the news. You might've heard about it."

Sonofabitch. Another famous missing person.

Ma was gonna fire me for sure.

CHAPTER FOUR

NOT THAT I had to get involved.

That's *right*. Why the hell did this serendipity or bad luck or karmic foul-up mean I had to get *involved*? Just because I had a beautiful wet minx parked on my lap?

Hell no.

She was right up against the door. I could whip it open and she would tumble out. We were only going eight miles an hour. I could slow it down to five and throw the door open, problem solved.

That would be a big step, though. I'd have to give it a bit more thought, not act impulsively. The truck might tilt onto its naked rim which would turn the steering to shit. I would have to stop, probably go back and pick her up, try to look contrite, maybe even apologize, and she'd end up right back on my lap again. No gain.

"The attorney general is your mother? Please tell me you're kidding."

"I'm not, but I'm sorry if it's upsetting. I mean, it isn't your problem. It's . . . I don't know. It's not actually mine either, if you want to know the truth. Except I guess it is. Sort of."

"Lot of circumlocution there, Harp."

She turned more toward me, which made me slightly more aware of a nipple bump than I had been. Good thing I'm tough. It would be better if I wasn't aware of things like that, but I'm a guy, not dead yet. Lucy would hear about that nipple too, not that she would care. She would laugh at me and tell me that under the circumstances if I *wasn't* aware of Harper, she would worry that my usual interests had changed and electroshock therapy was in my future. I've always hated electroshock therapy.

I knew my Lucy. She's secure in who she is. Jealousy isn't her thing. But, still.

"Circumlocution's a big word, Mort."

"Is, isn't it? Lot of syllables all crammed together. Try it out on one of today's teenagers, see what that gets you."

"Anywa-a-ay, I told you my mother being missing isn't actually my problem, but it sort of is. Which means you might be wondering about my relationship with her."

"That did occur to me."

"My mother and I aren't close. We aren't extremely far apart, either. Not like in some families. We're somewhere in between. I worry about her. I guess I love her, but it isn't the kind of love that . . . that . . . oh, hell. Not that things were great before, but she and I had a big falling-out over my marrying Brad. Huge, actually. It turned out she was right about him, but that's not the problem. It was the things we said to each other at the time. Not nice things. My mother speaks her mind. She doesn't pull punches. She has something of an overbearing, train-wreck personality, which I guess is probably excellent in an attorney general given today's world, but not so much in a mother-daughter relationship—ours anyway, especially when I was twenty and dumb and still in college. Since my divorce, my mother and I have been trying to patch things up, but it's been slow going, partly because I'm down in Vegas and she lives in Carson City since it's the state capital."

She fell silent.

The world is a minefield. Only two days ago, Friday, Ma told me if I came across Attorney General Leeman—her body or any disconnected body parts thereof since that's how I come across famous missing people—that I was well and truly fired this time, and I might as well drive straight to the unemployment office, but she would keep Lucy.

She's such a kidder. Lucy is mine.

"Your mother's been gone since Wednesday?" I asked to jumpstart the conversation again. Not that I wanted to, but avoiding it probably wouldn't make it go away.

"Uh-huh. Just . . . gone."

"No hint of how or why? Signs of a struggle? A ransom demand? Anything like—"

"Mort?"

"What?"

"Not sure how to say this since I'm sure it'll sound awful, but we can talk about Mom's disappearance all you want *if* you want, but later. She'll show up sometime. Right now, I'm more concerned about us."

I lifted an eyebrow. "Us?"

"Not *us* us, Mort—except that this has to be the most interesting situation of its kind I've ever been in."

"Of its kind?"

She smiled. "In the arms and on the lap of a strange guy, especially dressed the way I am."

"You think I'm strange?"

She gently slapped my face. "What I meant by *us* is this truck situation. And getting somewhere safe, getting dry, finding something to eat since I'm just about starving. There's nothing we can do about my mother right now. But if you're thinking I don't care at *all* about her, I was going to Ely to see Aunt Ellen, Mom's sister, to see if we can come up with some idea about what happened to Mom or where she might be. It's sad, but Ellen has been a lot closer to her than I have for the past eight years, so she might know something I don't."

"Relationships aren't always easy."

"Tell me about it. Actually, don't. I'd rather talk about us. Oops, I mean, you."

"Boring."

"And people think only women fish for compliments." She put a hand on my chest. "Tell me about you. You're a strong guy. You're in *amazing* shape for sixty-three."

"*Forty*-three," I snarled.

"Gotcha."

I smiled. "Good one, Harp."

"See? We can be friends. I think we *are*. Definitely. So how did you get in shape like this? Or stay in shape?"

I gave her a thumbnail sketch of my four and a half months in Borroloola, Australia, but not the reason why I went there.

"You dug holes for a *mile* of fence? One every eight feet? For room and board, no pay?"

"Told you I was boring."

"Uh-huh. Now that you mention it, you are, kinda. But you said that was a year and a half ago. How do you *stay* in shape, since being in shape at one time in your life doesn't last if you don't keep at it?"

"Yoga. And judo. Mostly judo, but I can almost touch my toes now because of the yoga."

"How close is almost?"

"I can get within three inches. Almost. I do it to keep Lucy from laughing at me. That doesn't work, by the way, hence the judo."

Harper smiled. "You and Lucy sound great together. So even without a gun in your hand, judo means you're not afraid of me?"

"Oh, I'm plenty afraid, all right."

Her voice changed slightly. "Of me—or us?"

"Huh," I said. "Are you flirting with me, lady?"

"I guess I am—have been. A little. Maybe I shouldn't since you're married, but this situation is something else, Mort. I don't mean anything *serious* by it."

I slowed the truck, came to a stop on a level straight stretch.

"What?" she said. "Why are we stopping?"

"Let's get out for a moment. Walk around, cool down, stretch, jog in place. It's not raining as hard as it was."

"Are you kidding? It's pouring. My top would get wet again, *soaked*. Unless, of course . . . that's the plan."

"It's a consideration, but it's not the plan. There is no plan. I think we need a little break, that's all."

She gave me a chagrined look. "I'm sorry. It's my fault for . . . for . . . being dumb. It's not like I'm trying to . . . to *seduce* you or anything. I'm just being . . . c'mon, Mort, a little bit of flirt is *fun*, that's all."

"That's all?"

"Yes. I'll stop if you want. I mean, like you said, this isn't going to lead to anything. I know that, but it doesn't have to be *dull*, either." She got a look in her eye. "I'll get out on the hood and be a counterweight ornament like you said earlier, if that'll make you feel any better."

"Okay, go."

She hit my chest again. "All I'm suggesting is that maybe my sitting on your lap like this isn't the worst thing that's happened to you in the past year."

"It's not. I did my taxes in March."

"Well, good. I was worried. But being compared to taxes is sort of a letdown." She smiled. "But funny, too."

"Not sure flirting is my thing, Harper. The only reason you're on my lap is so I can drive this thing. I will admit that your being a very good-looking girl is a plus." I got the truck going again, took it up to eight miles an hour.

She smiled. "Hey, you did it. Good for you."

"Did what?"

"Flirted."

"I did?" I can play dumb with the best of them.

"Without knowing it, it appears." She sighed. "Here I am in wet skimpy running clothes. Really, Mort, this has *got* to be flirt heaven, a once-in-a-lifetime thing. Don't you think it would be pretty weird to pretend it's not?"

I grinned. "Flirt heaven?"

"You know what I mean. You're not that obtuse."

"How do *you* know?"

"I just do. I know you're a good guy—and a freakin' Boy Scout."

My eyes jittered. There it was *again*, that Boy Scout image, poking its head out of a dark underwater cave like a moray eel.

"I am *not* a Boy Scout, sugar."

"Sugar. I like that. Okay, tell me something that tells me you're not a Scout in PI clothing. Not a bunch of failed attempts to build a fire in the wilderness, but something in your past that had to do with women."

"Really? I have to *prove* it?"

"Prove it, or say the Scout oath, take your pick."

Well, shit. Time to rack my brain and straighten this chick out. I kept wives, ex-wives, and fiancées off the list, then worked my way through what was left: Kayla, Winter, Holiday—*wow*, Holiday—Rachel, Danya, Shanna, Cheryl, Sophie, Rosa, Mira, Traci, Robin, possibly a few I'd lost track of in the mists of time. Christ, that was a lot of them. My life had become a whirlwind of unexpected women less than a month after I'd bid adieu to the IRS. *Adieu* sounds better than *shove it*, but it means the same thing.

"Can't do it, huh?" Harper said, grinning.

"Give me another minute here. I'm trying to narrow down the field."

"I've already given you three minutes. But you have a *field* to narrow down. That's something."

"Hush, child."

She smiled, settled in against me.

Winter. I backed up two years, all the way to Winter. She would do. She was twenty years old, wearing a black thong the size of a credit card when she asked me to hook up her bra in a dim second-floor hallway. That was after she'd made sure I got a good look at the undersides of her breasts in a scissors-cropped T-shirt outside the mansion where she and her mother, Victoria, who was also her half-sister—hell of a story, *that* was—murdered Reno's mayor and district attorney. Winter was a great-looking girl, but unfortunately psychotic, so we didn't hit it off.

I gave Harper the Winter story with enough detail to win a Pulitzer.

Harper smirked. "She wanted you to check out the underside of her tits, and you did for two whole seconds. Hold the presses."

"I didn't say tits, I said breasts."

"And, later, in a dark hallway you wouldn't hook up her bra."

"She was a very spooky girl, Harp."

She rolled her eyes. "A two-second look and you ran from hooking up a bra. If that's the best you can do, I rest my case, Boy Scout."

I sighed.

She put both arms around my neck, kissed my cheek, then snuggled against me. "Anyway, you're a dear."

Well, shit. A *dear*? Time to bring out a bigger gun so I said, "Yeah, I always end up with the booby prize."

She backed away and stared at me. "Holy cow! Maybe Boy Scout isn't right after all."

* * *

Still an hour out of Grange, Harper said, "I have to pee."

"Thanks for sharing."

She hit my chest, put a little muscle into it.

"It's still raining like a sonofabitch," I said.

"I know, and I wouldn't have said anything except that I'm getting kind of desperate."

I pulled to the right on what appeared to be a straight stretch, put the truck in park and left the engine running.

"See if you can get out on the passenger side," I said.

She levered herself off me, then scrambled over the center divider. As she went, the truck tipped gently to the right. She looked at me. "Will this thing be okay?"

"I think so. Go. Make it snappy, though."

"As if I was gonna dawdle. Uh, can you turn off the headlights?"

"We're still kinda far out in the road. If anyone comes along, I don't want them to slam into us. Shut the door and don't worry. I won't look."

She stared at me, then shrugged. "Fine."

Out she went. The truck reluctantly righted itself. I helped it by leaning as far to the left as I could.

She was back in less than a minute, water running off her head as if she'd stood under a waterfall for an hour. "Holy freakin' cow, Mort. That was *not* fun."

"I bet. My turn," I said. "Hold the fort."

I got out. Without my weight the truck tilted so far to the right that the half-flat left front tire lifted entirely off the pavement. Great.

I was about to unzip when a faint light appeared in the watery gloom. A vehicle of some kind was coming uphill toward us from the east.

I cracked the driver's door and said, "Lights coming. If you want a ride back west in something that still has four tires, now might be your chance."

"No."

"You sure?"

"Hey! I'm doing just *fine* with you. And why would I want to go back west anyway? Ely's east of here."

Good enough. Then I had a thought, or a premonition. You never know what these things are. "If that's the case," I told her, "then how about you get on the driver's side and hunker down. *Way* down. Out of sight and *stay* down."

She scooted over, which helped to right the truck. I put some weight on the left front bumper until the truck was upright and level, not looking like it had a problem.

As the vehicle got closer, my truck's headlights glinted off the big Ram symbol on the front of a glistening black pickup. It slowed, stopped opposite me, and the driver's window powered down.

"Trouble?" a big guy asked. In his early forties, one-inch aggressive salt-and-pepper beard. A glow off the dash lights gleamed off a bald head. He looked solid, with heavy shoulders and a thick neck.

"Nope. About to take a leak when you came along."

He chuckled. "When you gotta go, you gotta go."

"Got that right."

"Seen anyone else on the road out here, dude?"

A tremor rippled through me. "No. Yours is the first vehicle I've seen in a while, at least an hour and a half, two hours."

"Nothin' else, huh?"

"Like what?"

His eyes bored into mine for a few seconds, then he nodded. "Take 'er easy, man." He hit the gas and took off. I caught part of the rear plate as he pulled away. ZJX5. Missed the last two numbers. I might've gotten all of it if I hadn't had rainwater running into my eyes.

Who was the guy looking for? The answer might be in my rented truck, out of sight. But then, it might not.

Fuck.

The night and the situation had just hiked itself up a good-sized notch.

Maybe.

* * *

"Who was it?" Harper asked as I opened the door and got back inside, dripping.

"Some guy asking if I was in trouble."

Who might've been looking for you, I didn't say.

She crawled back onto my lap, squeegeed water off my face with a finger. "Hey, look at you. You got wet."

"How 'bout that. So did you."

"That rain was freaking *cold*, Mort."

"Uh-huh. I see that."

She smiled. "You *see* that? Exactly *what* do you see, Mister I-always-end-up-with-the-*booby*-prize?"

"What I *meant*, Drippy, is I see you got wet."

"Uh-huh. I'm sure that's all you meant."

CHAPTER FIVE

"It's nice when someone comes along right as you're trying to pee in the great outdoors," I said. I had a reason for saying that. Time to quiz this girl, see if that guy in the truck meant trouble for either of us.

"Which is why I asked you to kill the lights, Mort."

"At least the guy seemed friendly enough. Kind of a big dude. Full dark beard, bald head, might've been forty, forty-five. He looked pretty strong."

"Uh-huh."

No other reaction. Maybe my imagination had slipped into too high a gear. I gave it one last try: "He was driving a black Ram pickup. It looked fairly new."

"Whatever." She laid her head on my shoulder. "I've never been called a booby prize before."

"There's a first time for everything, Harp."

"Kinda nice, actually. You noticing." She lifted her head and gave me a look. "If you don't mind my saying so, that is."

"I don't."

"Good." Her head came back down. "I'm a *girl*, Mort."

"Noticed that."

"What I *mean* is, all of this is giving me a major flirty feeling. Just flirt, though. I hope that's okay."

"It is."

She didn't know the guy, but I would keep him in mind all the same. Some old guy dumps her off in the middle of nowhere and keeps going east. Another guy comes along hours later, headed west, wondering if I had seen anyone else on the road out here.

Strange, but the world is full of strange and this one didn't quite add up to two and two is four.

More like 3.9. Too close for comfort.

* * *

We reached Grange at one fifteen that night. I didn't know we'd arrived until we were almost opposite the general store, thirty feet off the highway. A single light was on inside, nothing else. Fifty feet from the store, I could hardly make out the 76 station, utterly dark, with only one service bay. Everything was buttoned up. If I hadn't seen that one light, we might've rolled right by the place.

Well, shit. I'd expected it, but it was still a letdown to see it looking so dark and deserted. Last thing I wanted to do was to push on to the next place down the line, Currant. Which might've been only another eight miles, but I was bushed, Currant wasn't much bigger than Grange, and the farther I pushed this gimpy damn truck, the more likely we would spend the rest of the night in a ditch.

I stopped in the middle of the road. "Grange," I said.

Harper turned to peer at the store over her shoulder. GRANGE GENERAL STORE was visible—barely—in faded, old-fashioned lettering across the front. Darn clever name for the place though.

"*Now* what?" she asked.

"I've got an old Frederick Forsyth paperback with me. *Day of the Jackal.* I could read it to you until morning."

"Okay, go for it."

Shit. She was onto me.

I babied the truck into a left turn and stopped beside the store, turned off the engine but left the headlights on. "We're staying here the rest of the night," I said. "One way or another."

"It looks like the store is only on the first floor. But it's a two-story building."

"You oughta be a private investigator."

That got me my tenth thump on the chest in the past three hours. "What that *means*, Mort, is it's likely someone lives there, above the store."

"I'm serious, you oughta be a gumshoe, get paid for all that top-notch detecting."

"Oh, for hell's sake. Are you gonna knock on the door, or shall I? No, wait, I'll go. You're gigantic and scruffy and wet—kinda scary looking, if you don't mind my saying. I might have better luck."

"You're wet and scruffy too, lady."

"I'm wet, but I am most certainly not scruffy."

"Says you."

"At least I don't look like Bigfoot."

She steeplechased over the center console and opened the passenger door. "Wait here. I'll see what's what."

She grabbed her purse and got out. I opened my door and followed her. The truck seesawed in place.

She came around the front of the truck. "I said wait here, Mort. Like—out of the rain?"

"You're a defenseless half-drowned waif, and I'm not going to let you pound on an unknown door after midnight without backup." I hadn't said anything more about the guy in the truck. Conversation-wise, that appeared to be a dead end. The guy wasn't likely to be her ex-husband since he was too old and she hadn't reacted to his description, not that it made any sense that her ex would be out here looking for her after she'd pulled a gun on some old guy who'd made a pass at her. Maybe nothing was adding up because there was nothing to add up.

"Backup?" Harper said.

"That's private-eye speak. I can't turn it off."

"Cool. But how about you keep out of sight? I don't want anyone to see you first thing and call the cops."

"Gotcha. If someone lives here, there's probably a door around back, not in front."

"Kind of obvious, Mort, but thanks anyway."

She headed toward the back and Mr. Obvious trailed along. We rounded the building, leaving the beam of the headlights. It was dark back there. Huge oak trees blotted out the sky, or would have if the sky hadn't already been blotted out. We squished through a puddle the size of Lake Erie. Cold water ran down my back, my front, into my eyes. I couldn't hear anything but rain hammering on wet leaves, the soggy ground, and the roof of a vintage Buick that looked, when I lit it up with my cell phone, as if it had hit a deer or two sometime in the distant past because the front-end dents had rusted.

Harper was about to bang on the door when I stopped her and pointed. "Doorbell," I said.

"You oughta be a private dick," she responded.

Damn, she picked things up fast. Including the lingo and, possibly, a bit of innuendo which didn't go unnoticed.

She rang the bell. I heard it go off inside. And again.

And again.

And again.

Finally, she pounded on the door.

"Okay, enough," I said. "No one's around."

And, of course, two seconds later a light came on in a room above us, faintly illuminating the backyard, the wet girl, and the guy who'd just said no one was around.

A window above us slid up a few inches. "Yeah, who's down there?" a woman's voice called down. Older woman, sounded like.

Harper backed away and looked up into the rain. She sputtered and said, "Our truck broke down. Is there any place around here where we can stay the night?"

"Who're you, child?"

"My name's Harper. I'm here with my husband."

News to me.

Harper shot me a look. "Let me do the talking. It'll be better that way."

Yeah, maybe. But still, I would have to let Lucy know she was a divorcée or I was a bigamist.

"What's his name?" the woman called down.

"Tell her I'm John," I whispered to Harper. "If she hears the name Mortimer Angel she might freak."

"John," she called up.

"John Harper?"

"No, *I'm* Harper."

"Hold on. I'll come down. I can't hear you so good."

It took two minutes while Harper and I treaded water, then the door opened and a woman in a baggy nightdress and bathrobe peered out at us.

"You two're almighty wet," she said.

Harper turned to me and said quietly, "Do *not* tell her she oughta be a private detective or I'll clobber you."

"Yes, ma'am."

Harper smiled at the woman. "Yes, we are. I'm sorry. Our truck pretty much broke down. I was hoping you could tell us where we might be able to stay the night."

"Nowhere around here," the woman said. "'Cept *right* here. I got a room upstairs you can use, down the hall from mine."

"Oh, thank you, Mrs. . . . ."

"Olson. Olivia Olson. Dimwit runs the gas station for me calls me Double-O-Seven, of all the fool things. Come in, get out of that rain. And let's get you out of those wet clothes, for heaven's sake. I'll stuff 'em in the dryer for you so they'll be dry by morning."

Harper shot me a huge grin, then she ducked inside.

I hung back. Double-O looked to be in her seventies, five-three, hundred sixty pounds, hair gray and worn long. She waved me in, but I said, "Truck's headlights are still on. I gotta turn 'em off. Be right back."

I slogged back to the truck, giving Harper and Olivia plenty of time to work things out.

Let's get you out of those wet clothes.

Sometimes you hear the train before you see it. The woman's comment circled around in my head like an angry hornet, stinger out and ready. I wondered if I could walk as far as Currant by morning. Only eight miles.

I could feel some sort of karma thing gearing up.

Shitfire.

I looked toward the highway, thinking about that big Ram pickup. I got in the rental, started the engine, then pulled it around to the back of the house out of sight of the highway in the slowest, iffiest left turn I've ever made. The ground sloped a little to the left, which might be the only reason the truck didn't capsize.

I grabbed my duffel bag and killed the lights. As I walked to the house, I saw a light moving through the rain to the west. I stood out of sight at a corner of the building and watched as a black pickup came trolling by at fifteen miles an hour. It stopped dead for ten seconds in the road opposite the store right where my truck had been moments before. I couldn't see anything inside the truck but I felt eyes searching the darkness.

Finally, it pulled away, headed east toward Ely.

I couldn't tell if it was the same truck I'd seen earlier, but it was similar. I didn't like that at all.

I hurried to the rear of the house. Olivia had left the back door cracked open half an inch. I went in and shut the door, water pouring off my clothes as if I'd fallen in a lake. The room was more mudroom than anything else. Washer, dryer, a deep sink, cupboards, an odor of laundry soap. A door led into what was probably the back of the store. Up a flight of wooden stairs, I heard women's voices.

I followed a trail of water up, enhancing it with more of my own. I found the womenfolk in a hallway. I also learned that Harper had solved the initial confusion about our names. I was Jonathan Harper and my wife was Angel Harper. "Angel" had a dippy smile on her pretty face under sopping hair, legs a mile long before they reached her skirt, nipples showing dark and prominent through a dripping translucent tank top.

Terrific.

Olivia smiled at me. "I was just telling Angel here that if you'll get outta them clothes, I'll run 'em downstairs to the dryer and get that going. This'll be your room for the night." She stood by an open door. "Belonged to my boy, Bobbie, before he up and joined the Marines twenty-six years ago, but I keep the place clean and neat as a pin all the same."

I peeked into the room past Olivia. One bed. *This* was going to take some kind of creative finesse. Maybe I could fake a heart attack.

"Thank you so much, Olivia," Harper/Angel said. "I can't tell you how much. You are *so* kind."

"Not a problem, dear. It gets kinda lonely 'round here what with Bobbie gone and my Rupert passed away these nine years. It's late so I expect you'll want to sleep in a bit. Don't you worry none about me. Take as long as you want in the morning."

"What do we owe you?" I asked.

Olivia gave me a shocked look that turned a bit sour. "Not a thing, John. I'm happy to do this for you."

Time for me to shut up and let the women talk.

"Thank you so much again," Harper said, reaching out to hold Olivia's hands. "You are truly an angel."

"*You're* the angel, Angel," Olivia said, chuckling.

"Oh . . . yes. I guess I am," Harper said.

"If you'll hand me those wet clothes out the door here when you're ready, I'll get that dryer going. Sheets on the bed are clean. Make yourselves at home. Oh, bathroom's that door, right there. You can use the shower if you want it. Kitchen's down the hall that-away, just past my room. There's food in the fridge and cupboards so don't be shy if you're hungry or thirsty."

"How will we get around?" I asked. "You'll have our clothes."

She eyed the duffel bag in my hand. "Got no clothes in there?"

"No. It's full of work-related things."

She pressed her lips together, gave me a look. "Been a long time since the sight of a naked man shocked me or revved my engine, but if you're worried, I'm a real sound sleeper. I'll be up at six, open the store at seven. I didn't get this old by being a featherbrained shrinking violet."

"Good to know," I said. "But—"

"But nuthin', John." She touched my arm. "I keep it warm in the house. Do what you gotta do and stop worryin' so much."

"Okay, thanks. We'll do that. Is there a phone I can use tonight or tomorrow? In case something comes up."

Harper arched an eyebrow and tilted her head at me. I had second thoughts about the phrasing of that comment—too late to take it back though.

"Got a phone in my room and in the kitchen," Olivia said. "There's a phone downstairs in the store, different number. You can use the one in the kitchen if you need it."

"I really don't think we will," Harper said. "But thanks for the offer. We'll get out of these soggy doggone clothes right away so you can get back to bed." She took my hand and pulled me into the room. Yanked me, actually.

"I'll wait right here," Olivia said. As Harper shut the door, I saw Olivia fold her arms across her chest.

"Well, *shit*, Harper," I said through my teeth. "What the hell are we gonna do *now*?"

"Strip," she said, kicking off one of her shoes.

"No."

"Yes." She kicked off the other shoe.

"No. I mean it."

"She's *waiting*, Mort," Harper whispered. "How long does it take to get clothes off? You gonna tell her you and I can't get naked even though we're married?"

"Is your phone in your purse?"

"Why?"

"Why do you *think*? See if you can get a signal."

"For chris*sake*, Mort." She glanced at the door. "All this hubbub wouldn't be because you're having interesting thoughts about me, would it? Because if you *are*, you can just put them right out of—"

"I'm not. Cell phone, girl. We haven't tried for a signal in the past two hours and yours has more battery left."

She dug her phone out of her purse, turned it on, then called out to Olivia, "It'll be another minute or two, Olivia. One of John's shoelaces is in a big wet knot. I'm trying to untie it."

"No hurry, dear."

"No signal," Harper whispered to me. "*And* we're out of time, so *strip*." She pulled her tank top up and off.

Shitfire. Her breasts were medium-small and shapely, and I was a pig for noticing. And admiring.

Things were moving fast. *Too* fast. I was going to tell all of this to Lucy, of course, every last detail, and I knew it wasn't going to bother her in the least because I know her. She was going to laugh and tell me I'm a dork—or worse—but wet or not, I wasn't about to give up my clothes. Well, I would take off my shoes, socks, and shirt, but that's all.

"Mort?"

"This is a bad idea, Harp." I took off my shirt.

She laughed quietly. "*I* think it's pretty funny."

"Why doesn't that surprise me?"

"And harmless. I mean *really*, Mort, what do you think's gonna happen if we get out of these clothes?" She pulled her running skirt down and off. She didn't have a thing on underneath, pubic hair neatly trimmed to half an inch in a narrow V.

Sonofabitch.

"No panties?" I said.

"That would be *so* weird. And uncomfortable. Panties *and* a liner?"

I shook my head. "The things I don't know."

Olivia called out, "I got you a couple of towels here. I'll just hand them in, if that's okay."

"Yes, please," Harper said.

The door opened six inches and a pudgy hand held out two towels. "If you've about got those clothes ready . . ."

"Give us another twenty seconds, Olivia," Harper said. "And thank you *so* much for the towels."

I could've kissed Olivia because I was thinking about staging a fight with my topless and bottomless wife and going out to sleep in the tilt-o-truck. The towels might be a game changer. Still, I hesitated.

"Mort?" Harper stood a foot away, hands on her hips. "I *know* we haven't known each other very long, but we can do this. I mean, *you* can; I already have. I really don't want to leave here and she's expecting wet clothes. If you don't get your clothes off right now, I'll take 'em off you myself. *All* of them. I'll give you two seconds, then look out."

I heard a faint snicker. I glanced up and Hammer and Spade were in a dim corner of the room, poking each other in the ribs. I hadn't seen those two clowns in months, but they often showed up when girls removed their clothes or things were about to get interesting.

I took off shoes and socks, tossed my wallet and keys on the bed, undid my belt, shucked off my pants and stood there for a few seconds in soggy underwear, then grabbed a towel. "Turn around, Harp."

She squinted at me. "Are you serious? Hard to believe, because . . ." She raised her eyebrows and smiled at me.

Aw shit, no. "Why?"

"Because those little red hearts on your boxers are *so* darn cute. I can't imagine why you think—"

"Turn around or I'll have to hurt you," I said. "That serious enough for you?"

I guess the threat didn't take because she stood there naked as an egg and smiled for five long seconds before turning around. "This isn't going to lead to anything, Boy Scout. We'll talk about it later. Pretty soon, actually."

Yes, we would—but damn, she had no tan lines, trim waist, and a solid shapely rear end. Hate to say any of that mattered, but . . . Okay, enough of that.

I stripped off my underwear and wrapped the towel around my waist. I gave it a tuck, which held but didn't feel secure. A bigger towel would've helped.

"Okay," I said.

Harper grabbed everything in a dripping bundle and opened the door. "Here you go, Olivia. Sorry it took so long. And thank you for being *so* nice and understanding about all of this."

"Not a problem, child. It's good to be of use to folks." She glanced at the soggy stuff in her arms. "Hearts, how adorable. You two make *such* a lovely couple." She turned and left.

Harper shut the door and spun around. She tried to stifle a laugh, but a little chirp squeaked out. "Adorable."

"Go ahead and laugh. I just grab what I grab from my dresser. So I got the ones with hearts that Lucy bought me. I wasn't expecting anything like this."

"I can tell."

So there we were. I wore a towel; she wore a smile. I wondered if she was going to wrap a towel around herself, or if I would have to pluck out one of my eyes like it says in the Bible, which, I have to say, would hurt like a son of a bitch. I'm not religious enough to actually do that, and my eyes weren't actually offending me—but still.

* * *

She wrapped the towel around her waist, didn't do the girl thing where it covers both top and bottom. It's not as if I haven't seen breasts before; in fact, I've seen a whale of a lot of them, big and small, in the past two years, but it still made me somewhat nervous.

Harper sat on the bed. "Mort?"

"*What!*"

"Oh, my, *that* came out a bit sharp."

"Did it?"

"Kind of. You should keep your voice down. Let me try to explain something here. That okay with you?"

"I wish you would."

"We didn't plan this, we didn't set it up, so we're not at fault. There is no blame here. You're still a nice guy, I'm not going to take any sort of advantage of you, and I'll bet you aren't about to take advantage of me, so quit whining."

Whining?

"That towel could cover a little more of you, Harp." Okay, that might be considered a whine.

"Think so?"

"I know so. I've seen it done before."

She canted her head to one side and gave me a long evaluative look. Which turned into a knowing smile.

Uh-oh. "What?" I asked.

"Methinks the gentleman doth protest too much."

That stopped me. "I thought that quote pertained to a lady, not a gentleman. Is that *Macbeth*?

"*Hamlet*. And it fits you perfectly. I have a feeling you aren't as distressed as all this moaning would suggest."

"I'm not?"

"It doesn't *really* bother you seeing me like this, does it? The truth, Mort."

Well, shit. Right then I knew I would have to suck it up and quit whining. This was right out of the PI manual, the chapter on unforeseen encounters with naked women. But I *was* going to tell Lucy about all of this as soon as I got my hands on a phone.

"Well, no. Not a lot." To prove it I gave her a good long look. She had dark brown nipples, a flat belly, gorgeous legs, no sign of modesty, so the hell with it.

"See," she said. "We really *can* do this. It doesn't have to be a big huge deal."

"Got it. But that towel *could* cover more of you. Just sayin'."

She gave an exasperated sigh, stood up and removed the towel. "These towels aren't very big, Mort. They were just to get us dry, not to cover up. Who knows—they might be the biggest ones she has. So observe—watch how this works. If I wrap it the short way around me like this to try to cover everything, it barely comes together on top, not enough to tuck so it won't stay up. If I wrap it the long way around—like this—I can tuck it, but it won't cover both my boobs and my pussy. So tell me what you want to see, or don't want to see, and I'll do it whichever way you like."

There was *that* word again. It had shaken me up when Lucy used it an hour after we met, not far out of Tonopah. I thought I'd gotten used to it, but apparently not. It was startling every time it popped up.

"Nice demo, Harp. I'm convinced. I'll let you decide if you want to wrap it high or low."

"Great. Let's go with this." She wrapped it around her waist then sat on the bed again. "Sometime later you can tell me why you think I'm supposed to be embarrassed, and I'll tell you why I'm not. I feel like we're friends. And if we *are*, this isn't really so terrible, is it?"

"Guess not."

"We're not going to do anything that we would regret later, but"—she grinned—"this *is* entertaining, isn't it? I mean, *I'm* not bored. How about you?"

I had to smile. "Not very."

"Good." She patted the bed. "Which side do you want to sleep on? Either side's fine by me."

I gave the bed a good look for the first time and knew right away it wasn't a king or a queen. "Is that a twin or a double? Not that it matters."

From below, I heard the dryer start up. Then Olivia's footsteps came up the stairs and went padding down the hall. Seconds later, a door shut with a faint thud and the house was ours.

Harper glanced at the bed. "It's a double. Or a full, which is the same thing, and why doesn't it matter?"

"Because I've got dibs on that easy chair in the corner. The bed's all yours."

"That is *not* an easy chair. That is a straight-backed wooden library-kind-of chair that might as well be a bed of nails or an antique medieval torture device."

"It's one thing for us to be hanging around in towels, Harper. But it's an entirely different thing to share a bed."

"You think something naughty might happen?"

"I know it wouldn't."

"So do I."

"Even so, it's not a good idea."

She sighed again. "Let's figure it out later. Right now I'm starving. Olivia said it's okay if we find something to eat in the kitchen, which is a fabulous idea. We can leave her some money to cover it. How about it?"

"Think she's asleep already?"

She listened for a moment. "I'm pretty sure I hear snoring. Although," she went on, "Olivia did say the sight of a naked man hadn't shocked her in a very long time, and that she wasn't a shrinking violet. That might've been an unconscious invitation. She would be totally fine with you in a towel. Probably even better without it."

"You're a riot, kiddo."

"You think I'm kidding? I know how to read between the lines." She stood up and patted my cheek. "She would be delighted. Let's go."

My towel wouldn't maintain a tuck and I didn't want to hold it all night with one hand. I opened a closet door, hoping Olivia's son Bobbie would have something in there I could wear. But Bobbie had been gone for twenty-six years and the closet was full of dresses that would fit Olivia and look positively dreadful on me.

"Mort?" Harper stood in the doorway and looked back at me.

"Yeah, yeah, I'm coming."

She grinned. "*Are* you? That's like . . . wow."

Shit. English is a brutal damn language.

CHAPTER SIX

HARPER WAS ONE thing, Olivia was another. I didn't know how soundly she slept. Before leaving the room, I whipped the comforter off the bed and wrapped it around myself, Indian style. If I had been thinking more clearly, I could've done it sooner, but Harper and our situation had my head spinning. Out in the hallway I handed her the towel I'd been wearing.

"Really?" she said.

"What do you mean, 'really'?"

"You need that comforter and I need another towel?"

"Did I guess wrong, precious?"

She rolled her eyes. "Thought we'd gotten past that."

"Past what?"

"What do you *think*?" She crept down the hall, holding the towel I'd given her as if it were an afterthought.

Rhythmic snoring came from Olivia's room. Sounded as if she might be able to sleep through a category-four, so we should be okay in the kitchen. It might get problematic if Olivia came in, but Harper with a towel around her waist was not offending my inner pig.

I turned on a light as we went into the kitchen. The room was roughly twelve feet square. Refrigerator, stove, countertops, sink, old linoleum floor. Basic and utilitarian.

Harper draped the spare towel over the back of a chair, then opened the refrigerator. I found an old cordless phone on a countertop by a pad of paper, bills and pens, catalogs, rubber bands, general household debris.

"Really?" Harper said quietly. "You're actually gonna call Lucy?"

"You bet. Got to give her an update. Let her know I'm okay." Among other things.

"Jesus, Mort. It's nearly two in the morning."

"I don't care. This won't keep."

She lifted her eyebrows, then shrugged and turned to sift through an antique round-shouldered Frigidaire, circa 1955, with a lever handle the size of a medium crowbar.

I could've taken the phone back to our room. But the food was in here, and I didn't have any reason to leave now that the issue of clothing or the lack thereof had been discussed and resolved to everyone's satisfaction, so I sat at a small pine table and punched in Lucy's number. On Olivia's phone the call might've been long distance, but I would leave sixty bucks in our room to cover it regardless, *and* the hospitality, which included the dryer, towels, and whatever we found in the way of food.

"Hello?" Lucy answered cautiously.

"It's me, Luce."

"Mort! Where *are* you? I expected to hear from you *hours* ago."

"I'm stuck in a dead zone, no cell coverage. I thought you'd be asleep by now."

"Is *that* why you called? To wake me up?" I picked up a smile in her voice.

Harper got a few things out of the refrigerator and set them on a countertop, then started opening cupboards.

"Yes," I said. "I like to catch you when you're mostly asleep. It puts us on a more equal footing."

"You *wish*. So what phone are you using? I didn't recognize the number."

"Got a real kickass story to tell you, babe."

"Oh, no. You ran off to the Caribbean with a girl and won't be back until mid-October."

"*Damn* close," I said. "I don't know how you do it."

Something in my voice caused her to hesitate for a moment. Then, "Interesting. How close is damn close?"

"This could take a while. How long have you got?"

"For you, sweetheart, forever."

"That's my girl. Okay, fasten your seat belt, Luce. This one's an E-ticket ride."

I launched into it, all the way from Tonopah, to the rain, the girl, the gun, the disabling of the truck, the flat spare, rain, the girl again, the girl on the lap, rain, tearing downhill at six to ten miles an hour, the Grange General Store, rain, Olivia, the *wife*, the wet clothes, the room, the girl no longer in wet clothes, the obligatory strippage of the Mort, the clothes in the dryer, the towels, the double bed, the comforter, the kitchen, and the girl in a towel who had just finished making two sandwiches. I left out sightings of the ominous black truck and its driver.

"Wowie, Mort."

"Yeah, wowie."

"Her mother is the missing attorney general?"

"Yup."

"Ma's gonna fire you for sure, this time."

I smiled. "I'll believe it when it happens, cupcake."

"Anyway, right now you're wrapped in a blanket?"

"A comforter."

"A towel wasn't enough? Why not?"

"Sugar plum . . ."

"I bet Harper's pretty. She is, isn't she?"

"Yeah."

"Good for you. And she's topless and right there with you as we speak?"

"As we speak, hon. She doesn't seem to think a second towel is necessary."

At that, Harper's head whipped around.

Lucy said, "Can you put the phone on speaker?"

"I think so. Sure you want me to?"

"Of course. Why not?"

Why not indeed? I waved Harper over. She set a plate in front of me, turkey and cheese sandwich on it, lettuce, mustard, and mayo.

"What?" she whispered.

"Got a surprise for you." I put the phone on speaker and said to Lucy, "You're on live with Harper, Luce."

"Hi, Harper!" Lucy said brightly.

Harper's eyes got big; her face went a shade whiter. I pushed the phone closer to her. "Speak up, Harper," I said. "Don't be shy."

Payback time, I thought.

"What . . . what . . . ?"

"She's not very articulate right now, hon," I said.

"I kinda got that. Are you there, Harper?"

"Uh, yes."

"Groovy. You have a nice voice. You heard everything Mort told me about where you are and how you got there, didn't you?"

"Um, yes, I did. I was making sandwiches."

"Okay, good. So you're wearing a towel and you and Mort are in a lady's kitchen getting something to eat?"

Harper closed her eyes and hung her head.

"Give her a moment, Luce," I said. "She's still in a bit of shock."

Lucy laughed. "Anyway . . . Harper?"

Harper took a deep breath. "Yes?"

"Has Mort been acting not very with it all the time, even a little bit stick-in-the-mud, especially after you got to Olivia's and she wanted to take your clothes?"

"Hey, hey, hey," I yelped. "Stick-in-the-mud? Where'd you get *that*, wife person?"

"At McGinty's, the first ten minutes when we first met. Anyway, Harper, from the way he told me everything that's happened, my guess is he's been kinda backward and self-conscious with you. Maybe even acting troubled."

Backward? I shook my head at Harper to shut her up, which didn't work.

Harper smiled at me. "He was. Quite a bit. Maybe not so much right now. It's hard to tell."

"It takes him a while. He's as trustworthy as a bank vault and you sound nice, so I'm fine with what you have to do there, but I realize he might not be. I'd like to make this easier for him. I don't like it when his blood pressure gets all spiky."

"My blood pressure doesn't get spiky, Luce."

"Yes, it does. So anyway, Harper, I don't want to keep you guys up all night, but after everything Mort's said, this might help. Have you ever heard of the WNBR?"

Oh no. *No, no, no, Luce. No.*

"The what?" Harper shot me a questioning look. I shook my head and stared down at my feet. One way or another, this wasn't going to be pretty.

"WNBR," Lucy said again. "That's the World Naked Bike Ride."

"Oh. I've heard of that. Is that when a bunch of people ride around on bicycles not, um, not wearing very much? Like in a city?"

"That's right. Most of the riders are naked or wearing body paint. Mort probably didn't get a chance to tell you he rode in the WNBR sixteen months ago in San Francisco."

Harper stared at me. "*Really?*"

"Yes. With a beautiful girl named Sarah, but she's also called Holiday. I'll let him explain why later. Ask him to describe her—that should loosen him up and maybe settle him down, *if* he describes her accurately. All he wore on that ride was a little bit of body paint that she put on him. Oh, and get him to tell you about a poster pinned to a wall in his business partner's office too."

Well, *shit.*

"A poster?" Harper asked.

"Yes. Anyway, Holiday wasn't wearing anything at all except a few words painted on her back. Her picture is still all over the internet, if you know where to look. So if the situation you're in right now is making Mort nervous and raising his blood pressure, I want him to just relax and be himself. Well, actually *not* himself, which is the point, but you know what I mean. And I know all of this isn't what you might've expected me to say, but Mort and I trust each other completely. If you tried to do anything serious with him, he'd run screaming into the night."

Enough. "I would not," I growled.

"Would too," Lucy replied. "I *know* you, cowboy."

Cowboy? Harper mouthed to me.

Shit.

Lucy said, "That was mostly hyperbole, Harper. I said it to help explain why I'm not upset or threatened by what you and Mort are doing. If you tried something, he might run into the night keening at half volume, but that's about all. Anyway, Mort, Mom says she wants to ride with us in the WNBR next March. I'm gonna sign her up, too."

"You gotta be kidding."

"Nope. In fact, she's right here. I've had the phone on speaker the whole time, which I guess you didn't know. Sorry about that. I should've told you, but . . . too late now. We were up late talking, but right before you called, we made up a pot of 'relaxed mind' tea, so we're getting kinda drowsy in spite of the breezy conversation. Anyway, Mom, you should say hi to Mort."

"Hello, Mort." Valerie's voice was uneven, as if she were trying hard to keep from laughing out loud.

"Uh, hi, Val. I . . . I don't know what to say."

"I'm not surprised. So, you drove a truck downhill in a thunderstorm on only three tires?"

"Two and a half, but who's counting?"

"That's amazing. And it sounds like you're still having a fascinating time."

"Pretty good understatement, Val. You're not *really* thinking about riding in the WNBR, are you?"

"Why not? I mean, why wouldn't I?"

"No reason. Just thought I'd ask."

"Hey," Lucy said. "Are you still there, Harper?"

"Yes."

"Do you want to ride with us? It'll be in March in San Francisco. I'll have to check on the exact date, but I could sign you up too. We could make it a foursome."

"That would be . . . are you sure?"

"Sure, I'm sure. If you can get away from teaching for a couple of days, that is."

"I can get a sub. I wouldn't tell them *why*, though."

"Say yes and I'll sign you up when the registration opens. They only take eighteen hundred people. It fills up fast. You in? It's a blast. You should know, we don't wuss out. The most we wear is a little bit of body paint, if that. Which is actually the whole point of the thing. I mean, how else are you gonna get nearly two thousand people to go on a bike ride? There has to be some kind of a *wow* in there."

Harper raised her eyebrows at me. "Yes, okay. I'm in."

"Great. Give me your number and we'll keep in touch. I hope we can meet before then, but you never know."

Right then a door creaked open. I heard the shuffle of bare feet out in the hallway.

"Hold on, Luce," I said. "Olivia's coming our way so don't say anything. I thought she was a sound sleeper. This could get pretty weird since Harper's topless and I'm doing a mummy impersonation."

Weird? Little did I know.

Olivia came into the kitchen. Her eyes didn't seem to be focused on anything and her face was slack. She was mumbling, nothing I could make out. She didn't look at me or Harper, just passed by us and opened the fridge.

Sleepwalking, Harper mouthed to me. *Omigod!*

A shiver walked up my spine.

Olivia got a carton of milk from the refrigerator and a glass out of a cupboard, then shuffled to the sink. She said something like, "Gar un ughk ongal uk," then gasped hard enough that her entire body jerked. She poured milk into the glass.

Harper and I stared at her.

Olivia drank the milk, rinsed the glass, shuffled back to the refrigerator and put the milk inside, then said, "Ina un inna garna too," turned off the kitchen light as she went out the door, then shuffled back down the hall and into her room.

"*That*," Harper said, as Olivia's door thumped shut, "is the spookiest thing I've ever seen in my life!"

Amen.

"Luce," I said, getting up. "You there?" I took the phone with me as I turned the light back on, returned to the table, and sat beside Harper again.

"I'm here. What's going on?"

"Olivia sleepwalked in here, got a glass of milk, then sleepwalked back to her room."

"You're kidding."

"Nope. Wish I had a video. Actually, nix that. I don't want to see that again. Once was enough."

"Are you and Harper safe, Mort?" Lucy asked, concern evident in her voice.

"I think so. At least she didn't have a gun."

"That's not funny, in case you didn't know."

"Sorry. No, I don't think we're in any danger. We'll hurry up with these sandwiches and get back to the room."

"Okay. But be careful. Anyway, Harper, I was about to get your number so I can call you sometime and set up this bike ride. If you're still interested in September when they open the registration, that is."

"I'm sure I will be."

"Good. It'll be fun. It's a blast, if you like being naked and free, which I do. I've been on four rides so far."

Harper reeled off her number. Lucy thanked her, then said, "Hey, this is gonna be a totally random question, which probably means I'm getting kinda loopy and oughta go to bed, but I just wondered . . . Have you ever seen the *Vagina Monologues*?"

Harper gave me a wide-eyed look. "I have, yes."

"I had a feeling you would have, don't know why. It just popped into my head. I probably oughta shut up and let you guys go."

"I've seen it twice, Lucy. It was at the student union at UNLV when I was getting my degree. It's funny you asked. I saw it again, recently, only about two months ago."

I ate my sandwich, let the girls chat. This happens to me a lot, don't know why. I'm a fifth wheel when girls get to talking. I get lost in all the loose verbiage, but it beats sticking my foot in my mouth.

"Cool," Lucy said. "I was in the play here in San Fran in a theater on Geary Street for three months. I performed two of the MONOLOGUES: *My Angry Vagina* and *Because He Liked to Look at It*."

"I *love* that second one," Harper said. "I thought it was the most, I don't know, *liberating?* For me, anyway." She tilted her head and smiled at me.

Uh-huh. Good deal. I took another bite.

"I still remember both parts word for word," Lucy said. "*Because He Liked to Look at It* is wonderful, even if the other one is more humorous."

"The guy's name was Bob, wasn't it?"

"Yes. What Bob did for her was great, his character, I mean, which wasn't an actual character in the play. He made her feel beautiful and set her spirit free."

"I *know*. Totally."

Yup. Free spirits. Totally. I took another bite. I was on board with the MONOLOGUES. Lucy dragged me off to see it in April when it came to UNR in Reno.

"Are you still there, Mort?" Lucy asked.

"Yup. Love the girl talk, hon."

"I know. You're hopeless even if you're a lot more like Bob than you care to admit."

"Okay, sugar plum. It sounds like your tea's kicking in kinda hard right now. How 'bout I call you tomorrow?"

"It *is* tomorrow."

"An impossible statement that would make Einstein's head explode. I should've said I'll call you later today."

"Do that. I better go, Mort. Mom left a minute ago. Bye, Harper. Get some sleep. If you need me for anything, Mort, let me know, otherwise I'll see you Friday."

"Will do."

"Also, tell Harper what interesting thing I did in that Mustang convertible about an hour after you and I met. If you remember."

"It's probably in the memory bank somewhere."

"I'm sure it is. It'll help explain you and me, the way we are."

"How are we?"

"We're great, Mort. Perfect. Okay, I really gotta go."

"Talk later, Luce."

We ended the call. "Well, *that* was fun," I said.

"I like her. A lot, Mort. And guess who phoned her, in case your saying it was fun had a faint ironic undertone?"

"I can't think that far back. I'm tired."

Harper slugged my shoulder, hard, too. "You rode a bicycle naked in a city of half a million people, *and* you did it with naked women all around, and you're getting your panties in a wad because *I'm* topless?"

"I'm not wearing panties, lady."

"Prove it."

"Nope. Take it on faith."

"Okay, Boy Scout, be that way. But seeing my tits had you freaking out not very long ago."

"I got over it." I took another languid bite. "And you make freaking out sound like a bad thing, Harp."

She smiled. "You idiot. Finish your sandwich and let's go to bed."

CHAPTER SEVEN

I STARED AT the bed. It hadn't gotten any bigger since I'd last seen it. "How the hell are we gonna do this, Harp?"

"You take one side; I take the other. Then we conk out. Easy peasy. You're probably overthinking it." She removed her towel and tossed it over the back of a chair.

"Overthinking it? With you naked as a cue ball? I'm not over-thinking a damn thing, woman."

"Sure you are." She grabbed the comforter and yanked it off me, fluffed it over the bed as I grabbed the towel off the chair and wrapped it around my waist.

She rolled her eyes. "You *really* need that?"

"In this situation it seems like a good idea."

"We wouldn't *be* in this situation if you hadn't slashed that tire thingie."

"That's right. You would be in a motel in Ely, and I'd be standing in the rain at the side of the road with a thumb out, trying not to freeze to death or get hit by lightning."

"Didn't I already say I was sorry?"

I shrugged. "Few times, yeah. I still like hearing it."

She smiled. "That's the very last time, so treasure it."

"I am. I will."

She gave the bed a thoughtful look. "How about this, since you're so skittish? You get under the sheet; I'll get on top of it. It'll be like short-sheeting. That way I can't touch you and you can't touch me, even by accident."

I thought about that. "Might work."

"Why wouldn't it?" She put her hands on her hips and gave me a serene look. "We'll be fine, Mort, I promise. But if you wear that towel to bed when there's a sheet between us, I will snicker all night and keep us both awake."

"Which would suck. I'll keep it in mind."

She went around the bed, adjusted the sheet, pulled the comforter back. She was an inch shorter than Lucy and a few pounds lighter, but they were almost the same size and shape. In the past year I'd gained a deep appreciation for the beauty of smaller breasts.

She caught me looking at her.

"What?" she said, straightening up, smiling a little as she looked at me across the width of the bed.

"Sorry, I didn't mean to stare. It's just that you look good, that's all."

She tilted her head. "Like Bob in the MONOLOGUES, you like to look at it. Lucy hinted at that."

I pulled the towel an inch higher. "I'm a normal male, Harp. I don't know how to turn it off, not that I want to."

She smiled. "I'm glad. I mean, I like it that you're not turning it off." She hesitated. "If you don't mind my saying, Mort, you're a sexy guy—not that that'll lead to anything. But you sure have a lot of scars. What's up with that?"

"Things got rough after I left the IRS. You'd think it would be the other way around, especially if karma works the way people think it does or should—but, no."

She came around the bed and stood in front of me. She looked terrific. She touched a gentle finger to a small round scar on my left shoulder. "How'd you get this?"

"Got a sword run all the way through my shoulder. A foil, actually. It's pretty much like a bullet wound, except foils don't expand as they go through."

"A foil? How the hell did *that* happen?"

"You remember me telling you about that girl in the mansion, Winter?"

"The one whose bra you wouldn't hook up in a dark hallway? She did that?"

"Yup. Under the house, right before I killed her. Well, *I* didn't, black widow spiders did, but I kicked her into a bunch of them, and they didn't like that, so I was nominally responsible."

"Not sure I want to hear all of that story." She touched another scar. "What about this one?"

"That's a real bullet wound, .38 caliber. That one came the closest to killing me."

"I'm so glad it didn't." She took my hand, turned it palm up. "And this burn on your wrist?"

"I had to stick my wrists in a flame behind my back to burn my way out of a zip-tie. That wrist got the worst of it."

She sighed. "I can't begin to tell you how strange that sounds. All of it. And the top of your right ear is missing, which I mentioned earlier."

"The same .38 that put a bullet in my shoulder clipped my ear. Happened about a year ago. It was sort of an ugly twenty or thirty seconds."

"You look like you've been through a war, Mort."

"A habit I'm trying to quit."

"I hope you do." She looked up at me. "You still look kind of tense, not sure why, now. But I'll put a towel back on if you want me to."

"Up to you, Harp. I'm okay."

"Just okay?"

"Quite a bit better than okay, if you must know."

She gazed at me for a moment. "You like women. *And* the way they look."

"Yes, I do. They're one of my favorite species."

She smiled. "When they don't pull guns on you, that is."

"It's better that way."

"You *do* realize there was a message in the things Lucy said in the kitchen, don't you?"

I smiled. "How about you parse it for me."

"That nudity is okay. It's harmless. It doesn't have to lead to anything. And Lucy trusts you implicitly."

"You're a pretty bright girl."

"Thanks. She was also connecting with me, making friends. Friends don't steal each other's guys."

"Actually, they do, then they're no longer friends, not that I think that was your point. But Lucy was turning you into a friend, period. She's like that." I backed a few feet away and looked at her. "You and she have the same body types. I don't suppose you're hyper-flexible too?"

She tilted her head and smiled. "Flexible physically or emotionally? Either one would be interesting."

"I said body types."

"Okay, then—physically. Still interesting."

"More like startling. Lucy is about ninety-nine percent boa constrictor. She can bend over backward and touch the back of her head to her rear end. Even worse, she makes it look easy."

Harper stared at me. "You're kidding."

"Nope. If they check her DNA, they'll find a reptile in the woodpile. Her lower spine bends almost double. There can't be any vertebrae in there. At least not bone. It might be a kind of tough, spongy plastic."

"That's . . . wow." She bent over backward, making it about as far as I thought most women her age would, able to see the top half of the wall behind her. Lucy could look down and see her own feet, put the palms of her hands on the floor beside her ankles and go right into a handstand from there.

Harper straightened up, then sat on the bed. "I'll have to see her do that sometime."

"It's a sight. It hurts to watch when she does it. And the splits, side to side, front to back, twice a day, every day, for fifteen or twenty minutes."

"She'd have to, to stay that flexible."

"Yep. I'm still working on touching my toes."

The evening was humming right along. I thought this was as good a time as any to see if I could shake anything loose, in case I was missing something important.

"Will anyone be wondering where you are?" I asked.

Her forehead knitted in a frown. "Like who?"

"Anyone. Boyfriend, ex-husband, brother, father."

"No. But it's an intriguing question, especially the ex or the boyfriend."

"I don't want our being together like this to run afoul of some guy in your life and give you problems." Like a rough-looking guy in a big-ass black truck, I didn't say, but I still wanted to know who he was.

She smiled. "Run *afoul*, Mort?"

"A phrase used by higher-class PIs. We get more per hour if we say things like that."

"I'm educated. I've read Agatha Christie. And Dickens. I know what 'run afoul' means, and no. My being here isn't going to be a problem that way. Or any other way."

"Okay. Good to know."

"I hope so. I do know a guy, though, but that won't be an issue—unless, of course, *you* think it is."

"Not me. If you're good, I'm good."

She sounded sincere. I was probably being paranoid. All the same, I was going to keep an eye out for a big black Ram pickup with a partial license of ZJX5.

She turned and looked at the bed, then back at me. "I don't suppose you'd have a toothbrush and toothpaste with you?"

"Matter of fact, I do."

"Oh, *good*! Gimme." She held out a hand. "If you can see me naked, I can use your toothbrush. That's gotta be a rule somewhere."

I rummaged in my bag and handed them to her. She opened the door and started to go into the hall.

"No towel?" I said.

"What on earth for?" Then she was gone.

Yup. What on earth for? But I wasn't giving up mine because I'm backward and my blood pressure gets spiky.

* * *

She returned and I left, with toothbrush. When I got back, Harper was in bed on top of the sheet, the comforter pulled up to her chin. I slid in under the sheet. *Under* it.

"Night," I said.

Harper made a little growling sound but didn't say a word. She got out of bed, came around to my side, reached under both covers and yanked my towel off, tossed it in a corner all the way across the room, then got back in bed.

"*That's* better," she said. "Maybe I can sleep now. Stay on your side of the sheet and everything will be hunky-dory. If you don't, everything will *still* be hunky-dory. Oh, and look. You didn't turn off the light."

"I forgot."

"So? Get it now. It's on your side."

"It was your turn to get the light, sugar."

"No, it wasn't. I kept track and it was *your* turn."

"The switch is way over there by the door. It's gotta be at least twelve feet away."

"So?"

"So twelve feet is a long way and you tossed my towel into the next state over—Utah."

She smiled. "Again, I ask, so what?"

Jesus. I got out, hit the switch, and came back.

"That wasn't so hard, was it, Mort?" she said. "At least it didn't look hard."

"Fuckin' English language," I muttered.

She laughed.

*   *   *

Dark as hades in the room. No streetlight outside, no moon out and not a hint of starlight making it through the dense cloud cover. Staring up at the ceiling, I might have been in a cave at midnight for all I could see. I was tired but still wide awake after the events of the past four hours. I stayed quiet so Harper could sleep.

She'd opened a window a crack to let in a little night air. It was cool, smelling of rain and wet earth.

She fit perfectly into the inexplicable karmic turmoil in which I'd become embroiled when I left the IRS and became a private eye, turmoil like an unending drumbeat—women, flocking to me like pigeons to a statue, one after another. I had seen more undressed women in the past two years than in the forty-one years previous. I had no way to account for it except karma, a reward for having managed, no thanks to the IRS, to cling to a functioning soul.

It was possible, even likely, that the dark pickup that had stopped for several seconds in the street outside was the one I'd seen up in the hills, that the bearded guy was still looking for . . . someone. If he was hunting Harper, then the older guy who had picked her up in Goldfield was connected to the guy in the Ram, *two* guys, in two different vehicles, which meant Harper was—

"Mort?"

"What?"

"I can't sleep."

Here we go. "Try harder, lady."

"You're not either, I can tell by your breathing. I know it's late, but we don't have to get up early, do we? I'm still kind of wound up."

"Wound up how, or shouldn't I ask?"

"Not *that* way. But maybe we could talk for a while."

"About what?"

"Anything. It doesn't matter." She moved closer and pressed herself against me. "Is it okay if I kind of hold you like this since we've got this sheet between us and the bed is so small? I'm right on the edge over here."

"I guess—since you're already doing it, and as long as the sheet stays put."

"Even if it didn't, it wouldn't lead to anything, which I think I've said about a hundred times. Lucy said to ask you about a poster on your partner's wall."

Great.

"Mort? A poster?"

I sighed. "It's a picture she took of me during that bike ride at the WNBR a year and a half ago."

Harper got up on an elbow. I sensed her looking down at me. "A picture of you without clothes, you mean?"

"I believe that's the gist of it."

"Cool. I'll have to see it sometime. This partner is the lady who's sixty something?"

"Sixty-three. Maude Clary. Ma."

"Wow. Uh, how naked were you?"

"We could talk about the last presidential election."

"No, we couldn't."

"Think of it as a sleep aid, Harp."

"Not ready yet." She sank down and snuggled closer.

"Enough about me," I said. "You said there's a man in your life. Tell me about that."

"Terrific segue. And, yes, as a matter of fact, there is. Kinda, sorta."

"Good guy? Kinda, sorta?"

Silence for several seconds. "I guess. It's only been five weeks so I don't know for sure. You know how it is."

"I know how it is with most people, but Lucy told me she'd marry me less than an hour after we met, so I'd say she and I aren't like most people."

Harper raised up again and I could tell she was trying to see me in the dark. "Are you kidding? An *hour*?"

"Yep. Ask her. I almost wish I'd taken her up on it so we'd have an even better story to tell. We were headed to Vegas at the time. We could've been married five hours after we first met in McGinty's Café in Tonopah."

"Wow." Harper settled down against me again. "Think she would have if you'd said yes?"

"At the time I didn't. Now I know she would have."

"That's so . . . romantic. *And* a little bit weird."

"It is, yes."

"I wish I had something like that in my life. Which I don't. This guy I'm sort of with isn't . . . isn't like that. He's eight years older than I am, kind of smooth and rich, into possessions and status, a lot more distant than you, though you were pretty darn standoffish when Olivia snagged our clothes." She laughed quietly as she said it.

I didn't know how to respond to that.

"You aren't smooth," she went on. "I like that. I don't know about possessions or rich, but my guess is you don't care about owning a bunch of expensive stuff to show the world how successful and special and wonderful you are. What I *do* know is you've got a tender, nice-guy streak in you a mile wide and a mile deep."

I smiled. "A tender streak. Right."

"I mean it. You're kind, considerate, easygoing."

"Aw, shucks," I growled.

"Nice try, but I *mean* it. Not just tender, which isn't exactly the right word, but trustworthy and honorable in a strange way. What I mean is, I can tell you like looking at me, but it's just *like*. It ends there. My being undressed around you doesn't make you lose your moorings or feel as if you have to *do* anything or even *want* to, which I'm sure is why Lucy trusts you the way she does."

Another "aw, shucks" would've been one too many, so I let the quiet take over, except for Olivia's distant snoring which made me wonder if I ought to get up and shove the back of a chair under the doorknob. I could visualize her sleepwalking with a gun in her hand, or an axe. Scary.

Harper said, "Actually, I think this thing I've got with this guy, Tony, is about on its last legs. But that's been my kind of luck with guys. At least I've got my own place. All I'd have to do to end it is say goodbye, not even pack up any clothes since we're not living together or anything."

Again, I didn't know what to say to that.

"You wouldn't happen to have a twin brother, would you?" she asked. "Someone exactly like you?"

"Uh, no, sorry."

"Just my luck. I shouldn't have asked." After a minute she said, "Listen. The rain has stopped."

"Huh. When did that happen?"

"I don't know. I just noticed it."

"Maybe we won't get drenched in the morning."

"And the dryer's stopped. You could trot downstairs and get your clothes, Boy Scout."

"Just mine?"

"Well, ours. Not that I need mine right now."

"Can't," I said.

"Oh? Why not?" I heard the smile in her voice.

"Someone threw my towel across the room. I'd have to turn on a light to find it."

"That's *right*. So you're stuck here like this."

"But you aren't. You could go get our stuff. You don't embarrass the way I do."

"Empirically true. But it's gotten kind of chilly in here, and I'm finally warm and perfectly happy right where I am. So, no. We'll cross that bridge in the morning, one way or another."

* * *

I remember the word *empirically* because that late at night it was as unexpected as a frog in a wineglass. And I remember her saying she was happy where she was, but I don't remember anything after that. I woke with a patch of weak orange sunlight on the wall to my right, a girl tucked against me to my left with an arm flung across my chest—which should have registered as impossible, but I passed out too quickly to analyze it. By then I'd only had three and a half hours of sleep and it wasn't nearly enough.

When I woke again, the sunlight had brightened and shifted down the wall almost to the floor. I got my watch off the night table. It was 8:45 in the morning.

I sat up, which lifted the sheet since I was under it. It was then that I discovered the girl was also under the sheet and the aforementioned arm had been across my chest, skin on skin. It would *still* have been across my chest if I hadn't sat up, but it wasn't. Somehow the sheet had ended up over both of us. I didn't know when that had happened, but I know *I* don't sleepwalk.

I decided it would be a mistake to panic about where her arm ended up. Instead, I tried to extricate myself with the kind of infinite care you see during brain surgeries, things getting moved and adjusted one micron at a time.

Which, of course, didn't work. Things like that never do. Check the PI manual, page 331, for the reason why the world fucks with you like that.

"Morning," Harper said sleepily.

"Good morning. Move your arm, woman."

"My arm is perfectly happy right where it is, thanks."

I laid down, dragged her arm up to my chest and said, "When did you get under the sheet that you were supposed to stay on top of *all night long?*"

"When this comforter slid partway off me for the third time and I got chilled and couldn't sleep. Once I got under the sheet with you, I dropped right off. You were warm and very cozy, so thank you."

"Uh-huh. *You* get to tell Lucy how and why you ended up under the sheet with me."

"Nothing happened, Mort, and nothing was *going* to happen, and nothing *is* going to happen as we speak. From what Lucy said last night, she'll be fine with this as long as your blood pressure doesn't skyrocket, so calm down."

"I *am* calm. I am the very *picture* of tranquility."

"If you say so, spike."

I snarled, then handed her arm back to her. But I still had what's known as a towel problem so I stayed under the covers.

"Your towel is over there in the corner if you need it," Harper said, reading my mind.

"Gee, I wonder how that happened."

"You gonna go get it?"

"Maybe, maybe not. What's it to you?"

She smiled. "The towel, Mort? If we're going to get up sometime today? If not, I'm warm and comfortable. This is a good bed. I'm quite happy here. I could sidle up a little closer to you. I've never actually copped a feel in my life. I might never get another chance, either."

Well, shit. Sometimes you have to give up and go with the fuckin' flow so your fuckin' blood pressure doesn't spike, or so I've been told. I swung my feet out of bed, then sat there for a moment.

"The towel, Mort?"

"Gimme a few seconds here, woman."

"Oh? Why is that?"

I gave up, got to my feet and started across the room, being careful to keep my back to her.

"*Finally*," Harper said, grinning, head propped up on an elbow, watching me. "Good boy."

I was halfway to the towel when the door opened and Olivia came one step into the room. "Here's your clothes, kids. I folded them. Oh, good, John, you're up. And don't worry, I seen my share of male plumbing." She looked past me to Harper. "And, my goodness, aren't *you* a lucky little gal, Angel?"

"Why, yes, I certainly am," Harper said.

Olivia gave me a wink. "Anyway, here you go." She set the bundle on a chair inside the door. "There's breakfast things in the kitchen.

I've been down in the store. I only popped up to get you your clothes. Come on down when you're ready. I have to keep the place open." Then she left. *Finally*. Proof that life is all about timing.

Harper convulsed with laughter. "Oh. My. God," she said, throwing the covers back. She got up, walked to the corner and picked up the towel, came over and put it in my hand. "My goodness! Aren't *I* a lucky little gal? Lucy will die when I let her know. Absolutely *die*."

Sonofabitch.

CHAPTER EIGHT

I STOOD OUTSIDE in the new day. Not a cloud in a bright blue sky. I don't know how clouds disappear so fast, but I knew it had rained because I remember being soaked, and twenty or thirty drowned worms were on the ground within ten feet of me.

Harper stood beside me, taking the fresh air deep into her lungs. She was back in her tank top and running skirt, looking good, hair brushed, eyes clear and bright.

"Nice," she said. "I could live here. *If* they had a mall somewhere nearby."

"If they had a mall, it wouldn't be nice, or maybe you never read *Catch-22*, city girl."

"I have, actually. It was pretty gross and not all that funny like some people said. Okay, no mall. What about a Costco? I buy a lot of clothes at Costco. And chia seeds."

"Still no."

The truck was a sorry sight, tilted onto its empty rim, canted like a torpedoed PT boat.

The 76 station was open. The door to its single bay was rolled up and an OPEN sign glowed in a grimy window.

Harper followed me over. A grizzled guy in his sixties was standing in the empty bay, smoking the last inch of a Marlboro, staring outside as the day warmed up. He gave Harper's outfit an appreciative look, then lifted an eyebrow at me.

"Morning," I said.

He nodded. "That your rig behind Double-O's place?"

"Yep. It's a rental. A real beauty, too."

"Be even better if they'd given you four tires. Bet you got a sweet deal on that."

"I did. Can you patch a leak?"

"Plug one, if it ain't too bad. I can't take a tire off its rim. Machine's broke. I'm expectin' a part in a couple of days. If you bring me a tire, I'll have a look at it. I'm Arlo. What's your names?"

"I'm Mo—John. This's Angel."

He gave her an even longer look this time, then he nodded. "Bring me that tire. Let's see what'cha got."

Harper accompanied me to the truck. I lifted the spare out and hauled it over to Arlo. He flicked his cigarette into a puddle where it hissed and died.

"This here tire's pretty much new," he said.

"And flat," I replied. "It's the spare."

He considered that. "You got here sometime last night on three tires?"

"More like two and a half."

"Better you than me." He put air in the spare, listened for a leak, then set it in a puddle, rolled it a bit, watched it blow bubbles the size of spider farts. He held it up, located the bubbles on the tread and gave it a closer look.

"It'll plug," he said. Which took about three minutes, then he waited a few more for the plug to dry and inflated the tire to 35 psi.

"Can you put a new valve stem on the other one?" I asked him. "Got damaged somehow." Like with a serrated knife blade.

"Nope. Don't keep any QuikStems in the shop and I can't take a tire off a rim. But that plug'll get you to Ely if you're headed that way—Tonopah if you're going west. I wouldn't want to drive all the way to Florida on a plugged tire, but that's just me."

I paid Arlo, put the tire on the truck myself, drove it over to the open bay and got air in the left front tire, then Harper and I went back to the house.

Upstairs in the kitchen, she phoned the repair shop in Goldfield to check on her Corolla. The mechanic told her nothing had changed and it would be at least another two or three days before it would be ready—more likely three than two.

She poked out her cheek with her tongue and thought for a moment, then looked at me. "Could you stand to have me around a couple more days? You said I might be able to help you find what's-'is-name, the stoner twerp."

"Well said. The twerp is Elrood. And yes, I'll survive since we'll be in separate rooms if I don't catch up to him today in Ely."

"Why separate? I mean, after last night, why bother?"

"Because that's how people do these things when the world doesn't gang up on them."

Her face fell. "I'm sorry you feel ganged up on."

"A poor choice of words. I take it back. I'm prone to that so you might want to get used to it."

"So the deal is, separate rooms if I come with? If you don't find Elrood right away, that is."

"That's right."

"And 'separate' wasn't just another abysmal choice of words on your part?"

"Not this time."

"Fine. If we must. But it seems so unnecessary. It's not as if I would try anything, Mort. *Or* you."

"Got it. Ready to hit the road?"

She sighed. "Sure. Let's go."

* * *

Fifteen minutes later we were a mile out of Grange—after I'd left sixty dollars on the dresser in Bobbie's room and we'd said our heartfelt thank-yous and goodbyes to Olivia. I'd also returned Harper's gun and bullets to her. And I'd reloaded my Ruger. A rock the size of a softball is as good a weapon as a gun without bullets.

"Um," Harper said, breaking five minutes of silence except for the hum of tires on pavement.

I smiled. "Um?"

"I, uh, had a thought."

"Let's hear it."

She looked over at me. "Not sure I should say this. I probably shouldn't but I want to. I mean, it's in my head and I'd like to get it out and be done with it."

"Go ahead. I'm as tough as scrap iron."

"Really?"

"No, but I can fake it. What's up?"

She pursed her lips. "You're a nice guy, Mort. Really nice. The past twelve hours—jeez, has it only been that long? It's been fun. Oh, hell. What I *mean* is, it's been sexy, risqué, and I liked it." She gave me an uneasy look. "I hope that's okay. Don't think I mean anything by that. It's been fun *and* unexpected, but I'm glad neither of us tried to turn it into anything more than that."

Whew. "I don't know what to say, Harp."

"You don't have to say anything. I wanted you to know that this was, well, *enjoyable*? I think that's the right word. Feels like it. At any rate, I'm glad you're the one who came along when you did, not some . . . some creep."

I still didn't know what to say. This felt like an area where a person could easily insert a size twelve boot in his size ten mouth. A person very much like me.

"One other thing," she said, looking into my eyes. "And don't worry, it's safe. It has to do with my marriage, which ended four years ago."

"Sounds safe."

She smiled. "It is. Quite a few women need a sense of danger to get, you know, worked up. I'm not like that. At least not now, not that I've been very worked up since you and I met. It's just that it occurred to me that back when I met my husband, I was into that enticing sense of danger. It felt masculine and erotic. But no more. I grew up."

"Good to know. I think." Not that I knew what to think about her saying she hadn't been very worked up. She had snuck the word *very* in there, probably inadvertently, but it was a nuance I didn't want to explore or even mention.

She looked at my expression and sighed. "I probably shouldn't have said anything."

I reached over and gave her hand a squeeze. "I'm glad you did. Now let's see about finding Elrood."

"Crap. Now *I'm* embarrassed."

* * *

Sixty miles from Grange to Ely. We had thirty more to go when Harper said, "You and Lucy haven't been married a full year yet? You must've gotten a divorce too, at some time in your life."

"You oughta be a detective. It's a good profession. No grading papers, keep your own hours, stop daydreaming about pepper-spraying kids."

She smiled. "You did, didn't you? Got divorced before you met Lucy. Was it messy?"

"Nope. We're still good friends."

"That sounds like you. So what went wrong?"

"Does it matter?"

She shrugged. "No. But here we are. We could get to know each other better as long as I don't have a car and we might hang out for a few more days. Especially after, well . . . last night. I mean, if that's okay."

"It's a lot better than the alternative."

She gave me a perplexed look. "Which is?"

"You being a mystery."

"I am?"

"On several levels, Harp."

"Name one."

"A tan, but no tan lines. Not that I noticed."

She smiled. "Yeah, right."

"Did I mention that I'm a private investigator?"

"I think so. Do you recall my telling you last night that I would tell you why I wasn't the least bit embarrassed to be around you without clothes?"

"Vaguely. Next time we stop for gas I'll check my notes and get back to you on that."

She smiled. "I'm a member of the Desert Sun Naturist Park. Twenty-five miles southwest of Vegas."

"Huh. That sounds like a nudist camp."

"Wow, now *there's* a term I haven't heard in a while. Desert Sun isn't big, isn't well known, and it's couples and single women only. It doesn't take single guys, for obvious reasons."

"Which explains why you don't embarrass easily."

"Or at *all*, Mort. When I'm undressed."

"Yeah, that—and the absence of tan lines. How long have you been going there? I've never heard of the place."

"Pretty much since my divorce. Desert Sun is a well-kept secret. They get new people by recommendations and interviews with people who came as guests of members. First time I went was as a guest of a science teacher at my high school, Karen No-last-name."

"No last name. Discreet, except for me being a hotshot world-renowned gumshoe. How many Karens are science teachers at your school, if you don't mind my asking?"

"Oop."

"That's right. But don't worry, her secret is safe with me."

"I hope so. Anyway, in the past four years I've gotten pretty good at tossing horseshoes."

"Nude horseshoe tossing. I'm impressed."

"It's better for tanning than nude chess. There's two guys in their sixties who play chess while their wives hang out around the pool and sunbathe. The guys butts are fish-belly white."

"Nude chess, white butts. The things I'm learning."

She grinned. "Uh-huh. Anyway, you were about to tell me about your divorce."

"I was? Since when?"

"It was in the works, until you sidetracked it."

I shrugged. "Hard to say why we got divorced. I was working for the IRS, which is like being given a daily dose of slow-acting poison that seeps in and turns you into a soulless thug. It might've been that."

"The IRS sounds like a wonderful career choice."

"I was stressed, unhappy, a little overweight. Not the best husband material at the time."

"You are now—just sayin'. What's your ex's name?"

"In high school it was Dallas Frick. Dallas Angel now. She kept the name."

"Yeah, I would've too."

I didn't respond to that since it might be like sticking my hand in a bear trap. But maybe not.

"*My* divorce was messy," Harper said. She glanced at me. "The sex was great at first. Very hot—for the reason I mentioned earlier. Then it sort of cooled off. Brad and I had been married three and a half years when he first hit me. He lost about thirty thousand dollars in an investment deal he told me was a lock, easy money, then suddenly it wasn't and he lost all but a thousand of it.

"He was pissed off, hungry, and I didn't have dinner ready on time, so he hit me, as if that would help. He was also drunk, which to me was—*is*—no excuse. At all. He was apologetic the next morning, classic abuser behavior, but I told him I'd give him that one freebie hit and if it ever happened again, he was going to be *so* damn sorry and I was going to be gone forever."

"Then, of course, he hit you again."

"Yes. But I was prepared for the possibility since I am nobody's punching bag, and I mean *nobody's*. I'm also a lot stronger than I look."

"You look plenty strong to me, miss pole vaulter."

"Thanks. That next day I got a pair of his nylon socks and wrapped two pounds of wet sand in layers of plastic wrap to keep it wet. I formed it into a kind of tube shape that fit into the end of one sock. Then I put the other sock over that, tied the two open ends in a knot so the whole thing was really strong and I could swing it, hard.

"A month or so later he was late paying a credit card that cost us almost forty dollars in a late payment fee. He got drunk at a bar and came home ranting about how that big investment was partly my idea because I didn't say no, so losing that thirty thousand was also my fault—except I didn't know he had invested anything at the time since he never told me. I didn't know anything about investing in general, except to put money in the bank and get six cents' worth of interest every month.

"So that night he came at me again, which was such a stupid stereotypical situation, so *trite*—being the abused wifey, I mean. He punched me and I fell down, but I got up and ran into the bedroom, slammed the door and got the sock out from under our mattress. I waited beside the door against a wall, and when he came in I swung the sock at the back of his head which knocked him the fuck out—pretty much like he had run full tilt into a brick wall. It surprised me, how well it worked. First time I've ever seen anyone knocked out so completely like that, like totally *gone*.

"I dragged him into the dining room and sat him up in a heavy wooden chair and cable-tied his ankles to the legs. Not just cable-tied, but *totally* cable-tied. I put six or eight zip ties on each ankle and tied a rope around his waist and around the back of the chair before he came to."

"You left his arms free?"

"Yes, but I kept the sock ready, and he wasn't about to get up and chase me. Anyway, he yelled bloody murder when he woke up and found himself trapped in the chair. He told me he'd kill me as soon as he got loose.

"I told him killing me wasn't going to be easy because he was never going to *see* me again, except in a lawyer's office or in court. He kept yelling while I was packing up my clothes and other stuff, and he was trying to untie the rope around his waist, reaching around behind him to get at the knot, so I said, 'Brad, sit still and shut up or I swear to God I will knock you the hell out again.'

"Dumbass kept yelling and cursing and he almost had the rope off, so I smacked the back of his head again with the sock, not all that hard, really, but that was that. I loaded up my car and got out. But before I took off, I retied the rope around his waist. I left a knife on the table beside him so he could cut the rope and the cable ties when he woke up. Or slit his wrists. Whatever he wanted to do."

"Remind me never to piss you off."

"Good plan, except you're *nothing* like Brad. Anyway, all that happened in Vegas during Christmas break which was good timing. I drove to Ely, to my aunt's place, which is where we're going now. I mean, we'll look for this Elrood guy you're after, but I'll also introduce you to Aunt Ellen. She's my mother's younger sister, younger by two years. She's divorced, so she's a member of the club. Divorce is pretty much a national pastime used to alleviate boredom or prevent assault."

"You didn't go see your mother after leaving hubby Brad tied to a chair?" I said. "And unconscious." Which, I didn't tell her, could've turned out badly if he had died like that. But she was an English teacher, not a paramedic.

Harper shrugged. "No. Mom lived in Carson City back then—and now. Ely was closer than Carson and, I have to say, friendlier. Anyway, that was my actual divorce. All the nauseating legal crapola came later."

"No trouble with Brad since?"

"Some ugly words over a big conference table in my lawyer's office. And he got a warning about coming by my apartment in Vegas one night, which violated a restraining order. He's not totally psychotic or anything. He's just a dumbass with limited self-control that I shouldn't have married in the first place, but there was that stupid danger thing at the time. I know a lot better now. Anyway, that's enough about my loser marriage, Mort. What about us?"

I frowned. "Us? What about us?"

"Don't look at me that way. I mean, you're looking for this guy, and we'll need a place to stay in Ely unless you find him in like twenty minutes and head back to Reno and . . . and then I don't know. I guess that'll be that, but until you find him do we *really* have to stay in separate rooms?"

"Last night wasn't unpleasant, Harp. Not at all. But it happened because it was necessary."

"I get it. I got it last night. You're married. Last thing I would ever do is get in the way of that or be a problem or anything. I like Lucy, Mort, even if I haven't met her yet. You and she and her *mother* of all things are going to ride bicycles around San Francisco naked, and it looks like I'm going too, so it's not like you and I are completely done with that, in case you forgot."

"Jeez. Lucy's mother. I might have to be sick that day, but thanks for the reminder."

She smiled. "You're welcome." She turned toward me. "Lucy wanted you to describe Holiday, the girl you rode with in San Francisco a year or so ago. Now's a good time."

"You sure?"

"Of course. Why not? Let's hear it."

I shrugged. "Holiday was twenty-five years old, five-six, very pretty. And, best guess, thirty-seven, twenty-five, thirty-six."

"Thirty-seven, huh?"

"I didn't use a tape measure so I could be wrong. And she's a civil engineer who can drive you batshit with math. You should see her T-shirts."

"Packed solid, huh?"

"Nope. Well, yes, but that's not what I meant. Most of them have obscure mathematical formulas on them, and math jokes so incomprehensible they aren't funny, except to her."

"So she's a gorgeous nerd."

"Of the first order on both counts."

Harper didn't say anything for a minute. Then, "I'm five three and a half. Thirty-three and a half, twenty-four, thirty-three. And trust me, I really need *both* of those half inches, which is why I mention them."

"Useful, if something weird happens and I have to buy you clothes. Which could happen."

She smiled. "Think so?"

"Unless we catch up to your suitcase."

"It's a sports bag, says REEBOK on the side. If what I'm wearing bothers you, I can buy more clothes in Ely."

"What you've got on doesn't bother me a bit, Harp."

She canted her head. "Good to know." She turned sideways in her seat. "Tell me what Lucy did—what was it she said? In a Mustang convertible an hour after you two met. She said it was interesting and for you to tell me."

"We were on U.S. 95, south of Tonopah. The top was down in the car and she took off her tank top and sat up on the back of the seat in the wind at fifty miles an hour."

"Topless? No bra?"

"Yup. Like you, she almost never wears one."

"Cool. Only an hour after you two met, huh?"

"That's right."

"Jeez. And you were freaking out with me at Olivia's. That is *so* wrong, Mort."

"I wasn't freaking out."

"Yes, you were, but only because you're married. I get it." She settled back in her seat. We rode without talking for a while, then she made a half groan, half laugh, so low I almost didn't hear it.

"What?" I asked.

She shook her head. "Nothing. I was thinking about your ex dumping the name Frick and keeping Angel, which got me thinking about names in general, that's all."

"Names?"

"When you teach high school, you become more aware of names and how they would work if you were a teacher. Frick wouldn't be a great name, especially for a woman. My name, Leeman, doesn't automatically and effortlessly lend itself to abuse, so I'm safe. Angel would be interesting, but it'd be better for a woman than a guy. Mr. Angel? I don't know about that." She smiled. "You probably shouldn't go into teaching."

"I'll take it off my bucket list."

"Good idea. But the reason I made a kind of *uck* sound a moment ago is there's a woman English teacher I met in another high school who married a guy with the last name of Wetmore. She's pretty and only twenty-four years old, which makes it even worse."

I thought about that, then said, "Bloody hell."

"You got it. I asked her how that was going and she said 'don't ask.' She didn't look happy. I would change my name legally or take up accounting or something."

Mrs. Wetmore. Damn. Sometimes life gets you with a claw and rips out your carotid.

Eighteen miles later, we arrived in Ely.

CHAPTER NINE

FIRST THINGS FIRST: Get the tire situation under control.

Doug's Auto Repair was the first likely place we came to. Doug himself put a new valve stem on the rim of the tire for thirty-eight dollars. A lanky grease monkey in his teens swapped the tire with the spare and put the spare back under the truck. I slipped him an extra ten for that.

Thirty-eight dollars. In Manhattan it would've cost a hundred sixty. To amuse Avis who'd given me a truck with a flat spare, I would've presented them with the receipt—if I hadn't cut the valve stem off to keep Harper from taking off with the truck. Hard to blame Avis for that.

"Where's your aunt's place?" I asked Harper. Elrood would have to keep for another hour or two.

"Up a ways, more toward the center of town, then left five blocks. Get going. I'll tell you where to turn." She faced me and smiled. "She has a house, not an apartment. Two-bedroom, and the second bedroom is an office, but there's a guest house in back, about three hundred square feet. Really cute. I stayed there two weeks last summer, got in a lot of high-altitude running. Elevation of Ely is sixty-four hundred feet. If we don't find Elrood right away, we can stay in her guest house tonight."

"We can't. You can."

"Mort . . ."

"No."

"There's a suit of armor in the closet. What if I wear that? *Or* you."

"That'd do it, except one of us would clank in their sleep and no one has a suit of armor in their closet."

She sighed. "You're really . . . different."

"First time anyone's ever said that about me."

"I doubt it. Okay, turn left here."

We headed west on Campton Street then south on Elysium Drive, a quiet residential street. This wasn't like trying to find an address in L.A. The population of Ely is 3,960, down from about 5,500 in 1990. People are leaving, probably because Ely doesn't have a Costco to keep them happy. The nearest Walmart is 180 miles away. Good luck trying to find another town this size in the contiguous United States where that is true. White Pine County is larger than the state of New Jersey with its nine million people. The population of the entire county is about the same as West Eighty-Second Street in Manhattan.

Typical rural Nevada.

Ellen Moore's place was a single-story ranch-style house, maintained somewhat better than average, cream with blue trim, maple tree in the front yard, three more in back. Kids eight or nine years old were riding bikes in the street, banging away at each other with finger guns, four boys, two girls. This was not PC country. In Reno, a kid in first grade pulling a finger gun on the playground would get a three-day suspension. In California, he or she would get three years in San Quentin. California is a train wreck, governed by imbeciles.

The driveway was empty so I pulled in and turned off the engine. We got out and went around back, not to the front door. Harper rapped on one of six glass panes set in the back door.

We waited.

Waited some more.

Harper knocked on the glass again, harder.

Nothing.

"Must be out," I said, because I've been trained to add up clues and connect dots.

"A startling conclusion for sure." She dug a key out of her purse, opened the back door, and we went in.

"Aunt Ellen?" she called out.

No response, so we went through the house. Nothing was out of place. Bed made; kitchen clean. We went into an attached garage. Her aunt's car was still there.

Harper frowned at the car, then shrugged. "She rides her bicycle a lot. One of those fat-tire bikes."

I aimed a finger at a dark corner. "One fat-tire bike, bright red."

Harper pursed her lips. "She might be out walking. Also, last I heard, she's got a boyfriend somewhere in the neighborhood. Guy by the name of Jeff, so there's that."

"They do sleepovers? Not that it's any of my business."

"I believe so. She's only fifty-four, Mort."

"Doesn't have one foot in the grave, huh?"

"No, and neither do I."

I kept a mile away from that one. We went back in the house. She tried to call Ellen's cell phone, got no answer. She took a set of keys off a peg by the back door. "Let's go have a look at the guest house. You'll like it."

"Uh-huh."

"Really, Mort. You and I would be fine there."

"I'm trying not to let any lines get blurred."

"They're *not*. Try to get funny with me and I'd knock your freakin' block off, mister."

"Ouch. That'd hurt."

We walked to the cabin on flagstones set into a well-kept lawn. As advertised, the cabin was tiny, sixteen by eighteen feet. Small bath and an alcove kitchen. The living room and bedroom were one and the same.

"Cute, huh?" Harper asked.

"Very."

"And look, the bed's a queen, not a full."

"Yup."

"And the cost is right. As in free."

"Best deal in town."

"It *is*, Mort. Anyway, I'm glad you're *so* excited about the possibility of staying here tonight." She stared at me. "Think about it while we're out hunting Elrood. How're we gonna *do* that, by the way?"

"I'll talk to this Zola person. Elrood used her phone to call the girl in Tonopah. Ma used Zola's number to come up with an address. How familiar are you with Ely?"

"Fair. It's not a big place."

I gave Harper the address. "East side," she said. "Little bit south of here."

"Want to buy some clothes first?"

"What for? It's already ninety out, probably get close to a hundred today."

"That's still a hell of a short skirt, Harp."

She turned and faced me. "I pole vault and long jump, which is tomboy, but I'm still a girly-girl in my head, which is where it counts. So, yes, the skirt is short. I like how it feels. If that's not okay with you, I'll cover up. If it *is* okay and you're not thinking about tossing me into a bed, then let's go find this Zola person."

I smiled. Had to. "Look out, Zola, here we come."

"*Thank* you. I mean, jeez Louise, Mort. Last night you saw a whole lot more of me than this."

Guess she told me.

We went out to the truck and headed east toward the main drag, then went south, turned left before reaching a McDonald's, traveled two blocks, then left for one block. In that short mile, I spotted three black pickup trucks, a Ram driven by an older guy with an older woman beside him, a crew cab Ford F-150, and a Chevy Silverado. Popular color, black. It gave me the willies, seeing them in the distance, knowing one of them might be last night's black truck and I wouldn't know it until it was too close to avoid. Last night I gave Harper a description of the night-riding guy and got no reaction. I hadn't told her he was hunting for someone up in the hills. She didn't seem to have any idea she might be a person of interest to anyone, but if I saw that bearded guy again, she and I were going to have a lively discussion about it.

Zola's place was a two-story apartment building of pale green cinderblocks. It had wrought-iron railings and a tired look, as if it had seen too many winters, not enough paint. I parked on the street in the shade of an elm and we piled out.

"Apartment 2D," I said.

We hiked over, then up a flight of outside concrete stairs, turned right, went down to 2D, and rapped on the door, got no answer.

No answer after another good rap, which was how the day had gone, how it was continuing.

Harper turned and looked out toward the street. "Now what?"

"Now we play detective."

"Cool. How?"

"Knock on doors. Ask around."

Two doors got us no response. The third door was opened by a girl about twenty years old in denim shorts, a torn and cropped knock-off Rolling Stones T-shirt, bare feet, tattoos, pierced tongue and belly button, and a whiff of happy weed powerful enough to knock us back a foot. She was five ten, a hundred fifteen pounds, if that, a sallow skeleton with eight rings on her fingers.

"Zola in 2D, sure. It's not like we hang out 'cause she's, I dunno, like almost forty? Or maybe thirty, I'm not sure. But I kinda know her okay, like sorta."

Didn't sound like it.

"She's not home. Do you know where she is?" Harper asked.

"I bet she *is* home. Asleep. She's a cocktail waitress at the Jailhouse. Works nights."

"Jailhouse?" I asked.

Harper put a hand on my arm. "A motel-casino on Highway 50, middle of town." She turned to the girl and said, "Thanks. We'll try to catch up with her later."

"That's the shortest skirt I've ever seen," the girl said, still in the doorway. "Or is it a skort?"

"No, it's a skirt."

"For real? You're brave."

"It's a running skirt."

"What's that?"

Harper rolled her eyes. "A skirt for runners. It's meant to be extra short."

"Still brave. I'd be afraid of wind gusts." She stepped inside and shut the door.

We left, headed back to the truck.

"You smoke that stuff?" I asked.

"No more. I tried it a few times, didn't care for it. It's been a while, like six or seven years. How about you?"

"I'm the guy in North America who's never tried it."

She laughed. "Don't bother, Mort. Really, it's *totally* not you."

Huh.

* * *

"Where to next?" she asked.

"How about we buy clothes, since what we're wearing is all we've got?"

She shrugged. "Might as well. For later anyway. Right now I'm good."

Before we took off, I dug through my duffel bag and came up with a dirty blond wig—about the shade of Robert Redford's hair back in the day. I put it on.

Harper stared at me. "Really?"

"Yes, really."

I found a reddish-blond moustache and put that on too, and a Budweiser ball cap, and dark glasses. "If we're going to be in and out of stores I need to hide. I'm fairly recognizable in this state, Harp."

"Actually, I was commenting on the fact that you have a wig with you. Not many people carry that kind of thing around, in case you didn't know."

"Not everyone has a shifty politician's hand FedEx'd to them, either." I probably shouldn't have said that, but I wanted to see how she would take it. In this PI business it's good to have an assistant who isn't squeamish.

She rolled her eyes. "I get *that,* but that wig makes you look, well . . . kinda peculiar, Mort."

Okay, not squeamish. Good thing, considering how the world has been treating me the past two years. "Kinda peculiar is what I'm shooting for. It's even euphemistic. You might've meant bizarre. Let's go find a store."

We ended up at a place called The Garnet Mercantile, half a block from the Jailhouse Motel-Casino. They had a decent small-town selection of clothing. Harper bought a pair of black jeans and blue shorts, long-sleeve and short-sleeve button-up-the-front shirts, a T-shirt with *Lehman Caves, Great Basin National Park* on the front, panties, no bra. I got jeans and a black T-shirt, a green shirt with a collar, socks, underwear. At the last minute I bought his and hers lightweight jackets.

"Thanks," Harper said. "But do I need that?"

"We're over a mile high. It'll get chilly tonight."

"Which means we're staying. Goodie."

"Have to. I haven't bumped into Elrood yet."

"Bumped into. Is that an investigative technique I've never heard of before?"

"Don't make me hurt you, girl."

She laughed. "Yeah, *right*."

I'd parked the truck on Second Street, a quarter block off Highway 50, the main drag through town past bars, casinos, hotels, chamber of commerce. I was about to open Harper's door when a big black pickup rolled by on the highway. I stared at it until it disappeared.

"What?" Harper asked.

"Nothing. Thought I saw a guy might've been Elrood, but it wasn't."

We got in the truck. "Where to?" Harper asked.

I started the engine. "Check on your aunt again?"

"See, there's this kinda new thing called a cell phone."

"Smart ass."

She swiped the screen, hit a few buttons and listened for half a minute, then put the phone away. "No answer."

"Are you hungry?"

"Getting there."

"Got an interesting question for you then."

"What's that?"

"If you sit in a chair in that skirt, say in a restaurant, what might people see?"

"Wow, the things you ask. It depends on *how* I sit, and where people are in relation to the direction I'm facing."

"Want to change into the pants you bought?"

"Not really, but I guess I'd better. If we're going to be in a restaurant full of uptight old fogies, that is."

"Let's go check on your aunt. You can change there."

It took three minutes to get to Ellen's house. No sign of life from outside. We went in the back door and Ellen still wasn't home.

Harper traded the skirt for tight black jeans but kept the body-hugging tank top.

"What?" she said when she saw me looking at her.

"That's a mighty snug top, lady."

"Uh-huh. Comfortable, too. What's your point?"

"Just sayin'. So, you know this town better than I do. Got a preference about where we eat?"

"Not really. But the Jailhouse restaurant is okay and Zola might pop in."

Good enough.

I parked in the Jailhouse parking lot and we walked half a block to the casino, found a table in the restaurant. My wig got a long look from a woman in her forties who told us her name was Beth and she would be our waitress. We got menus and drinks, then I fired up my phone and called Lucy. I kept my voice down and didn't put the phone on speaker.

"Hi, Mort," she said. "Everything still okay?"

"Great. My clothes are dry and Harper and I are in the Jailhouse in Ely." Thought I'd give her a tweak.

"Jailhouse Casino, huh? In the restaurant? It's about lunchtime."

So, no tweak.

"That's right, sugar plum. You oughta be a detective."

"I am, kinda. How's Harper?"

"She's fine. Also dry. We haven't run across her travel bag yet so we bought a few clothes to tide her over. I got a few things too since I didn't bring anything with me. How's your mom?"

"Really looking forward to chugging a big bottle of magnesium citrate tomorrow afternoon to, you know, get things started."

"I bet."

"Guess what's in your future in about ten years, Mort."

"In ten years I'll be married to the most flexible forty-two-year-old girl in the entire country."

"You're so sweet, reminding me that I'll be over forty in just ten lousy years."

"They'll be good years, cupcake."

"Okay, then. Anything else goin' on, Mort?"

"Trying to hook up with Harper's aunt Ellen. She's out right now. Harper thinks there's probably a boyfriend in the vicinity."

"Cool. Every woman should have one of those to take out garbage and unplug drains—unless she finds herself a shithead, then no. Okay, looks like I gotta run. Mom wants to Uber us over to Union Square to buy some stuff."

"A pre-colonoscopy shopping spree, huh?"

"I'll tell her you figured that out."

"Good luck with that."

"Talk to you soon. Haven't found Elrood yet, huh?"

"Nope. He's a slippery lad."

We ended the call. I hadn't mentioned the guy in the Ram truck. If I had, Lucy would've been on her way here within minutes. I didn't want her to abandon her mother for no reason.

Our waitress took our orders, then left.

I phoned Ma. Had to do it, but the conversation was likely to cause Harper and me to have more conversation and I wasn't looking forward to the damper it might put on what was so far a pretty good day.

"Mort! What's going on with Elrood Wintergarden?"

"Ma! How're you? I'm fine, thanks."

"Yeah, yeah, I figured as much since I ain't seen you in the news."

Ma—Maude Clary—still gets nervous when I phone after I've been out of her sight for more than twenty-four hours. I've found so many bodies and body parts of famous missing people in the past two years that she cringes when I call, so this could get interesting.

"Funny you sayin' that, Ma."

"No. Uh-uh. I'm hanging up now, bye."

"Don't. Not that you shouldn't, but I've got something of a problem you might help me with."

Harper stared at me. I shook my head and mouthed, *Not you*. She gave me a questioning look.

"A problem?" Ma said. "I'm hangin' up, Mort."

"I would only call back, so don't bother. I, uh, ran into a person you need to know about."

"Oh, shit. Who?"

I looked at Harper. "The daughter of Nevada's missing attorney general."

"You're fired." She hung up. She's such a kidder.

I smiled at Harper, then called Ma back.

"Hola, Miz Clary. We were cut off."

"No we weren't, boyo."

"Okay, cool, you sure showed me. But here's the thing. I haven't come across any . . . you know. What I sometimes come across."

"Body. Bodies. Body parts."

"That's right. Those. So we're good, Ma. I need you to find out whatever you can about a black Ram pickup truck, partial Nevada license ZJX5."

"Why? What's with the truck?"

"It might be involved somehow."

"With what? The missing attorney general?"

"Not likely, but I guess it's possible."

"So it's got nuthin to do with Elrood, does it?"

"Not a thing."

"Which is what you're supposed to be working on."

"I *am*, Ma. I've been tracking that dimwit all over the state. You didn't ask where I am, in case that got by you."

"Where are you, Mort?"

"So glad you asked. Ely."

"Which means you're checking out the address I got you from that phone call to that girl in Tonopah."

"You're a sharp old—"

"Be very careful how you finish that sentence, boyo."

"—cookie."

"I'll get back to you if I get anything on that truck. But here's a thought: Try to locate *Elrood Wintergarden*."

"Will do, Ma. You're the best."

She hung up.

"What black truck?" Harper asked, eyes boring into mine like augers.

I knew that was coming but I'd had to get Ma looking into that truck. I wanted the name of the guy driving it. "Funny you should ask, Harp."

Her eyes narrowed. "Maybe not so funny? It must be the one that came by last night in the rain, which you never said anything more about. Until *now*."

So I told her about the Ram pickup and the rough-looking character behind the wheel who'd asked if I'd seen anyone up there in the mountains that night, but didn't say who, or under what circumstances—in a car, walking, riding a bike, holding out a thumb. And I told her about the black truck that stopped outside the general store while she and Olivia were on the second floor, plotting how to get me and Harper stark naked in one small bedroom.

"Plotting," she said. "As if you and I didn't look like drowned rats. You're something else. I don't know anyone with a black pickup or anyone matching your description of that guy—and what's *that* all about, anyway?"

"If you don't know, it's probably nothing."

"You've got your partner checking out a partial license because it's probably nothing? Isn't trying to track down a partial plate a lot harder than an entire plate?"

"It is, yes."

"You want to give her something to do, keep her out of mischief? You don't think this truck is anything serious, is that right?"

"Right. I'm hyper-cautious. It's a personality fault." I looked around. "Don't see our waitress anywhere, do you?"

"Nice try. So the guy was asking if you'd seen anyone up in the hills and you think he was looking for me?"

"He might've been, but I didn't ask. It didn't seem like a good idea at the time."

She frowned. "You had me duck down and hide *before* he got close, before his truck stopped or anything."

"Did I mention that I'm a bit cautious at times?"

"You mean paranoid? Yes, you did."

"Well, then. I don't know what you're getting at."

She fell silent, but I doubted that that was going to be the end of it. In fact, if she didn't bring it up again, I would, now that the elephant was loose in the room.

Our food arrived and we filled up. Lucy had me off large doses of red meat so I had a grilled chicken breast and veggies. I don't call 'em veggies, but she does. Harper had a salad, which is how the womenfolk around me eat and why they weigh less than a hundred twenty pounds.

Our waitress returned and asked if we wanted dessert. "My wife here said something about a banana split," I told her. I recanted when I took a warning shot to a shin. "But I think we'll pass. I wouldn't want her bloating up like she did last year. Ouch! What time does the shift change in the bar?"

Her eyes jittered. "Did she just kick you?"

"Sort of, but not really. She has restless leg syndrome. I'm used to it. Shift change?"

"Five o'clock. Is that a no on the dessert?"

"Yes, that's a no. Does Zola work there in the bar?"

Asking for her by name was a bit of a risk, but I didn't know how else to get the information.

"Zola? Sure."

"Is she on this evening?"

"I think so. Are you looking for her?"

"I'm supposed to give her fifty bucks a friend of mine borrowed from her a few months ago." Another risk, but probably worth it now that I'd put Zola's name out there.

She shrugged. "Come back any time after five. She'll be here." She took a couple of twenties and left.

"*Bloating?*"

"Hush, little lady. People are staring."

"Lucy must be a saint."

* * *

It was 1:35 when we went outside into blazing sun and a temperature of 98 degrees.

"Hot out," Harper said. "I'm going to change back into my running skirt, if that's okay with you."

I looked around. "Go ahead, but be quick. I'll keep an eye out for cops."

"How about I do that at my *aunt's house*, not out here on the street?"

"If you insist, Prudence."

"I thought you wanted us to keep a low profile."

So we went back for the third time. Ellen still wasn't home, wasn't answering her cell phone. Harper peered out a window at the street. "If she's with boyfriend Jeff, she's probably having a good time."

"No comment."

She turned around. "'No comment' *is* a comment."

"Do you know Jeff's last name or where he lives?"

"No. He's something of a new item. She's mentioned him, but I haven't met him yet."

"A new item. That's always exciting. How about you change and we take off again?"

"Where to?" She undid the button of her jeans and ran the zipper down. Being immune, I didn't bat an eye, didn't look away.

"No idea. Drive around. Get a feel for the town. Maybe see if Zola's up yet."

"Might as well."

She hooked her thumbs into her jeans and panties and stripped them off so fast I didn't have a chance to turn around before the *fait* was *accompli*. She stepped into her running skirt and pulled it up.

"Man, that was fast," I said, impressed.

She smiled. "I'll do it slower next time if you want."

"That wasn't the point of my comment, but what you said has its merits. I'll let you know. Ready to go?"

"In a minute. I want to give my hair a quick brushing."

"I'll be outside." My truck was parked in the driveway. A middle-aged woman diagonally across the street was in a three-point kneeling stance, weeding a flower bed.

I walked over. "Howdy, ma'am," I said.

She looked up and shaded her eyes. "Yes? Hi?"

"Don't want to take up much of your time since you look like you're having an awful lot of fun there . . ."

She smiled, sat back on her haunches. "No, I'm not. Please, take up some of my time."

"Will do." I pointed toward Ellen's house. "You know the woman who lives over there?"

"Of course. Ellen and I have been friends for years. I'm Peggy. Peg. Who're you?"

"Mort. Friend of Ellen's, sort of indirectly."

"Uh-huh." Peg wasn't sure how to take that.

Harper came out from behind the house, spotted us and headed our way.

"Oh, are you with Harper?" the woman asked me.

"More or less."

She tilted her head. "How curious. Hi, Harper," she said as Harper came up and put an arm around my waist. Peg looked up at me and grinned. "*That's* more or less?"

"What's more or less?" Harper asked.

"You being with me," I said.

"Yeah, that sounds right. Hi, Peg. Hey, have you seen Ellen around yesterday or today?"

"I spoke with her day before yesterday. Or maybe it was the day before that." She gave it more thought. "I saw Jeff's pickup in her driveway earlier this morning, but I didn't actually see him or Ellen. When I looked over there ten minutes later, it was gone again."

Huh. "What make and color is his truck?" I asked.

"Gee, I wouldn't know the make. I don't know trucks. They all look the same to me. But it's big and black."

I didn't like that, and by the way Harper's face lost two shades, she didn't either.

"Ready to go?" I asked her. I didn't give her a chance to respond. I took her by the arm, about to spirit her away, but then I turned and asked Peg, "About what time was it, when you saw his truck over there?"

"Well, I'm not sure, exactly. I guess it must've been about nine, nine-thirty. Something like that."

"Thanks. Do you know Jeff's last name?"

"Nickel. Jeff Nickel, spelled like the coin. He's been good for her. Ellen's been happy lately." She smiled. "*Very* happy."

"Thanks. It was nice meeting you, Peg. Harper and I will probably be around. In and out, looks like."

"Good. Ellen will like that. And," she said with a bit of the devil in her eye, "she's got that cute little guest house in back—more or less."

I smiled, then led Harper away, trying to make it look as if she were coming along willingly, not being propelled away before she could say too much.

"There was a black pickup in her driveway?" Harper said when we were back at my truck. "This morning?"

"Jeff Nickel has a black pickup."

"So does that guy who might've been looking for me last night."

"Uh-huh."

"Maybe we should go to the police."

"It's much too early for anything like that, Harp. We need to find this Jeff guy first."

She thought about that. "Okay, that makes sense. I'm sorry. I'm kinda worried, that's all." She hugged my arm.

I glanced over at Peg. "Forgot to ask her where Jeff lives. Gimme a minute."

I walked over, asked Peg about Jeff.

"He'll be in the phone book for sure, but he doesn't live far from here. Within walking distance, anyway. Ellen has been going over to his place on foot a lot. I've never been there so I don't know. Somewhere east, though."

"Great. Thanks."

So far it added up. Jeff had a black pickup. Ellen was out. She was a walker. Jeff and Ellen were an item. Ellen has been happy lately—very.

Inside Ellen's house Harper took a phone book off a kitchen countertop. Jeffrey Nickel was on Avenue H, about ten blocks away, a decent stroll.

We hopped in the truck and I drove over. Jeff's truck was in his driveway—a black crew-cab Chevy Silverado, not a Ram. So far so good. I got out with Harper and rang the doorbell.

A woman in her mid-fifties answered. Heavy-set with a pleasant, open face, wisps of hair in her eyes. "Yes?"

"Sorry to bother you, ma'am," I said. "We're looking for Jeff."

"I'm his sister, Carol. What do you want him for?"

"Actually," Harper said, edging around me, "I'm trying to find Ellen. I'm Harper, her niece. I was hoping she'd be over here."

Carol smiled. "It's nice to meet you, Harper. Ellen has mentioned you quite often. But you missed her. She and Jeff took off for Idaho yesterday morning."

"But she's okay?"

Carol frowned. "Of course. Is everything all right?"

"I'm just surprised she left. She knew I was driving up. I was in her house, but she didn't leave a note."

"She might've been rushed and forgot. This trip was one of those last-minute things. Jeff wanted to use his time off to take Ellen to Boise to see his other sister. Maybe to get Sara's approval, which I've told him he doesn't need. Or maybe just to introduce the two to each other."

"His truck is here," I said. "So it wouldn't have been at her house earlier this morning, would it?"

"Oh, heavens, no. I haven't driven it since he left. He took the Forester so they could put more stuff in it and lock it up if they had to. Gets better gas mileage too."

"I'm glad she finally met someone," Harper said. "And I'm very glad to have met you, Carol. Did they say when they'll be back?"

"Jeff thought by Thursday." She looked at Harper, bit her lip and said, "I really don't mean anything by this, but is that a skort? I've never seen one that short."

"No. It's a skirt. A running skirt. Tennis players use them too." Harper shrugged. "It's hot out, and I like my legs to be free when I run. And, just free generally. The sun feels good."

Carol nodded. "I'd wear it too if I had your legs. Don't mind me, dear. I'm something of a busybody."

"No you're not. Really. Everyone asks about this skirt. Well, I guess we'd better get going. I want to do some more looking around."

"If I hear from Ellen before you do, I'll let her know you're asking about her."

"Thanks. I tried to call her on her cell, but no answer."

"You wouldn't. She dropped it a few days ago and . . . well, killed it. It was an older phone anyway. She said she'll get a new one when she and Jeff get back."

"Can I have Jeff's number? In case I need to call her."

"Of course." She reeled it off and Harper put it in her phone.

We left. We didn't mention the black pickup that had been at Ellen's that morning. No sense trying to explain it, getting Carol worried, having her pass that along to Jeff and Ellen. This needed more thought.

If things didn't shape up soon, however, we might end up talking to the police, though I had no idea how to tell them about the black truck without sounding a bit loony.

CHAPTER TEN

WE GOT BACK in the truck and Harper looked at me. "I don't like this, Mort."

I didn't either. Attorney General Annette Leeman had disappeared four or five days ago. Her sister, Ellen Moore, was probably okay, but there was a rough-looking guy who might—*might*—be looking for Harper, a guy who might've been at Ellen's house for a few minutes that morning, then took off. A guy who could still be around.

None of that constituted proof of anything, but things weren't shaping up well.

I didn't think I was going to be leaving Ely anytime soon. Certainly not today, which hinted at my next move.

I started the engine, pulled away from the curb.

"Where to?" Harper asked.

"See if Zola is up, then check out that Nevada Hotel-Casino."

"It's called Hotel Nevada, which is kind of backwards, I know. What're you gonna do there?"

"Get a couple rooms for the night."

"Seriously? We've got that great little guest house and it's free and we're gonna go to a hotel?"

"Yep. I'll give you a few minutes to think outside the box and figure out why."

"I hate that expression."

"So do I."

"So why'd you use it?"

"I was speaking outside the box."

"Oh, jeez."

She sat with her arms folded across her chest for a few seconds, then she looked at me. "You don't think it's safe for us to stay at Ellen's, do you?"

"I have my doubts. I don't know what's going on. It might be nothing and your aunt and Jeff will show up and we'll never see that pickup truck again and everything will be fine, but until that or something like it happens, I don't want to take chances."

"Okay, but how about we get *one* room so you can save me if a big bearded, Yeti-looking guy breaks in."

"How about two rooms, with an adjoining door?"

She squinted at me. "We've seen each other without clothes, Mort. And we both know that's *absolutely* as far as that'll ever get, *and* I think we're friends—"

"All of which is true."

She glared at me. "I hear a 'but' in there."

"*But*, we'll get two rooms anyway."

"Well, shoot. Whatever you want, Mort. I give up."

Probably not.

Zola didn't respond to a light knock on her door, so we let her sleep. Next stop, Hotel Nevada.

The place was a rectangular box, six floors of red brick built in 1929. For a number of years, it had the distinction of being the tallest building in the state. I left the truck in one of their parking lots, a plot of hot cracked asphalt half a block east of the hotel. Ely wasn't big enough to want or need multilevel or underground parking. Everything was out in the weather, sautéing in the summer, accumulating ice and snow in the winter.

We took the clothes we'd bought, cell phones, guns—with bullets—and bags to the hotel. I kept an eye out for a black pickup as we hiked toward the building. We went in a back entrance and down a short hallway to the casino.

The hotel's interior was cool, but not chilled. I wasn't sure the suggestion of "fine dining" was going to pan out since the main restaurant was a Denny's, but it looked as if it might be a cut above a Reno or Vegas Denny's. The bar would've been dark as a crypt except for half a dozen flat-screen TVs lining the walls.

A tour of the ground floor took two minutes, then we hit the hotel's reservation alcove.

A lone girl was behind the desk. "Got two rooms with a connecting door between them?" I asked her. She had a silver ring in one nostril, another through an eyebrow, ears full of shrapnel. Her upper left arm and what I could see of her left shoulder were inked so solid it looked like a bruise she'd gotten running an ATV off a cliff. Tattoo regret was probably in her future, once the novelty wore off, which it tends to do. A plastic name tag on her shirt read "Aurora." Pretty girl except for the self-destruction.

"Do you have a reservation?" she asked, ready to pounce on a computer keyboard.

"Nope."

She dropped her hands. "Oh, well, then I'm sorry. It's summer and we're almost full."

"But not completely full?"

"No. But we don't have rooms with a connecting door. There's not many of those in the hotel anyway."

In a high corner behind the reservation alcove, Spade and Hammer guffawed and nudged each other, knowing how this was about to play out. The jerks.

"How about two rooms on the same floor?" I asked.

Aurora glanced at her monitor. "Uh, no. I've got one on the fifth floor, one on the fourth, and one on the second. That's all we have right now. Just those three rooms." She gave me an apologetic look.

Spade let out a high-pitched giggle.

Harper eased around me. "We'll take the one on the fifth floor." She turned to me. "How's that? It probably has the best view, honey."

"No good." I turned to Aurora. "We'll take the rooms on the fourth and fifth floors."

Harper laughed. "My husband kids around like this all the time. You should hear him at family gatherings. He's a riot." She gave me a cross-eyed look and bumped my hip with hers. "That fifth-floor room will be fine," she said to Aurora. "It sounds like you need all the rooms you can get. No sense in us taking two when one will do."

"Fifth floor, room 512, comes with a single king bed." Aurora looked up from her computer. "Is that okay?"

"Fabulous," Harper said.

"What's on the fourth floor?" I asked. "In the way of beds, I mean."

"404 has two queens. And it's nonsmoking."

"That'll be fine," I said. "We'll take it." Aurora looked between me and Harper, trying to decide who was in the lead. "She tosses like . . . like a person tossing *horseshoes* in her sleep," I added, pulling ahead by a nose.

"I do *not*," Harper said, struggling to contain a laugh. "We'll take the room with the king bed." I got another hip bump as she held out a credit card.

I plucked the card out of her hand and glanced at it. To Aurora I said, "We'll take the room with two queens. 404? How much is it?"

"Honeeyyy . . ." Harper said.

I held up a forefinger to Aurora. "Excuse us for a few seconds. Need a little conference here." I took Harper ten feet away and held up her credit card. "Read the name on this card. Quietly."

She pursed her lips. "Harper Leeman."

"We're trying to fly under the radar. How does waving your name around help us?"

"Oop." Then she said, "But why is your card better, Mr. Mortimer Angel?"

"Hold that thought." I kept her card and took her back to the desk. "We'll take 404 with the two queens."

"Are you *sure*?" She looked at Harper, who nodded reluctantly.

Aurora tried not to roll her eyes, then she sighed and said, "That'll be ninety-six fifty. That's with the room tax. And it includes two free breakfasts in the restaurant."

Two Denny's All-American Slams? What a bargain.

"Great," I said, handing over a Visa card.

She read the name. "Stephen Brewer. I'll need to see some ID, and I have to have a vehicle's license plate."

As I handed over my fake license, Harper gave me a questioning look. I slipped an arm around her waist, slid my hand up and pressed two fingers against the underside of her right breast to keep her quiet. Or occupied.

She jumped slightly. "Yow!"

Aurora looked up. "Excuse me?"

"Nothing," Harper said. "Something kinda hit me. I'll have to talk it over with my darling husband later."

Aurora went back to her computer. Harper looked up at me and lifted an eyebrow. I gave her a little head shake. Ever since a certain trip to Paris, Ma and I had fake IDs and credit cards, passports. Lucy still had a fake ID her father got her for an entirely different reason. The three of us had made good use of our bogus paper last year when we went down to Phoenix and Ma stole a hundred twenty thousand dollars from a bank, but that's a different story.

I didn't want a record of Mortimer Angel registering at Hotel Nevada, so it was Stephen Brewer and his wife, Tammy. Tammy, since only one of us had to show an ID. I thought I'd have "Tammy" tell Lucy about "Steve's" latest wife *and* room 404, a conversation I would record to play back during those riotous family gatherings.

This, I thought, was likely to end the Brewer identity. When we got back from the "Phoenix job" last year, my partner, Maude Clary, got Doc Saladin in New Mexico busy whipping up new identities for the three of us—Lucy, Ma, and me, so I had one more to fall back on: a driver's license and a MasterCard in the name of David Peterson. I didn't want to use the Peterson identity, at least not yet. For now, the Brewer ID would have to do. I didn't think it had been burned, but odds were this was its last gasp. I only hoped I hadn't pushed it one time too far. Given what Ma and I had done in Paris over a year and a half ago, it might have been smart to retire "Steve" right then, but it's hard to give up a good fake ID.

Once the paperwork was completed and we got card keys for the room's electronic lock, Harper led me over to the stairs.

"Got an elevator over here to the left, honey," I said, pointing.

"Yeah, but over *this* way they've got this bitchin' in-house Stairmaster, *honey*."

So we trooped up, Harper in the lead which meant I had a view of panties much of the way. Or a panty liner. I still didn't see that there was any significant difference, but that was one hellacious short skirt and it didn't quite cover a hundred percent of a perfectly rounded fantail.

The room was reasonably okay. They probably didn't have anything that basic at the Taj Mahal, if the Taj has rooms. I'll have to Google that sometime.

Harper sat on one of the beds and bounced. "Down at the check-in desk you copped a feel, Mort."

"Did I?"

"Uh-huh. I'll take my turn later." She got up, went into the bathroom, came back out. "Got an okay shower in there, in case you're interested."

"Jeez, this place has running water too?"

"Don't know. I didn't turn it on."

Pretty quick comeback. I liked this girl.

I eased back a curtain and peered out the window. We had a nice view of the street below, a head-on view of the Jailhouse Motel-Casino directly across from us, distant brown hills to the north. A black pickup truck rolled slowly by, headed east. I turned back to the room.

"You have a credit card in someone else's name. Why is that?" Harper asked me.

"That's not worry I hear in your voice, is it?"

"Just . . . curious."

"I'll tell you later. Right now, how about you take the battery out of your phone."

"Why?"

"We're broadcasting our location." I got out my cell phone and pulled its battery. "We should've gone dark before leaving Grange."

Gumshoe in the dark. That was me the past two years, the world throwing me curveballs I didn't see coming. All this subterfuge might not be necessary—cell phones, fake IDs, wigs, and moustaches— but it didn't hurt to be safe.

Harper got her battery out. "You really think someone might try to track our phones?"

"It's possible. The guy in that black truck still has me worried. We're gonna have to buy a couple of burners."

"Burners?"

"Cheap disposable cell phones. No GPS, not registered to anyone, in particular not to us."

"My aunt won't be able to contact me if we do that. If, you know, she tries to call."

"Can't be helped. We need to go dark, at least until we get this figured out. Some old guy hits on you and you end up at the side of the road. Then *another* guy comes along a few hours later and asks if I've seen anyone up there. He didn't say who, just anyone. Those two events appear to be connected somehow." I looked at her. "You still don't know what any of that might mean, do you?"

"No. I never saw the old guy before yesterday, and I don't know anyone with a black truck like you described."

"Your mother is missing. She's political, in the public eye. The country has never been so divided, ideologically speaking. She'll have a lot of enemies."

She pursed her lips. "I know. It's a mess."

I gave her an appraising look. "You need to get out of those clothes and into something less recognizable."

"Well, shoot. I *like* what I'm wearing."

"Wear whatever you want in here, Harp, but walking around a town this size in that outfit is like waving a flag."

She smiled. "Well, good. You're on record saying I can wear whatever I want in here." Then her face grew serious. "Tell me again how long it was before Lucy said she would marry you."

"Why?"

"Just . . . tell me. Unless you were kidding before."

I didn't need to think back. That day was embossed in my memory. "The marry word first came out of her mouth ten or twelve minutes after she plopped down in a booth with me in McGinty's Café. Without asking if it was okay, by the way. I don't count the twenty minutes before that since she was my waitress, but she got fired for dropping my plate of fried chicken. What she actually said was she would *probably* marry me if I asked, so I think that counts. The actual proposal, or something very much like it, came when we were about ten miles south of Tonopah on U.S. 95, headed for Vegas."

"Was it real? The proposal?"

"Must've been, since she meant it. Not that I knew it at the time, but I'm slow that way."

Harper sat cross-legged on the bed. "Less than an hour after the two of you met. That borders on spooky. It's also so darn romantic I can hardly stand it."

"Speaking of spooky, what do you get when you take the 'k' out of the word 'lucky'?"

She thought for a moment. "Lucy."

"There you go. She was born when four planets were lined up and Mars wasn't one of them. She has intuition or luck like you wouldn't believe. Whenever she says anything that relies on intuition, premonition, or luck, I listen. And I act on it."

"She has you," Harper said wistfully. Then her eyes widened. "Sorry, that came out *so* wrong. What I mean is, you have each other and nothing at all can come between you. Which is totally wonderful."

"That's right."

She smiled. "Including me, so I'm not a threat. I like that. That must be why she doesn't worry about how I'm dressed around you. Or not dressed."

I shrugged. "Okay by me too, as long as *you* tell her what you're wearing or not wearing so I don't have to. She and I don't keep secrets from each other, but I'd rather you do the telling since she razzes me unmercifully."

"Cool." She got off the bed. "I really want to meet her. She has to be a completely amazing person."

"She is that."

* * *

Harper changed into blue shorts and a T-shirt. We hiked downstairs and went outside. The day was still hot. We headed west on foot. I felt exposed on the main street like that, but there wasn't anything we could do about it except move quickly. I still wore a wig, a moustache, dark glasses, a ball cap. I hoped we could pick up disposables at the place where we bought clothes, the Garnet Mercantile, a block from our hotel on our side of the street.

Before we ducked inside, I looked up and down the street, didn't see a black pickup, which didn't make me feel better since I still felt as if we had targets on our backs.

I might've been wrong about that. My paranoia gene flares up when unexplained things happen.

The store had burners, so we didn't have to wander up and down the street hunting for them. We bought two, and Harper bought a used paperback and a man's large T-shirt, sky blue, with mountains drawn on the front, then we went back to the hotel and up to our room.

Our new phones came with wall chargers. We got that going, then Harper stripped off her clothes—two items so it wasn't a big production and didn't require music. She put on the T-shirt which fell to mid-thigh and looked like a tent on her. She spun a three-sixty in the room and struck a hip-shot pose. "What do you think?"

"No underwear?"

"What on earth for?"

"Up to you. But you might want to be careful how you sit or lie on the bed, not plop down any old way."

"Uh-huh." She gazed around the room. "*Now* what, Mort?"

Now I didn't know what. It was 2:45. Zola wouldn't be in at the Jailhouse until after five, so the search for the opportunistic vanishing Elrood was on hold. I didn't want to put the battery back in my cell phone to call Lucy, and my new burner wouldn't be ready to go for another hour or two. I didn't want to go back to Ellen's place for the fourth time that day. We were better off staying out of sight in the room.

I looked at Harper. "How about a game of chess?"

"Got a set in your duffel bag?"

"Nope."

"So . . . mental chess?"

"Looks like."

"Okay, then. I've got white. Pawn from E2 to E4."

Shit, it figured she was a ringer. "I fold," I said. I dug *The Day of the Jackal* out of my duffel and settled into one of two easy chairs by the window.

"You're just gonna read?" Harper said.

"You oughta be a detective."

"I wonder if there's a naturist park anywhere around here. Seems like there oughta be."

"Google it, hon. Report back."

She grinned. "Would you go if I found us one?"

"Nope."

"Figures."

* * *

I phoned Lucy at 4:10.

"Where are you?" she asked.

"Hotel Nevada, room 404."

"You and Harper?"

"Yup. Had to. Hotel is about full up."

"It's fine, Mort. Is the room nice? I've driven past the place but never stayed there."

"It's okay. Not the Taj Mahal but it has running water and everything."

"Wowie. So what's with you getting a new burner?"

"I left the old one in Reno. Didn't think I'd need it. Harper has one too. I'll get you her number in a while."

"How's she doing?"

"Same old same."

Lucy laughed. "Really?"

I glanced at Harper. "Actually, no. She's in a T-shirt that would fit someone eighty pounds heavier, reading a Barbara Parker novel she picked up for a dollar. We're on hold, waiting on a waitress."

"You're waiting on a waitress in your hotel room?"

"An incredible bit of irony, I know. Even stranger, she doesn't know we're waiting on her. I'll put you on speaker so Harper can keep up with this."

"Groovy. Hi, Harper."

"Hi, Lucy. Hey, you should get a man's large T-shirt. Best lounge-around shirt ever—though maybe I should've got a medium. This thing's huge."

"I'll have to do that. So, Mort, how'd you get a waitress in your room, and why are you waiting on her? Though I have to say that sounds *so* much like you."

I had to explain about Zola and the shift change.

"Sounds like you're having a good time. I will too, in a while. Mom and I are going out to dinner. Last one until after she . . . you know."

"I'm sure she's fine with you telling me all this."

"I wouldn't know. I'm just giving you an update."

"Thanks. Keep 'em coming."

"They probably won't be very detailed, but keep me in whatever loop you're in. Especially tonight after you and Harper get settled in."

Harper shot me a look.

"Worried?" I asked Lucy, knowing how that would go.

She laughed. "I'm more worried about earthquakes. I think Ely had one last century that knocked a brick or two out of the wall of the hotel you're in."

"Yeah, we're on the fourth floor. Hate for this thing to lose another brick in a quake."

"Anyway, what're you doing next?"

"Zola's supposed to get in at five over at the Jailhouse. With luck, we'll get a bead on Elrood."

"Great. Gotta run. Keep me posted. Bye, Harper."

"Bye, Lucy."

Lucy said, "I love you, Mort. Be safe."

"Always. Love you too."

We ended the call on that mushy note. Harper looked over at me. "She's more concerned about an earthquake than us being here together? I *really* have to meet her."

She went back to her novel, smiling faintly.

* * *

We didn't wander over to the Jailhouse until 7:50. I wanted to wait until dark, but hunger drove us out of the room. Harper wore blue shorts and her skin tight tank top. She looked great, but she stood out, drawing appreciative and envious looks. We didn't see the black pickup or the guy who'd been in it so maybe we were okay.

Zola was a buxom brunette in her early thirties in a one-piece outfit—a tight-fitting body suit with a push-up top that . . . pushed up. She was five-ten and wore five-inch heels, so she topped out an inch shorter than me.

"Yikes," Harper said as we got closer to Zola. She was gliding by a bank of slot machines offering free booze to the players. Turns out, alcohol makes slot machines more festive. Harper and I had been aimed in Zola's direction by the older of two bartenders behind a thirty-foot mahogany bar. Ugly video slot machines had been embedded in its surface. The casino owners evidently decided that preserving the old-time ambience of the place wasn't as profitable as having voracious slots within easy reach of bored, tipsy customers.

Harper held my hand as I spoke to Zola. Zola had never heard the name Elrood before so I showed her his picture.

"He said his name was Sam," Zola said. "You want to find that sweet-talking asshole?"

"Yep." I liked the identifier, especially since he wasn't giving out his real name.

"He jump bail, or what?" Zola asked.

That spun my head around. "He's awaiting trial?"

She grinned. "Not that I know, but it wouldn't shock me, the jerk. Sounds like you don't know him."

"I don't. I've been hired to find him, that's all."

"Well, good luck, since he left sometime yesterday, as far as I know."

The jerk.

"Where to?" I asked.

"Elko, last I heard."

I sighed. I was getting a tour of rural Nevada courtesy of Elrood Wintergarden. "Any idea where in Elko?"

"No. All I heard was he was gonna see a girl named Olga. I only know that because he borrowed my phone to call her and I heard him talking."

"Is her number still in your phone?"

"Uh, no. Sorry. I deleted it right after he made the call. I didn't want it in my phone."

No phone number. Nothing is easy.

Olga. I wondered how many Olgas lived in Elko, but it could have been a lot worse. He might've gone to see Mary Something.

"Any idea who she is or what she does, anything? A last name would be great." And too much to hope for.

"No. All I heard was the name Olga. I wouldn't have remembered it except it's uncommon, like Russian or East European or something."

"Did you know 'Sam' before? I mean in the past?"

"Never met him before three days ago. He was in here. The guy wouldn't shut up, had a mouth on him like one of those old windup chattering teeth. Wish I didn't have to be nice and smile to every customer who comes in. Fact is, I wish they would let me carry a gun." She put a hand on my shoulder. "Kidding."

"Don't worry. Your secret's safe with us. How long did you talk to the guy?"

"Too long, lemme tell you. Maybe thirty minutes total, on and off over a two-day period. I'd go behind the bar to get away from him, but I'm supposed to keep circulating so he would find me again. He tried to borrow five hundred dollars. Five *hundred*." She looked around, lowered her voice. "The dimwit also wanted me to take him home and let him stay the night."

"And, don't tell me, when he borrowed your phone, he made not one call but two."

She smiled. "Hey, you're pretty good. He did, now that you mention it. I checked right after, saw that he also called someone in Tonopah. I deleted that number too."

So. Dead end, except for the name Olga in Elko.

"Thing is," Zola said, looking around again to make sure no one was listening, "he's a very good-looking guy, a little over six feet tall, sort of boyishly sexy. Not my type, but a lot of women would really go for him. I can see him scamming around for money, which is the impression I got. Can I get you guys a drink? They're on the house if you drop a quarter or two in a slot machine. Cheapest way to drink in town, if you don't keep at it, thinking you're gonna leave a winner—not that I told you that."

"No thanks. Not yet anyway. We gotta get something to eat. Can't drink and gamble on an empty stomach."

"Smart. Anyway, I'll be here 'til two in the morning if you change your mind."

"Good to know. See you around."

Harper still had my hand. We left the Jailhouse, jaywalked across the street to Hotel Nevada and went into the Denny's restaurant.

We got a booth with a window seat, a nice view of the sporadic traffic on the street, the front of the Jailhouse, and a pair of drunks evidently trying to decide which way they wanted to go. We were almost through with dinner when the bearded guy who'd been driving the black pickup came in and spoke briefly to the hostess, a girl in her teens.

Oh, shit.

He was a few inches shorter than me, but built like an NFL tackle, or a jackhammer. Probably had me by twenty pounds, not that we were gonna box or wrestle. The girl was showing him to a table in the middle of the room when he paused and a smile broke out. He stopped at our table. "Hey, man, small world. Hell of a storm last night on that road, wasn't it?" He gave Harper a glance, then turned his attention back to me.

"Sure was," I said. Beneath the table I gave Harper's calf a warning touch. Her eyes locked with mine for an instant, then she looked down at her food.

"Your hair looks different now," the guy said to me. It would've been the strangest comment ever by a stranger but for the subtle hint of awareness and duplicity lurking in his words. He had to know I was wearing a wig.

"Must've been the rain," I said, lying back at him. "I probably looked like a half-drowned golden retriever."

"Actually, your hair looked shorter."

"Huh. You find what you were looking for out there?"

"Yeah. My dad. Took a while. He's gettin' up in years. Turned right instead of left when he reached 93, made it all the way to Pioche of all places. He called me on his cell. I ended up driving most of the night. Anyway," he nodded toward the young hostess who was still trying to seat him at a table, "Gotta go. Take 'er easy." He left.

So that was that. He'd lost his dad.

Or not. How likely was it he would give Harper a one-second look, gorgeous girl like that? She was getting looks from almost every guy and girl in the room.

But that might also be nothing. It could depend on his "orientation"—a word or concept that had eased its way into the social consciousness and lexicon of the country in the past two or three decades. I glanced over at the guy. He dipped his head at me, then opened his menu.

"Don't look at him," I said to Harper.

She nodded unhappily.

Right then, my burner rang. I recognized the number. It was Lucy. "What's up?" I said quietly.

"I think you should leave, Mort."

"Leave?"

"The hotel where you're staying. It doesn't feel right. Get out now. I'll call back in like ten minutes, but you need to leave right away. Bye."

The hair stood up on the back of my neck. I tossed two twenties on the table and Harper and I got out of there, leaving an eleven-dollar tip.

We piled into the elevator. "What's goin' on, Mort?" Harper asked on the way up. "That was the guy in the pickup truck, wasn't it?"

"Yes. Lucy told me, us, to get out of here."

"What? The hotel?"

"Yes. I doubt that she knew why. But when she says things like that, I don't ask questions, I just do it. It had to be because of that guy."

Her eyes were wide. "That's . . . spooky."

"I know. *She's* not, but the way she feels things is. Anyway, we're gettin' the hell out of here, now."

We hustled to the room, grabbed our stuff, which took less than a minute, and were headed toward the elevator when I heard it start up down below.

"C'mon," I said. I led her toward the stairs, opened a fire door to the stairwell, and we went in. I stopped, peered through a small window in the door, and saw the big guy come out of the elevator and head down the hallway in the direction of our room.

"Time to go," I said. "*Fast.*" We went down as if the place were on fire, or at least smoldering, through the hallway to the back of the hotel and out the back way. We jogged to my truck, got in, I started the engine, slammed the lever into drive, and we headed east.

Fast.

CHAPTER ELEVEN

HARPER TURNED AND looked out the rear window. "What the hell is going on?" she asked breathlessly.

"Dunno. But that guy got off the elevator and headed toward our room."

"Omigod. Are you sure?"

I gave her a look. "I'm sure. I didn't wait to see if he kicked in our door or if he had a room on that floor, so I'm not absolutely certain he was after us." Only 99.9 percent, I didn't say.

"What're we gonna do now?"

"Dunno. Give me a moment."

We were still headed east. If the guy was in the hotel it was probably safe to check Ellen's house one last time, see if she'd come back early from Idaho—not likely but worth a quick look. I headed over there, pulled into the driveway. We bailed out, went through the place fast, still no sign of Ellen. We locked up and took off again.

"Where to now?" Harper asked.

My burner rang. It was Lucy. I pulled to the curb and answered, put it on speaker.

"Are you out of there?" Lucy said.

"Yes."

"Good. I just hope I did the right thing. I mean, I don't know why I got that feeling, Mort. I just did."

"You did good, babe."

"Really? Sometimes I don't know. Not for sure."

"You were right this time."

"Good. I guess. I mean, I wish I *wasn't*, but as long as it helped, I'm glad." She paused, then said, "What's going on, Mort? What was I right *about*?"

I didn't want to get Lucy involved. I had to soft-pedal this one. "Harper is trying to avoid some guy. He might be trouble. She and I were in the hotel restaurant when you called. We got out of there right before he came in." She would beat the shit out of me when she found out what had really happened, but this three-quarters lie was for her, not for me. I didn't like doing it, but I had to. "We're out of the hotel now," I told her, "and not going back."

Harper remained quiet, watching me. She knew I was giving Lucy half-truths, and she knew why.

"Well . . . good, Mort. I had the weird feeling it was something like that. Anyway, I Googled motels in McGill and got you a room there at the Desert Rose Motel under the names John and Britany Taggart. I told the guy on the phone I was Britany and that you and I were in separate cars but we were going to meet up there later and that you would get there first—*and* your wallet was stolen in Vegas, which is why I was making the reservation. While you're there, Harper will be Britany Taggart. I told him what you look like, Mort, so go to the office and give the guy there the story. He's expecting you. Leave Harper outside while you get the room. He's not expecting Britany to get there until later. The room is paid for. Stay in the room and . . . be safe. You've got room fifteen, by the way."

For the past few years, she had an ID and credit cards in the name of Britany Taggart. This business with the guy in the black pickup is why Lucy, Ma, and I have fake IDs. You never know when you'll need them.

"Good work, hon," I said. McGill was a small town about fifteen miles north of Ely on Highway 93.

"I'd really like to be with you right now," Lucy said. "But I don't know what good I would be, and Mom's sort of . . . you know."

"I've heard how that goes. You stay put. Harper and I will be okay. I've got something of a lead on Elrood. He might be up in Elko so we'll head up there in the morning, get out of the area here."

"That sounds like a good idea. Can I do anything more for you from here right now?"

"Not that I can think of. If I do, I'll let you know."

"Okay, Mort. Keep Harper safe, *and* you."

"Will do." I ended the call.

"Keep me safe," Harper said, swiping at a tear. "She is . . . really amazing."

"On many levels," I said.

* * *

The Desert Rose at dusk was pink stucco illuminated by pink floods. Other than the color, it looked reasonably inviting. More than inviting, under the circumstances.

I parked well away from the office and Harper stayed put while I went in. Lucy's story got me by the gaunt fifty-something gray-haired guy behind the desk. I signed the registration form in the name of John Taggart and got a key for room 15.

"Sorry about you losing your wallet," the guy said.

"Thanks. Worst thing isn't losing the eighty bucks, it's the license, credit cards, all the stuff I've got to replace."

"I hear that."

I got Harper and our bags into the room, then drove the truck a quarter mile north to the only other motel in town, the Silver Hills, left the truck in a dirt lot behind a Texaco station next door. I hiked back in the dark, ducking into side streets and behind bushes every time a vehicle came by, long before it could hit me with its lights.

Paranoia R Us.

With a population of eleven hundred, McGill was less than a third the size of Ely. It was good to be out of Ely, but this was only a stopgap measure. I wanted to get to Elko, far away from Ely and the guy in the black Ram.

I gave the door three knocks then one before opening it with the key and ducking inside. I shut it quickly, then turned and Harper gave me a hug. Not so much a hug as like someone clinging to a rock as the tide came in. She'd changed into her too-large T-shirt. Didn't feel like she was wearing anything under it, but what did I know? Anyway, I'm tough. I'm okay with large fast-moving bugs, spiders, and braless women.

I let her hang on until she was ready to turn loose. I took the time to gaze around. The room was a standard small rectangle, bathroom at the far end, a single queen-size bed against a wall in the middle, facing a TV and desk, wall lights on either side of the bed, single light overhead in a generic fixture. Only one wall light was on. Harper's gun was on a night table at the side of the bed nearest the bathroom.

She looked up at me. "This is just so . . . awful."

"I know."

"It's like someone really is after us. After me, actually, and you pretty much got in the way."

"We don't know that for sure, but . . ." In fact, we did. I tried to sugarcoat it. Big Guy had been seated at a table in the restaurant for one minute when we got up and left. Three minutes later he's up on our floor? That didn't come close to passing the smell test.

"We need a name for that guy," I said. "We can't keep calling him 'big guy.' How about Max?"

I felt her shrug. "Okay." She took a deep breath, then turned me loose and sat on the bed. "I guess I'm kind of a wuss, letting all of this get to me."

"It's getting to me too, kiddo."

She gave me a dim half-smile. "Kiddo. I feel like a kid. I mean, I can face a class full of hormone-driven freshman hellions, but this is . . . different." She took another deep breath. "I'll try to keep it together, Mort. I haven't been a teacher for five years for nothing."

"Take your time."

She closed her eyes, hung her head. Then she looked up at me. "I still feel kinda shaky. I'm gonna take a shower. Maybe that'll help."

"Go. Enjoy. I'll take one later. Didn't get one last night at Olivia's."

She gave me another half-smile. "We should've."

We? Nope, not gonna touch that one.

She took a wad of clothes into the bathroom, left the door partway open, turned on the water. I couldn't see into the bathroom from where I stood. Good enough.

I paced for a minute, out of sorts, then phoned Lucy. "We're at the motel," I told her. "Got safely out of Dodge, so thank you."

"Who is this guy Harper's avoiding, Mort?"

"She doesn't know him. She's never seen him before. He pretty much showed up out of the blue."

"Could it have something to do with her mother who's missing?"

"We don't know. Anything's possible."

"That all sounds so weird. I mean, you were off to find that Elrood guy. No big deal. Now this."

"You've got your special abilities, I've got mine."

"Yeah, well, I like mine better. Harper's there with you now, is she? Doing okay?"

"In the shower as we speak."

"Groovy." I heard a smile in her voice. "So you two are gonna head up to Elko in the morning?"

"That's the plan. How's your mother holding up?"

"She doesn't start with the fun stuff until tomorrow. We haven't been talking about it very much. Avoiding it, actually. Looks like we're gonna watch a movie tonight. Or two movies. Call me in the morning? Not too early, I might be up kind of late."

"Will do." I ended the call, looked around the room, didn't see a billiard table or dartboard to occupy the time, so I dug out my Forsyth novel and read a few pages.

Five minutes later Harper came out in a tank top and panties with a towel wrapped around her head.

"Look at you," I said. "All dressed up, no place to go."

She smiled. "I don't have to be. All dressed up, that is."

"Uh-huh. It's a free country. Do whatever you like."

"Wow. *That's* a huge improvement."

"Right. I'm gonna hit the shower. How's the water?"

"Wetter than usual. You'll totally need a towel after. Just to get dry, though."

"Part of this PI shtick I've got going is that I run into women with razor-sharp wits."

"Do you? That's gotta be annoying."

"It is. Also, I didn't get any useful information out of you, which doesn't surprise me. But I'm glad to see you're back in form."

She looked down at herself. "You noticed? Cool."

I smiled, opened a three-pack of underwear, took out one, and went into the bathroom, shut the door.

* * *

10:05 p.m. I came out in jeans, no shirt, bare feet, hair wet. Harper was under the covers on the side nearest the bathroom, shoulders bare, sheet across her breasts and tucked under her arms, reading the novel she'd picked up: *Suspicion of Malice.* Her clothes were on a chair against the opposite wall.

She looked up at me. "You look very clean."

"An illusion I create with smoke and mirrors to fool the teeming masses."

She patted the bed beside her. "If you want to get in here and read, I won't bite or even grope. But leave your jeans off, if you don't mind."

"I like these jeans."

"Do you regularly sleep in long denim pants?"

"Not regularly, not every night."

"Then take them off, hop in and read for a while or conk out. I won't touch you, I promise. And if you touch me, I'll scream and call 911." She went back to her novel.

Good enough.

I got my gun out, checked its load, set it on the night table on my side of the bed, then checked the door one last time, made sure the deadbolt was thrown and the security gizmo was set. Even so, one good kick and the door would blow open so I jammed the back of a chair under the knob. At least it would make a hell of a racket if Max tried to break in.

I stripped off my jeans.

"Jockeys," Harper said. "And here I thought you were a boxers man."

"I'm nothing if not versatile." I got between the sheets and picked up my novel.

Harper turned a page. "Next question: Do you go to bed in underwear on a regular basis?"

"Not usually. Sometimes I make an exception."

"I don't either. *Ever.*"

"Interesting, but irrelevant."

"Couldn't find undies with little red hearts, huh?"

"Hey, I'm trying to read here."

She smiled without looking at me. "This is a pretty good novel. How's yours?"

"Mine's a classic. Well, a classic thriller, not one of the *classic* classics like *The Scarlet Letter.*"

She kept her eyes on her book. "That's an interesting choice of classics to pull out of thin air."

"Hawthorne and I never really hit it off. Only reason I mention him is because my therapist suggested aversion therapy whenever I run into certain things."

"What kinds of things?"

"Stray naked women in my bed for one."

"You have a therapist? That sounds like an excellent idea. Hope he or she is good."

"It's hard to read with all this talking," I said.

"I *know*, right? I wish you'd shut up."

"You and Lucy will get along great."

"I'm sure, since we have something in common. Sort of, anyway."

I didn't ask what.

* * *

Harper put her book aside at 11:00, got out of bed, turned off the light on her side, and walked six feet to the bathroom. And, no, she doesn't wear anything to bed, but I knew that.

On the other hand, my underwear was going to stay in place as if super-glued.

I read until she came back. She slipped into bed. I got up and heard a snicker, but I'm used to it so . . . water off a duck's back. I didn't even break stride as I went into the bathroom.

When I returned and was about to get into bed, I heard that snicker again. I turned off the light on my side, kept the jockeys on, and got between the sheets.

Someone sighed, sort of loud too, but it was dark so I couldn't tell who it was.

* * *

We were out of the motel by 6:40 the next morning. I was in jeans and a T-shirt. Anticipating another hot day, Harper wore blue shorts and her contour-revealing tank top. "Let's go back to Ely," she said. "I want to see if Ellen is home yet."

"Maybe not a good idea. Also, you could call her. You have Jeff's number."

"I know, but I'd still like to go. We could grab a quick bite to eat at her place. Something actually healthy. Isn't there a way to do it safely?"

Safely? Safely would be to get a quick unhealthy bite right here in McGill and head straight for Elko. "Maybe," I said, not listening to a little voice whispering in my head. Which I should have.

"A quick in and out?" she said hopefully. "Anyway, I have another tank top at her place. I left it there last time I came to visit. I could use it." She gave me a smile. "It's thin too. And tight."

"Two very fine qualities in a tank top."

"I thought you'd think so."

I shrugged, put the truck in gear. "If we see a black pickup anywhere around her place, we're outta there."

We got to Ellen's at 7:02. The sun was up but it wasn't hot yet, temperature in the sixties, birds in the trees, a dog trotting along a sidewalk, and a white sedan of some kind parked in Ellen's driveway.

"Huh," I grunted. "Looks like she's got company."

"She better not mind us barging in on her. She's got some explaining to do since she took off when she knew I was coming to see her."

"She's got Jeff on her mind, Harp."

"Even so."

I parked at the curb and we got out. We ambled over to the car, a Nissan Altima. I peered in a window and there was a dead guy on the floor in back.

CHAPTER TWELVE

TURNS OUT, THE White Pine County Sheriff's Office is a beige, one-story, nondescript, no-frills architectural blah with dull red trim around its windows and doors.

But we didn't see that for over an hour.

"Don't look," I said to Harper, trying to keep her from seeing what was in the car.

"Why not?" She muscled around me, bent down, and peered into the Altima. She straightened up fast. "*Oh!*"

"I said 'don't look.' You should listen to me." Gaping holes in foreheads are never pretty. This one hadn't bled excessively, probably because the guy had died quickly and his heart quit pumping—but still. He lay face up, crumpled on the floor with his head against the passenger-side door, eyes open, staring into a different world.

I got out my phone, about to call 911.

Harper had backed away. Her face was pale, but then her eyes narrowed and she came closer and took a longer look. "Omigod, Mort. That . . . that's the guy!"

"No, it's not."

"Not the guy in the restaurant last night. That's the old guy who was driving me to Ely. The one who hit on me, then left me out there and took my bag and clothes."

Time to slow down and think. I put the phone away.

"You sure?"

"Sure, I'm sure. This is the car I was in. Which might mean my bag is here, like in the trunk."

"This's a crime scene, honey. We can't disturb it. We can't touch anything."

She bit her lip. "If it's in the trunk, the police might take it and keep it for a while. I'd really like to have it. It's not like it's *evidence* or anything. It's just a bag. It has my clothes and toothbrush and stuff, that's all."

I looked around, didn't see anyone watching us, but there were a lot of windows in the neighborhood. I circled the car and looked in at the ignition. The keys were in it. A fob dangled from a short chain.

Damn. Maybe I could punch the trunk release without removing the keys, not touch many surfaces. If her bag was in the trunk, it shouldn't be a crime to get it.

I went back to the truck and got a pair of nitrile gloves out of my duffel bag, first time I had occasion to use them. The driver's-side door was unlocked. I opened it then said, "I'm not doing what you see me doing, Harper."

"Got it." She backed away and watched what I wasn't doing.

I leaned in far enough to reach the fob, hit the button for the trunk, heard a faint *thunk* from in back, got out and beat Harper to the trunk, which meant I was the one who lifted the lid and found the folded nude body of Nevada's missing attorney general, Annette Leeman, crammed inside—a woman who was also Harper's mother.

I found her. Me. Mortimer Angel. The foremost finder of famous missing persons in the country.

Son of a *bitch*. I would never again open the trunk of a car that didn't belong to me. And maybe not even if it did.

* * *

Harper had been behind me when I opened the trunk. Her legs gave out when she saw what was inside. Good thing I was close enough to get an arm around her and ease her to the grass beside the driveway. I lowered the trunk lid, didn't latch it. In with Harper's mother was Harper's duffel bag, navy blue with a big white *Reebok* on the side.

She shuddered and made something of a whimpering sound then put her face in her hands, but didn't cry. She took several deep breaths, sitting cross-legged on the grass, rocking slightly, looking down at nothing. I held her for a minute, but I had things to do before making a 911 call, a call that had to be made soon.

But not yet.

"You okay?" I asked. Dumb, but nothing I might have said at the moment would've been right. She needed time. All I wanted was a response of some kind.

She nodded.

My mind spun as I continued to hold her. This was a ripe mess. I wanted to close the trunk to make the police think they were the first to find Leeman's body, but no way would Harper be able to feign surprise and shock when they did, not after she'd been hit with it for real. The trunk was going to have to remain open.

Not forty hours ago, the dead guy in back had left her at the side of a lonely desert road as night was falling. Harper's fingerprints were most likely still in the car. It wasn't my inclination, but the only thing I could think to do was tell the truth and hope the local police were smart enough to realize we had nothing to do with this. In general, that was a long shot. I wanted to get the hell out of Ely. We had to get through the next few hours unscathed and keep out of jail. I gave us a fifty-fifty chance.

This was complicated. It was still early morning, not yet seven fifteen. We had a room at Hotel Nevada under the name Stephen Brewer, an act that had subterfuge and guilt written all over it. But would that come to light if we didn't mention it? Maybe not. Why would it? We had spent the night at a motel in McGill, miles away. A White Pine or Nevada state detective would want to know where Harper and I were when the Altima was parked in the driveway, so they would have to know about the Desert Rose Motel, room 15.

My brain surged onward, picking this apart. The room in McGill was registered to John and Britany Taggart—not to me or to Harper Leeman. Why? Because Harper and I were avoiding a big guy in a black Ram pickup truck who had been acting in a suspicious manner. "Britany Taggart" was a close friend of mine in Reno. I'd asked for help and she had made a reservation for me in case the guy we were avoiding knew my name. She used her credit card to get the room. That would have to do, but it was likely that we'd now burned Lucy's Taggart ID as well as Brewer's, so this was getting expensive. Too bad, but it was what it was. I might be able to use Brewer's credit card as misdirection if it was being tracked, so I wouldn't toss it. Yet.

And wasn't it a merry fucking coincidence that Harper was right there on the spot when her mother was found in the trunk of a car that had her fingerprints in it?

Shee-*it*. This pot was about to boil over.

I finally remembered that I was wearing a wig and a moustache, not easy to explain with Halloween still two months off, so I stashed them in my truck, *and* the nitrile gloves because they shouted that I knew opening the trunk was a big no-no.

"Harper?" I said.

She looked up at me. "What?"

"Are you going to be all right?"

She took a deep breath. "Yes."

I nodded at the car. "That's your mother in there," I said as gently as I could.

"I know." She took another deep breath. "I know, and I'm . . . I don't know what I am, but right now I'm not . . . not what I probably ought to be. I'm not heartbroken. It's been months since I've seen my mother. We haven't been close for such a long time, pretty much since I became a teenager. She was always so . . . tight, controlling. Felt like it anyway. I might not have been the easiest teenager out there, but I wasn't such a bad kid either."

She was rambling. "I'm going to call 911," I said. "The police are going to ask a lot of questions. We need to get through that without getting hung up."

She struggled to her feet. "What should I say?"

"It's more about what you shouldn't say."

She nodded. "Okay. What shouldn't I say?"

"Tell them everything just the way it happened, but *do not* mention the room we got at Hotel Nevada—or your gun, or mine, nothing about fake IDs or credit cards. If they bring any of that up, then, okay, tell it like it is. But it's very unlikely, so don't offer it to them. Can you do that?"

She nodded. "Yes."

"You'll have to tell them about the guy who picked you up and hit on you, because here he is. He was fine when he drove off and left you. That's all you know about him. And we'll tell the police about the guy in the black pickup truck. We were in the restaurant when he came in and spoke to me, which is why we got out of there and got that motel in McGill. That hostess in the Denny's might remember him talking to us. Are you okay with all of that?"

"Yes."

"Is your gun still in the truck?"

"Yes. It's in my purse."

"They would need a warrant to look in our bags. Let's hope it doesn't come to that." I smoothed her hair. "If you tell a lie, it'll come back to haunt you, so don't. Not even a little one. Just don't give them any information they don't ask for."

"Okay." She held her arms across her body as if she were cold. She shivered slightly. Then she raised her eyes to mine. "I can do that. I'll be okay, Mort."

"I opened the trunk because you recognized the guy in the back and he'd taken off with your things. That wasn't smart of me, but it wasn't criminal. I'll weather that storm when it hits. You don't have to worry about it, so don't."

"Okay."

"I'm going to call 911 now."

"Okay. Go ahead. I'll be fine. I'm . . . I was sort of in shock. I imagine I still am, a little. She's my mother. We weren't all that close, but still. This will probably hit me in a while, but . . . not yet." She touched my arm. "Call the police. I'm gonna go sit on the porch steps. Do you think I can get my travel bag out of the trunk now?"

"Better not. It's part of the story, but the police will probably give it back once they've gone through it. If not, we'll buy you more clothes and things in Elko."

If we're not in jail, I didn't say.

I hit 911, got a dispatcher and gave her my location but not my name—might've created a beehive of activity when I told her I'd found two dead people—then I hung up.

I locked my truck, then sat on the porch with an arm around Harper to await events.

* * *

It didn't take long. Sheriff Ben Taylor was among the first to arrive. He was in the lead vehicle, with two others following, lights, no siren.

Taylor was in his forties, six-one, two hundred thirty pounds, barrel chest, thick moustache, black belt loaded down with gun, handcuffs, half a dozen other things. He climbed out of his car, left the lights flashing, and headed our way at a fast shuffle, trailing a deputy, Zack Niemeyer.

I got to my feet.

"Oh, please, no," he said, pulling up short when he saw who I was. "Dirty son of a bitch. Mortimer Angel." He glanced past me and saw Harper, hesitated a fraction of a second too long when he saw her in shorts and a tight tank top, then his gaze came back to me.

"Sorry about this, Sheriff," I said.

"Well, *shoot*. I was hoping you'd never get around to White Pine County, you with your goddamn reputation."

Which was about to get another good-sized boost.

Now was not a good time to smile, nor did I feel like it. "I don't do this on purpose, Sheriff."

"I'm Ben Taylor. Who's the girl?"

"Harper Leeman." I held out a hand to her. She came over and took it, stood quietly beside me. A deputy popped out of one of the other cars, hurried over, looked at the house and the front yard. Sheriff Taylor waved a hand at the place and the deputy went into the back to have a look around, check for criminals.

"Leeman?" Taylor said. "Sounds familiar but I can't place it off-hand." He shrugged dismissively. "Where's the body? Bodies."

I pointed. "In the car. Back seat and the trunk."

He sidestepped ten feet, looked inside at the guy in back on the floor, then glanced at me and Harper. "Either of you armed?"

I held my arms out. "No. We found them, that's all. House here belongs to Harper's aunt. She's in Idaho, last we heard. With a guy named Jeff."

"That'd be Jeff Nickel," Taylor said. "Good guy, Jeff."

He was on top of things, knew his people. Good small-town sheriff. He got a pencil out of a pocket and used it to lift the trunk, which was up two or three inches. His eyes widened and his lips tightened, but nothing else about his face changed. He took a breath, looking in at the attorney general. "Aw, jeez, I don't need this." He looked at Harper. "Leeman. *Your* name is Leeman?"

"Yes. That's my mother."

"Aw, shit," Taylor said so quietly I barely heard him. He looked at me. "Who's the guy in the back seat?"

"No idea. But this is probably his car and he comes with a story."

"A story?"

"Harper here had something of a run-in with him."

"Huh. Where and when? And how?"

I gave him the two-minute version with Harper filling in gaps as needed. I also told him about the guy in the black Ram pickup who might be looking for Harper, but we didn't know that for certain and neither of us had ever seen him before.

Sheriff Taylor took it in, said, "Huh," then strode over to Deputy Niemeyer, who'd glanced into the back seat of the Altima, and into its trunk, then backed off, watching us. "Otis on the way?" Taylor asked.

"Alma said he's five or ten minutes out."

Taylor nodded. "Need the coroner, too. And tell Alma to contact NDP, see if she can get Dick Vales out here, if he's available. Tell her that's a hurry-up job."

He looked at me and Harper. "Nevada Department of Public Safety, investigation division. I'd rather have Vales than some newbie runnin' around screwing things up." He took another peek in the trunk of the car. "This's gonna be a long goddamn day."

* * *

He wasn't wrong.

To get things going, he took preliminary statements from Harper and me. Niemeyer listened in as a witness.

The coroner arrived. Larry Norton, a white-haired wisp of a man in his late sixties. He determined that the two in the car were indeed dead, thought the hole in the old guy's forehead was much too big for a bullet wound, no exit wound, didn't know what had done it right offhand, but said he would know more after an autopsy. He found the old guy's wallet on the floor and tentatively identified him by the photo on his driver's license as Chase Eystad, sixty-eight years old, with a Reno address.

"Eystad," Taylor said. "Never heard of the guy before he gave you that lift?" he asked Harper.

"No. First time I saw him was in Goldfield."

"And here he is again. Attorney General Leeman too." He gave the two of us questioning looks, but Harper and I didn't say anything to that.

His gaze turned casual. "Tell me again about the guy in the pickup. Got a license plate, description, anything?"

I didn't see a downside to giving him the partial plate and my thoughts about who might have killed Eystad and Leeman. It would slow Max down if he were picked up for questioning. I didn't tell Taylor that Harper and I had been calling him Max. That would've been too confusing.

"Late model jet-black Ram pickup," I said. "Crew cab, partial license of ZJX5. Didn't get the last few numbers in all the rain when he took off west."

Taylor looked over at Niemeyer. "That it, Zack?"

"Close enough, Sheriff. License was ZJX583."

"Huh." Taylor turned to me. "Got a description of the guy in that pickup?"

"Thick beard about an inch long, dark with some gray in it. Bald head, thick neck. Strong-looking guy, six-two, about two hundred thirty pounds. Jeans and boots, short-sleeve shirt, nothing fancy."

"And you saw him again in the Denny's at the hotel?"

"Uh-huh. He came in while we were eating. I had a bad feeling about him that night in the rain and there he was again, so we left, got a room in McGill for the night."

Taylor squinted at me. He thought for a minute then shrugged. "There's a law enforcement maxim that says we—the law—shouldn't give out information we don't have to. But I've known Russ Fairchild going on twenty years. We golf together a couple of times a year, here and in Reno, so I'm gonna go out on a limb and hope it doesn't bite me in the ass."

He chewed thoughtfully on his lower lip, which gave me time to ask, "You and Russ are friends?" Russell Fairchild was the senior detective at RPD in Reno.

"Same class in the Academy. Last person I wanted to show up here is you, Angel, given your record. Back when you found those two heads, Reno's mayor and the DA, Russ badmouthed you up one side and down the other. But something changed last year, about the time you and that other girl took down those two serial killers south of here around Caliente. Now he can't speak highly enough of you." He gave me a hopeful look. "Don't suppose you know why Russ changed his mind, do you? That's not like him."

I sure did. It was because I know who really killed the gangsta rapper Jo-X, and it wasn't who the police or the FBI thought it was. Russ and I have a relationship based on the Cold War—mutually assured destruction—that has evolved into something approaching real friendship.

"I've bought him a few beers," I said. "Russ likes his Bud Heavy. Maybe that's it."

Taylor gave me a look. "Don't think so. It's more than that. Anyway, about that pickup truck. We got a call about a vehicle fire three miles up Highway 6 at four in the morning. Black Ram pickup. That partial plate you gave me matches. It was stolen off a Ram pickup down in Vegas, but the owner doesn't know when it happened. The truck was still too hot an hour ago to get at its VIN number, but I'll bet you a month's pay it's stolen too."

"No bet, Sheriff."

No need for Ma to keep working on that partial plate now. I would have to give her a call when I got a chance. In fact, I would have to tell her about my finding the attorney general, see if it was worth a bonus.

Taylor looked at me. "You never met this Eystad guy before either, huh?"

"No. Don't know what to tell you," I said. "But it looks like this is all connected to the attorney general somehow. She was missing; now she isn't."

"And here *you* are. Again."

"It's all my fault, Sheriff. This wouldn't happen if I'd stuck it out with the IRS."

He grinned. "You call Russ Russ. Might's well call me Ben, keep it friendly." He put his hand out and I shook it. He glanced at Harper, then gave me a subtle eyebrow lift. "Desert Rose Motel, huh?"

"Room fifteen."

"Might've gone into the wrong line of work back when I was twenty-four." He shook himself, then said, "I'll need a formal statement from both of you back at the office. Don't see a problem with what you told me right offhand so I won't put you in cuffs—kidding—I mean *not* kidding—but you know how it is with paperwork."

"I was with the IRS for sixteen years. The U.S. tax code is the most ambiguous, circular, contradictory dung heap of paperwork ever created by a bunch of criminal lunatics. God couldn't unravel it, so we had ample opportunity to put anyone behind bars we didn't like. Which was actually the point of it. Still is, too."

Ben Taylor grunted. "There are feds and there are feds. FBI is full of prima donnas; IRS is full of . . . of what?"

"Thugs."

"Yeah, those. Anyway, *this*"—he glanced again at the Altima—"is a hell of a mess. And that black pickup, which might be part of this based on what you said happened up there thirty miles west of Grange." He turned to Niemeyer. "Did you get that description of the guy Mr. Angel saw in the pickup?"

"Wrote it down while he was givin' it."

"Get Alma to put it out on the air right away. Just to detain the guy for questioning, but be damn cautious about it. Request backup before approaching."

Niemeyer trotted over to his patrol car.

Sheriff Taylor frowned at the Altima. "I'll be happy to turn this over to the state boys. And girls," he added. "How about you go over to the office. I'll get over there soon as I can after Otis shows up. Otis Kuska, the county detective. He'll want to talk with you. He can get a look at this, then we'll be over. He'll probably want to leave this for the state guys, too. You two can follow Niemeyer over to the office in your truck there."

All of this had gone easier than I had any right to expect. I would have to thank Russ later, buy him enough Bud Heavies to have to drive him home, but not so many I would have to tuck him into bed. There's a reason to be on good terms with the law, but not *that* good.

On the way to the sheriff's office, I reminded Harper of what not to say. She held my hand the entire trip, which was less than two miles and didn't take five minutes.

"I'm okay, Mort," she said. "I don't think this will be very bad."

"You heard what I told the sheriff. Just tell it again."

"I've got it."

*   *   *

And she did. We told our story to Ben and Otis when they showed up. They never mentioned Hotel Nevada, so neither did we. No one asked about guns. A phone call to the Desert Rose Motel did bring up the question of who Britany Taggart was, but that had nothing to do with Max or the black pickup, Chase Eystad, or the attorney general. In fact, the guy in the pickup made my use of a friend's credit card sound reasonable. I would have to thank Max for setting his truck on fire if I saw him again since it gave our story more heft.

During a ten-minute break in the Q & A, I phoned Ma.

"Hola, Ma," I said.

"Mort. Where are you? What the hell're you doing?"

"Funny you should ask." Harper put her ear next to mine so she could listen in.

"No. Oh, fuckin' no. I hate it when you say that."

"Anyway, the attorney general is no longer missing."

"Oh, Lord. Please tell me you didn't."

"I did. Harper and I are currently at the sheriff's office in White Pine County. In Ely."

"Good luck, then. I ain't posting bail and you're fired." She hung up.

Harper looked at me. "Really? You're fired?"

"Nope. Ma's a kidder. She thinks firing me is a kick. She does it all the time." I called her back. "Hola, Ma."

"You're fired." She hung up.

"Three's a charm," I said, dialing. "Ma! Don't hang up."

"Why the hell not?"

"Got some good news for you."

"What? They're lockin' you up and tossin' the key?"

"You don't have to worry about that partial plate, so you can move on to other, more lucrative stuff."

"Why? What's with the plate?"

"It was on a truck that was torched a few miles west of Ely this morning."

"Is that related to you finding the attorney general?"

"Yup. I'm ninety-nine percent sure of it, anyway."

"Is she dead? I forgot to ask."

"Well, yeah. You know how it is with me."

"You are *so* fired." She hung up.

We left it at that. I figured I'd let her absorb what I'd told her, give her time to cool off, then try again later. I phoned Lucy. By then it was 10:35 a.m.

"Hey, Mort. What's happening? How are you and Harper?"

"Just peachy, cupcake."

"Uh-oh. *Now* what?"

"You know how I drift around the world minding my own business and end up coming across things?"

"You mean 'things' like Harper?"

"That, yes, but, you know, other things as well."

She sighed. "Yes."

"And you know who's been missing and in the news of late. Other than those two teenage girls."

Another sigh. "You found her, didn't you?"

"Yes, I did."

"And of course, she's dead, because that's how they are when you find them."

"That too, yes. Sadly."

"Are you all right? Not hurt or anything?"

"I'm fine. So's Harper."

"How's she taking it? I mean, the attorney general was her mother, wasn't she?"

"Yes. But they weren't close, not like you and your mom. She's doing okay. I'll let her explain about that later sometime. Right now, we're in the sheriff's office giving statements. We'll be here a while. Eventually they'll cut us loose and we'll head up to Elko, see about finding Elrood."

"What about that guy Harper's been avoiding? Do you think he might've killed her mother?"

"No idea. We're keeping away from him all the same. We don't know anything about him, including his name. We've been calling him Max."

"Max. Groovy. You don't know where he is now, huh?"

"Nope. But I told the police he appeared to be stalking Harper so there's an APB out on him. He might get picked up. That would slow him down, but I don't think it'd stop him for long. We don't have proof that he's stalking her. We'll keep an eye out, but Elko ought to be safe. I'll try to get us up there by tonight. Hey, how about you talk to Ma, get her to get Doc Saladin working on a new ID for me, and make it snappy."

"I thought you had one you haven't used yet."

"I do, but I have a feeling I might need more than one with all this going on, and Max is out there. Just a feeling, but I'd rather be safe than sorry."

"You *better* be safe. And why don't *you* tell Ma to get on it?"

"She hung up on me three times in two minutes. You know how she gets when I find people and our agency ends up in the news again."

"Uh-huh. Little bit grouchy."

"Yup. And right now, I've got a detective staring at me. Gotta go. Talk to Ma about getting me a new license and credit card. Soonish."

"Okay. I love you, Mort. Be safe."

"Love you too, sunshine."

She laughed. "Sunshine? That's new." Then she was gone.

I opened a can of Diet Pepsi. Harper got her travel bag back after it was checked out and nothing was found that could have the slightest bearing on the two murders. We went back to the Q & A stuff and the day wore on.

A young reporter for *The Ely Times*, Megan Howard, hung around and eventually cornered Sheriff Taylor in the lounge by the coffee machine, got as much of the story as he was willing or able to tell her. He included the possibly newsworthy fact that Reno private investigator Mortimer Angel had located the body of another missing person—as if some sort of remarkable skill were involved. Ely being in the middle of nowhere, young, likeable, fresh-faced Megan out-scooped the likes of ABC, NBC, CNN, and all the other alphabet news-vulture agencies.

A little before noon I learned that Chase Eystad had once been a high-dollar criminal defense lawyer in Reno. He'd retired three years ago. Somehow it figured that one or more lawyers would stumble into this morass, whatever it was. Eystad's liver temperature indicated that he'd been killed an hour or two after midnight, about five hours after Max had seen us in the Denny's.

I also heard that no one in the neighborhood had seen the Nissan as it was driven to Harper's aunt's place and left in the driveway.

Engine temperature indicated it had been run an hour or two before Harper and I got there, but after Max's pickup was torched. That told me Sheriff Taylor was trying to connect the two events. Given those things, I felt the presence of the ghost of an accomplice lurking in the background, someone other than Eystad since he wasn't in any condition to drive at the time the truck was set on fire. If so, there'd been at least three people hunting Harper.

At 12:55 p.m. I heard the distant beat of helicopter blades. It got closer, finally landing outside in the yard in a hot cloud of dust, and two people got out.

Dick Vales was a lead investigator for NDP, a thin, sallow guy of fifty with buck teeth and blue eyes like lasers. His cohort, Alice Jacobs, was in her forties, stocky, hair pulled back in a bun and held in place with something that resembled a short dark chopstick, but what do I know? The two of them had come from Winnemucca. Evidently the discovery of the state's missing attorney general warranted immediate, high-level action.

Vales and Jacobs were first driven to the crime scene where a forensics crew was still hard at work. They nosed around, got what little there was to get, then returned to the sheriff's office. Harper told the story to Jacobs, I told it to Vales, then the two of them compared notes. We got a late lunch and learned that Max's torched pickup had been stolen in Vegas three days ago.

Then the team players switched sides. I told our story to Jacobs, Harper told it to Vales. At one point I think my eyes rolled up in my head and I passed out. If not, I don't know where those missing minutes went. The story wasn't getting any better with the telling, as stories are supposed to do. I got another Diet Pepsi to stay awake—at taxpayers' expense.

But Harper and I must have passed inspection on the Q & A because we finally got cut loose at 4:15 p.m.

"Omigod," she said when we were back in the truck. "I never want to do *that* again." She set her Reebok bag on the floor at her feet.

"Stick with me, kid. You'll do it at least twice a year."

"Let me out now. I'll walk back to Goldfield and wait for my car to get fixed."

"Walk? Dressed like that you'd catch a ride easy, so if you want out . . ."

"Drive, Mort. But don't find any more . . . you know."

Good enough. I pulled out of the parking lot, headed north. As we left Ely, Harper called Jeff's number and got her aunt in Idaho. She put the phone on speaker.

"Hi, Auntie," she said.

"Hello, Harper. Sorry about this last-minute trip, but Jeff and I will be back day after tomorrow. Did you get settled in at my place? I fixed up the cabin for you."

"Uh, no. I guess I won't for a while."

"Oh?"

Harper gave her aunt an abridged version of recent events, but there was no way to soft-pedal the death of her mother, Ellen's sister.

Silence on the other end. Then, "Jeff and I will come back right away."

"No, don't."

"Why not?"

"It, uh, might not be safe. Right now."

So much for soft-pedaling. Harper had to get into it in more detail. She told Ellen there was a guy running around who might be targeting family members for some reason, but she wasn't sure about that.

"So you're headed to Elko with . . . who?" Ellen asked.

"This nice guy, his name is Mort. But you should stay where you are, Auntie, since you're family too. If you come back, stay with Jeff for a while, until this gets . . . resolved."

"Resolved how, for goodness' sake?"

"When they catch the guy, I guess. Anyway, I hate to ask this, but could you deal with the police, you know—releasing mom's body, funeral arrangements, that sort of thing? I would, but . . . right now I . . . well, I can't."

More silence. Then, "I can do that."

Hesitations and subdued conversation, but no tears. Interesting. Annette Leeman must not have been an easy person to be around. They ended the call with Aunt Ellen on board with taking on the necessary arrangements.

We passed through McGill without stopping at the Desert Rose, picked up a Red Bull for me and some sort of raspberry-flavored vitamin water for her, a bag of cashews and another of sunflower seeds, then we got the hell out of the area and far away from Max. I hoped.

But as we were leaving McGill, I wondered where Max was and what he was doing now that he'd killed Chase Eystad and Annette Leeman. He might bore easily. I didn't think he was done with that sort of thing—*if* he'd done it—and I had the feeling he was a slippery son of a bitch and wouldn't be picked up by the police anytime soon.

Just a feeling, but my feelings are right at least two or three percent of the time. Less than that, however, when it comes to figuring out women—like the one sitting a few feet to my right as we barreled north on 93.

CHAPTER THIRTEEN

HARPER WAS QUIET, pensive. The road had little traffic and the desert looked the same whichever way you looked, mile after mile. I had time to think about everything that had happened the past two days, about coincidences that couldn't possibly be coincidences.

Attorney General Annette Leeman had been missing for several days. Then the radiator in her daughter's car blows and Harper is picked up by an old guy, Chase, who dumps her at gunpoint—hers, not his—at the side of a lonely road. Then Max comes along looking for someone, which pretty much had to be Harper. So Chase and Max were connected. Max comes into the Denny's restaurant; Harper and I leave. Three minutes later Max is up on our floor after sitting down in the restaurant, which meant Max was interested in us, not food. Chase and Annette end up dead in Chase's car in Harper's aunt's driveway, and Max's stolen Ram pickup is burned to a crisp a few miles west of Ely. Things were happening. As usual I was in the dark, no idea what was going on. But what I circled back to, over and over, was that Harper's part in all of this started with a blown radiator.

Radiators don't pop seams on the whim or the prayers of bad guys. Which didn't add up if Eystad and Max were in this mess together. Not yet, anyway.

I looked over at her. "Tell me again how that old fart, Chase, picked you up. If he and Max knew each other, him giving you a ride couldn't have been an accident."

"It was, though. I mean, it had to be, didn't it?"

"It couldn't have been. Run through it again, from the time right before your radiator blew."

"Well, I was driving along and it just . . . *blew up.* It must've overheated and it was old and the pressure or something got to be too much and it . . . *bang.*"

"Bang?"

She smiled. "Bang. You know, sort of like a gun went off."

"Half a mile south of Goldfield."

"Yes. The guy at the gas station said he couldn't fix it with some sort of radiator leak-fixing stuff you pour in. He couldn't even fix it with some other stuff like putty that would fix a split seam an inch or two long. He said it blew a seam eight or ten inches long and some of the rest of it was sort of shredded. He said he'd never seen anything like it. So like I told you earlier, I was lucky it happened that close to Goldfield."

"Uh-huh. A happy coincidence."

"What else could it be?"

"A setup."

She stared at me. "How is that possible?"

I thought about it. How would I do it if she were in a car and I wanted to get her into my car, get her alone? For a while nothing came to me, then a glimmer appeared in the mist. I worked on it, but it never exceeded a glimmer, never felt at all likely. Still, I had nothing else to work with.

"Did you stop anywhere before you left Vegas?" I asked, clutching at the only straw in sight.

"I filled the tank at a gas station."

"Did you leave the car, go inside the store there?"

She pursed her lips. "Uh-huh. I bought some water for the trip north."

"Where was your car when you went inside?"

"Not by the pumps, if that's what you mean. They don't like that. I parked it at the side of the store."

"Could you see your car from inside?"

"I didn't try, but . . . probably not. I was only inside for a few minutes."

Long enough, if Chase had exactly the right thing, the only thing that fit what had happened, and which seemed so unlikely as to be laughable. And if not laughable, then absolutely frightening.

An idea slowly filtered into my head like a sunrise chasing away the dark. A chill went up my spine. Up ahead I saw a few buildings at a place called Currie, sixty miles north of McGill. I checked the rearview mirror, didn't see anyone behind us. I pulled off the highway and into a dirt lot beside a Texaco station that stood next to a ramshackle country store.

"What're we doin'?" Harper asked.

"I gotta check something."

I climbed out. Harper got out on her side. I lifted the hood and looked in at the radiator. Didn't see anything I didn't expect to see. I got on my back under the front of the truck and looked up at the radiator, didn't see anything for a moment, then my eyes adjusted to the dimness, and I saw something on the underside I couldn't identify. I touched it gently. Hot. I got out from under the engine compartment and trotted into the station. A guy in his late twenties, red hair, in greasy bib overalls, was kicked back in a wooden chair reading a paperback. He looked up as I came in.

"Got some gloves I can borrow for a minute?" I asked.

"What kind of gloves?"

"Whatever will take engine heat."

He found me a pair of filthy leather gloves, then came outside with me. His face lit up when he saw Harper in shorts and her body-hugging tank top.

I slid back under the truck and got hold of the thing I'd seen. Hard to get a grip on it and it didn't want to come off, but it didn't look like part of any radiator I'd ever seen before. I had to pry it off. It was attached with some sort of sticky gunk that might've hardened on the hot metal, but it eventually peeled loose.

I scooted out from under the truck. In the sunlight I looked at what I'd found. A small black plastic box the size of an old matchbox, two wires coming out of it into a foot-long strip of something that looked like grimy black cord half an inch in diameter covered in gray putty.

"Huh," the station guy said. "What's that?"

"I don't know. I heard a strange noise under the hood and stopped to have a look, then I found this."

No point in bringing this guy into it. The noise story was pure cross-eyed bullshit, but I had a good idea of what I'd found, and I didn't like it. I didn't want to toss the thing, but I didn't want it in my hands, either. Not if it was what I thought it was. The black box had a tiny switch on the side. I wasn't about to mess with that.

"Got wire cutters in your shop?" I asked, holding the thing by its box, letting the cord dangle. I didn't even want to hold it that way.

"Sure. C'mon."

He found a greasy wire cutter. I used it to clip the wires that led into the black cord, thanked him, then went out to the truck and put the pieces in the bed of the pickup by the tailgate. Then I got Harper and me out of there.

"What was that thing?" she asked when we were a few hundred yards down the road.

"A coincidence."

"Huh?"

"That's what blew your radiator as you were getting near Goldfield. A receiver and very likely a battery wired into an explosive strip—probably a small shaped charge of some kind. Chase could've been half a mile behind you on the highway, hit a button on something that might look like a garage door opener and blew your radiator."

"A shaped charge? What's that?"

"An explosive that cuts in one direction. A big one can cut through a steel plate two inches thick. This one wasn't that big, but it was big enough to take out a radiator."

"That's . . . unbelievable. Also *amazing*, Mort. I mean, you finding it like that."

"Every so often I impersonate someone who has a vague idea of what they're doing."

"Maybe more than 'every so often'."

"What this *means*, Harp, is that you've got some very serious people after you." After *us*, now, I didn't add. "It has to be related to what happened to your mother. This is a lot more than you being given a ride to Ely by some nice old guy. If he hadn't hit on you, no telling what would have happened to you, so be thankful he did. I have the feeling it cost him his life. We knew something more had to be going on when Max came by that night looking for you. Now we find that these people, whoever they are, can come up with remotely detonated explosives."

"That's *crazy*, Mort."

"Yes, it is. We've got a lot more trouble than we knew about five minutes ago—except now we do know. It would be a big mistake to underestimate people like this."

"You keep saying 'we.' You shouldn't be around me if this is really dangerous. Maybe I should go to the police."

I looked at her. "And tell them what?"

"You put that bomb thing in the back. If I show them that and ask for help, maybe I'd be safe then. *You* would, anyway."

"I hate to say this, but the police weren't able to keep your ex away from you and he's a nobody. They don't have people hanging around for long-term assignments like that. Anyway, I'm in this now. I found your mother, not that I want to keep bringing that up, but I did and that's already in the news, so like it or not, I'm in this. I can't say I'd be more effective than the police in protecting you, but at least I care and I can stay with you full time."

"My very own full-time bodyguard."

"In a manner of speaking."

She smiled. "Guarding my body."

I looked over at her. "Are you taking this seriously?"

"Of course. I'll expect you to stay *real* close, Mort."

She might not realize how much danger she might be in, not that I did, but it's hard for people to wrap their heads around something like this if they haven't been in the kinds of situations I've been in the past two years. I've had three concussions, two mild, one bad; I've been buried alive, tied to a chair in a burning building, and my fiancée, Jeri DiFrazzia, was murdered two feet away from me by a homicidal woman who blew Jeri's head off and dumped her body down a mineshaft. This PI gig wasn't what I had thought it would be when I first started out in my nephew's PI firm. Three days after he told me how boring PI work was, I found his decapitated head on his office desk. So much for boring. This job had a dark side.

What I didn't tell Harper, yet, is that in addition to a device to blow the truck's radiator, we might have picked up a tracker, something so small and easily hidden that we wouldn't find it in an hour—and if we searched for an hour and found nothing, we might conclude we weren't being tracked, which could be even more

dangerous. I could see Max there in the parking lot sometime before we left Hotel Nevada, putting the shaped charge on the radiator so he could blow it anytime he wanted. That would be safer than
trying to grab us—or her—in a hotel room. I could also see him
installing a highly sophisticated GPS tracker. It could be anywhere.
If he opened the cab of the truck like a locksmith, he could've slit
the upholstery and inserted a tracker in the padding of a seat, sealed
it inside.

Sometimes I let my imagination run wild.

Sometimes that's a good thing.

* * *

I didn't like the idea of hauling around a bomb or whatever it was in
the bed of the pickup, so I left both the receiver and the explosive in
a plastic bag hidden in weeds behind mile marker 3, south of Wells.
That switch on the receiver must've been active when it was attached
to the radiator, otherwise what was the point? It was safe to turn off
now, no longer connected to the charge, so I switched it off to save
its battery, but I would remember where I'd left it. You never know
when an explosive will come in handy, like to crack a safe or blow
through a locked door.

Harper and I pulled into Wells at 6:45 p.m. My burner phone
had a signal so I called Lucy.

"Are you okay?" she asked.

"Never better. Harper and I are in Wells at the Flying J, getting
gas, about to head over to Elko."

"So you're safe? No sign of that Max guy?"

"I haven't seen him since yesterday, and now we're a hundred
forty miles north of Ely, so yeah, we're safe." If we hadn't picked up
a GPS tracker, I didn't tell her. I also didn't tell her about the

explosive on the radiator. I didn't want her anywhere near this. I didn't want me or Harper near it either, but she and I didn't have that option.

"Good. And Mom chugged a big bottle of magnesium citrate a few hours ago, so things are underway here."

"Tell her I wish her joy and luck."

Lucy laughed. "I don't think that would go over very well. I sure wish I could be with you right now, but it's not a good time for me to take off. She's practically drowning in that other crud she has to drink. Eight ounces every ten minutes and she's still got more than a liter to go."

"Don't worry about it. We're fine."

"You're bouncing all over the state. The way things are going, that's probably a good thing. I'll catch up with you when I can."

"Soon, I hope." No, I didn't.

"Me too. But it won't be tomorrow. I'm thinking I'll pass on colonoscopies. Mom has to drink two liters of icky crud in three hours. Then she gets a break, but she has to be up at four in the morning to drink the last two liters. Her procedure is at twelve fifteen tomorrow afternoon."

"I can't imagine that much fun," I said.

"I'm sure. Say hi to Harper for me, okay?"

"Will do."

"Gotta go, Mort. Talk to you later."

I gassed up the truck, then Harper and I took off for Elko. Maybe we were being tracked, maybe we weren't, but one way I was being tracked was on the radio. Ten miles from Elko, the big news on a local AM station was that private investigator Mortimer Angel had found Attorney General Annette Leeman, dead. More to come.

I wondered if Max was catching the news. If so and if he didn't know my name before, he did now.

* * *

Nevada is a big empty state, which is why the forever-benighted folks in D.C. think it's a terrific place to dump the nation's radioactive waste. Empty? Only three cities in Nevada are big enough to have a car rental agency—Reno, Vegas, and Elko. Our first order of business was to return the truck to Avis. If it had been infected with a tracker, I wanted to be rid of it, fast.

Note to self: Mortimer Angel had rented the truck, so returning it to Avis in Elko would put Mortimer Angel in Elko for anyone with the ability to track credit cards and car rentals. These days, it's not easy to get around without leaving digital footprints, especially when credit cards are king, not cash.

Avis was inside the terminal of Elko Regional Airport. Harper and I exited I-80, went south on Mountain City Highway, turned right on Terminal Way, and found Avis's parking lot. The time was 7:25 p.m. I donned a dirty blond wig with hair over my ears, glasses with thick black frames, topped it off with a ball cap, and we went inside.

The rental desk at Avis was buttoned up. A sign on the countertop gave instructions, so we went back outside and I parked and locked the truck, left its keys and the rental agreement in a lockbox, and we went back in the terminal with our bags. Enterprise car rental was shut down but a sign on their counter indicated they would be open for one hour, from 8:00 to 9:00 p.m.

"We can stick around awhile and get wheels," I said, "or Uber off to a motel and come back tomorrow."

"A room would be great, and a personal bodyguard would be super, but wheels sound like a necessity."

We stuck around. No sign of Max so the Z71 might not have picked up a tracker. No way of knowing, however.

By 8:20 we were rolling toward downtown Elko in a dark blue 2020 Ford Explorer. To rent it, I had to use my last fake ID, the one for David J. Peterson. I didn't want to do it but I didn't have a choice. Stephen Brewer had rented the room at Hotel Nevada in Ely, and the same guy had found Annette Leeman and Chase Eystad, and his name, according to the police and the news, was Mortimer Angel. If Max was still around and listening to radio or TV, it would take him three seconds to put two and two together—if he hadn't when we did that do-si-do in the Denny's and the fourth floor of the hotel. I hoped it would take him longer—as in never—to connect Brewer and Angel to David Peterson. Fake IDs that hold up under close scrutiny are damned expensive, at least Doc Saladin's were, currently running about ten grand each. Even so, I thought I might need another one, maybe sooner than later. If not, I would have a new fake ID in a few days. I could think of worse things to have ready to go.

"Hungry?" I asked.

"Pretty much starving."

"How about we hit a Denny's for a Grand Slam since we didn't get our freebie pancakes this morning?"

"How about we don't?"

We ended up at a Mexican place half a block off the main drag, Idaho Street, that was doing a brisk business. A lot of the customers were Hispanic, so I figured the food would be good. It was. We left forty-five minutes later.

Six blocks away on Elkhorn Road I spotted a tiny red neon VACANCY sign. Ruby's Hideaway was a motel so out of the way it was almost invisible—eight dark, narrow units tucked beneath three good-sized oak trees.

An obese woman in her fifties was behind the desk peering at a cell phone when we came in. She looked up, gave us a smile and an eager look. Good. I liked eager.

"Got a little problem," I told her. "We're trying to keep Angela's ex from finding her, so I don't want to use a credit card. I'll pay extra if we can use cash, keep off this guy's radar since he's something of a nutcase."

"Works for me," she said. "I'm Ruby, by the way. I own the place, so I make and break the rules as I see fit."

I leaned on the desk. "How much for a room, Ruby?" I didn't ask about the bed situation. Personal bodyguards are not only flexible, they're as tough as railroad spikes.

"Seventy-five fifty with a credit card."

"How about a hundred, cash? And if some guy comes around asking about us, you never saw us."

"Works for me. Trouble, I don't need."

We got room 6, two doors down from a grumbling ice machine and a vending machine tucked into an alcove in the middle of the Hideaway.

Another queen bed, basic bathroom, small flat-screen TV on a wall, his and hers lamps bolted to night tables on either side of the bed. It wasn't easy to tell Ruby's place from the Desert Rose, or vice versa. I had to look twice and ignore the déjà vu.

"These places are starting to grow on me," Harper said as she kicked off her shoes and stretched out on the bed. She looked up at me. "Now what?"

"It's still early. I might try to find Olga, see if that gets me any closer to the dubious and itinerant Elrood."

"What's the population of Elko these days, anyway?"

"Somewhere around twenty thousand. Why?"

"About half will be women, and half of those might be around the right age, so you only have to ask five thousand of them if their name is Olga. Shouldn't take more than a month if you get right on it and go like gangbusters."

"I might do it differently."

"If you go, I'm coming with. No way I'm staying here by myself with Max out there somewhere, even if I have a gun ready to mow him down."

"Mow him down. You sound very Eliot Ness. But you should try to avoid that. When you kill someone, even if they're trying to kill you, the paperwork is murder. Also, they take your gun away and don't return it until they're good and ready."

"Another reason for me to tag along. And you're not totally bad company. Besides, you might need my advice or help. What if this Olga is pretty, has a fantastic body, and you get sidetracked since you're so impressionable?" She looked at me for several seconds, then said, "*Not.*"

I didn't follow up on that.

"You can't go dressed like that," I said.

She looked down at herself. "What's wrong with it?"

"It's too . . . hell, are you really gonna make me say it?"

"Yes. Too *what*, Mort?"

"Sexy, girl."

She smiled. "You really think so?"

"Okay, let's get this straight. Yes, you're a hell of a girl. As such, you'll attract attention. People will remember you. That's exactly what we don't want. So if you're going to help me find Olga, I want you in the black jeans you got in Ely, and this." I tossed her the black T-shirt I'd bought at the mercantile, which I still hadn't worn.

"No freakin' way. This thing's an extra-large."

"Exactly right."

"Ugh. I'll be super baggy, and dressed all in black."

"Right. And I want you to wear a wig, too."

"Which, luckily, I don't have."

"Which, luckily, *I* do." I dug a straight black wig out of my duffel bag and tossed it to her. The longest wig in my disguise arsenal, it would cover her blond hair nicely and hang halfway down her back.

"You're kidding," she said, holding it up like a freshly killed muskrat with a hair problem.

"Nope. Put it on. Let's see how it looks."

She settled it on her head. "It doesn't fit very well."

"It looks fine, makes you look different. Sort of like Cher, back in her Sonny days."

"Seriously? *Cher?*"

"Or Stallone when they filmed *First Blood*. Although we might want a second opinion on that."

"How about I give you an opinion right now?"

"It wouldn't count. You're too close to the issue."

"I'm gonna get up at three in the morning and slap you silly when you're dead asleep."

"Jeans," I said. "And the shirt." The front of which had an impressionist drawing of a huge Harley on it, the kind of thing a terrorist foaming at the mouth might ride.

She held it up. "I'll get *lost* in this thing. And I'll look like a biker chick, sort of a dumb one, too."

"Uh-huh. If we get a chance, I'll buy you some black lipstick and black eyeliner."

"I thought you didn't want me to stand out."

"You will, but you won't look at all like you, and that's really what we want."

She sighed, got off the bed, took off her shorts and put on jeans, then hesitated with her hands gripping the hem of her tank top. "Should I wear this top under the T-shirt, or take it off?"

"Up to you. It'll get cool later tonight."

She shrugged, put the shirt on over the tank top, then stood in front of a mirror on a wall outside the bathroom. "Awful. I don't recognize myself."

"Again, that's the idea." I put on the latest and ugliest in a long line of ugly wigs—silver hair slicked straight back with the ends flipped up at the back of my neck, the Wild Bill Hickok look. "How's this?"

Harper gaped at me. "Mesmerizing."

"Thanks." I put on wire-frame glasses with amber lenses and a battered green ball cap. I snugged a black ball cap on Harper's head that had NAPA AUTO PARTS on it, and we went out the door. We took our guns, but they would remain in the car.

"I'm *way* overdressed," Harper said as we got in the Explorer. "Not overdressed as in high fashion, but this clothing is too warm and bulky. Fair warning, I'm gonna take a shower when we get back and I'm not going to wear anything afterward. I'm gonna be who I am, period."

"Miss Nudist."

"That's right, cowboy."

"Good deal."

She smiled. "You think I'm kidding, don't you?"

"No. I might run screaming into the night and I might not. Time will tell."

Right then, Lucy phoned. I told her Harper and I were fine, that we'd gotten a room in an out-of-the-way motel, Ruby's Hideaway.

"That's not a house of ill repute, is it? What I mean is, you're in Elko and . . . you know."

"How would *I* know? And a house of ill repute costs something like a hundred bucks an hour, sweetheart."

"How would you know *that*?"

"Because I'm a private investigator?"

"Oh, right. Sometimes I forget."

She told me her mother had polished off two liters of crud, and Ma had already contacted Doc Saladin in New Mexico. Lucy would bring me a new ID the next time she saw me, if she got it in time. We spoke a while longer then ended the call.

The new ID was a rush order, twelve thousand bucks, Lucy had said. Doc would overnight the documents to Ma in Reno and Lucy would get them to me once Val was done with her "procedure." For now, I had to make do with the David Peterson ID. I might be able to use the Brewer credit cards as misdirection, but that would take some thought.

The sun had gone behind the hills. Pink and lavender clouds were backlit by a fading glow as I took us to Idaho Street and headed east.

"I gotta see how you find this Olga person," Harper said.

"This is where pure, blind, staggering luck comes in," I told her. "All part of being a private eye. I give us about one chance in fifty of getting so much as a whiff of her this evening."

"A whiff of Olga. That's fabulous, Mort."

CHAPTER FOURTEEN

Elko is a strange place. I'd never really gotten a handle on it. A third of it catered to traffic on I-80 and a third was for the locals. The last third, its backbone, Idaho Street, catered to both. Streets meandered around. You could buy tires, go grocery shopping, and three blocks later drive past 24-hour brothels. You can't do that in Iowa.

Cruising Idaho Street, I found a CVS pharmacy that would have what we needed to complete Harper's so-called goth look.

"Really?" she said when we were inside at the makeup aisle. "Black lipstick?"

"And eyeliner and maybe purple eye shadow. Purple's a good look."

"I could also black out two of my front teeth."

"If you want, sure. That'd be great. I'll send a picture to Lucy so she knows what you look like."

She slugged my shoulder.

One of Lucy's favorite disguises is the goth look, but with short lacy black skirts, black leggings and boots, cleavage-rich bodices with huge safety pins and buckles. She might be a goth chick at heart. We weren't going that extreme with Harper. We didn't have the right clothes, and she would've hit me harder. She got the poor-goth look.

After the CVS pharmacy and after Harper had put on purple eye shadow, I went looking for another motel.

"Why?" she asked, applying black lipstick.

"Misdirection. Watch and learn."

"As a teacher, I understand misdirection, Mort."

"Then this will make sense. I returned the truck to Avis, which might register with someone. So that someone would know we're in Elko, or that we were here recently. I'll get a room using what might be a blown ID and credit card to keep them off balance in the wrong part of town."

"Kids in my classes never did anything like that."

"How do you know?"

I used the Stephen Brewer credit card to get us a room at a motel right off the interstate, Shilo Inn. The room was nicer than what we had at Ruby's, but we weren't tempted to stay. We went in, messed the place up a bit, then left.

First up that evening for the Elrood hunt was a lounge at the Red Lion Inn. He had a habit of finding women in bars, although the girl in Tonopah said Wintergarden had met her in the produce section of a supermarket, so the lad was a versatile, low-rent, scamming, half-assed gigolo.

I wasn't about to buy booze at each of the myriad bars we were likely to hit that evening, but drinks are a form of camouflage. I got a bottle of Pete's Wicked Ale and Harper ordered a margarita to get the evening started off right and to prime the bartender. Harper looked eighteen and had to produce some ID.

"Yum," she said, cheeks pulling in as she sucked on a little red straw. "When're you gonna investigate?"

"We've already started." I waved the bartender back over, a girl in her mid-twenties in black pants and a black vest over a white shirt. "Refills already?" she asked.

"Not yet. I wonder if you know a gal by the name of Olga here in town. Or," I pulled out a picture of Elrood, "if you've seen this guy around." No point in mentioning his name since he didn't use the same one twice.

She gazed at the picture. "Nope on him, and I don't know anyone named Olga, so you probably shouldn't play the slots this evening."

"Why's that?"

"You're not lucky, ducky."

What a gal.

She wasn't done yet, however. She waved the other bartender over, a guy in his thirties. He pulled thoughtfully on a short goatee, then shrugged and shook his head.

"Worth a shot anyway," I said. Then I had a thought. I described Max to the two bartenders. Again, they shook their heads. It was possible Max was in Elko by now. If so, he would be looking for Harper. And me. We didn't know who he was, where he was, or anything about him except that he was dangerous and we were on his radar for some reason, a reason that had gotten Nevada's attorney general killed.

"This's one bar down," Harper said, stirring her drink with the pygmy straw.

"A hundred ninety-nine to go," I replied. "Drink up. Let's keep moving."

"Two *hundred* margaritas? I'm gonna be *so* drunk, Mort. You'll have to undress me when we get back and put me in the shower and scrub me then toss me into bed." She glanced at me out of the corner of her eye.

"Guess what ain't happenin', little lady, no matter how drunk you end up."

She smiled. "We'll see. Where to next?"

"Anyplace with neon. The night is still young."

I glanced up at a television above the bar, and there I was in some ancient stock footage from when I'd found the decapitated head of Reno's mayor. I got the bartender back and asked if she could turn up the volume. She hit a button on a remote. Seeing myself on the little screen, I felt Max's presence here, close by. If he knew which room we were staying in at Hotel Nevada, he had gotten to the girl at the desk, which might mean he'd found the Stephen Brewer identity. If he could plant explosive charges, I had to assume he could track credit cards and that he'd made it here to Elko. Was he working alone? Was someone with him when he'd torched the truck? I didn't think he would set it on fire and walk away. It would be too easy to get picked up. Again, I felt the presence of an accomplice.

They had no video of my latest missing-person coup, so it was all footage from the past—a split screen with a pair of talking heads telling viewers that Reno's infamous PI, Mortimer Angel, had located Nevada's missing attorney general. He'd found yet another person in the trunk of a car. They made a big deal of that. They had very little real information so they winged it, filled three minutes of air time with conjecture and compared it to my finding Mayor Jonnie in the trunk of Dallas's Mercedes two years ago. A shot of my face looked like a mug shot, but with a caption under it—shit, a *caption*: "Reno's Finest," which might piss off every RPD officer in the city since they would assume, automatically, that they were the finest. My fifteen minutes of Andy Warhol's idiot fame got yet another three-minute boost. In fact, what Andy had *tried* to say is that all fame is fleeting, even for the famous.

He was wrong, of course. I only wish he'd been right in my case. Who the hell needs fame except fools?

A new story started up. My favorite Reno detective, Russ Fairchild, was speaking into a bunch of microphones, telling reporters that the bodies of two teenage girls who had gone missing several days ago had been found in the basement of a house between Locust and Kirman Streets in one of Reno's older neighborhoods.

"What two girls?" Harper asked.

"Couple of teenagers," I said with a sigh.

Vicki Cannon and Cathy Jantz had been missing for five days. They'd been found in an unoccupied house that had been on the market for several months. The coroner estimated they'd been dead four days. They'd been hung. They were found by a realtor who was showing the house to prospective buyers. A sale unlikely to go through.

"Hung," Harper said. "Two young girls. What a lovely world we live in."

"It can be. It isn't always. Let's get out of here."

We went out to the Explorer. I got us on Idaho Street and we went looking for more neon.

Next up was the Gold Country Inn. No luck, no booze.

Then the Ramada Elko Hotel and Casino. No Olga. No one recognized the photo of Elrood or the description of Max.

Then, in order of appearance: the Stray Dog Pub and Café, Silver Dollar Club, Star Hotel, Jr's Bar and Grill.

We got a nibble at Good Times Charlie's. A bartender named Karen leaned closer and said, "I know where there's an Olga." She took in Harper's goth outfit then gave my slicked-back silver Hickok hair a look and a smile. "If it's the one you're looking for, she works housekeeping at the Red Lion."

"Housekeeping," I said. "Making beds and vacuuming, leaving little mints on the pillows, that sort of thing?"

"Uh-huh. Anyway, that's the only Olga I've ever heard of around here. I don't actually know her, but my brother's been dating Bridget, the sister of an Olga, says the two of them work together at the Lion."

Which had been our first stop of the evening, but it wasn't surprising a bartender wouldn't know a room maid. Different hours, different locations within the hotel-casino complex. Red Lion was a good-sized operation.

I showed Karen the photo of Elrood.

"Good-looking guy," she said. "I would remember him if I saw him, which I haven't." She left to whip up a basic rum and Coke and a blue Hawaiian in a hurricane glass for a man and woman in touristy clothes to our left.

"Got a whiff there," I said to Harper.

"That felt like more than a whiff. Now what?"

"It's getting late. Back to Ruby's unless you want to get plastered. Not the royal 'you' meaning both of us, but *you* could get plastered and I'll watch and get the video."

"That'd sure be fun, but, nope. Unless you want to get me plastered for a reason you haven't mentioned, in which case I'll consider it."

"Nope."

"Okay, then. Let's go."

We approached Ruby's Hideaway cautiously. The PI manual says it's a good idea to be careful around guys who have access to remotely-detonated explosive devices. Last thing I wanted to do was underestimate Max. He might be hundreds of miles away, or he might be right here in Elko.

The night was quiet around Ruby's as we drove by. I didn't see anyone obviously watching the place, but that didn't mean much. I went by at a normal speed and we looked for movement in the parked cars we passed and in the shadows around the buildings.

"Nothing," Harper said as we left the area.

"Nothing obvious, anyway." I parked the Explorer six blocks away in the back lot of a Budget Inn. Places like that tend not to tow unknown cars. It might piss off a paying customer, and they have plenty of spare parking. We got out and I locked the car with the key fob.

"We're leaving the car here?" she asked, looking at me over the hood of the car.

"Observant. That's why I hired you."

She rolled her eyes. "And what, we're walking back?"

"That's right, Miss marathon-running, cross-country and track coach lady."

"Fine. Race you back?"

"Take off," I said. "I'll give you a head start."

"I'm sure." She grabbed my hand and headed out, but I held back which, given our weight differential, gave her a pretty good yank. "*Now* what?" she asked.

"We forgot our weaponry."

"Oh. Good idea."

I unlocked the Explorer. My .357 revolver went in a jacket pocket, her 9mm automatic ended up in her purse. We walked back, keeping on a dark side street.

We stood across the street in deep shadow, watching Ruby's for several minutes, then finally went in with guns drawn but not in plain view, fingers outside trigger guards. We weren't exactly a full-on SWAT team, so it was a good thing Max wasn't inside with an Uzi aimed at the door. He could've mowed us down.

"All that sneaking around for nothing," Harper said once I got the door shut and locked.

"Be thankful."

"I am." She whipped off the T-shirt I'd given her. And the tank top and all the rest of it. "Dibs on the shower," she said, "unless . . ." She gave me a look, then disappeared into the bathroom.

Unless what? I failed to ask, which might be why she poked her head back out, gave me a three-second look and ducked back inside.

I can't explain it. I've tried, but other than some sort of post-IRS karma, I come up with nothing. I've never asked Lucy, but it might be time to do that, get this figured out. She might know because she got topless with me an hour after we met. Maybe she'd heard a little voice in her head, like Ted Kaczynski but with a different message. If so, I wanted to know what it said.

It was after midnight. Late, but she might still be up. Probably was, given what Val was doing, so I called her.

"Hi, Mort," Lucy answered. "You still okay?"

"Why wouldn't I be?"

"Got a few possibilities, but you sound okay, so what's happening?"

"Really want to know?"

"Uh-oh. Is your phone on speaker?"

"Nope. And Harper's in the shower."

"Groovy. So what's up?"

"I'd like to know why women take off their clothes in my presence more than, say, any other guy in the country."

"*Any* other guy? Do you have proof of that?"

"I took a poll. It's true."

"And you called to ask me why?"

"It was on my mind."

"Is it a serious problem?"

"Nope, not serious. I'm acclimating, toughing it out, and there's no accompanying drama."

"Right, toughing it out. How's that goin'?"

"I don't have to fend her off, not even close. But she'll be great on that World Naked Bike Ride next year."

"As will I, Mort. *And* Mom."

"Which isn't the point, but good to know. *And* a little disconcerting, that last part."

"My mother going with us, you mean?"

"Yup."

"So let me guess—the point you *were* making is that Harper's not dressed to the nines all the time."

"Or to the ones, sugar plum."

"Got that. But without drama."

"That's right. She's not being the least bit pushy and I'm in Zen mode, detached, able to block out all kinds of irrelevant stimuli. You know how I am."

"I do. But it's not Zen mode. It's something else."

"Whatever. A bit of playful innuendo has picked up in the last twenty-four hours, but that's all."

"Related topic alert—do you remember what Danya was wearing when you knocked on her motel room door that second time in Caliente last year and we sort of barged into her room the moment she unlocked the door?"

Danya. Russell Fairchild's daughter, married to a girl named Shanna. For a moment I replayed the scene in my head. "Panties," I said.

"Good memory. What else?"

"Well, nothing. Not even a smile since she was angry."

"That's right. And you didn't freak out or stare, but I don't think Zen is the answer. Are you sure you didn't call because you wanted to hear my voice?"

"You got me, Luce. I miss you."

"Me too."

I took a deep breath. "Anyway, how's Val doing? She havin' a blast?"

"Sure you want to phrase it that way?"

"Oh. No, I take it back. She having a good time?"

"It's been a laugh a minute around here. I'm not going to have a colonoscopy until it's too late to care if they find anything.

And—gotta go, Mort. I'm being paged. Enjoy the sights, such as they are, and don't worry about it."

"Will do."

She hung up. I still hadn't told her about the bomb on the radiator or the incinerated truck. If I had, she would abandon Val and drive all night to Elko. Not fair to Val and I didn't know what Lucy could do here anyway. I didn't know what I was going to do either, except find Olga and keep after the girl-hopping Elrood.

"Mort?" Harper called from the bathroom.

"What? Before you tell me, you should know I charge ten bucks a minute to scrub anything." Which was pretty good innuendo, if I say so myself.

Silence for a few seconds, then a girlish laugh. "That's not it, dope, though I might take fifty dollars' worth to see what happens. I just wanted to know if I should leave the water on for you. I'm about to hop out and it's at a perfect temperature, which wasn't easy to get."

"Sounds like that would result in a first-degree traffic jam—the two of us trying to shuttle past each other in that little room. Think I'll step outside for a few and watch the street, make sure no one's lurking out there."

"You're going to leave me all alone in here?"

"If anyone comes to the door, I'll see them and come charging to the rescue. Also, you've got a gun. Don't shoot me when I come back."

"I might . . . just because."

I didn't follow up on that bit of innuendo. There was a lot of slippery talk floating around. I went outside, not sure what I thought I might see. Max could be driving anything if he was still around—anything but a Smart car, that is. He couldn't squeeze into one of those naked and greased.

The truck had been torched three miles up Highway 6, southwest of Ely. He could've hiked back to Ely in an hour. An accomplice could've picked him up. He could've flagged down a ride at some point—though that would be a sloppy move for a killer since someone could get a description of him, or at least a sighting. He would need transportation if he was still after Harper. Or me, since it had no doubt occurred to him that I had lied to him up in the mountains that night in the rain. He would be miffed about that.

Not that it was essential, but an accomplice seemed likely. Max might not be in this alone, even now, after he'd eliminated what had to be one accomplice: Eystad, retired shyster. It depended on how big a deal this was, how many people were involved, who they were, what they wanted.

Why hadn't Max dumped Eystad in the desert instead of leaving him in his car in the attorney general's sister's driveway? Why leave the attorney general there too? Was he sending a message? If so, to whom, and what was the message? As usual, I was so far in the dark I couldn't even make out dim, shifting shadows.

Speaking of which, I was in darkness beneath a huge oak tree that was blotting out the stars, nothing moving on the street, it was nearly one in the morning, cool outside, Harper was inside wearing nothing but an overall tan, and I was male, a pig, and it appeared that karma still owed me one. Far be it from me to spit in the eye of karma and upset the balance of the universe.

I went back to the room.

* * *

She was in bed, reading. I brushed my teeth and took a quick shower, no innuendo involved. I crawled into bed beside her, wearing jockeys.

"Undies off, please," she said with a little sigh.

"Hah."

"It's not as if I'm gonna molest you, Mort."

"Yup. You had your chance in Grange. And McGill."

"Well, then. You might as well be comfortable. *I* am."

I thought about that, then gave up. I got naked, set my jockeys on a nearby chair. "Happy?"

"Very." She rolled onto her side and reached under the covers, gave me a two-second squeeze.

"Yowzer!" I yelped.

She rolled back, smiling. "Copped my feel. We're even now." She picked up her book, then said, "Revenge is a dish best served cold. And, yes, I will tell Lucy."

Well, shit. Guess karma really did owe me one.

CHAPTER FIFTEEN

BEFORE LEAVING RUBY'S the next morning I donned an unkempt dishwater-blond wig, John Deere ball cap, non-prescription glasses with thick black frames.

"Nice," Harper said. "Very Farm Bureau. A lot better than last night's nasty-awful wig."

By 8:45, after breakfast at a place called Marlene's Kitchen, Harper and I were wandering the hallways of the Red Lion Inn, tracking down Olga.

Which turned out not to be difficult, even for a newbie PI backed up by an English teacher in jeans and a tank top. I asked a pretty Hispanic girl in a maid's outfit if she knew Olga, and she gave me a blazing smile of even white teeth and said, "No entiendo, Señor."

Yeah, right. No entiendo.

I didn't follow up on that and we kept going. Harper asked the next maid, in a pale blue dress with a name tag that read *Bridget*. "My sister?" she asked.

"If her name is Olga, yes."

"Um, what about?"

I said, "We're trying to find a guy who might've called her a few days ago from Ely."

Bridget's eyes narrowed. "You mean the butthead?"

"That sounds right. Is Olga somewhere around?"

She pointed. "Down in 205. They always put us on the same floor. We work good together."

Good thing English Nazi Lucy didn't hear that. Harper gave me a look, smiled, didn't say anything.

Bridget came with us as we went into room 205. Olga was a plain girl in her early twenties, five-seven, with thick eyebrows, mouse-brown hair in a chunky pigtail, wearing a pale blue uniform dress like her sister.

It took a minute to get past the butthead part of who and what Elrood was, and that Olga had given him a loan of four hundred dollars which she would never see again. "Then he took off," she said. "He was supposed to come back in two hours, but he just— *took off*, the butthead."

So we weren't done with the butthead part, but I'm a patient guy.

"Took off for where?" I asked.

"Jackpot, I think. I mean, I'm pretty sure, probably. And he took my car."

Now we were getting somewhere. "With your car?"

"Yeah. He said his car needed new tires and he had to have four hundred to get new ones, and then he would pick me up after work and take me to Jackpot with him to see this guy who owed him like *eight* hundred and he'd, uh, you know, get me, well, us, a real nice room there at Cactus Pete's, and we would come back the next day and I'd have my money back, and an extra fifty. But he didn't show up after work yesterday, so maybe he's still in Jackpot and, I don't know, maybe not."

A muddled story with logical difficulties, unlikely to be true in any of its particulars, but it was the only lead I had so Jackpot was in my—*our*, I amended because I had acquired an assistant— immediate future.

"What make and model is your car?" I asked.

"A Toyota Avalon."

"*Our* car," Bridget piped up. "It's mine too."

Olga rolled her eyes. "That's what I *meant*."

"Which means now we have to walk like a mile to get to work here," Bridget elaborated. "And a mile back to our apartment when we're done. With sore feet."

"I said I was sorry," Olga said. "And it's only been one day. He took off yesterday morning after he dropped us off at work here."

I was closing in on the butthead. "What year car?" I asked.

"A 2011. I think. I—we—paid almost seven thousand for it. It still runs real good."

"It would if we *had* it," Bridget said, and Olga gave her a look that would set a flying duck on fire.

"Color?"

"Green, kinda."

"*Mint* green," Bridget said, arms folded across a fairly substantial chest.

Probably not a lot of mint-green Avalons on the road, and Jackpot was nothing but a wide spot on Highway 93 on the Nevada-Idaho border—a casino town that siphoned money out of the wallets of folks around Twin Falls who'd succumbed to the gambling bug. Elrood might be up there, or might not, but we had to check it out. No choice, and keeping on the move wasn't a bad idea.

Something wasn't adding up. I thought there had to be a bit more to the Elrood story. I asked Olga, "He phoned you from Ely a few days ago?"

She looked down at her feet. "Um, yes."

"So he knew you from sometime before that?"

"Yeah."

Time to tread gently here. Elrood had probably taken her for money in the past. Elrood was a classic scamming shithead and

Olga was a classic patsy—nice girl, not overly bright, a soft touch, and, best guess, emotionally needy.

"How long ago did you know him?"

"Like about a month. Then he called and asked if we could like get together again."

And of course, she'd said yes. Elrood was making the rounds. No telling how many girls he had on a string, and accumulating more along the way, the cad—which is an antique, underutilized word that means shithead.

Or butthead.

* * *

"So we're headed to Jackpot?" Harper asked as we walked back to the car.

"Uh-huh."

"Keeping an eye out for a mint-green Toyota Avalon?"

"You really oughta be a detective."

She slugged my shoulder, then hugged my arm. "Are we staying the night in Jackpot?"

"One never knows."

"Depends on what we find when we get there, right?"

"You oughta be a—*oof*!"

"Anyway," Harper said, as if she hadn't hit me twice in ten seconds, "I've never stayed overnight in Jackpot. I've been through a time or two on the way up north. I think there's at least one hotel-casino that doesn't look too icky."

"That would be Cactus Pete's."

She looked at me. "You've stayed there?"

"When I worked for the IRS rounding up tax dodgers. We used to ship them off to federal penitentiaries without any of that habeas corpus, fair-trial nonsense."

She stopped walking. "No, you didn't."

"We wore black jackboots and an armband, a luger in a leather holster on a wide belt, the whole nine yards. You should have seen the salute we gave the commissioner's picture on the wall Mondays before we headed out."

She sighed. "I take it you *really* didn't like the IRS."

"Smashing understatement, Harp. I gave them sixteen years. I haven't gotten over it yet." We reached our car and I opened the door for her. "Next stop, Jackpot."

* * *

Was Elrood a car thief? He was opportunistic, but car thief didn't seem to fit his usual M.O. I wondered what had happened to Judy Alcott's Pontiac Vibe. Elrood might be a serial car borrower.

Thief, however, did fit, but in an understated way. He didn't use a gun. Women gave him money of their own free will. The law might not see it that way, though. Elrood was flirting with jail time if a few of these girls would testify, which I doubted. I wondered what the charge would be. Failure to stick around? Misrepresentation? He'd found himself a lifestyle that worked for him, got him from girl to girl, bed to bed, wasn't going to make him rich, but maybe he was in training for the big time when he would go after an older woman who had millions, not that he could think that far ahead with a brain the size of a kidney bean.

Which wasn't my problem, but I was feeling less and less like completing this assignment. Elrood didn't deserve a five-dollar bill, much less seven hundred grand.

We were on Idaho Street headed toward I-80 when I slowed abruptly, came close to standing on the brakes.

"What?" Harper asked, one hand on the dash.

I pointed. "Is that Max?"

She looked. A big guy with a beard was headed for a McDonald's up ahead.

"Oh, shit," she said. "I think so. At least it's a definite maybe."

The guy opened the door then stopped and glanced back at the McD's parking lot, the street, the sidewalks. His eyes passed over us but didn't linger. After that scan of his surroundings, he went inside. Gone.

"Omigod," Harper breathed. "That's him for sure. He found us."

"Probably not. But he made it as far as Elko."

"Which is *way* the hell too close, Mort."

"I agree."

"So, now what?"

An interesting question. Call 911 on a burner phone and tell them . . . what? *I think the guy who murdered the attorney general is in the McDonald's on Idaho Street here in Elko.*

First thing they would ask is, *Who are you?*

Then what? Hang up? Tell them I'm Mortimer Angel? Give a bogus name and hang up? Fake a signal dropout?

Suppose police went into the McDonald's and spoke to the guy? What evidence would they find *on the spot* that he had killed the old guy and Leeman? That he had ever been driving that Ram truck? Would they hold him long enough to find evidence? Would they detain him at all based on an anonymous call? I doubted it. I was the only one who had seen him up in the hills, asking if I had seen "anyone else" up there. What did "anyone else" mean? It could mean any number of things. It didn't necessarily point to Harper, and even less to Chase Eystad or Annette Leeman. Even a bumbling half-assed defense attorney would laugh at any such suggestion. I'd given Sheriff Taylor a fair description of the guy, but I was only one person. Was that enough? How many guys would fit that description?

And if Max were picked up, did he have an accomplice I might've been getting a glimpse of from time to time? A glimpse that might be nothing at all, or an accomplice who might keep after us, someone we wouldn't see coming?

"You don't know what," Harper said after a while. I had gone past the McDonald's and pulled to the curb eighty yards away, watching the place in the driver's-side mirror.

"You got it. I'm at a loss here."

"Want a little advice from your assistant?"

"As if I don't know what that'll be."

"Let's get the hell outta here. Now. Go to Jackpot. I bet Max doesn't know anything about Jackpot."

"Might do that," I said.

"Might? What *else*, Mort?"

"I could drop you off at the airport. You could catch a flight to Vegas, keep out of this."

"What terrific advice, since my mother was in that car. I'm *already* in this, more than you. If he finds out I'm not with you, the first place he'd look for me is in Vegas since that's where I live and work."

"Uh-huh."

Five seconds of silence, then she said, "Are you trying to get rid of me?"

"No, I'm trying to keep you safe."

"You don't think I'd be safer with you instead of on my own in Las Vegas?"

"Hell, Harp, I don't know. We don't have the slightest idea what's going on."

She was quiet for a moment. Then, "Keep your friends close, your assistants closer."

I smiled. "Not sure that's an exact Sun Tzu quote. It sounds a bit off."

"Sun Tzu? Where are you getting that?"

"Judo lessons. I know fifty Sun Tzus. It's part of my training. I actually used one of them last year." I didn't add that a few weeks later I had to kill the guy I'd used it on. With a big rock, too. Better to leave that for another time.

"You're taking judo?"

"I'm up to a green belt."

"Huh. I've got a brown belt in Tae Kwon Do. Another year and I'll go for my black."

"Tae Kwon Do, cross country, track. No wonder you're so, so . . ."

She smiled. "So what? Let's hear it."

"Solid?"

"Gee, thanks—I guess. You and I ought to go to a gym and spar sometime. Judo versus Tae Kwon Do."

"Or not."

"We can think about that. But right now, what are we gonna *do*, Mort?"

While we'd been talking, I'd been keeping an eye on the McDonald's. Max hadn't come out yet. "I'd like to find out what he's driving so we'll know what to watch for."

"Now that he cremated his stolen truck."

"Yeah, that."

I pulled away from the curb, went up a hundred yards and turned around, came back facing the McDonald's and hugged the curb again. I was still wearing a wig and a ball cap, glasses with black frames. I reached into my duffel bag and handed Harper a shoulder-length black wig.

"Seriously?" she said.

"Seriously. Put it on. Last thing we need is for him to recognize you."

She sighed, stuck it on her head, then stared at me with her lips pushed out. "It doesn't fit."

"It's better than your blond, lady. Tough it out. And put on sunglasses."

She did. She toughed it out and we waited.

And waited.

"Think he's still in there?" she asked after a while.

"Probably. Unless he went out a bathroom window."

"No one actually does anything like that, Mort."

"Little do you know."

She gave me a strange look, but I didn't tell her about the Mexican Chickadee, Sophie, in Bend, Oregon.

Ten minutes later, Max came out. He gave the street a long look then headed away from us. He went past the side parking lot and kept going. I had to fire up the engine and trail along behind, pulling to the curb every hundred feet or so. It wasn't an optimal solution to the problem, but I had no choice.

Max strolled three blocks up Idaho Street, then into a first-floor room of a generic-looking place called the North Elko Motel. Spiffy name.

"Now what?" Harper asked.

"One of us could go knock on his door."

"Yeah, *right*. I'm serious."

"We wait a while, see if he comes out and gets into a vehicle of some kind."

So we waited.

Ten minutes.

Fifteen.

Twenty.

"Boring," Harper said quietly.

"Such is the PI's life." Unless someone's trying to kill you, I didn't say.

"Boring," she said again.

"You should have that echolalia checked out."

She sighed.

Ten minutes of blessed silence later she said, "I'll bet Mike Hammer never had to do anything like this."

My head whipped around. "Say what?"

"Mike Hammer. You've heard of him, haven't you?"

"Hell, yes. He and I are on almost a first-name basis. He and Sam Spade."

She smiled. "Those are fictional characters."

"Says you."

She rolled her eyes. "How long are we gonna sit here and stare at that place?"

"We'll give it another half hour."

"Great. If he doesn't show, then what?"

"Jackpot."

"Which we could do right now." She looked over at me. "I read *I The Jury*. Mike Hammer would go kick in his door with a drawn gun and beat the snot out of him."

"Hush, Bubba."

That got my shoulder backhanded. Like Lucy, she was a testy critter and prone to violence.

* * *

We gave it the half hour, then gave up. No sign of Max. Not so much as a twitch of a curtain.

"Probably asleep," I said, starting the engine.

"Like me."

"And you an English teacher. Shame on you."

She laughed. "Drive."

* * *

Fifty miles to Wells on I-80, then sixty-eight more to Jackpot on U.S. 93. Harper and I got there at 12:55 in the afternoon, temperature 96 degrees, about typical for mid-to-late August. Two crows were dining on roadkill ten miles south of town. They hopped four feet to one side as we blew on by, then hopped back and kept at it. Yum.

My burner phone rang when we were a few miles from Jackpot. It was Lucy. She'd stepped out of the room where her mother was in the midst of her colonoscopy and was calling to give me an update.

"Not holding her hand, sweetheart?" I said.

"She's so gorked right now, she's like comatose. She doesn't know I'm out of the room. I doubt that she knows her own name."

"Probably a good thing, considering what's going on behind her back."

"For sure. Anyway, are you all right, Mort?"

"Of course. Why wouldn't I be?"

"Oh, you know—dead bodies, some guy trying to find Harper. She's still with you, isn't she?"

"Still is."

"Where are you now?"

"About two miles south of Jackpot."

"Jackpot? That mean you're still trying to find that Elrood character?"

"Yup. He's a slippery little eel."

"No match for my favorite PI, though."

"No comment, since he's been as elusive as a Denver omelet in Saudi Arabia."

"You'll get him. Love you, Mort."

"Love you too."

We ended the call and I cruised the highway through town, speed limit 25 past the casinos, keeping an eye out for a mint-green Avalon. We made it to the last place in Jackpot, then pulled over, hung a U-turn and headed back.

"Now what?" my assistant asked.

"You say that a lot."

"I'm seeking professional guidance here."

"Good luck with that."

"Uh-huh. Now what?" she asked again.

"Now we cruise the casino parking lots."

"After hitting a bathroom in one of them, right? And maybe finding something to eat?"

"What a terrific little assistant."

"And, look! There's a casino right *there*, Mort!"

"What sharp eyes." It was seven stories tall, biggest one in Jackpot—Cactus Pete's. I took us into a parking lot and we got out, headed for the casino and bathrooms and a restaurant, looking for a mint-green car of any description, but didn't see one. It wasn't a common color.

We ended up in the Desert Room, a café more elegant than the Denny's in Ely, though "elegant" was subjective and defined regionally. I had a Monte Cristo sandwich and Harper had what girls have to keep the poundage under control—a salad with a bunch of inedibles on it, like beets, sprouts and something like watercress or unfresh seaweed.

Harper settled back in the booth when we were done. She grinned and said, "Now what?"

"You're fired. Turn in your badge."

"Don't think so, flyboy."

We hit the parking lots around Cactus Pete's, and the upper and lower RV parks. No luck, so we went off to the other casinos, cruised the parking lots of Barton's Club 93, the Horseshu, which had a spelling error on the sign out front that would be expensive to fix, the Four Jacks casino, and the lowest-rated hotel in town, the West Star.

Still nothing.

"Maybe he's not in Jackpot," Harper said.

"Possible, since Olga wasn't the most reliable source of information I've ever come across."

"Well, then—"

"If you say 'now what,' I might have to hurt you."

"Uh-huh. *Now what*, Mort?"

I had to smile. "Now we cruise the neighborhoods."

"This place has neighborhoods?"

"It's almost like a real town, Harp."

"If you say so."

We headed east and motored along Poker Street, Ace Drive, Casino Way, Keno Drive, Lady Luck Drive, Twenty-One Drive.

"It's as if there's, you know, like a *theme* to the way they named the streets here," Harper said.

"Really? I hadn't noticed."

"I'm sure. Hey, look!" She pointed at a mint-green Toyota Avalon parked beside a trailer broiling under the white-hot sun. Heat waves roiled the air above the trailer's metal roof around a big swamp cooler.

I slowed as we went by, stopped forty yards up the street, then backed up and parked on the street in front of the trailer. I couldn't see anything inside. All the curtains were pulled.

Harper smiled. "Now what, Sahib?"

* * *

Now I was conflicted. I'd probably caught up to the twerp, but I didn't want to do what I had been hired to do. Odds are, Elrood was in that trailer, scamming some poor girl out of a few hundred bucks. He didn't deserve a dime of Mildred Castle's money. But it wasn't my call because it wasn't my investigative agency. It was Maude Clary's.

"Now I go knock on the door and say howdy to the shithead," I said, opening the car door.

"Oh, boy. This I gotta see."

We walked to the side of the trailer, and I knocked on the door. It was a smallish double-wide, eighteen by thirty-two feet. Thirty years ago, it might have been maroon and white—back when things like this were called trailers. Now they're manufactured homes, as if that's better. The Avalon was right outside what passed for the front door. An old Honda Accord was parked farther in on a cracked concrete pad, blocked in by the Avalon. Overhead, the swamp cooler rumbled diligently.

I knocked again. With two cars in the drive someone had to be home. Probably. I knocked a third time.

A minute later, the door opened a few cautious inches and a woman in glasses and tangled hair peeked out.

"What?" she asked.

"I need to talk to the guy who's driving this car." I nodded at the Avalon.

"Um. Juss a sec." She sounded sleepy.

The door closed. I looked at Harper. She arched an eyebrow. "We might've interrupted something important," she said.

"One never knows. You should ask."

That got me a poke in the ribs.

Three minutes later, the door opened and the woman said, "Um, who are you guys?"

"I'm a private investigator and this is—"

The door shut.

Shitfire.

"Maybe you should wave a gun around," Harper said.

"I might do that."

Two more minutes passed. Hot minutes, even though we were in shade on that side of the trailer. Then the door opened and the woman said, "C'mon in."

She stood aside and we trooped in. Not knowing what was in there, I took the lead. The temperature inside was twenty degrees cooler, the air humid enough to grow mold. The lady was in a bathrobe, bare feet, hair mussed. She was in her early thirties, plain, twenty pounds overweight, toenail polish bright blue and chipped on splayed toes.

"Where's Elrood?" I asked.

"Um, he'll be out in a few minutes. Can I get you some water or something?" She had to speak loudly to be heard over the swamp cooler blasting air overhead.

"I'm fine."

"Me too," Harper said.

So we all looked at each other, which took some doing since the room was dim with the curtains pulled.

"Do you want to sit?" the woman asked. "I'm Beth, by the way."

"I'll stand," I told her. "I've been sitting all day."

"Me too," Harper added.

So we stood and stared at each other, gazing around the room. Then the front door opened and a kid about ten years old came in, thin, big feet, needed a haircut.

"You do what you was told?" Beth asked him.

He stared at me and Harper. He had a goofy grin on his face, a devilish light in his eyes, then he looked down at his feet. "Yes'm."

"Okay, good, Bobbie. Now go on in the back an' play or something."

The kid opened a door and disappeared into a back room. Seconds later I heard another door close softly.

"Now what?" Harper asked Beth, then she looked at me and smiled.

Beth shrugged. "I don't know."

Weird.

About then I heard a car's engine fire up. It sounded close, right outside, so I flipped a curtain aside in time to see the Avalon back out, fast. I went out the front door like a shot, right as the Avalon's tires threw dust as the car took off, headed north.

"Let's go," I called out to Harper.

"Right behind you," she said. She'd bailed out of the place right on my heels. What a great assistant.

We ran to the Explorer. As we approached, I saw that it didn't look right. And, slumped in front, it wasn't. The two front tires were flat on their rims.

Sonofabitch.

You do what you was told made sense now. I caught the last two seconds of mint green as the car whipped to the left and roared west toward Highway 93.

"Next time," Harper said, "use your gun."

* * *

Across a field and beyond Cactus Pete's we could see intermittent stretches of the highway. Half a minute later the Avalon was visible, heading toward Wells, Ely, Elko, and points south. Gone. I went back to the trailer, didn't knock, just went in and said, "Your kid flattened the tires on my car."

Beth shrank away from me. "Eddie tole him to."

"Eddie?"

"The guy you called Elrood. His name is Eddie Tower, but he tole me some guy calling him Elrood was after him, thinking Eddie knew where his sister was."

"Whose sister?"

"*Yours*. I just said."

I could tell I wasn't going to get through to this lady any time before the Second Coming. No point either. "How much did you give him?"

"Huh?"

"Money. How much did you give him?"

Her eyes narrowed. "Like that's any of your business."

"He's a good-looking guy, been scamming women all over the state. Three hundred here, four hundred there. I hope you didn't give him anything."

She stood there, lips working as she thought. "He said you might say something like that."

"Didn't that strike you as strange?"

"Strange? Why would it?"

I sighed. "How long have you known him?"

"Like that's your business."

"How long?" Harper asked gently.

Beth looked at her, then sagged a little, sat heavily on an old couch as reality hit home. "Since . . . since yesterday afternoon." Then she looked up at me with sad eyes. "Shit."

"Yup. How much did you give him?"

"Six hundred."

"If I catch up with him, I'll try to get it back to you."

Beth started to cry. "He . . . he said . . . back there in the back when you came to the door . . . he said he'd come back after you was gone."

"Don't count on it," I said.

"Well . . . shit." She left the room, went into the back, and we could hear more crying.

Harper took my arm and we went outside. "Elrood is one rotten, slippery fucker," she said. "Lady in there has a kid, too. What the hell was she thinking?"

"She wasn't." I stared at the cross street where Elrood had disappeared. "And I'm trying to get him almost seven hundred thousand dollars."

"Don't."

"There's a thought."

*　*　*

I went house-to-house and finally found someone who had a tire pump. I didn't think a garage or gas station in Jackpot was hooked into Triple-A. I might've been wrong, but sometimes it's best to work out frustrations doing physical labor. Like using a cheap bicycle pump to inflate two big-ass tires enough to limp to the nearest gas station.

I got one tire up to maybe 10 psi—good enough for a half-mile trip to the Chevron across from Cactus Pete's, disconnected the pump and attached it to the other tire, then Harper said, "My turn."

"Go get 'em, girl." I handed her the pump.

She went to it, hard, sweat starting to glisten on her forehead, muscular arms working like pistons. I could see her sailing over a bar thirteen feet off the ground. She was a hell of a sight. She looked up at me. "We sure are having a lot of trouble with tires, Mort."

"Terrific observation. Keep at it. You're a dynamo."

"Yeah, right. Are you gonna keep after Elrood?"

"Have to. After today I've got to beat the tar out of the lad then get myself a cold beer."

"Cool. Can I watch?"

"You get to take the YouTube video."

"Even better."

* * *

Before we took off, I went back inside and gave Beth six hundred dollars from the stash in my lockbox. Made her cry again. I wouldn't miss six hundred, but she would, and I might recover it from Elrood, you never know.

Back in the car, Harper said, "You old softie."

"Watch who you're calling old, teacher."

CHAPTER SIXTEEN

WE WERE BACK in Elko at 4:45 that afternoon. I drove the length of Idaho Street, wondering if Max was still in town. He was the last person I wanted to run into but I wanted to see what he was driving.

"Back to Ruby's for the night?" Harper asked.

"You like that place, huh?"

"After pumping up that tire, I need a shower." She gave me a look. "You need one too."

Wouldn't touch that with a non-conducting pole the length of a first down in the NFL. "I think we oughta move around, not stay in the same place two nights running. Not with Max out there somewhere."

"As long as we end up in a place with a decent shower and a bed, I'm good."

Uh-huh. Still not touchin' it.

Right then I saw a mint-green Avalon, parked outside a place called Bud's Discount Tires. I hit the brakes, pulled into the lot, and parked beside the Avalon. Harper and I got out and went inside. It might not be the same car Elrood was driving, but I was playing the odds.

"Help you?" a scruffy guy behind the counter asked.

"Hope so," I replied, looking around the front room. No sign of Elrood. "There's a green Toyota Avalon outside. I'd like to talk to the guy who's driving it."

The guy shrugged. "He drove up in it an hour ago, paid for the tires I put on his other car, a Pontiac Vibe, and took off, left the Toyota."

Slippery butthead.

"He say what you should do with the Avalon?"

"Nope. Paid for the tires and hauled ass."

"Did he leave its keys with you?"

"Nope. Probably left 'em in the car."

"Thanks." I took Harper by the arm and we went out to the cars. I glanced in the Avalon. Keys were dangling in the ignition. He wasn't a thief, just an asshole. Time to be a good Samaritan again. "Might as well return the car to the girls," I said.

"Of course. Cleanin' up after the rude Elrood."

"Nice."

Right then my phone rang. It was Lucy.

"Hola," I said. "How's Mom doin'?"

"She's fine. Still a little ditzy right now, but she knows her own name. And mine."

"Sounds like progress."

"Like you wouldn't believe. How're you doin'?"

"Great. I gave six hundred bucks to a lady in Jackpot then Harper and I pumped up two car tires with a cruddy bicycle pump. She and I are about to return a not-quite-stolen car to a couple of dippy girls in Elko."

Silence for two seconds. Then, "I'm not even gonna ask why—about any of that."

"Good idea. It would take a while. You still planning on staying with your mother tomorrow?"

"So far, since Dad's still gone. Unless you need me."

"I always need you, sugar plum." I glanced at Harper. She smiled at me. I put the phone on speaker.

"I mean, need me like with a billy club or a gun," Lucy said. "Not . . . you know."

"Things haven't gotten that serious yet." I still hadn't told her about the bomb on the radiator, which would've qualified as *that* serious and more.

"Uh-huh. How's Harper?"

"She's smelly, needs a shower."

"Wowie." Lucy's voice held a smile.

"Here. You talk to her." I handed the phone to Harp.

"Uh, hi," Harper said.

"Hi. It sounds like Mort is being Mort, Harper."

"He is, yes. I don't know how you stand it."

Lucy laughed. "I take Valium when he's not looking. He gave some lady six hundred dollars?"

"Yes. That Elrood guy scammed her out of it."

"And, don't tell me. Mort gave it to her because she needed it. That sounds like my Boy Scout."

Harper grinned at me. "Boy Scout is *so* right. Actually, I'm starting to think *Eagle* Scout."

I grabbed the phone from her before that got out of control. "I'm back, sweetie pie."

"Groovy. Anyway, Mom's looking good for the next ten years, colonoscopy-wise."

"Good to know. Tell her I'm thrilled for her."

"Yeah, probably not."

"I gotta call Ma now, Luce."

"Oh? Why's that?"

"Need an address for two girls here in Elko. Got to try to return a car."

"That'll take Ma about thirty seconds."

"If that. Call me later?"

"Sure. As long as you aren't in the shower."

"Sugar plum . . ."

"Yes?"

"I miss you."

"Miss you too, big guy. A bunch."

We ended the call and I punched in Ma's number.

"What now, Mort? I'm soaking in the tub so this had better be nothing so I can hang up on you."

"You're soaking? What timing. How about I give you a car license and you get me an address here in Elko?"

"As if that's gonna happen with me in this tub, boyo."

"See, Lucy told me something about you."

"Oh, shit. What?"

"You keep your iPad within arm's reach 24/7 so you can investigate at a moment's notice. Like right now."

"Well, shit. I'll have to have a talk with that girl. So gimme the flippin' plate so I can relax here."

I read it off to her. Thirty seconds later she was back with an address. "Thanks, Ma. You're the best."

"I'll take it out of your pay. And if you find any more bodies, being fired will be the least of your worries."

"Yeah? What will?"

She hung up.

* * *

Looking back, my big mistake was in going over to the Red Lion first, thinking the girls might still be there. They would be happier driving home than walking.

Harper drove the Avalon and I drove the Explorer. We pulled up outside the Red Lion. As we walked toward the hotel Harper said, "He put new tires on someone else's car. What a nice guy."

"With someone else's money."

"Okay, there's that."

"Which might mean he's thinking about keeping the Vibe. Pretty much stealing it."

"Why, that dirty rotten son of a bitch."

We went inside and ambled down the same hallway where we found Olga and Bridget that morning. Then we quickly walked all the hallways.

No luck. The maid work was done for the day. A few guests were coming and going—a family of four; two ladies in their seventies; a kid of nineteen, red hair, crotch of his pants shuffling below mid-thigh, several inches of boxers showing, face pierced in half a dozen places. A cool dude and every mother's nightmare.

No maids, but we had an address. We went back to the cars, watched the redheaded kid get into a beat-up '83 Volvo and sit there with the stereo system pounding out bass notes loud enough to loosen sphincters.

I found the girls' street on an Elko map, then took off with Harper following in the Avalon. After a mile, I pulled up at an apartment building. Harper parked beside me and we walked to number 7B, knocked, and a few seconds later Olga opened the door.

I handed her the Avalon's keys. "Your car's parked in a visitor's spot," I said. "No charge."

"You did . . . you . . . you *got* it?"

"Yup. Gotta run. Oh, and Elrood, or whatever name he gave you, is a scammer. Don't give him the time of day, much less money."

We turned and left. Olga's voice followed us. "Thank you. You . . . I mean, this's great."

I held up a hand in a wave as Harper and I went back to the Explorer and got in. Somewhere in the distance I heard an idiot-thumping of bass, like someone pounding on an empty ten-thousand-gallon steel tank with a sledgehammer. Hard to believe anyone thinks that's music; all it does is club your brain stem farther down your neck.

* * *

I asked Harper to drive, had her pull onto Idaho Street and head west. "You should think carefully before saying, 'Now what?'" I said to her.

"Should I?"

"Yup. Very carefully."

She pondered that for a moment. "Okay, now what?"

"I thought you'd ask. Now we get out of Elko."

"Cool. A road trip. Where to?"

At this point I didn't think it mattered. We'd lost track of Elrood. I didn't know how to pick up his trail again. Or did I? I knew who had a shot at it.

I put my phone on speaker and called Ma. "Hola, Ma. You out of the tub yet?"

Harper smiled.

"What's it to you?" Ma asked.

"Just keepin' track, doll. Someone has to. I need you to put a trace on a plate, different plate than before, see if it shows up anywhere."

"You ain't gettin' nowhere, callin' me doll, boyo."

"A trace, Ma?"

"This better be about that fuckin' Wintergarden. Who, by the way, according to the DMV, doesn't own a car."

"It is, Ma. I'm all over Master Elrood. And good call. You're the best."

She sighed. "Gimme the plate."

I read off the tag of Judy's Pontiac Vibe then Ma hung up on me. As she does.

Harper smiled at me then looked back at the highway. "You're lucky the women in your life haven't throttled you yet, Mort."

"And lose all that comic relief? No way. I'm safe."

"Yeah, right. So . . . road trip. Where to?"

"Ever been to Battle Mountain?"

"Oh . . . shit. Do we have to?"

* * *

I bore easily, so I played around with my new burner phone and discovered I could download free ringtones. I located a new tone as Harper drove. This, I thought, was a surefire winner, best one yet.

* * *

Battle Mountain sits between Winnemucca and Elko on I-80. On the side of a mountain overlooking the town, in white for all to see, possibly as a warning, are the letters *BM*. The town was probably named long before it became popular to put the town's initials on nearby mountains in letters a hundred feet high. If not, then someone didn't think that one through all the way.

We pulled into the Big Chief Motel at 7:42. I parked in a temporary spot outside the office and we went inside. An old guy behind the reception counter was reading a worn Travis McGee paperback, *Bright Orange for the Shroud.* Which was interesting, because Hammer and Spade were up in a corner, ogling Harper and ignoring McGee, waiting to watch me order up a room with a damn good-looking girl by my side. Jealous, of course, the swine.

"Got two rooms next to each other?" I asked the guy, at which point Hammer's and Spade's mouths dropped in disgust. They blew raspberries and took off.

"Mort . . ." someone to my right said.

"Up on the second floor overlooking the pool," the old guy replied. "Two eleven and two twelve."

"We'll take them."

"Mort?"

I turned. "Overlooking the *pool*, Sis. That's great. I can watch you swim." I gave the old guy a smile. "My sister-in-law. Swims like a dolphin, does she ever."

Harper stared at me. "Well . . . hell. I thought—"

"Hold that thought," I said. I slid a registration form over to her. "Fill this out while I work on mine—Sis."

She emitted a low growl, rammed an elbow into my short ribs, kinda hard, then picked up a pen. "We'll have to talk about . . . about where to *eat* tonight, brother dear."

"Sure thing, kid." I paid cash for the rooms, used the name John Hansen, the quarterback of our football team when I was a senior and a gridiron hero. An easy name to remember if I were asked. I checked Harper's form. She'd put down the name Emma Ennui.

Jeez. English teachers.

"Those rooms wouldn't have an adjoining inner door, would they?" she asked the old guy.

"Nope. Got a few like that on the first floor, but they're taken. You got the last two rooms that're next door to each other. It's summer. We fill up most days."

"That's wonderful."

"Sure is. Takes care of the lean winter months."

"I'm so happy for you."

She didn't look happy when we left the office. I waited for it; when it came, she said, "As a bodyguard, you suck."

"Except you'll be right next door. Shouting distance. Or thumping."

"*Why*, Mort?"

"I'm something of an idiot, that's why. And married. We might call this a reality check. Lots of fine reasons."

"Hasn't it been working out okay with one room?"

"So far so good." I handed her a key to room 212.

She stared at it, said, "*Cub* Scout," as she marched off toward the outside stairs to the second floor. "I'll be up in my *private* room, Mort. You park the car."

A bit curt, but I'd expected it. She would get over it, and I'd weathered worse storms. I'd also been demoted to Cub Scout. Sheesh.

I parked the Explorer closer to the stairs, retrieved our bags and took them up to my room. Now was not a good time to give her her travel bag. I gave the room a cursory look. Not much to see—two queen beds, a TV, chair, desk, bathroom, all generic so I kicked off my shoes, stretched out on a bed, closed my eyes, and . . .

Half an hour later she knocked on my door. I got up, a bit bleary-eyed, and opened it.

She came in dressed in ankle-length slacks and a long-sleeve shirt. "Okay, Mort," she said quietly. "I get it. Sorry for acting kinda pissy."

"No problem. And you should know, Harp, I'm not a Boy Scout or a Cub Scout. Not even close."

"I didn't really think you were. At least not very." She looked into my eyes. "Is that why I'm in the other room? Because you aren't a true-blue Scout?"

I smiled. "Partly."

"Good to know. I think. Anyway, if I yell at night when Max is attacking me, will you come running?"

"Guns blazing, lady. You hungry?"

"Pretty much."

"How about Mexican? There's a good place on East Front Street. El Aguila Real."

"Mexican food two nights running?"

"Best place in town."

"Sounds like you've been here before."

"Yup. Rounding up tax dodgers for Uncle Sam. Train goes almost through the middle of town. We loaded 'em on boxcars and shipped 'em straight off to Leavenworth."

"Hope their relatives don't remember you and come after you with pitchforks and torches."

"Wow . . . talk about a déjà vu moment."

She smiled. "When we get back, can I hang out in your room and read for a while? Just, you know, to be safe for an extra hour or two."

"Why not? I'm an old softie."

*　*　*

We were back at the motel at 9:05. The sun was below the hills in the west, nice sunset starting to fire up. Harper showered in her room while I showered in mine. She came over in slacks and a short-sleeve shirt, book in hand. She was still working on *Suspicion of Malice* and I was halfway through *The Day of the Jackal*. She propped herself up on pillows on one bed to read and I took the other bed.

Forty minutes later I hadn't turned a page. Nothing registered. Words floated without meaning in front of my eyes. I thought about Max in the pickup truck in the hills, in the Denny's at Hotel Nevada, in the fourth-floor hallway soon after he was seated in the Denny's, arriving seconds after Harper and I had gone out the door to the stairwell. Then, two days later, there he was in Elko.

Who was he? What was he after? What did he want with Harper? No answers.

I thought about the bodies in the Nissan in Harper's aunt's driveway, one of them Nevada's attorney general *and* Harper's mother—a woman of substance likely to have a list of enemies the size of a small phone book, a woman whose disappearance had made national news in the past few days, a woman connected somehow to retired criminal defense lawyer Chase Eystad—a connection that may or may not run deeper than her being found in the trunk of Eystad's car. No way of knowing at this point. I could turn on the television and get a rehash of all that, but television in the last decade has become so annoying and inaccurate that I and millions of others no longer had any use for it, a fact that should give advertisers and network executives second thoughts, but they were conspicuously immune to anything so obvious. Television had about run its course. "Reality" TV and propaganda "news" was killing it.

I glanced over at Harper. Engrossed in her novel, she didn't notice that I was looking at her. Was she who she said she was and nothing more? How did I know?

I didn't, really, other than trusting my gut.

But add this up: The attorney general is missing, then her daughter, Harper, is targeted, and the A.G. ends up at her sister's house in Ely, dead in the trunk of a car. All of that meant something, and the attorney general was the focus, the primary target, not Harper. And now that the attorney general was gone, who was left?

Harper. The secondary target.

And, of course, the A.G.'s sister, Ellen Moore, but she was probably safely out of the way in Idaho. For now. The target had shifted to Annette Leeman's two closest family members.

My role in all this was only a disturbance, a fly speck, an accident.

The tie-in between Max and Eystad was tight, but not rock-solid. Late Sunday afternoon, sun low in the west, Chase is forced at gun-point to leave Harper at the side of a lonely highway. Later, Max cruises the road in the rain and dark, looking for someone, doesn't say who, but who else could it be but Harper? Good enough for me, if not for a jury. Eystad and Max were in cahoots, even if I didn't know what a single cahoot was. I looked over at Harper. "What the hell is a cahoot?"

She stared at me. "A *what*?"

"Cahoot. Singular."

"I don't know. A kind of weird little cigar?"

"I think that's a cheroot."

"Isn't that what you said?"

"Never mind."

She shrugged, went back to her novel, and I went back to my contemplation of this Max mess. His truck is burned to a crisp a few miles up Highway 6 early Tuesday morning. It looked like arson, getting rid of evidence, but it might've been a battery gone bad, a serious ignition problem. *Hah* to that. Not long after, Eystad is found in the back of his car, dead, with a hole in his forehead bigger than that of your garden-variety bullet hole. And Annette Leeman is in the trunk, also dead.

None of which made sense. Yet. But it had to be one big nasty interconnected mess.

It was too good to be true that Harper's Corolla just happened to blow its radiator when Eystad was right there to pick her up, Eystad being connected to Max, Max being connected to Harper via Harper's mother via the trunk of Eystad's car. Eystad was not an accident. He was in this up to his rheumy eyeballs. And a bomb or shaped charge had been attached to the radiator of my rental truck, possibly with a remote detonator. Coincidence? I stifled a laugh.

I tried to add it all up, but it was gumbo, disconnected bits and pieces. I was missing the glue that would put it all together. I still sensed an accomplice lurking invisibly in the background, but Max looked like the main player, the guy for us to avoid at all costs.

I'd given up all pretense of reading my novel when my phone played the first ten seconds of the original "Li'l Red Riding Hood" by Sam the Sham and the Pharaohs, starting with the wolf howl. My new ringtone.

"That's so nice," Harper said, not bothering to look up from her book. "What the hell is it?"

"A classic from 1966—don't knock it." I checked the screen. It was Ma. I put the call on speaker—no secrets from my assistant. Better to keep her in the loop. "Hiya, Ma," I said. Harper looked up and set her novel aside.

"Jesus. Okay, boyo, you got lucky. That Pontiac with the license you gave me got a speeding ticket in Tonopah at seven forty-five this evening. I was checking license plates, not names, but the ticket was issued to Elrood J. Wintergarden."

"Might've been a different Elrood Wintergarden, Ma. Did you check that?"

Silence for six seconds. Then, "You're fired." She hung up.

I smiled, waited, and Harper shook her head. "You're lucky you're still breathing, Mort. I mean it."

"I've heard something like that before."

It took almost a full minute for "Li'l Red Riding Hood" to fire up again.

"We were cut off, Ma," I said. "So—Tonopah, huh?"

"He was doin' forty-eight in a twenty-five zone."

"That's gotta be our boy. In a hurry to scam another gal out of a few hundred bucks—but the ticket will cost him a few hundred bucks. Karma, balancing her books."

"Her?"

"Gotta be. Karma's a bitch."

"Je-*sus*. Seven forty-five this evening, Mort. Which means he might still be in Tonopah, if you get my drift."

"Too late now. I couldn't get there before two in the morning. He's probably after more money from the girl he scammed a few days ago. We'll drive on over tomorrow, try to get there before he moves on."

"We?"

"Harper and me. That son of a bitch is running us in circles, Ma. I'm gettin' dizzy."

"Don't shoot him when you catch up to him. I mean *if*."

"*If*? It's only a matter of time, Ma. He's mine."

"Whatever. Just don't shoot him. If you do, we don't get paid. It's in the contract." She hung up.

Harper stared at me. "Karma's a bitch?"

"Near as I can tell."

"And we're headed to Tonopah in the morning?"

"That's the plan. Evidently." I phoned Lucy, gave her the news.

"Tonopah," she said. "Groovy. You should see if they still have that heart-attack fried chicken at McGinty's. If they do, don't eat it. You *do* remember McGinty's is where you and I first met, don't you, Mort?"

"As if I could forget. That entire half hour is burned so deeply into my neurons it still gives me that eerie robbing-the-cradle feeling."

"Sweet talker."

"I mean it. How's your mom doing?"

"Better. A lot. Hey, if you end up spending the night in Tonopah, you should stay at the Stargazer Motel. It's only fifty yards from McGinty's."

"Will do, cupcake. If."

"Mom and I are watching a DVD, got it paused right now. I better go so we can finish it without losing track of who Bruce Willis is supposed to be killing or whatever he's up to since I'm not entirely sure. Love you, Mort."

"Love you too, jailbait."

She laughed and we ended the call.

"Jailbait?" Harper said, frowning. "I thought you said she was thirty-two."

"Wait'll you see her. It'll make more sense then."

* * *

Harper shrugged and went back to her book. I gave it another try but wasn't successful. I lay there, trying to assemble the pieces of this Max/Eystad/attorney general mess in a way that made sense.

At 10:50 my thoughts were interrupted by a deep bass pounding, somewhere outside. It started slow, easing into my consciousness stealthily, finally registering maybe ten seconds too late. I opened the door a crack and looked out, didn't see anything, then went out on the catwalk, heard the bass thudding somewhere off to my right, beyond the structure of the motel, slowly fading, finally gone.

I waited.

Harper came out and stood beside me. She looked out over the pool, the parking lot, the street, the starry night. "What're you doing out here?" she asked.

"Came out to see what that dumb-ass bass thudding was a minute ago."

"What about it?"

"Heard it in Elko. At the Red Lion, and later when we were returning that car to the girls."

"Dipshits trying to be deaf by the time they're forty. It's everywhere now. They want everything to be as quiet as the inside of a cave in their sixties. They'll communicate by sign language and texting. So what?"

"So I don't like coincidences. Even little ones."

"Paranoia R Us?"

"Paranoia R useful."

She laughed. "Maybe it's time to get some sleep. How about you walk me to my room? If you want to."

"Nope."

"Seriously? It's twelve feet away. That's a long way. I could get mugged walking that far in the dark all alone."

"You're staying the night in my room. Or we'll stay the night in yours, but we're staying together."

"Oh, my. This is kinda sudden. Is your Scout gene on the fritz?"

"My gene is fine and working overtime. It doesn't like that bass pounding. Let's get whatever you want from your room, then lock ourselves in mine."

She tilted her head at me. "Okay. I'm not going to look a gift horse in the mouth." She hesitated. "I suppose you're thinking we'll sleep in separate beds, huh?"

"That's right."

"Which means it's okay if I sleep in the nude."

"Sleep anyway you want, lady."

"Cool. I will. You should keep that in mind, *and* that I'll be only six feet away."

"Huh. Something to think about if I can't sleep."

"That's the idea, cowboy."

* * *

She took the bed closest to the bathroom. I had the one closest to the outside door. My .357 revolver was on the nightstand, arm's length away. I turned out the light.

"Don't shoot me by accident in the dark," she said.

"I never do that."

"Okay. Good."

CHAPTER SEVENTEEN

I WOKE UP at 5:48. Daylight was seeping in around the sides of the blackout curtains.

I got quietly out of bed and made it most of the way to the bathroom before I heard, "Excellent. I'm not the only one who slept naked last night."

"I thought you were asleep."

"Nope."

"The hell you weren't. You were snoring."

"Faking it."

"Great. Anyway, keep the histrionics to a minimum. I hate it when women lose it." Amid laughter I went into the bathroom and shut the door. Three minutes later I came out in a towel and got back in bed. "Your turn," I said.

I heard her get up. I was asleep by the time she came back.

* * *

I woke again at 8:10 and dressed in clothes I'd left on a chair near the bed.

"Morning," Harper said drowsily as I was buttoning my shirt.

"Sleep well?"

"I had a great dream. There was this naked guy—"

"Time's a-wasting, woman. Up and at 'em."

She got out of bed, stretched—quite a sight—then said, "Don't suppose I have time for a shower, huh?"

"Nope."

"Great. Thanks. I won't be long."

"Why'd you ask, if you don't mind my asking?"

"It's that karma thing you've got going. I didn't want to disappoint her since she's a bitch."

Sonofabitch. She got me.

* * *

For one of us breakfast supported life: Spanish omelet with hash browns, couple of sausage links, orange juice, toast and coffee. For the other it was unbuttered rye toast, two scrambled eggs, and tea.

"Not sure why you're still alive," I said.

"I could say the same about you."

Touché.

The day was warm, headed for hot. Harper was in her short running skirt and tight tank top. She got a moue of distaste or envy from our waitress, twenty years old who looked size twelve, working on fourteen.

By 9:50 we were on Highway 305, straight shot south past Mount Lewis to Austin, middle of the state, then Highway 376 through Kingston and Carvers to Tonopah—205 miles of emptiness that gives folks in New York City nightmares when they make it out this way and take a wrong turn.

We arrived at McGinty's Café at 2:20 p.m. A Texaco station was next door to the left and Lucy's seven-year-old Mustang convertible was parked in front of room 8 at the Stargazer Motel to the right.

"Huh," I said when I saw it.

"What?"

"Lucy's here."

Harper looked around. "Where?"

"Room at the Stargazer, looks like. The Mustang there in front is hers."

"Cool. Looks like I finally get to meet her."

"Looks like."

"Does that worry you?"

"Not a bit, but I usually miss out on hugs when one of my girls meets another one."

She smiled. "I'm one of your girls?"

"In a strange way, yeah."

"Even cooler."

I parked next to the Mustang and we got out, headed to the motel room opposite Lucy's car. She came out of McGinty's Café and called to us.

I spun Harper around and we waited as Lucy ran up like a colt and threw her arms around me and gave me the kind of kiss that stops traffic. She had on white shorts and a white tank top, no bra, white sandals. All in white, Lucy looks like a million bucks. And eighteen years old.

"Wow," I said when she pulled back to let us both get enough air to support life.

"I really missed you, big guy."

"I can tell. I've missed you too."

She looked to my right with her arms still around my neck. "You must be Harper."

"I am."

"I figured. Mort's never been big on introductions."

"I am when I don't have someone attached to my lips," I said. "Makes it sound funny when I talk."

"Excuses, excuses." Lucy looked at me. "You didn't tell me she was so gorgeous."

"If I remember, I sort of did, low key. I certainly didn't say she looked like Wilford Brimley."

"Um," Harper said. "Nothing happened, Lucy. I mean, nothing the least bit serious, between Mort and me."

Lucy smiled at Harper. "I know. He's a bit backward but, after all, this's Mort we're talking about here."

"Hey, hey, hey," I said.

"Hey, hey, yourself," Lucy said. "I *know* you, Mort." She gave Harper a brief hug. "I'm so happy to finally meet you."

"Me too." She looked at Lucy. "You can't be anywhere near as old as he said you are. Please tell me you're not a day over twenty. Or even nineteen."

"Can't do that. I mean, I could, but I'd be, you know, lying. But thanks. I'm thirty-two."

"I might have to kill myself."

"Okay," I broke in. "No one here has to kill herself or, I hope, himself. I'm with two of the most beautiful girls in Nevada, either of whom would make Magnum so jealous he would have to kill *himself* if he saw you with me. Now how about we go over to McGinty's and have a bite to eat? I'm hungry."

Lucy looked at Harper. "He's such a sweet talker."

"Yeah, I kinda got that the first hour we met. Not so much a sweet talker, but he was mellow and nice. It was sort of weird, since I'd pulled a gun on him."

"He gets over little things like that pretty quick."

"It could also have been because I had to, you know, sit on his lap for three hours, dripping wet."

Lucy grinned. "I had trouble figuring out why you had to do that when Mort told me about it, or tried to. But it sounds like the kind of thing that happens to him. It was something about the tires. Tell me again in the restaurant, okay? You might have to draw a diagram."

* * *

So we sat in a booth and caught up on everything that had been going on—Chase Eystad leaving Harper up in the hills, two flat tires and the balancing problem, the store at Grange, Olivia, Max in the truck, Max in the Denny's, the Desert Rose Motel, the bodies in the trunk, the drive to Elko. When I got to the remote-controlled bomb attached to my truck's radiator, I got a stare that would boil water.

"You didn't tell me that," Lucy said. "When you were in Elko, *supposedly* telling me what was going on. And you didn't tell me about Max following you up to your room in the hotel."

"I didn't want to drag you away from your mother."

"As if I would've left her."

"As if you wouldn't."

She was silent for a moment. "Okay, I would have, but you *really* need to tell me stuff like that, cowboy."

"Not when a colonoscopy is on the horizon."

"How often does that happen?"

"Logically, that's a non sequitur. See, sugar plum. I told you about the explosives so we're all good now." I kissed her cheek. "Aren't we?"

"I'll think about it." She turned to Harper. "About the World Naked Bike Ride. You're still going with us, I hope. It'll be March 14 next year. I checked."

"Wouldn't miss it," Harper said, looking from her to me and back again. "Especially now that I've seen how you two are together."

"Oh? How's that?" Lucy asked.

"A couple. Inseparable. Perfect together."

Lucy smiled. "I'm glad he found you on that highway, not some idiot girl, nothing but trouble."

"Anyone want dessert?" I asked. "Or shall we go find ourselves an Elrood and beat the crap out of him."

"Great segue," Lucy said. "First let's go get Harper a room, then we can beat the mud out of Elrood."

"Mud," I said. "Nice."

* * *

It was 3:35 by the time the three of us walked over to the Stargazer's office and Harper got a room for the night, next door to ours.

We all freshened up, then I suggested a little powwow in our room, Lucy's and mine.

"A powwow?" Harper said.

"A confab," I said. "A meeting of the minds."

"Don't listen to him," Lucy advised. "He says things like that all the time."

"I pretty much got used to it, actually," Harper said.

Lucy was still in her white shorts, white tank top, and Harper had on the short running skirt and thin top she was wearing when I'd first seen her at dusk in the hills. Both of them had nipple bumps showing. That appeared to be fine with them and I know it was with me. Lucy and I sat side by side on a bed, Harper on the other bed facing us.

Right then, a gentle knock came at the door. I got up, opened it, saw a blur of motion, and lights kaleidoscoped through my head as I tumbled back into the room and hit the floor.

Then all the lights went out.

CHAPTER EIGHTEEN

I REGAINED CONSCIOUSNESS before Lucy. I was lying on my side on a carpeted floor, trussed like a Christmas goose. My eyes refused to focus. The room was dim. I was seeing double.

Another concussion? Fuckin' things were going to be the death of me yet.

I lay there for several minutes, trying to get my head right, feeling my fingers, hands, legs. And listening, which told me a television was on. I finally identified the voice of Sergeant Schultz of *Hogan's Heroes* when he said, "I know nuthink, nuthink."

Sonofabitch. Maybe I'd been knocked back to 1968.

More inane talk, then canned laughter.

I tried to sit up, didn't make it. My hands were held behind my back, ankles bound. I felt weak as a kitten.

I waited a few minutes, then tried again.

Finally, I made it, got into a sitting position with my back against a bed, knees bent, feet flat on the floor. The curtains were pulled but light spilled around the edges. I turned my head. Green glowing digits of a clock on a night table beside me showed 4:42.

All I could see were curtains, a table and chair, a door eight feet to my left. Everything was shifted a little, side to side. I closed one eye and one of the images disappeared, which helped. I couldn't see or hear Lucy or Harper, or anyone else, but most of the room was behind me, out of sight. A faint sound of traffic on the highway outside came though the walls, a few sporadic cars passing by. The only sound in the room was Schultz and Hogan. Then Colonel Klink.

Maybe I was in hell.

I struggled to my feet, almost fell over, then Harper said, "Oh, thank God."

A young man's voice said, "Take it easy, dude. Take it the fuck easy or I'll put you down again."

I squinted into the gloom. The flickering light of the television illuminated a guy lying on the bed closest to me. Hard to tell his age, but he looked young. Too young for what was taking place, not that I knew, yet, what that was. Harper was on the other bed, closer to the bathroom. Lucy was beside her. Both were on their backs, hands tied in front of them. Lucy's right ankle was held to Harper's left with duct tape, which would make it all but impossible for them to run or fight. Harper was awake. Lucy wasn't.

The kid on the bed watched me but didn't get up. He had a black device of some kind in one hand, a gun in the other with a silencer on the end.

"Gun," he said, wagging the automatic. "And Taser. I prefer the Taser. No blood, no noise. But I'll use the gun if you make me, so sit down."

I did a foot shuffle to move backward then collapsed onto a chair four feet from the outside door.

"Who are you?" I asked.

"Joe Blow. What's it to you?"

Weird kid.

"That mean I can call you Blow?" I said.

He stared at me, eyes bright. "Do that and I'll put a bullet in your knee and fuck the blood. That'd hurt. I doubt that anyone would hear it, but you might yell so . . . Taser first, then bullet."

I believed him. His voice was lifeless, like he was dead inside. I decided to keep still, not give him any trouble, but I finally recognized him as the redheaded kid I'd seen at the Red Lion, the idiot with the too-loud stereo in his car. He still looked nineteen years old, no more than twenty.

"Someone hit me. Was it you?"

"My uncle. He was first in the door, tagged you with a Taser and a billy club—one, two. I was right behind him. I punched one of the bitches, got the other one with a Taser. Easy. Whole thing took like four seconds."

"Other than your name, Joe, who are you?"

For a moment he didn't answer, then he grinned and sat up straighter. "Vicki Cannon. Cathy Jantz."

The guy was nuts. In fact, my head wasn't right, so the names didn't mean anything to me. Yet.

"Harper," I called softly to her.

"What?" She sounded terrified.

"Are you okay?"

"Pretty much. He Tasered me, but I'm not hurt now."

"How's Lucy?"

"She . . . she's breathing. He hit her when they came in, then he hit her again, later."

I looked at the guy. He shrugged. "She got loud. She's got a big mouth so I decked her. But screw her, it's the other one we want."

We. His uncle—at least that's what he called the other guy, who wasn't there at the moment. Right now, it was one-on-one, except that I hardly counted as one. I might not count as a half, even if my arms and legs were free and the kid didn't have a gun.

But they wanted Harper, whoever *they* were. Which made sense. This was still about the attorney general, not about Lucy or me.

"Let the other girl go," I said.

The guy laughed. "Shut up or get Tasered." He gave me that flat stare and a faint eerie smile. "I like Taserin'. It's a blast and a half, dude. Give me a reason."

So I shut up.

* * *

The digital clock read 5:20.

Vicki Cannon. Cathy Jantz. The missing teenage girls who'd been found dead in a basement in Reno. Hung.

Shit.

The television played on.

* * *

5:35. Lucy woke up.

"Mort?" Her voice was weak.

"I'm here, honey."

"Where?"

"Over here by the door."

"Are you okay?" she asked.

"I'm . . . fine. Not too bad. How are you?"

"My head hurts."

Joe sniggered. "You two shut up."

Lucy struggled to sit up with her back against the wall. With their ankles taped together, Harper had to sit up too. Lucy looked at Joe. "Who're you?"

"I'm the guy with the gun who's gonna put a bullet in this guy's kneecap if you don't shut up, bitch."

She shut up, but kept her eyes on me. They looked big and luminous in the dim room. And *very* angry. She knows when to zip it and when to pick her battles, but she doesn't take shit off anyone for a minute longer than she has to.

*   *   *

6:45.

7:52. I still had a headache, but I was no longer seeing double.

At 8:35 someone knocked on the door, three raps, one, three. The door opened and Max came in. He had a key, so 3-1-3 meant *don't shoot me.*

It had to be Max, but he'd changed. No longer bald, he wore a medium-length dark brown wig, glasses with wire rims, and he'd lost the beard, probably knew there would be an APB out on him. But the meaty shoulders and neck were the same, still solid muscle.

He had a pizza box in one hand. Within seconds the smell of cheese and pepperoni filled the room.

"*Finally*," Joe said, getting off the bed. "What the *hell*, Uncle Jake. Where've you been?"

Jake.

Jake's eyes whipped snakelike toward the kid. "I told you not to use my name. Ever."

"Like, what's it matter? It's not like they're gonna get a chance to tell anyone."

"It's a principle. A *doctrine*. We do it because we do it. You need to do what I tell you, bud."

The kid shrugged, then said, "Sure, okay."

"You tell 'em your name?"

"I told this guy I was Joe Blow."

Jake hesitated, then said. "Okay. Keep it that way."

So Joe wasn't Joe. Except he was, for now.

Jake, no longer Max, turned to me. "Mortimer Angel." He grinned. "That was a hell of a surprise, you gettin' into this deal."

I didn't answer.

"You're famous for finding famous people who end up dead," he said. "Now it's your turn."

Funny guy, except he didn't smile.

They opened the pizza box and each grabbed a slice. "How about giving us some of that?" I said.

Jake stared at me. "No point, man. Now shut up."

Like uncle, like nephew.

* * *

They took us out to two vehicles at 10:15 that night, the kid's Volvo and a white Suburban. Lucy's and Harper's hands were flex-cuffed behind their backs. I had a chain around my waist, wrists flex-tied to the chain at my hips. The three of us had our feet hobbled by lengths of nylon cord ten or twelve inches long; we could only shuffle out to the cars. Duct tape covered our mouths.

"Struggle, fight, try to run, or make any sound at all," Jake said to me, "and I'll bust you up so bad you'll wish you were dead, man. I'll break both your legs and both arms. I don't see that I'll have any use for you." He gave me a cold look. "Better yet, how about I bust up that other girl if you get wild ideas? Not Harper, though. She and I have got us some talking to do first."

I didn't have any way to fight or run so I went quietly as I was put in the front passenger seat of the Volvo. Jake strapped me in using the seat belt, flex-tied my ankles to the seat supports in the floor. He stripped off the duct tape, which might have made a sharp-eyed highway patrol officer suspicious. Once we were on the road I could yell or spout obscenities, but . . . probably not a good idea.

Lucy and Harper were strapped into the Suburban, Lucy in back, Harper in the passenger seat up front. Jake removed their duct tape before we left the motel parking lot, but I heard him tell them what would happen to me if they screamed for help. If you need to control someone, don't threaten them, threaten someone they love.

Another doctrine, if you were a murdering sociopath.

* * *

"You ready?" Jake's voice came over a handheld two-way radio on the console between the front seats.

"We're good," Joe said.

"Get going. Pay attention to the speed limit. I don't want to have to kill some cop."

We left Tonopah at 10:20, Joe's Volvo in the lead, the Suburban following. We were eight miles out of town when Dipshit Joe hit the stereo and the nightmare thud of bass rattled the windows and set up a pounding in my head that almost loosened my eyeballs. The lyrics were putrid—he'd put on a Jo-X rap CD, cranked up to 120 decibels.

Jonnie-X, Jonnie Xenon, whom I'd last seen hanging in the rafters of a garage with a bullet hole in his forehead, another one in his chest—an unattached garage at a house rented by two girls, Danya and Shanna. Danya Fuller was the daughter of RPD Detective Fairchild, and Shanna was Danya's . . . bride. Or she was Fairchild's daughter-in-law. That was a year ago and I still didn't know how to define their relationship so the PC police wouldn't drag me away.

"Where to?" I asked Joe in a five-second gap between the thundering rap crap.

"Reno. Now shut up."

* * *

We did the speed limit the whole way and didn't pass through towns bigger than Hawthorne or Fallon until we reached the outskirts of Sparks on I-80. We went through Sparks and into Reno, the stereo off, silent, not drawing attention to the car at 2:20 in the morning. My head was still throbbing from all the pounding it had taken. Jo-X's gangsta rap was worse than Jake's Taser or billy club. My brain felt like mush. I would be partly deaf for two hours.

We got off I-80 at Wells Avenue, then headed south, turned west on Vassar Street.

"Pull over," Jake's voice came over the two-way. "Get some duct tape on him."

Joe pulled over, ripped off six inches of duct tape and stuck it over my mouth. The Suburban took the lead. We went across Virginia Street and into the older tree-shaded neighborhoods west of Arlington Avenue. As we crossed Arlington, we passed within a quarter mile of Ma Clary's house, south of California Avenue.

Two and a half blocks west on Monroe, the Suburban pulled into the driveway of a two-story house, not a light on in the place. A FOR SALE sign was on the lawn in front. Jake stopped the Suburban by a side door to the house and Joe pulled in behind him.

We sat in the dark and quiet until Jake walked back to us, opened the passenger door, cut the straps holding my feet, and hauled me out. He had a heavy canvas bag in one hand. He left Joe to watch Lucy and Harper. As he walked me to the door, I thought about trying to kick him to death since he had freed my feet—small chance of succeeding and I didn't see how that would help Lucy and Harper, still with Joe. Jake opened the side door with a key and pushed me into the house.

We went through a laundry room and into a kitchen. It had no countertops, no sink or cabinets, no plumbing or wiring. The floor had been torn out all the way down to the floor joists. Strips of plywood were laid over the joists as a pathway. In another room, probably the dining room, I saw furniture draped in ghostly pale sheets.

"Place is for sale," Jake said. "Seller ran out of money for the kitchen remodel two weeks ago, so the contractor's on hold. When the cabinets were torn out, rot was found in the subflooring, joists, and an outside bearing wall. The price of the remodel jumped by thirty-five grand. I don't expect buyers to come through anytime soon. The seller and his wife could show up, in which case they're gonna have a real bad day, same as you."

He pushed me through an arch, down a dark hallway, opened a door, hit a light switch. We went down a flight of bare wooden stairs into a musty basement. The floor was forest green Berber. A billiard table stood in the middle of the room, cue sticks in a wooden holder on a wall, flat-screen TV, a recliner, two leather couches, small bookshelf loaded with Blu-ray discs and paperbacks. A man cave. To the left of the stairs a door was open to a half bath—toilet and sink.

When we reached the bottom, Jake stripped the duct tape off my mouth. "Yell if you want," he said. "No one'll hear you, but I'd deck you anyway, because—"

"It's a principle," I finished the thought for him.

"You pay attention. Interesting, not that it'll matter."

The basement was divided into two rooms. Jake led me to a door to the right of the stairs. It swung inward. He pushed me inside and flipped a switch revealing an oblong room somewhat larger than the man cave. It had concrete walls and floors, heavy wooden beams overhead, a rusty drain in the floor by a good-sized hot water heater, a big workbench with tools on a pegboard on the wall behind it. It was set up as a wood shop, with an expensive Jet floor model drill press, Jet band saw, table saw, sander, jig saw, shop vac, dowels standing in a bin, wood on racks on the walls. A battery-powered clock on a wall showed 2:50.

Jake set the bag on the floor. "I read about you," he said. "Internet search. Among other things, you're some kind of a hotshot escape artist. This time you're not going anywhere, guaranteed."

He shoved me and I stumbled, hands still held at my sides to the chain around my waist. "Lay on the floor, facedown," he said. "Feet straight out."

I did, and he tied my feet with a length of nylon cord, looping it around my ankles in figure eights, tying the ends in a square knot. Then he rolled me over, lifted me to my feet like I was a bale of hay. *Strong* goddamn guy.

He stood me against a concrete wall fifteen feet from the workbench. Eyebolts had been put in the walls around the room, purpose unknown, but they had obviously been there for years. From his bag he removed a quarter-inch-thick steel cable, loops in both ends, a little over three feet long, and a heavy-duty padlock. He showed it to me, held it at both ends and gave it an experimental pull, as if it were a garrote. Thick one.

"Seven-thousand-pound breaking strength," he said. "That oughta hold you."

He looped the cable twice around my neck, held the end loops together, and padlocked them both to a heavy eyehook in the wall, five and a half feet off the floor. He stood back and checked his work. The cable had almost no slack in it.

"Good deal," he said. "I had a guy in a hardware store in Tonopah make that up for me. That's what took me a while to get back with the pizza, that and picking up a few other things. Figured you for a seventeen-inch neck, stud. You're probably gonna die right where you are now. The only way you're getting out of that hook-up is by removing your head."

I'd never felt so helpless. My hands were still held to the chain around my waist. Whatever Jake had in mind, I wasn't going to be able to help Lucy or Harper. At all. I was now an observer, irrelevant, useless.

Jake went out the door. I heard him go up the stairs to the first floor. For the moment, I was alone. I struggled a little, a hopeless gesture, trying to loosen the cable or pull the eyehook out of the wall using my neck. There wasn't the slightest give in any of it. Even if my hands were free, I couldn't do anything about the cable around my neck.

So I waited, looking around the room. Nothing was within reach. He'd attached me to a bare concrete wall.

Two minutes later he returned with Harper, guiding her by the flex-cuff holding her hands behind her back. Joe pushed Lucy ahead of him. She and Harper were wearing what they'd had on at the Stargazer Motel, which wasn't much. Both had duct tape over their mouths, but the rope that had held their ankles had been removed so they could walk. When Lucy saw me and how I'd been cabled to the wall, her eyes got wide with dismay.

"Sit 'em down against the wall over there," Jake said. He removed his wig, tossed it on the workbench. His head was bald, reflecting the fluorescent lighting. "I've got work to do, call it home improvement. Unless," he said, sinking into a crouch in front of Harper once she was on the floor with her back against a wall twenty feet from me, "you want to tell me where it is, avoid all this." He stripped the duct tape off her mouth, then did the same for Lucy, two feet to Harper's left.

"Where—" Harper coughed, tried again. "Where what is?" She held her legs straight out in front of her, together, trying to keep her short skirt from showing too much. Her hands were still behind her back, as were Lucy's.

"We can play that game for a while if you want, girl," Jake said mildly, "but if you don't tell me where it is, this is gonna turn into a pretty rough deal."

"Where *what* is?"

He shook his head, stood up.

Harper and Lucy looked at me with frightened eyes. I wanted to signal that we would get out of this, but I didn't have it in me. Lucy closed her eyes and leaned her head against the wall, but there was something tough about the set of her mouth. Her teeth were working on her lips. She was a fighter and her feet weren't tied. If we had any hope down here, Lucy was it.

Jake went through the billiard room and up the stairs. He came back with a chair that might have come from the dining room, plopped it down in the middle of the room beneath a wooden beam. He got a new eyebolt out of the canvas bag, and a cordless drill and a set of drill bits. The eyebolt was shiny steel, three-eighths of an inch thick with a wood screw formed in one end. He compared drill bits to the eyehook screw, selected one, then got up on the chair and sunk a vertical hole in the beam. He screwed in the eyebolt, then stuck a screwdriver through the eye and used it to crank the bolt deep into the beam.

"Go get those stools," he said to Joe. "They're in back of the Suburban." He looked at Lucy and Harper. "These two babes aren't goin' anywhere."

Joe left, footsteps clumping up the stairs, then he was gone. Jake stood in front of Harper. "Where is it, girl?"

"I don't know what 'it' *is*." Her voice rose in pitch at the end, like a cry for help.

Jake shook his head again. He turned to me. "Guess you found what I put on your truck's radiator, huh?"

I stared at him for a moment. "Saw something when I lifted the hood to check the oil, halfway between Ely and Elko. I showed it to the guy at the gas station. He didn't know what it was, but he pulled it off. What was it?" No sense telling Jake I had a good idea what it was.

"Shaped charge. That's an explosive that cuts in one direction. It'd tear a fair-sized chunk out of that radiator. Which reminds me." He took something like a pager off his belt and dropped it on the workbench. "Don't need this anymore. Not right now anyway. Been carrying it around so long I forgot I had it on me."

"Remote detonator?" I asked.

"You got it. Has a range of two miles, line of sight."

I appeared to think about that, as if I didn't already know. "Is that how you disabled Harper's car?"

"That's affirmative, dude."

"Where do you buy something like that?"

He smiled. "You don't. It helps if your brother is an ex-SEAL, demolition expert. He'll be here in a few hours. You can meet him. If you think I'm tough, wait'll you meet Kyle. What he might do is put a charge around your neck, see if it'll take your head entirely off. My guess is it won't. There's a lot of strings and gristle in a neck. But you never know until you try. I'll have to get him to hold off on that until we're about done here. Fact is, we're not going to get this party really rockin' until he gets here. You don't want that to happen. It'd be a lot better if you told me where it is now." He yawned, then glanced at a watch on his wrist. "Damn, stud, I've been up thirty-six hours. I could use a little sack time before Kyle gets here."

I didn't say anything.

Joe returned, carrying two three-legged stools made of cheap pine, twenty inches tall with round tops.

"Got some interesting history here," Jake said, taking one of the stools from Joe. "These are the stools I used on those two high school girls."

Harper made a gagging sound. She looked away, into a corner of the room. Lucy didn't.

Jake stared at the girls. "You first," he said to Harper. He set a stool under the eyehook he'd sunk into the beam. He took Harper by an arm and hauled her up, pulled her toward the stool, grabbed her under the arms and lifted her like a sack of dog food, no problem, no hesitation, and stood her up on the stool. Lifted a hundred twelve pounds in a modified military press as if she weighed ten pounds.

He stood a few feet from her. "That's a hell of a short skirt, girl. Kinda slutty, but I like it. Now don't move." He took a length of half-inch nylon rope out of the canvas bag, measured off about thirty feet, cut it, sealed the ends with a butane lighter. After it cooled, he tied a knot in one end. "This here's a bowline," he said, showing it to Harper. "In case you're interested. Anytime you want me to stop, all you have to do is tell me where it is."

"I don't know what you mean. I promise. I really really *don't*."

He shrugged. "Have it your way, girlie. So here we go—bowline's got a small loop, pass the other end through that loop, pull the rope through until you've got a bigger loop, which"—he stood on the chair next to Harper—"goes around your neck like this, tight enough but not too snug because I'm a nice guy, then the free end goes up through the eyehook in the beam, like this." He stepped off the chair. "Then it's tied to an eyehook in the wall behind you, leaving a little slack, not enough to matter, not enough that your feet would reach the floor if you fall off that stool, but it'd jerk the hell out of your neck if you do. And, of course, you'd strangle yourself, so you oughta stand still."

When he was finished, Harper was on the stool with a noose around her neck. The stool looked rickety, just three slender pine legs keeping her alive.

I glanced at Lucy. Her eyes had narrowed, taking in Harper, the rope, the stool. I could tell that her brain was working, hard. Mine was too, but I wasn't coming up with anything useful. All I could do was hope that Jake would die suddenly of a heart attack or an aneurysm.

He looked up at Harper. "Anytime you want to end this, you know what to do."

"But I *don't*," she wailed.

Jake shrugged. "We'll see." He got up on the chair and installed another eyehook in the beam, six feet from the one he'd put in for Harper.

He looked down at Lucy, thinking. He looked around the room then back up at Harper. "That's an idea," he said to himself.

He got a pair of scissors off the pegboard above the workbench, then cut Harper's tank top off, slicing up the front from bottom to top, then across her shoulders. He pulled it off her, not bothering to give her a second look. Joe, however, ogled her breasts until Jake said, "Get that bucket over there and fill it with water. There's a bathroom in the other room."

Joe grabbed the bucket and went out the door. Harper gave me a despairing look.

Jake slung Harper's ruined tank top over his shoulder, then grabbed Lucy by the back of her neck and lifted her off the floor. She made a startled squawk and got her feet under her. Jake walked her over to the drain in the floor, shoved her down, faceup, hands still behind her back, and straddled her, forcing her down with his weight.

I struggled against the neck cable but got nowhere. If looks could kill, he would've gone up in a puff of sulfur.

"Turn around, Harper," he said. "Do it now. You need to see this. Call it motivation."

Harper shuffled around on the stool. She made a tiny cry of horror when she saw Lucy on her back, Jake on top of her.

Joe came in with the bucket of water. Jake told him to stand by Lucy's head. Jake covered Lucy's face with the top he'd cut off Harper. "Anyone here ever see someone waterboarded?" he asked. "No? No one's got anything to say? No one wants to tell me where it is?" He looked up at Joe. "Pour water on her face. Not too much, just enough to soak the material real good."

"Stop," I yelled.

Jake turned. "Where is it?"

"It's . . . I've got it."

He stared at me, shook his head. "Don't think so, stud. Right about now you'd lie to God. But if you've got it, you know what it is. So what is it?"

I couldn't answer that.

Jake turned away from me. "Do it," he said to Joe.

Joe tipped the bucket and poured water on the ruined tank top covering Lucy's face.

Lucy gasped, then choked as she inhaled water. She arched her back and tried to buck Jake off, but he was too heavy. He shoved her shoulders into the concrete floor.

"More," he said to Joe.

"Omigod, *stop*!" Harper screamed.

Jake took Harper's top off Lucy's face. She took big wet gulps of air, coughing, sputtering. "Got something to say, girlie?" Jake asked Harper. "If you tell me you know where it is and I find out you don't, I will rearrange your face with a blowtorch, and Lucy's, and this big guy's. So what'll it be, sugar tits?"

"I . . . I don't know what it *is*," she sobbed.

"So be it." He arranged the material over Lucy's face again, then nodded to Joe. "Do it."

Water splashed. Lucy bucked, choked, drummed her heels against the floor. Joe eased up on the water. "Keep going," Jake said, and I wanted to kill him, I *had* to kill him. I bit the inside of my mouth and tasted blood, willing him to die, to spontaneously combust.

"Okay, stop," Jake said. He took the wet top off Lucy's face. She gagged, dragged in a little air, coughed, gagged some more, then cried, "Mooooort," in a little girl's voice. She sounded five years old.

My heart broke. My eyes bulged with white-hot rage. I lunged against the cable. I spit blood.

"Mooort, help...h-h-h-*help*. I-I *can't*—" She let out a soul-rending keening wail of misery, as if all the innocence were leaving her mind and body.

I felt a part of myself die inside.

Jake looked up at Harper. "What say you, girlie?"

She was crying, tears flooding her face. "You are going to burn in hell. You are gonna—" She couldn't finish.

Jake shrugged. "One more time," he said to Joe. "See if we can't loosen something up here."

"No, no, no, no, *please*!" Lucy wailed, tearing my heart apart. Then more water, more choking, gagging. I couldn't watch, couldn't listen. I sagged against the cable, felt it bite into my neck.

"Enough," Jake said after almost a minute, removing the material from Lucy's face. He stood up.

Lucy gagged. Her chest rose and fell, hitching as she tried to breathe, coughed, retched, spit water, finally got a little air. She lay on her side, breath coming in strangled coughs and gasps.

Jake looked down at her. Then he strode over to me. "How long was that? Total of two or three minutes? How about we do it on and off for half an hour? How about *two* hours, stud? Two hours and she'd never again be the girl you once knew. She wouldn't know her own name. I'll give you a while to think that over. You too," he said to Harper.

Lucy was still curled on her side, coughing. She looked like a rag doll, hair drenched, eyes closed.

Jake left her like that. He set the second stool under the eyehook he'd put in the beam six feet from Harper. He gave Lucy a few minutes to recover, then got her to her feet and lifted her onto the stool. He got a noose around her neck, up through the eyehook, then over to a second hook in the wall, tied it off.

He turned to me. "Seriously, stud, if you know where it is, now would be a real good time to speak up. If I don't get it, all of you are gonna die. Badly."

All I wanted to do was kill him, but I said, "It? What the hell is *it*? The problem is, none of us *knows* anything. We might, though, if we had some idea of what the hell you're looking for."

A moment of silence. Then: "The *recording*, man."

"What recording?"

He stared at me. "If you don't know, you're not worth spit. But you get to watch. Although," he said, giving me a closer look, "one of these gals might be willing to tell me where it is if they don't want to watch me put out your lights. One never knows which key will fit the lock."

"You murdered those two teenage girls a week ago," I said.

"So? I've done worse."

His cell phone rang. He answered, said, "What's up?" He looked at me. "Yeah, got him hooked up to the wall the way you said. The girls got ropes around their necks. We're cool. What time you gonna get in?" He listened, then said, "See you then," and ended the call.

He stood in front of Harper and Lucy. "If either of you makes trouble, Joe has permission to kick Lucy's stool out from under her.

You two might want to think about that." He glanced at Joe. "Jesus, kid, lose the gun. You don't need it now. Put it on the workbench over there."

I could tell Joe didn't want to do that. He liked having the automatic in his belt, especially with the silencer on the barrel, which probably made him feel like a bad dude, but he did as he was told. Jake went out the door. A minute later the toilet flushed in the other room. He went up the stairs. For a while I didn't hear him. Joe strolled through the gap between Lucy and Harper. With a foot, he tested a leg of Harper's stool.

"This thing's pretty old," he said. "Kind of unstable."

"Speaking of unstable," Lucy said. Her voice still had a wet sound. It didn't sound like her. Her tank top was wet, partly see-through.

I warned her with my eyes. She looked at me for a few seconds, then gave Joe a diamond-hard stare. Still tough, but I didn't see any way out of this.

Jake returned. He had something like an axe or a rock hammer in his hand. He showed it to me. "Ever see one of these before, stud?"

I didn't reply. It was a nasty-looking weapon—a sharp angular spike on one end of a black steel head, cutting edge on the other. Sixteen inches long overall.

"No?" He smiled. "Browning Black Label tomahawk. They call it Shock 'N Awe. American made. Sitting Bull or one of those guys back then would've loved this puppy.

"Kinda cool, huh, calling it a tomahawk?" He touched a finger to the tip of the spike. "Got a needle-sharp point on this end. I used it on that dipshit lawyer, put a hole in his forehead you could stick your thumb in. He went down like I'd dropped him with an elephant gun. Here, check it out." He rested the spike on top of my head and let the weight of the weapon press the point into my scalp. It hurt. I felt it dig in.

"Stop it," Lucy said, voice almost back to normal.

Jake turned. "You got something to say, girl?"

"Don't . . . don't do that."

"You know where that recording is? Guess you didn't get a chance to say much. Waterboarding's like that. How about now?"

"I don't know what it's a recording of or what it's on."

"It might be a DVD, or on a flash drive. That give your memory a boost?"

Lucy stared at him, silent.

Jake strolled over to Harper, tomahawk in hand. "But *you* know, don't you, sugar tits? You know *what* it is and *where* it is. You've got that million bucks in your head and you're not talking. Not yet, but you will."

"*Money?* I . . . I don't know anything about anything like that. Really, I *don't*."

"That'd be too bad. I'll waterboard you next. It'll be bad, real bad. It won't kill you, but you'll wish it did. Think about telling me where that goddamn recording is, not go through all of that."

"A recording of *what*? I don't know *anything*."

Jake sighed. "Those two girls made a video, put it on a thumb drive, mailed it to . . ." He paused, thought about it, then went on. "They wanted five hundred thousand each. Dumb kids, didn't know what the fuck they were doing. I had them in a basement on stools like you two now, but I had to leave for a while. Joe wasn't there, but my leaving for a lousy twenty minutes should've been okay.

"When I came back, they were both hanging, gone. I should've waterboarded them right away, probably could have avoided all this. I figure one of them started fussing and fell. I might've had them too close together so the one who fell knocked the stool out from under her girlfriend." He shrugged. "Live and learn. I put you two far enough apart so that's not likely to happen, and Joe is gonna watch over you. I've got the ropes tied off behind you in a fast-release knot. If you fall before it doesn't matter anymore, he can pull the knot. Which means you oughta be real nice to him."

"Nice the way I asked you?" Joe said to Jake. "I mean, look at this one." He stared at Harper's breasts. With her hands behind her back, she couldn't hide herself at all.

Jake shrugged. "I don't care, as long as you don't hurt 'em." He stood back and looked at the two girls. "This would be a lot easier for all of us if you'd cooperate."

"Are you getting paid for this?" I asked, hoping for more information. Anything that might get us out of this.

"Sure am. Pretty good payday, stud. I'm also returning a favor. Gotta pay stuff back, keep folks happy, but I don't work for free. Neither does Kyle. It's bad for business. You gotta set parameters or you get screwed over."

He yawned again. "Jesus." He glanced at his watch. "I gotta get some shut-eye. Kyle said he'd be here about nine." He looked at Joe. "I'll be upstairs, got that bed in the back room. Watch these girls. Don't let anything happen to Harper or I'll skin you alive, boy." He smiled, knuckled Joe's head. "Kidding, but I'd kick the living shit out of you. You best pull that knot damn fast if she falls off that stool."

He glanced at the tomahawk in his hand, then set it on the workbench. From his utility bag he took out a gun in a nylon holster. It looked like a Glock. He left and I heard him stomping up the stairs. Then things got quiet. The hot water heater came on, making a faint hissing sound off to my right. I couldn't hear anything from outside the house. The time was 3:55 a.m. Kyle would be here in five hours.

"I'm sorry," Harper said, looking over at me, then to her right, at Lucy.

"Not your fault," I replied.

"All of you shut the hell up," Joe said. He roamed the room, bored. He picked up the scissors and looked at Lucy, ambled over to her.

"This chick's got fine tits, kinda small though. Let's have a look at yours."

He cut her top from waist to neck, same way Jake had cut Harper's. Her tank top fell open to either side.

"Nice," he said, checking her out. He cut through the shoulders and stripped it off, then glanced over at me as he tossed the scissors and her top on the workbench. "Guess you were doin' all right for yourself, *stud*."

I didn't respond to that.

Joe looked at Lucy. "What are you, like eighteen?" He nodded toward me. "What're you doin' with that old guy? Is he like your dad or something?"

"Or something," she said. "Hey, listen. I have to pee."

Joe shrugged. "Yeah? Then go."

"Up here? Like this? That's stupid. I mean, why don't you pull it out and pee on the floor?"

He grinned. "Not with you watching, bitch."

"There's a bathroom in that other room, isn't there? Let me use that."

"No way, girl. You're not gettin' off that stool. If you gotta go, go. You want, I'll cut your shorts off so you don't piss yourself. How 'bout that? Maybe you'd like me to see the rest of you, not just tits. Lot of girls get off on that."

Lucy took a breath, then stared at the wall in front of her as if to put him out of her mind, but she'd already set the hook.

Joe glanced at the open doorway to the other room. "Be right back. Don't go away, and don't fall." He went out and Lucy went to work the instant he was out the door.

She knocked both sandals off. She stood on her left leg and lifted her right leg up, felt around near her throat for a few seconds and hooked the nylon rope with her big toe. She pushed the front of the noose up toward her mouth. She caught it in her teeth, held it while she lifted her leg behind her neck, got the rope with her toe again and edged the noose partway over the back of her head. She switched legs, got the rope with the big toe of her left foot and lifted the noose entirely off.

Off. It didn't take forty seconds, start to finish. After having been waterboarded.

Tears fractured my vision.

"Omigod," Harper breathed. "How—?"

"Shhh," Lucy hissed as she jumped off the stool. She ran to the workbench and got the scissors, ran over to me, turned her back and put the scissors in my right hand, held out her wrists. No words necessary.

Flex-cuffs are damn tough. It took more effort than I thought it would to cut through the loop holding her right wrist, but I was motivated. The cuff parted three seconds before the toilet flushed in the other room.

The flex-cuff still hung from Lucy's left wrist, but her hands were free. She darted to the workbench, grabbed the tomahawk and ran to the door. She ducked behind it a few seconds before Joe came through. He stopped when he saw the empty stool. It was the last fraction of a second of startled thought in his short, sorry life, then my true love buried the spike of the tomahawk in the top of his skull, all the way to the hilt.

CHAPTER NINETEEN

JOE WENT DOWN as if poleaxed. I would have to Google "poleaxe" someday, find out what that is, exactly, but the concept has always been clear enough.

For a moment Lucy watched Joe with the tomahawk in her hand, ready to deliver another blow if needed. She decided it wasn't so she ran behind Harper and pulled the quick-release knot at the wall and yanked the rope through the hook. Harper jumped off the stool, safe. She bent over to shake the noose from around her neck then hurried over to me. I cut the flex-cuff off both her wrists, then she used the scissors to cut the two flex-ties holding my wrists to the chain around my waist.

Lucy had Joe's .22 in one hand, flex-cuff still attached to her left wrist, watching the stairs through the open door, listening for Jake. Once Harper and I had our hands free, Lucy gave me the gun.

I checked the stairs. No sign of Jake, but if he came down the first thing he would see through the door would be Joe on the floor, dead. Not good.

I cut the remains of the flex-cuff off Lucy's wrist, then nodded at Joe who was leaking blood on the concrete. "Get him out of sight. Then see if he has a key for this padlock." I couldn't get free and Jake was a beast. I didn't think the girls could handle him alone with a gun and an American-made tomahawk. A .22 isn't a man-stopper; the automatic Jake had taken upstairs with him probably was.

The girls each grabbed an arm and dragged Joe to a far corner where he couldn't be seen from the other room. Lucy went through his pockets. She came up with a wallet, tossed it on the floor. Finally, she shook her head at me and stood up. No keys. Harper had gone through Jake's utility bag and pulled out an assortment of tools, wire, duct tape, eyehooks, rope, trash bags, more flex-cuffs, but no phone, no keys.

Therefore, Jake had the key. He probably didn't trust Joe; I wouldn't. So I wasn't going anywhere soon.

"Quiet," I said. For a moment the three of us listened to the house, didn't hear Jake moving around up there.

"You two get out of here," I said. "Get to a phone, call the police."

Lucy shook her head. "No way. I'm not leaving you alone with that psycho."

"Me either," Harper said.

"And . . ." Lucy said, then she looked away.

"And what?"

She glared at me. "I want to kill him. I *have* to, Mort. You don't know what it was like. I felt like I was drowning, dying." Her voice was ragged. Her eyes glistened. "I don't want the police to get him. *I* want him."

"No. That's crazy. Scram. Get out now," I said. "I can hold Jake off with this." I held up Joe's pistol.

"No," Lucy snarled. "That's a popgun. Psycho's got a real gun and you're stuck there. You're a sitting target. And he said some guy is coming. His brother. We don't know for sure when. We've got a gun and this tomahawk thing. Let's take that asshole down *now*."

She was tough, furious to the point of being deranged, not about to leave me here with a popgun.

"Get out of here," I said, one last time. I didn't raise my voice, but I put a lifetime's worth of feeling into it. I wanted her out of here. I wanted her safe.

"Not happening, Mort."

Shit. "Then you better have a damn good plan, Luce."

"Thinkin' about that," she replied.

All three of us thought about it. Finally, I said, "What you need is a half-second delay as he comes through the door, like with Joe here. Once Jake is down the stairs, the first thing he'll see is me, stuck to the wall. That'll make him relax a little. Harper needs to be back on the stool with a rope around her neck, hands behind her. As he gets close to the door, he'll see her first because of the angle. He'll come through thinking nothing is seriously wrong."

"We can't wait around for him to wake up," Lucy said. "Not if his brother is on the way."

So I laid out the rest of it.

She thought about it, lower lip caught between her teeth. "Okay, that oughta work."

"What *would* work," I said harshly, "is if you two get the hell out of here, now, and call the cops like I said."

"Maybe not," Harper said. "He's up there somewhere. What if he hears us? Also, we're topless, Mort."

"Topless won't matter to the police, Harp. That's not a consideration. You might even get faster service."

She rolled her eyes.

"Okay," Lucy said. "Mort's plan. Let's go over it one more time then get goin'." She looked at Harper. "Are you okay with a gun?"

"I pulled a nine-millimeter on Mort when we first met, remember? And I have a concealed carry permit."

Lucy smiled. "Okay, then. Don't miss."

I unscrewed the silencer and gave the .22 to Harper. A silencer would slow the bullet a little and I wanted all the velocity we could

get. A little noise didn't matter. I would have taken a silencer off
a howitzer.

* * *

Harper got back on the stool with the rope around her neck. Lucy
doubled the end of the rope and put it through the eyehook in the
wall like that. The slightest tug and the rope would pop out of the
hook. It only had to look good for one second. Harper had the .22
behind her back, safety off. Lucy stood behind the half-open door,
not immediately visible from the outer room, but far enough out of
the way that if Jake slammed the door open when he came through
it wouldn't hit her.

We were ready. I hoped. We were betting the entire pot here, all
or nothing. I nodded to Harper.

She took a breath and half screamed, half yelled, *"Stop it!"* She
gave it two more seconds, then, "Stop it! What are you *doing?"* She
shrieked again, fairly loud.

We listened.

Floor rumble from somewhere above.

My heart was pounding so hard I could barely hear Jake overhead. This *had* to work.

Jake charged down the stairs, which was Harper's cue to yell
again, but not too loud, "Get your hands *off* me!"

Jake ran inside, barefoot and shirtless. He banged the door open
as he came in, missing Lucy by inches. He had his automatic in one
hand, but it was aimed at the floor. Lucy swung the tomahawk into
his chest, spike first. Jake lost the gun as he spun partway around,
which ripped the tomahawk out of Lucy's hand. Harper jumped off
the stool as Jake staggered away from Lucy. She fired three rounds,
putting one bullet in his hip, another in his right arm, and a third
into the wall behind him. She ran closer and put a round in his

neck, another one in the wall. She raised the barrel of the gun as Lucy leapt at Jake with the backup weapon in her hands—a claw hammer. She swung it at his head, didn't get in a killing blow but clipped his skull hard enough to put him down.

Poleaxed.

Bleeding in four places, but still breathing.

Lucy raised the hammer high over her head, about to finish him off with the claw end to his temple.

"No!" I said sharply.

She paused, eyes blazing. "Why *not*?" She still held the hammer high, ready to put him down forever.

"We've got to interrogate him, Luce."

"Interrogate him *after* I fucking kill him!"

"Lucy! Get some duct tape around his ankles. A *lot* of it. And around his knees. Around his wrists too, behind his back. Or flex-cuffs. Or both. *Then* search him for keys, not before. Do it now, *fast*!"

The girls went to work on him. In three minutes, Jake looked like a fly wrapped by a spider. At least he no longer posed a threat of any kind.

Blood leaked from his bullet wounds but nothing was pumping so no arteries had been hit. The neck wound was through-and-through, not much more than a furrow to one side. It had gone through muscle, hadn't hit his carotid or jugular. Blood from the tomahawk wound ran off his chest and under his right armpit onto the floor. He looked as if he'd been through a war. Which he had. And lost.

Lucy searched his pockets, came up with several keys, a set for the Suburban outside, and a key to the padlocks, the one holding the cable to the wall and one for the chain around my waist. And a cell phone, a wallet, and a spare magazine for the Glock.

She hurried over and opened the lock, unwrapped the cable from around my neck, then cried as she gave me a long, hard hug. A few seconds later, Harper got in on that.

Two topless girls full of adrenaline after what they'd been through? I've had worse hugs.

* * *

I backed out of the group hug. "We need a cell phone," I said. "A burner, not this guy's phone." I was still able to think, which surprised me.

I picked up Jake's automatic, a Glock G20, which fired ten-millimeter rounds. Pretty serious gun. It felt good in my hands. I've always liked Glocks.

"What we *need*," Lucy said, "is to kill this cretin and get out of here *now*." She glared at Jake who had regained consciousness. He glared back at her, hurting, full of holes, but I didn't think he would die on us anytime soon. "Better yet, let's waterboard him 'til he's *gone*. I want him to know how it feels."

"No. We've got to call Ma, and I don't want a record of Jake's phone calling her."

"Ma?" Harper asked. She'd forgotten who Ma was.

"Maude Clary, my partner." I dragged Jake fifteen feet and sat him up, wrapped a double loop of rope around his neck and tied the ends to a sturdy leg of the workbench.

"*Our* partner," Lucy said.

"Sorry, I misspoke. *Our* partner and employer. It's her detective agency."

"We can't stay here," Lucy said. "This guy's brother is supposed to get here in a while."

"Good point, but he said the guy won't be here until around nine, and I want Ma's help with this."

Lucy thought about that. "Like that time with you and Holiday in her apartment after—you know?" I'd given her the entire story of what we had to do after Julia killed Jeri. No secrets from Lucy.

"Something like that. Ma saved us back then."

I nudged Jake with a foot. He gave me a baleful look, then grimaced as a wave of pain rolled through him. The tomahawk wound looked worse than the bullet holes in his hip and arm. I wasn't sure about the one in his neck.

"There's a recording," I said to the girls. "Of what, and where it is, we don't know, so this isn't over yet."

I crouched near Jake. "But it's over for you, chief. One way or another, you're done."

"Whatever," he snarled. "I want a hospital, now."

"If you think that's happening anytime soon, you're an idiot." I turned my back on him and took in the room. "I want a cell phone. A burner. We also have to get this mess cleaned up. You two might get started on that."

"Or not," Lucy said, picking up the tomahawk. She gazed thoughtfully at the blood on the spike.

I raised an eyebrow at her. "Or not?"

"It's not our mess," she said. "No one knows we were here, except him." She stared at Jake. "We get rid of him, then we get out of here." She and Harper were still topless, but they didn't seem to notice, or care.

"We don't want the police to know we were here," I agreed. "For several reasons. We can call it in later, if at all. I still want to see what Ma thinks about it." I glanced at Joe in the corner. "He can stay, get the cops involved. I don't know how far they'll get since I have the feeling these two were hired by a third party to do this and one of them is dead, but the way this room is set up, it'll connect Joe to those two dead girls. And Jake, *and* maybe his brother."

Lucy stared at Jake. "I want to waterboard you for an hour on and off. I mean it. I want to *drown* you, make you die fifty times then send you straight to hell."

Like I said, tough. And furious.

I checked the clock on the wall. 4:25 a.m. "We have a window of opportunity here if this guy Kyle isn't supposed to get here 'til sometime around nine. Let's use it wisely."

Jake's gaze swiveled from Harper to Lucy. "One of you got loose. How the *hell* did you do that?"

Lucy stared back. "Magic." She thought for a moment, then said, "You're big, but you have a midget-size brain. I'll show you how stupid you were."

She picked up the rope that had been around Harper's neck, draped the noose around her own neck and put her hands behind her back. She raised her right leg, caught the noose with her big toe and lifted it off her neck. She stood on one leg and held her foot six inches above her head for five seconds, giving Jake an unblinking stare, then lowered her leg, in perfect control the entire time. "Easy," she said.

"Fuck." He looked away.

I noted that his bleeding had slowed, almost stopped. I didn't think he was about to die, which, in a way was too bad. He was a problem. I didn't want to think about it now, but as long as he was alive, it wasn't going to go away.

"Let's get goin' here," I said. "It's probably still dark out but it won't be for long. Our bags are in the Suburban. I'll get clothes for you two, and a burner to call Ma." I got Jake's keys, waved a hand at the room. "Make yourselves useful, but don't kill this dimwit."

I left, taking the Glock with me in case I ran into Kyle. Jake might still be alive when I returned. If not, problem solved. I wouldn't blame Lucy one bit. It was dark outside, quiet, almost no sound except for a distant thrum of traffic on I-580 and maybe Virginia Street. The Suburban and the Volvo were in the driveway. Lights were on in a few nearby houses but they looked dim, like night-lights. I didn't see any signs of activity in the windows.

I found a burner in my travel bag and took Harper's bag inside. She should have at least two shirts in there, and maybe her Beretta. The more firepower the better. I noted the street address on the front porch in black numerals. The lock on the side door was new, most likely installed by Jake or Kyle, which explained how Jake had a key.

Downstairs, Lucy had the contents of Jake's wallet spread out on the workbench. Harper was going through Joe's.

"Hospital," Jake said. His voice was strong. He wasn't going to be nice and kick off. Too bad. I ignored him.

"Jacob Michael Anza," Lucy said to me. "That's this guy's real name, so maybe Kyle is Kyle Anza. And there's an Arizona driver's license in the name of William Burke with Jake's mug shot on it. He also had twelve hundred dollars, mostly in big bills, hundreds and fifties."

Harper held up a license. "Joe is Joseph Anza."

"So they really were related," I said. "Good to know. I have clothes for you two naked ladies, if you're interested."

They were, but they didn't make it a mad scramble. They took their time sorting through the available shirts and pants while I called Ma.

"You got any freakin' idea what time it is?" she said, sounding groggy and not in the mood.

"Got a situation, Ma. It's bad."

At the tone of my voice, she came awake fast. "Where are you?"

I gave her the address, told her to bring her .45, same gun she'd used a year ago to blow the brains out of Arlene Hicks, a crazy lady trying to kill me at the time with a .38. With Ma helping out we could really take Kyle down if he showed up. I also told her to bring another burner phone to make anonymous calls—like to 911.

"Jesus," she said. "I'll be there in five." She hung up.

By then Lucy and Harper were dressed in slacks and shirts from Harper's bag. The two of them were very nearly the same size. Jake was still sitting on the floor, tied to the workbench. I dragged the chair over to him and sat down. "Who hired you? What's on the recording?"

He stared at me. "Christ. You really don't know?"

"None of us knows *anything* about this, moron. Now who are you working for?"

"She's not—" He stopped dead, then said, "The guy bankrolling this is *connected*, dude. You think you're home free? You're not. None of you are. You're all walking dead."

"She. You said she. I want a name."

"It's not a she. My head hurts like a son of a bitch. I need medical attention."

"Uh-uh. Not buying it." Though he had a lump rising on his skull where Lucy got him with the hammer. "You're lucid enough. You said she. Who is she?"

His eyes wandered. "*Screw* you."

"You waterboarded my wife. I want you dead. Think about that before you mouth off again, dimwit."

"Your wife, shit. What is she, seventeen? What'd you do, raid a high school for the homecoming queen? Or did you buy yourself a sweet little trophy wife?"

"Not going to tell me who you're working for?"

His eyes spit sparks. "Fuck you. I want a hospital and a lawyer."

"Have it your way. I warned you about mouthing off. Think you're tough, waterboarding girls? Let's find out." I had seen a spring-loaded clamp with plastic jaws on the pegboard on the wall above the workbench. It was similar to a clothespin but larger, used to hold small projects together while glue dried. I ripped off a length of duct tape and pressed it over Jake's mouth then pinched his nostrils shut with the clamp.

"*Really* pissed," I said, and walked away.

After twenty seconds he started to thrash. Distressed grunting, squealing sounds came from his throat. He tried to shake his head, but was only able to bang it against the leg of the workbench. I let that go on for another twenty seconds then removed the clamp about the time his eyes were frantic, bulging.

"You're not that tough, bucko," I said. "The price of air is a name. If I put the clamp back on, it'll stay on for a full minute. If you can't think of a name after that, we can try a minute fifteen. I'll give you time to think about that. Call it waterboarding without water." I looked down at him. "You tortured my wife. I can't *begin* to tell you how furious I am about that, but I can show you."

I left the duct tape over his mouth and walked away, not particularly proud of myself, but *pissed*.

No one does what he did to Lucy. *No one.*

*   *   *

Maude Clary lived five blocks north and two blocks east of the house on Monroe Street. She called my burner when she left her place. I went outside to have her park the Chariot of Fire a block west on Monroe.

The Chariot is Ma's '63 Cadillac Eldorado. Its top safe speed is fifty due to a combination of soft springs and good shocks. Above fifty, it has an eerie floating sensation and the steering feels loose enough to give you the willies.

As we walked to the house, I gave her a synopsis of the situation, short on detail, but I hit the highlights.

"The son of a bitch waterboarded Lucy?" she said.

"Yes. I will remember how she sounded for the rest of my life. She felt like she was dying."

Ma's eyes turned to stone.

As we went down to the basement, I told her about the duct tape and the clamp I'd used on Jake. She stopped dead when she saw him sitting on the floor. Her eyes were ferocious, feral. "Clamp him again," she said curtly, then she turned to Lucy and gave her a hug.

Jake made muffled squealing sounds through the duct tape over his mouth, eyes wide and screaming as I picked up the clamp. "She's the boss," I said. "She's also tougher than I am. You're the one who thinks waterboarding is a kick, stud. You might reconsider. And think about giving us that name."

I clamped his nose, then turned my back on him. I willed myself to hear Lucy's shrieks again as she was being waterboarded, to feel her horror, lungs locked, unable to breathe as she felt her life slipping away. Behind me, Jake sounded much the same. Still wrapped in Ma's arms, Lucy stared at him without expression.

After a minute I removed Jake's clamp. By then, Lucy was introducing Harper to Ma.

"That's what you did to my wife," I said to Jake when he quit gasping for air. "You won't get any sympathy here. This was your idea. Come up with a name or you'll get the clamp again. Next time'll be longer."

I turned to Ma. "Powwow," I said. "We've got a lot to do and not much time to do it."

"Do what?"

"Not sure. That's where you come in."

* * *

We ended up calling RPD Detective Russell Fairchild. I had him in my pocket, so to speak, since I happened to know who killed Jo-X last year and he knew I knew. I told Russ to get his butt over to a house on Monroe Street, gave him the address, then Ma took the phone out of my hand and told him to bring the behemoth with him. I wasn't sure that was a good idea, but I'd trusted Ma with my life in the past, so I trusted her now.

The behemoth was Officer Clifford Day, six-foot-six and now three hundred forty-five pounds, having gained a ham hock or two since I'd last seen him. Cliff was Russ's brother-in-law so they were close. They were together in the Arlene and Buddie Hicks deal, *all* the way in, including evidence tampering and withholding evidence. They knew who'd really put the bullets in rapper Jo-X.

But Day knows how to keep his mouth shut and he's proven useful in the past, especially when he kept me from bleeding to death during a hundred-mile drive to Vegas after Arlene put a bullet in my shoulder that hit a fair-sized blood vessel. Day and Ma were once an item, and I wasn't sure they weren't still.

Which was cool. It meant Day was in Maude's pocket too, so the five of us, and Harper, were now a cabal.

Russell's inclination after he and Day showed up and found a dead body and another body with severe puncture wounds was to get RPD involved, and the FBI, and maybe DHS. Ma nixed all of that so fast Russ's eyes jittered. She and I were on the same page here.

I recapped the events of the past few days. I had to do it quickly so I left out details that didn't matter much. But I hit the highlights, one of which was wrapped in duct tape, bleeding, hands flex-cuffed behind his back, neck held to a leg of the workbench with nylon rope. The other highlight was dead, leaking in a corner of the room.

"This is Jacob Anza," I said, nudging Jake's foot. "His brother, Kyle, is due to get here sometime around nine this morning. He might be our best shot at figuring out what's going on since Jake here isn't saying much."

"You say he waterboarded Lucy?" Day's voice sounded like thunder on the horizon. "And he had these two girls up on those stools with ropes around their necks? Bet I could get a word or two out of this shitworm."

"We should probably hold off on that," I said, though I thought "shitworm" was a winner.

I told them about the shaped charges on the radiator of Harper's car and on my rental truck. "Which means, as this guy told me, he's connected, or the person who hired him is. He's got access to things the public doesn't—he or his brother, Kyle, who might be an ex-SEAL, unless Jake was blowing smoke. The two of them were hired, probably by a woman, to retrieve some sort of a recording. Who the woman is and what's on the recording, he isn't saying."

"Not yet," Ma said. "But he will unless he's willing to take it to the grave." She gave Jake a glacial stare.

"He might," I said. "He murdered those two girls who were found hung a few days ago in a basement, so that's a place for us to start. Why capture and threaten a couple of high school kids?" I looked at Jake. "You thought they had the recording. Which means all of this started with them."

He was silent for a moment. Then, "They sent a copy to . . . to someone who cared. A lot."

His tongue was looser, now that he was facing death or imprisonment.

"Why?" Ma asked. "What did they want?"

"Half a mil each."

"They thought some woman had that much and would pay up?"

"They did. And she *would*. If she had to."

She again. No doubt, this time. We were starting to get somewhere. "Who is she?" I asked him again.

"Blow it out your ass, dude. I want a hospital and a lawyer, like I said. I'm hurt, especially my neck. My chest, too. I'm not saying another fucking word about any of this until that happens. I'm keeping that name to myself 'til I get a deal, and you can take that to the bank."

"Cliché," Lucy said. "Boring."

His eyes swiveled to her.

"Let's wind it up here," Ma said. "We've got things to do if we're going to sanitize this place so none of us were here. We can get together and figure out what to do about the Anzas, who hired them, and what's in that recording later." She snapped half a dozen photos of Jake's face with her cell phone.

"I still think RPD needs to get involved," Russ said.

"Here's the problem," I said. "And it's a big one. This guy is connected to people with power. The minute RPD gets involved, he gets a hospital and a lawyer. He clams up and—"

"Clams up," Lucy said. "Wow."

"Quiet, sweetheart. He doesn't tell us anything. All we get is his mouthpiece yammering at us, keeping us in the dark, trying to make a deal. We nail Jake, but his brother, Kyle, is still out there. Grab Kyle and he'll lawyer up. His lawyer will claim Kyle was coming to the house here because his brother called but didn't say why, Kyle doesn't have a clue, doesn't know anything about anything and we have no proof that he does, then Kyle goes free. *That's* our problem. Kyle would still be out there and someone would still want that recording and they're willing to kill to get it."

"So what're we gonna do with this guy?" Russ asked. "And that body over there?"

"The body stays here," Ma said. "And I'll handle Jake."

"Handle him how?"

"Don't worry about it, Russ. I've been thinking about it. I'll take care of it."

"Probably a good idea not to ask her," Day said. "You might not want to know. In fact, I'd bet on it."

Which meant Day knew Ma better than I thought.

CHAPTER TWENTY

MA AND RUSS collaborated on how to leave the crime scene, got the rest of us to set the place up a certain way. We hustled around, thinking about fingerprints. We put up new nooses to keep Harper's and Lucy's DNA out of the place, not that their DNA was on record anywhere. We rubbed the nylon rope on Jake's hands. The crime scene was a basement; nooses would put Jake and Joe with the dead girls, Cathy and Vicki, and make things hot for Kyle. I pocketed the remote detonator Jake had carried around. When we were finished, Ma ordered everyone out of the house, said she would catch up later at Gil's Café, three blocks from her office near the municipal courthouse.

We all trooped out.

Outside, dawn was breaking. I stayed behind on the driveway, but the girls, Russ, and Day left in the Suburban and the Volvo. They drove to Ma's office, parked the cars, then walked to Gil's. The girls were starving. So was I, but I had to know what Ma was up to, and if Kyle showed up, I wanted to be there with Jake's Glock to protect her.

I went back inside the house and down the stairs in stocking feet, not making a sound. I crept to the door to the wood shop, pushed it open a few inches, and listened. Ma had the duct tape hanging half off Jake's mouth.

"—if you give me a name," Ma said. "I don't have a lot of patience, just so you know."

"Fuck you, bitch."

I heard her sigh. "That girl you tortured is worth ten thousand of the likes of you. You're human garbage. I'm not going to play around here. If you think I'm a softie because I look like your grandma who used to give you milk and cookies, you're wrong. Give me a name so we can clean this mess up, or—"

"Or what? Or *nothing*, bitch. I need a hospital and a doctor, you crazy old crone."

Another sigh, deeper this time. Then she said, "One last chance, and I mean it. I won't put my friends at risk to save your miserable hide, buster—"

The hinges made a faint squeak as I opened the door another inch. Ma turned, saw me looking in at them.

"Aw, Jesus. Get the *hell* out of here, Mort."

"No. We've always been in it together, whatever *it* is."

"Not this time."

"This time, every time."

"This isn't gonna be like Paris. This's me, no one else."

I came in and stood beside her. "Whatever it is, you're not in it alone, Ma. You and I are partners."

"Get out of here, Mort. I'm serious."

"No." My heart began to pound. I didn't know what she had in mind, but I couldn't leave her, couldn't let her do this alone, no matter what it was.

She lowered her head.

"What're you up to?" Jake asked her. His voice held a tremor, bravado evaporating like ice on a hot plate.

Ma stared at him. Softly, she said, "We have crossed the Rubicon, Jake. You and I are done here. I'll try not to kill you, but five minutes from now you will no longer be you." She pressed the tape over his mouth, made sure it was on tight. "Goodbye," she said.

He squealed, shook his head, then Ma put the clamp on his nose. She took my arm and pulled me toward the door. "Let's get out of here, Mort."

We watched from across the billiard room. When Jake stopped trying to yell through the tape and went limp, Ma checked her watch. It had a second hand. "Twenty seconds after five forty-two," she said quietly.

I didn't say anything. I held her hand as she stared at the floor for half a minute, eyes closed.

"He shouldn't have waterboarded Lucy," she said so softly I could barely hear her. "He shouldn't have said he would waterboard her so long she wouldn't know her own name afterward. I can't have him putting that horrible idea in his brother's head, or telling it to someone else."

I squeezed her hand. "I'm right here with you, Ma."

She looked up, gave me a dim smile. "Thank you." A single tear leaked out of her right eye. She wiped it away. "That's not for him," she said. "It's for me."

I squeezed her hand again. "I know."

At 5:45 I followed her back into the room. She gave it another twenty seconds then took the clamp off Jake's nose, the duct tape off his mouth. Ten seconds later Jake's chest spasmed once, twice, then he started to breathe.

"I shut him down for three full minutes after he lost consciousness," she said in a flat voice. "If it hasn't killed him—and it looks like maybe it hasn't—I don't think he'll be the same guy who threatened Lucy. Hope not anyway."

We watched Jake a while longer. He kept breathing, but his eyes weren't right. They looked vacant, no context or understanding to anything his eyes were taking in.

Too harsh a punishment for what he had done to the attorney general, Lucy, the two teenage girls, *and* what he would have done to Harper? Too much judge and jury, tap-dancing on both sides of the scales of justice? I didn't have answers to any of that. I'm not that smart. But now it was what it was. No takebacks.

Ma and I trooped upstairs.

*　*　*

She phoned Day on her burner as I put my shoes back on. "Get over here," she said to him. "Just you, no one else. Bring the Suburban."

He arrived eight minutes later and we gathered down in the basement. "Everyone just ordered," he said, looking at what was left of Jake. "I did too. My pancakes are going to get cold, Maude." I knew the comment was an attempt to lighten a somber mood. It didn't work.

"Sorry about that." She nodded at Jake. "We have to get this guy out of here."

He stared at Anza. "Where to?"

"My house. We'll stash him in the garage for a while." She didn't say for how long, and Day and I didn't ask.

"He's quiet," Day said. "Guess his morning didn't go so good. I parked the Suburban right outside the door."

Ma stepped out of the way. "Can you two get him out of here and into the car?"

"No problem." Day looked at me.

"I'll take his feet," I said.

As Day and I lifted him, Ma set a burner phone on the worktable, turned on, ready to receive a call.

"Insurance policy," she said.

* * *

Day and I followed Ma as she drove the Chariot of Fire back to her place. We left the Suburban in an unattached garage behind her house, a three-story place she shared with two other ladies about the same age. Jake Anza was awake, sort of. Not easy to tell since he was unresponsive. We locked the Suburban and left him tied up, duct tape over his mouth to keep him quiet, a tarp covering him in case anyone tried to peek inside.

"His brother's supposed to get to the Monroe house around nine," Ma said before we left the garage. "After he's gone, we'll put this guy back in the basement and call 911 on a burner, get the police going on it."

"We could've left him there," Day said. "Not put him in here."

"His brother would've seen how Jake ended up. Not sure I want that. And he might've taken him away. I didn't want that either. I want Kyle to be off balance, not knowing what's going on. I want the police to ID Jake, start putting pressure on his brother, which might put pressure on the person or persons who hired them."

"Let's hope it was Jake and Kyle, no one else," I said. "Joe doesn't count. He was a shitbird, brought into this by his uncles. It might be a family thing, to keep it tight. Jake didn't mention anyone other than his brother."

"Then maybe there isn't," Ma said. "But someone else is in this. There's a recording that has someone panicking, someone with a lot to lose if it comes to light. Whoever it is probably didn't hire anyone else. They would want to keep this as quiet as possible."

"Let's hope."

Day said, "My pancakes are probably stone cold."

* * *

Gil's Café had been open less than a year. It had a bright, appealing retro look—red Naugahyde booths, tables with red-and-white checkered tablecloths, a long counter with ten stools on a low, raised dais, milkshake machines, '60s neon jukebox loaded with '50s and '60s rock and roll.

At 6:10 all of us were in a booth closest to the restrooms, as far from other patrons in the room as we could get. We held a powwow, keeping our voices down. Ma had pulled up a driver's license photo of Kyle Anza from the DMV site so all of us could ID him if we saw him. Lucy had dropped a small fortune in quarters in the jukebox to keep our conversation private. Chuck Berry was singing "Johnny B. Goode."

I sat across from Lucy and Harper. Both of them gave me questioning looks, wanting to know about Jake. I gave them a slight head shake in return. *Not now.*

Lucy handed Harper the $1,200 she'd found in Jake's wallet. Harper gave it back. "No way. That's too much like blood money. I don't want it."

Lucy shrugged and pocketed the roll. "No problem. I'll launder it."

Ma stared at her, then said, "We'll try to follow this Kyle guy if he shows up. And I want to put a tracker on his car."

"No," Day said. "That's too dangerous."

"He'll go in the house. We'll leave the door unlocked. I'll be nearby. An old lady out walking will barely register with him and not as any kind of a threat. I'll put the tracker on his car as I go by, keep going. It won't take ten seconds. When he leaves, we'll follow him. We'll be in three or four cars, all of us talking on a conference call. If he meets the person who hired him, we might nip this thing in the bud."

"Not likely to happen," I said. "Especially once he sees what's in the basement."

"Which is what?" Harper asked. She gave me and Ma a look, wanting to know what we'd done with Jake. I would never tell her. Lucy yes, but Harper had to go back to her life, back to teaching. It wouldn't do her any good to know what had happened to Jake.

"He'll find Joe dead on the floor," I said. "Nooses hanging from the beams. Two wooden stools, Jake's duffel bag of equipment, a few pools of blood. But no tomahawk or wallets. We'll put those back after he's gone. It'll help tell a story once the police get there."

Russ leaned closer. "What about Jake? He'll be there, won't he?"

I figured Russ would get around to that. Ma had left Russ out of it; didn't think he could handle what she had done to Jake. Clifford Day was tougher. Russ would find out later, one way or another, but now was not the time.

"No," I said flatly. "Jake's not there now and he won't be there when Kyle goes in."

Lucy lifted her eyebrows at me. I gave her a look that said *later*. "With Jake missing, Kyle is gonna be worried," I said. "And hyper cautious. He won't know what's going on. He won't stick around the place for long." Ma's insurance would make sure of that.

"We don't know what he'll do after he leaves," I went on. "He might contact the person who hired him, but if he does, it'll most likely be by phone, no way to trace it."

"Nothin' we can do about that," Ma said. "But we need to keep tabs on him, which is why I want a tracker on his car. So here's how we'll work it . . ."

* * *

Kyle Anza showed up at 8:54 that morning in a silver Lexus GX SUV. Ma had been strolling up and down the street for an hour, taking it slow and easy, acting her age on a nice day. A breeze was blowing, temperature in the mid-seventies, headed for ninety-five, scent of honeysuckle in the air.

I had Jake's cell phone in case Kyle called before going in the house. Which he did. The phone erupted with the sound of bamboo wood chimes, startling me. The screen showed the letter K. "About time, man," I said. "Get in here," then hung up. I could only hope I'd sounded like Jake, that they didn't have a code word or phrase worked out, and that the brusque response wouldn't scare him off. If he called back, I didn't know what I'd do, other than to sound angry and fake it again.

I let everyone know he was on the way. Ma watched as his SUV passed her, moving slowly on Monroe. He turned left into the driveway. The Volvo was still there, locked, far enough from the house that Kyle had to leave the Lexus close to the street. The Suburban was still in Ma's garage.

Ma watched as he got out of the car. He gazed around, but didn't take note of the older woman slowly ambling up the sidewalk across the street—or the white-haired fellow out walking a dachshund on a lavender leash, or a woman trimming rose bushes half a block west.

Kyle wore black jeans, a gray T-shirt, ball cap. He was a solid-looking guy, six-two, two hundred forty pounds. He opened the side door and went inside. Ma crossed the street and headed for the Lexus. She gave us all that on the conference call, and the license of the Lexus when she got closer to it.

It took her eight seconds to stick a tracker under the SUV's right rear wheel well and keep going. Seconds later I drove by in my nondescript '94 Toyota Tercel. No sign of Kyle yet, as I'd expected. I didn't slow down or speed up. I dialed the number of the burner Ma left on the worktable. I gave Kyle one minute to look around the basement before hitting the SEND button.

It rang five times, then, "Who's this?" he answered in a guarded tone.

"Cops will be there in two minutes, Kyle." I ended the call. I smiled, having probably sent his blood pressure into orbit.

Ma and I had talked over the timing. She strolled by on the far side of the street, keeping one eye on the house.

Kyle came out, moving fast, looking around. He had Jake's utility bag in one hand. He tried to open the Volvo's doors, gave up, then stopped by the back of the Lexus and scanned the street. He looked both ways, took out his cell phone and tapped the screen. I got all that from Ma.

Jake's cell phone rang in my Toyota. I didn't answer. It was better to keep Kyle guessing, wondering where Jake was, wondering what had happened. Wondering who had answered the phone not four minutes ago since it couldn't have been Jake who'd told him to "get in here," and wondering who was on the burner telling him cops were on the way. He would be on edge, on guard, sweating bullets.

He got in his car and backed out, took off fast.

"He's leaving," Ma said. "He's got Jake's bag of tools, but he left Joe in the basement. Right now, he's headed east on Monroe."

I was two blocks west and headed west, too far away to get on him. Day was in a blue-gray Taurus a block north on Nixon Avenue. "I've got him," he said.

The tracker was up and running according to Ma, but that wouldn't tell us who Kyle met, if he met someone, so the chase, such as it was, was on.

It didn't last long.

In a rented Chevy Sonic, Harper took over from Day when Kyle's SUV turned right onto Arlington. She kept on him down to Plumb, stayed two cars back, and followed him all the way to the Grand Sierra Resort on Mill Street with Lucy one car behind her in a '98 Plymouth Breeze I'd borrowed from Velma Knapp, my former neighbor up near Ralston Street. Velma is eighty-eight years old. I told her we needed to track a bad guy, a *very* bad guy, and she was thrilled. She'd wanted to come along. Feisty old gal.

Harper parked in a slot a hundred feet from Kyle. He was in row G. Harper took row E. She got to the front door of the hotel-casino thirty seconds before him, kept an eye on him as he came in, then handed him off to Lucy. Lucy got a profile shot of him at the registration desk as he got a suite on the eighteenth floor. The girls lost him when he went into an elevator. So much for tracking him to see if he met anyone. But . . . *c'est la vie.* We had other pressing matters to take care of.

*   *   *

First up was getting Jake out of Ma's garage and back into the basement of the Monroe Street house, leaving the Volvo in the driveway. We returned wallets to Joe's and Jake's pants and tossed the tomahawk on the workbench with Jake's fingerprints on it. The police might be able to track down who had bought it and where. The spike end of the tomahawk would match the hole in Joe's head and the wound in Jake's chest. It might even match the hole in Eystad's forehead. Food for thought—something for the FBI to ponder, if RPD got them involved. Jake's eyes were vacant, drool on his chin. His shirt was still upstairs and he was bare-chested. He was untied, no duct tape on him. A nice puzzle for cops or feds. No point in leaving the Glock with Jake, so it was mine now.

The two girls had a ten-minute delay getting out of the Grand Sierra. Lucy led Harper over to a high-limit roulette table. She watched for two rounds without betting, then set five hundred on red, five hundred on a 14, 15, 17, 18 corner, and the ball landed on fifteen black. She cashed in the chips, gave $3,000 to Harper, a hundred to the girl running the table, and pocketed the rest for traveling money.

"Keep it," she said to Harper. "It's clean now."

"Uh, okay, I guess. How did you do that, and why do I get three thousand dollars?"

"Answer to the first is I was born on April Fool's Day when four planets were lined up. The second is, you need it to pay for your car and travel expenses and I don't."

"Huh. Neither of those makes any sense, Lucy."

"Life is often like that."

"Okay, but the guy said the new radiator is only going to cost three-forty. Three thousand is *way* too much."

"Keep it anyway—to get to San Francisco next March. Fly first class, it's great. Let's get outta here."

* * *

They had to do a car shuffle, returning Velma's car and Harper's rental, then they were off to Tonopah in the Suburban. They would leave it in the Raley's supermarket parking lot. Lucy's Mustang was in front of the Stargazer Motel. Harper had gotten word that her Corolla was ready in Goldfield. I gave Lucy a long hug and an even longer kiss, then watched as the Suburban rounded a corner of Washington Street, headed for I-80 and points south. Ma stood beside me as they disappeared.

"Now what?" I asked her.

"Print the cell phone photo of Kyle that Lucy took, and his driver's license picture, and the best one I got of Jake down in the basement, then I'll get on the computer and see if I can get a line on the Anzas which might tell us who hired them. *And*," she said, eyes narrowed in thought, "see if we can get a handle on those two girls who were found in a basement a few days ago. All of this started with them. They got hold of a video of something they shouldn't have, something that got them killed."

"And call 911?" I said. "Get the police scurrying over the Monroe house like beavers building a dam?"

For a moment she stared at me. "That too. Cops will ID Jacob Anza and his nephew, which might put them on Kyle. That could also turn up the heat on the broad who hired 'em—if it really was a broad."

She hesitated, then shook her head at me. "Beavers buildin' a dam. I don't know how you come up with stuff like that, Mort."

"It sounds like what cops do, doesn't it?"

"In a strange way." She took a deep breath. "Hope that asshole Jake doesn't wake up and start squawking. That'd be a bitch and a half."

CHAPTER TWENTY-ONE

NOT MUCH CHANCE of that. Last time I saw Jake, he wasn't saying anything or trying to. He gave me the heebie-jeebies as Day and I sat him on the floor and propped him up against the workbench. I wore nitrile gloves as I tied a rope around his chest under his armpits and around a leg of the bench to keep him upright. One more thing for the crime scene techs to chew on.

Ma had stayed out on the street, watching for people and traffic as Cliff and I hustled Jake into the house, and as we left. In Gil's Café, Ma had run the Suburban's VIN. It was registered to a Harold Barnes in Elko, but the plates were for a Nissan Titan in Sparks. More hanky-panky with the vehicles. Someone in the Monroe neighborhood might remember a Suburban coming and going in the driveway, but I doubted anyone would connect it with the one about to be abandoned in Tonopah.

Ma also ran the plates on the Lexus Kyle was driving. The plates were for a Lincoln Navigator that belonged to a Walter Corbell in Sparks. Kyle Anza owned a Lexus, so he might have been using his own car—stealing plates being easier than stealing a car—driving safely to keep the police from running the plate and pulling him over. Ma got him in a DMV database. He was thirty-eight years old and had a home address in Reno. Ma gave Officer Day the address.

He went by the house, but the Lexus wasn't there, and no one an-swered the door when he rang the bell and knocked.

Jacob Anza was forty-one, with an address in Sparks. No one was at that house either, nor would Jake ever be there again.

Forty minutes after Ma called 911, I drove past Monroe on a cross street, Mark Twain Avenue. I glanced to my left as I went by, saw four police cars with lights flashing, a coroner's wagon, and a para-medic van.

I kept going. Russ was in there. Police Chief Menteer had put him in charge of the crime scene. Russ had given me a flash call on a burner, told me Jake was awake, sort of, and breathing, which I already knew. Jake's eyes would track lights moving from side to side in front of him; otherwise he was as unresponsive as a carrot. Russ didn't ask what had happened to him, but a question was in his voice. Given time, he would figure it out on his own.

I drove to Ma's office on Liberty Street, parked in back and went in. First thing I saw was a poster of a Coca-Cola ad circa 1927. Swing that out of the way and there I'd be, in the buff, full frontal, on a poster behind the Coke ad.

I stood there for a moment, hoping Ma had gotten rid of the poster. I swung the Coke ad aside and—nope—there I was. The only thing hiding what should remain hidden was a little red body paint, put there by a gorgeous girl, Sarah Dellario, also known as Holiday, when we rode in the World Naked Bike Ride in San Francisco a year and a half ago.

Ma was in front of a computer, engrossed, scrolling through a database.

"When are you gonna retire this goddamn poster?" I growled at her.

"When hell freezes over, boyo. It's mine. Keep your grubbies off it."

"I worry about you, Ma. So what can I do to help out?"

"Get on the other computer and see who owns that house on Monroe. Probably nothing there that'll help us, but you never know."

I booted up a laptop and got into the Washoe County property tax database, put in the address for the house on Monroe Street, came up with a Bernard and Natalie Watts. I gave the names to Ma.

"Never heard of 'em. Find out where they work, what they do."

That took one of the several restricted databases Ma subscribed to as a private investigator. Bernard was thirty-six with an MBA in accounting, an assistant director in the Department of Corrections, making sixty-seven five a year.

Natalie didn't appear in that database. I got her using a special program written by Ma's best and most expensive hacker, a program that, as I understood it, scurried around to several databases and other sources compiling hard-to-find data, which meant we weren't going to announce that we had obtained the information. Natalie was twenty-nine, had two children, Denise and Mark, ages four and six. She didn't have an outside job. On the family's 1040 last year her occupation was listed as housewife.

Bernard's salary wasn't enough to keep the kitchen remodel going after so much of the underlying structure had been found rotten. The remodel was on hold, along with the sale of the house. That might be causing trouble in paradise. Bernard was a mid-level worker bee in Nevada's government. I wondered if that could have anything to do with the attorney general being murdered.

I gave all that to Ma.

She swiveled in her chair. "Not sure what to do with it, but good job—we'll keep 'em in mind and dig deeper if the name pops up again. Now see if you can find anything on those girls the Anzas killed last week."

"What kind of things?"

She stared at me. "What part of *anything* did you not get?" She went back to her computer.

Jeez.

Okay, a couple of teenage girls, found hung in a dank basement. That sounded like fun.

Not.

But I got online and got to it.

Vicki Cannon was a month over seventeen years old when she'd been found. Cathy Jantz was sixteen and ten months. They would have been seniors at Reno High the coming school year. They'd lived half a mile from each other in a good part of town. Vicki's father was a dentist. Cathy's was a senior executive at the Golden Goose Casino, of all places. The Golden Goose was the biggest casino in Reno. It was also site of the Green Room, a bar Lucy, Ma, and I used as an informal office where Patrick O'Roarke tended bar with a hot girl, Traci Ellis, his live-in girlfriend, twenty-six to his forty-seven, which meant I'd had to revise my opinion of the lad. Upward, of course.

"As if any of that matters," Ma said when I told her.

Rebuffed, I dug deeper, using several of the special techniques I'd learned from Ma. "Special" actually meant illegal, but we didn't use that sucky terminology.

Vicki was a B-plus student with a 3.32 GPA, and Cathy had been running a solid A with a 3.96, taking more math than Vicki— trigonometry in her junior year. Cathy had registered for AP calculus the coming year. Both had been homecoming princesses. I pulled up last year's yearbook pictures. Very pretty girls. Gone now.

I sat there and stared at the screen.

Now what?

Facebook, that's what, since against all odds, it was still the crown jewel of social media, if *crown jewel* makes the slightest bit of sense, referring as it does to a place that competes with messages left on bathroom walls—parents take note. If I got nowhere with FB, I might try Instagram, Weibo, and Reddit. Meetup would be a last resort. I hoped I wouldn't get that desperate or that the girls had ever been that desperate for attention either.

But first, Facebook—if the parents of the girls hadn't thought to remove their accounts, and if the girls hadn't created bogus accounts, if they hadn't password-protected their accounts so their parents couldn't see what they were up to. How to do any and all of that would be "well, *duh*" information to every high-school teen in the country.

I typed in "Vicki Cannon" and got a list of potentials. I scrolled through, weeding them out, one by one, then came up with a Vicki Cannon at Reno High. I went through her pictures and comments by her friends, much of it illiterate unless your okay with *your* replacing *you're*. I slowed to read more carefully when I found an exchange between Vicki and Cathy that took place less than a month ago:

Cathy: i'm with d-m 2nite

Vicki: lucky u. i'm w/ q-j-e

Cathy: xlt$$ but yuk. pt's out 2gether?

Vicki: i think so

Cathy: not sure? c$ mite show

Vicki: not w/o u i hope ☺ ☺

Cathy: not safe now! d upset ttyl

Vicki: tl

I read it again. And again. Then I called Ma over, had her take a look at it.

"The world is goin' to hell," she said when she'd read it through twice.

"Got that, but what do you make of it?"

"They were talkin' in code. Or shorthand, or both. Or what passes for language by today's youth."

"Any idea what it's about?"

She went through it again. "Hard to say."

"Dollar signs indicate money. And that 'not safe now' is intriguing."

She shrugged. "They're into something there. Keep at it." She scooted back to her computer.

My phone rang. It was Lucy.

"Hola, cupcake," I answered.

"Hola, yourself. Harp and I are a few miles south of Fallon. Probably hit a dead zone soon. She and I didn't get a good chance to talk before. Now we do, just sayin'."

"Uh-oh. That can't be good." And she'd called Harper *Harp*. So, friends. They might talk about any damn thing.

"She told me about that lady, Olivia, coming into the room with the clothes she'd dried and you were up, getting a towel Harp had thrown across the room. She said Olivia was impressed by the sight since you'd gotten out of bed right before she came in."

"You should gag her until you reach Tonopah."

"No way. Laughing keeps me awake. I'm really tired, but I've got to get my car before someone at the Stargazer has it towed or something."

"I'm tickled to be a source of humor and derision for your amusement."

"Just humor, Mort. Oh, and she told me why she had to throw your towel across the room."

"That's bogus. She didn't *have* to do anything of the sort."

"She said it was so she could sleep. Giggling keeps her awake. Anyway, she says she's got more stories like that so I'll be okay all the way to Tonopah. Not sure I'll be able to drive back today, though. I'm exhausted. I think she and I will stay the night in Goldfield. I miss you, but there's no way I can drive all the way to Reno from Goldfield without getting a decent night's sleep."

"I miss you too, but do what you gotta do."

"Um, how is that guy, Jake?"

"Unresponsive, according to Russ."

She was silent for a moment, then, "That's good. Is he likely to stay unresponsive a while longer—like forever?"

"I would bet a six-foot pile of gold bars on it."

"That's good. Okay, I better go before I lose the signal. Anyway, like I said, Harper's got more things to tell me."

"Don't believe a single word she says."

"Why? So far it sounds just like you. But don't worry, I get it. Bye, Mort. Be safe."

"You too, Luce."

I ended the call, then went back to the computer and read the exchange between Vicki and Cathy a few more times, couldn't make sense of it, so I saved a screenshot of the conversation since things on Facebook tend to show up then disappear forever. I read it one more time, feeling as if I were missing something that was right in front of me.

I found more cryptic exchanges between the two girls going back six months. In one of the earliest ones I saw the figure *$500!* and the return comment *OMG!*

The most recent exchange, not two weeks ago, was a short one:

Vicki: hear a-t yet?

Cathy: no. talk on zx!

Vicki: not safe here?

Cathy: not for $$$$! Jeez v

Vicki: k…@zx

That was it. I saved a screenshot of that, too, then had Ma take a look at it.

"They were into something bad," Ma said.

"It involved money. It got them killed."

"Obviously. And someone hired the Anzas to fix it."

"They made a video. Probably blackmailed someone they thought had deep pockets. Someone, it turns out, who had enough to lose that murder seemed like a reasonable option. Jake said something about the two girls asking for half a million each."

"Greedy," Ma said. "And smart, but not nearly smart enough to get away with something like that."

* * *

Jake knew about the remodeling problems with the Monroe Street house. He had insider knowledge, which meant he had an in with the realtor, the contractor, or with Bernard or his wife, Natalie. Someone had scouted around for an empty house with a basement. A realtor would be a good bet if a person wanted to locate a house with certain amenities. Like a place to waterboard girls.

I phoned Russ.

"What?" he growled.

"Kinda brusque, Russ. I need a name or two."

"I'm in the middle of something here."

"And I'm your good buddy. You've probably got what I need. Who's the realtor for the Monroe house, and the contractor who's doing the remodel? I don't want to drive by to get a look at the *for sale* sign out front. I might get pulled over for rubbernecking."

"Ah, jeez. Hold on." I heard voices in the background, then Russ said, "Realtor is Sue Harvey at RE/MAX. Like all realtors, she's polite as hell, always on the lookout for a new client. I had a guy speak to her already. The contractor is a Robert Edman, E&L Contracting out in Sparks."

"Got phone numbers for those?"

"Look 'em up, Detective."

"Okay, Detective."

We disconnected in the same nanosecond.

I phoned Sue Harvey first. We got through the usual pleasantries in short order, then I said, "I wonder if we could meet in person. Are you free sometime today?"

"I'm in the office right now, but a prospective client is due here in twenty minutes."

I got an address; told her I'd be there in ten. I grabbed a print of Jake's face, Kyle's too. "I'm goin' out, Ma," I said. "Back soon."

She didn't turn around. "Find more dead people and unemployment is at 4001 South Virginia Street, boyo."

What a great sense of humor.

* * *

Sue Harvey was a pleasant-looking lady of forty-five. She did a professional job of masking a hopeful look as I came in the door, so I knew she'd been a realtor for a long time. She was one of two realtors currently in the office, and a young girl was at a reception desk. When I told Sue I was a private detective, all trace of the hopeful look went south and she was all business. I had the feeling she hoped I would wrap it up quickly and leave.

I sat in front of her desk and showed her a picture of Jake Anza. She gazed at it, then said, "No. I've never seen him." So I showed her the picture of Kyle that Lucy took. "Could be," she said, so I showed her his driver's license photo. "Yes," she said, nodding. "He was in here. Edward Vale. I remember the name."

Of course, he'd give her a fake name, and of course, she would remember names. That was her job. And she'd just tied Kyle into the murder of the two teens. I would have to tell Russ, though that might not lead us to the woman who was bankrolling this operation, so I would hold off on that for a while.

"Can you tell me when he came in? And what he was looking for," I asked.

She checked her cell phone, which doubled as an appointment book. "I showed him a house five days ago, at three thirty in the afternoon." Her eyes widened. "I spoke to a Reno detective not long ago. There was a murder in that house, but"—she slumped in her chair—"I guess that's why you're here." She closed her eyes. "What a disaster. That house already had problems. It'll never sell now."

"Yes, ma'am. I'm trying to find out where Edward Vale got a key to the place."

She stared at me. "He had a key?"

"Evidently. He went in through a side door." I didn't tell her I watched him do it and my hands were tied behind my back at the time—and it was his brother, and his name was Anza, not Vale.

"Well, I don't know. He certainly didn't get one from me—or us. We don't do that. Ever."

"Could he have unlocked a window and left it closed while you were showing him the house?"

"Oh. I . . . I guess that's possible."

"He could've come back later that night, gone in and changed that side-door lock. It was brand new."

"I . . . I've never heard of such a thing."

I stood up. "Not your fault. You can't check twenty or thirty windows every time you show a house."

"No, no I couldn't. But still . . ."

And that's when the gold-plated thought occurred to me, out of the blue, as they do. "I don't suppose you keep a record of who refers a seller to you? Or a buyer. Not cold-call walk-ins, but personal referrals?"

"We do, yes, whenever possible."

"I wonder if you could tell me who referred the Wattses to you—if anyone did."

She looked up as two people in their fifties came into the office. She called out to the receptionist, "Anne, could you please help this gentleman?" Meaning me. She offered her hand. I shook it, then she turned and greeted the new arrivals.

Anne was in her early twenties, very pretty, all smiling teeth, blue eyes, and enthusiasm. "What can I do for you?"

I told her. She said, "Easy," and asked her all-knowing computer, squinted at the screen, tapped a few keys, and a printer whipped out a single sheet.

"Here you go," she said.

I gave the sheet a quick scan, had to work to keep my expression from giving anything away.

Anne gazed at me. "Um, aren't you that . . . that guy who . . . ?"

"I know who you mean, and I've been told I look a lot like him. It causes me no end of trouble, let me tell you."

"You even have that same scar." She ran a finger from the bridge of her nose across her left cheek.

"That's my biggest problem. Gotta run, kiddo. We'll have to do lunch sometime. Bye."

I got the hell out of there.

* * *

I sat in my car and stared at the sheet Anne had given me one more time. It had addresses, a few dates, a brief in-house comment by Sue, and a name.

The referral had been made by Nevada's lieutenant governor, Sylvia MacKenna Haas.

Hot damn.

Sometimes investigations slog, but sometimes a piece breaks loose and the whole thing unravels like a cheap sweater. Okay, this sweater hadn't exactly unraveled, but I had what looked like a nice loose end to pull.

Maybe.

CHAPTER TWENTY-TWO

Sylvia MacKenna Haas was a woman with more than the usual amount to lose. Currently she headed a list of five or six people being considered as the running mate of presidential hopeful William Jackson Price next year. At the moment, "Billy" was the front-runner in his party, but nominations were still nine or ten months off.

Sylvia didn't need a scandal. The definition of *politics* is image over substance. A video of any sort getting loose, especially a black-mail video, would cut her off at the knees.

But wait. A video of what? What would a pair of dippy high school girls have gotten a video of?

I could think of only one thing.

* * *

Ma was still at her computer when I walked in. "Hold the presses," I said.

She swiveled toward me. "You found another stiff and I need to find a new assistant. As if I want one."

"Nope. Even better."

"Jesus, I hope so. All I got is Janet Anza Miller, sister of Jake and Kyle. She's got a kid, Katie, age four. Janet's married to Thomas

Miller, an electrician. They're in Sioux City, Iowa, probably not involved in what's goin' on with Jake and Kyle. What've you got?"

I wagged my eyebrows at her. "Sylvia Haas."

* * *

"Okay, I'll bite. What about her?" Ma asked.

"She's our lieutenant governor."

"As if I didn't know. What about her? And what're you doin'
about Elrood Wintergarden?"

That stopped me. "Elrood?"

She smiled. "Gotcha. Screw Elrood. We've got bigger fish to fry.
What's up with Haas?"

"She referred the Wattses to Sue Harvey of RE/MAX."

Ma screwed up her face. "So?"

"So Haas has a lot to lose, Ma. Especially now."

"You think a VP hopeful hired the Anzas to put the kibosh on
what might be a blackmail video?"

I gave her a narrow look. "In the unlikely event that you don't
remember, I once received the shaking hand of a presidential hopeful via FedEx."

"Well . . . shit. So you did. So what?"

"So, karmically I'm tied into all kinds of oddball crud. Excluding
hot women, of course. I'm tied into that, but it's a different kind of
karma."

She gave that more thought. "Teenage girls. It's *just* like you to
come across something as bad as that, Mort."

"Thanks."

"That wasn't a compliment, boyo, but, okay, good job. Don't
know how you do it. I'll check out Haas, see if I can connect
her to any part of this horror story." She turned back to her
computer.

I watched her for a moment, then thought about Kyle. He was still loose. I wondered what he was up to. Might be nice to get eyes on him, if possible. In fact, I thought it was time to monitor the tracker on his car, make sure he was still at the Grand Sierra Resort.

The tracker worked with an app on Ma's cell phone. I loaded the app on mine, found Kyle's Lexus at GSR. Good deal, but maybe I should keep an eye on it. He'd been in there long enough to have decided on a plan of action. And it was almost eleven o'clock. He could have a television on in his suite. By noon, Jake and Joe would make the news. Kyle and the mystery woman who'd hired him might set up an emergency meeting. If so, I'd like to get in on it—from a distance. I could set up surveillance on his car, follow him if he went somewhere, get a line on this dame.

"Goin' out, Ma," I said.

She waved a hand over her head, didn't turn around. I went out to the parking lot, hopped in my old nondescript Toyota, and drove to the GSR. Harper had reported that Kyle parked in the G row. I drove the row and . . . no Lexus SUV, no Kyle. But the app said the tracker was still there.

I didn't like that one bit. It took a while, but I finally found the tracker stuck inside the left rear wheel well of a Prius. I cruised every row in GSR's parking lot, which took twenty minutes. I found several Lexus SUVs but none with Kyle's stolen plate on it.

He had found the tracker, reassigned it to folks from Wisconsin, and disappeared.

* * *

I phoned Lucy, but it went to voice mail. She might be in a dead zone, somewhere on U.S. 95, south of Hawthorne. I left a voicemail message for her to call me.

Now I wasn't sure what to do.

I went back to Ma's, told her that Kyle had slipped his leash.

"Well, *fuck*," she said, which summed up the situation nicely. "Get Russ to put out a BOLO on that Lexus. See if he can round him up or at least get eyes on him."

"Think he'll do that?"

"Get hold of the brother of the guy in that basement who is either a murderer or a victim? He'll do it."

I called Russ on a burner.

"What?" he answered cautiously.

"Kyle's gone. He found the tracker and took off in his Lexus. He's in the wind."

"And I should do what about that?"

"Put a BOLO on his car. Pick him up or at least find out where he is."

Silence for a moment. "Okay, I can do that." He hung up. He'd sounded distracted.

Now what?

I didn't know. I couldn't go out, drive around hoping to come across Kyle's Lexus. I looked at Ma. "Got anything interesting yet?" I asked.

"Not much. Sylvia is forty-four. She's been married to a Dr. Carl Haas for twelve years. Her first, his second. He's fifty-one and an orthopedic surgeon in private practice in a medical group with two other MDs. They've got three kids, Quinn, Jenny, and Ethan, ages seven, eight, and ten."

"Forty-four? That seems kinda young to be up for vice president."

Ma shrugged. "Kennedy was elected president at age forty-three. Also, it's a godawful lousy field this year, and she rounds out the ticket. So say the pundits."

"Still."

"Yeah. Politics." She went back to her computer.

So, a government bigwig and a surgeon. Pillars of the community. I tried to picture them, and the family. When I did, kids rose to the surface. That quickly morphed into babysitters for the tots, Quinn, Jenny, and Ethan.

"Well, I'll be a son of a bitch," I said.

Ma turned. "No argument there. What's up?"

I pulled up the screenshot I'd made of the Facebook conversation between Vicki and Cathy. I pointed to the line where Vicki had said: *lucky u. i'm w/ q-j-e*

"Quinn, Jenny, Ethan," I said. "I think this has to do with babysitting."

"Jesus."

"What're the Wattses kids' names again?"

Ma found it. "Denise and Mark."

In the first line Cathy said: *i'm with d-m 2nite*

"It's coming together," Ma said, smiling.

"I get a nice big bonus for this, right? No lump of coal in my stocking for Christmas like I got last year?"

*   *   *

In all the excitement, Jake had let slip that the person who'd hired him and Kyle was a woman. Which meant we had her now: Lt. Governor Sylvia Haas.

Maybe. Likely, but not a hundred percent. We didn't have enough to go hammer on her door, drag her out into the street and slap on handcuffs. Yet.

Kyle was still running loose.

Lucy wasn't answering her personal cell phone or her burner.

I decided Ma could handle the computer search now that we had a direction, a target. I wanted to be with Lucy. And Harper, of course, but Lucy was my life. I had to make certain she was safe.

Which meant a trip to Tonopah or Goldfield. I didn't want to trust my antique Toyota for a trip like that. It wasn't fast enough or reliable enough. At sixty miles an hour the driver's-side mirror whistles, sounding too much like Madonna. That was a problem, but the bigger problem was that the car was closing in on two hundred thousand miles. And it didn't have air-conditioning.

I phoned Avis, ordered up an SUV, settled on a Toyota Sequoia.

I slowed down long enough to really think about what I wanted to take on a trip like this. It wasn't likely that Lucy and Harper were in any kind of trouble. They were probably still in a Verizon dead zone. But Lucy and I have a poor track record when it comes to trouble, so I wanted to be with her, prepared for anything. I came up with a few items not on most shopping lists, one of which was an S&W .44 Magnum revolver loaded with "critical defense" rounds. Man stoppers.

By 12:25 I was on I-80 in a red Sequoia, headed east toward Fernley. Half an hour later I was nearing Fallon on U.S. 50 when my phone rang. It was Ma.

"I think Sylvia Haas and Kyle Anza are an item," she said without preamble.

"How'd you get that, Ma?" I reached a 45-mph sign at the west end of town so I knocked it back from sixty-five.

"I already mentioned Thomas Miller, married to Janet Anza Miller, Jake and Kyle's sister. But then I worked on Sylvia Haas's family tree and found that Tom Miller is her third cousin, so it's likely Sylvia knows the Anza boys."

"Jury-wise, that's thin, Ma. And how does that make Sylvia and Kyle an item? Which, of course, would be huge if we had proof."

"I'm gettin' there, boyo. I've got Kyle in a suite at the Peppermill on the fifteenth a month ago, paid with a credit card in his name. So I got into the hotel's video and caught Sylvia in a poofy blond wig and dark glasses at 8:25 that same evening near the elevators."

"Sure it's her, Ma?"

"Better than ninety percent."

"We can't go before a jury with that either. Not that we were actually thinking that far ahead."

"No, we can't. But the point is, we're sneakin' up on those two. By the way, Kyle Anza was Navy, a SEAL, ended up with a bad conduct discharge, BCD. Got that from his DD214. He did six months in a naval brig in Jacksonville on an assault charge, got out with his BCD eight years ago. His 1040 has him as a laborer, whatever that is. Last year he claimed a gross income of forty-two thousand, which doesn't spell a mortgage *and* a year-old Lexus to me."

"Keep on it. I'm in Fallon, about to head south. Let me know if you get anything else."

"Will do."

An ex-SEAL with a BCD. Shit. Still no Lucy and I was about to hit a bunch of Verizon dead zones on U.S. 95.

* * *

I pulled into Tonopah at 4:05 that afternoon. I had a signal on my cell, but Lucy still wasn't answering hers. No sign of her Mustang anywhere, including at the Raley's parking lot. But the Suburban Jake had been driving was there, doors locked, a little engine heat wafting from under the hood that might've been nothing but the sun blazing down on it. I made a quick circuit of Tonopah's motels and business district—still no Mustang. I gassed up the Sequoia and took off for Goldfield, twenty-six miles farther south.

I breathed a huge sigh of relief when I spotted Lucy's Mustang in front of a unit at the Goldfield Inn. In the slot next to it was a Toyota Corolla, which would be Harper's. The two cars were in front of units 5 and 6. Two other cars were in the parking lot, no silver Lexus in sight.

I parked, got out, knocked on the door to 6, got no answer, knocked harder. Still nothing, so I knocked on the door to room 5. Hard.

Still no response.

I didn't like that. I walked to the office and went in. A woman of sixty was in a room behind the small reception area. I hit the bell and she came out in a tired housedress, tired eyes, tired half-smile, cigarette burning in one hand.

"He'p you?"

"I was supposed to meet the girl in the Mustang who came in this afternoon. My wife. Which unit is she in?"

Her eyes narrowed. "I don't give out information like that without some kinda ID." She glanced at the register, then back up at me. Not being mulish, just careful.

I showed her my driver's license. Same last name.

"Okay, then. She and the other girl are in six. Both of 'em tired as all get-out, looked like."

"I knocked. No one answered."

"Like I said, they was tired. Couldn't keep their eyes open. Probably asleep by now."

"I knocked pretty hard. Can I get a key, see if they're in there, make sure they're all right?"

She thought about that, then took a key off a rack and came around the counter. "I'll go with. That okay?"

"Fine by me. I really appreciate this."

I followed her past rooms along a covered walkway. We were ten feet from the door to room 6 when my cell phone rang, not the burner Russ would use, but my regular phone. I grabbed it from a pocket. The screen showed a picture of Lucy.

"Hola," I said. "You had me scared, sugar plum."

"No one's ever called me that before," Kyle Anza said, not a trace of humor in his voice. "Let's you and me talk."

CHAPTER TWENTY-THREE

"First," he said, "get rid of that old lady who's with you. Send her back to the office. Whatever you told her, tell her you changed your mind."

I looked around. "You've got eyes on me?"

"Remote camera, dude. I'm fifty miles away. Lose the broad right now or Lucy gets a broken finger."

I stopped dead and held up the phone. "This's her," I said to the woman. "My wife. She and the other girl aren't in the room right now, so I don't need to go in."

She shrugged. "Suit yerself. You need something or want another room, you know where to find me." She U-turned and went back to the office.

I felt my heart fluttering. My vision darkened for a few seconds. Kyle had Lucy and Harper. They were fifty miles away. "She's gone," I said into the phone.

"I see that. And I see you've got a red Sequoia. That's good. You'll be needing that four-wheel drive."

I didn't respond to that. I was having trouble getting enough air.

"Where's Jake?" Kyle asked.

"Renown Medical, last I heard. The police have him. Kidnapping and murder are against the law."

"How'd you get past him? He told me he and Joe *had* you guys in that basement."

It's unlikely he would know what condition Jake was in. "I got the upper hand, that's all. I sucker punched him. Guess I hit him kinda hard. He might have a concussion. I think they were doing tests."

A lengthy silence. Then, "I don't see that happening, you handling Jake one-on-one. No way, Sally, not with you cabled to that wall the way I told him."

Sally?

"But it is what it is. I'll have to ask him," Kyle went on. "I might be able to see him at the hospital. I thought about it. Cops don't have a thing on me."

Not yet, I thought. He didn't know Sue Harvey had ID'ed him as the guy who'd asked about the Monroe Street house several days ago. When that came out, Kyle would be *número uno* on the FBI's to-do list.

"Listen up," Kyle said. "I'll tell you how this is gonna play out. If it doesn't work out *exactly* like I tell you, Lucy and this Harper chick are dead. You got that?"

"Yes."

"You've got the recording, the video?"

Now what? Say no and possibly get the girls killed? Or lie and maybe get them killed anyway, but later?

No good choices, but I chose later.

"Time's wasting, Sally," he said. "Say something."

"Yes," I replied. "I've got it. It's on a flash drive. I don't have any way of knowing if it's the only copy, though. For all I know, that girl, Cathy, the younger and smarter of the two, could've made a hundred copies."

"Doesn't matter. I'm in this for two mil, then I'm out of the country. All I need is the video. Did you look at it?"

How to answer? No didn't seem likely, so I said yes.

"What's on it?" Kyle asked.

I'd given that some thought on the drive from Reno to Tonopah and added it up. Two prom-princess babysitters, $500, danger, big$$, and a video came up Carl Haas, MD and blackmail. At least one of the girls babysat the Haases' kids. If Carl Haas were caught up in a big scandal, Sylvia Haas could kiss that VP running mate thing goodbye, no hope of ending up a heartbeat away from the presidency. It made sense. People into power would kill to keep it or get more. It's how dictators see the world. D.C. was full of it. Anyone wanting to be a U.S. senator was automatically unfit for the job. Need proof? Look at the senate.

I took a chance and said, "The lieutenant governor's husband and those two girls. It's pretty raw."

"Figured it had to be something like that. Okay, here's how it's gonna work. I've got cameras in a few places. If I see a bunch of black Suburbans, police, anything like that, I off these two and split, take my chances.

"At 10:00 a.m. tomorrow, you're going to turn left off U.S. 95 exactly 34.6 miles northwest of Tonopah to a place called Silver Peak on road number 265. I'll have eyes on that intersection. Be there right at ten, not before, not after. If I see anyone but you in that red Sequoia, the girls die right then and I'm gone.

"Fifteen point two miles south on 265 you'll see a dirt track to the right that goes up into the Silver Peak Range. Four miles up that track it forks. Take the left-hand fork and follow it into the hills about sixteen miles. It'll wind all over but no more forks. Twenty miles from 265 you'll see a cabin in a clearing. End of the line. Stop at a log across the trail about a hundred feet from the cabin and get out.

"Here's where it gets interesting, dude. Now we'll see how much you love your cute little wife. You get out of that SUV and strip, and

I mean all the way down to bare metal, no jockeys, not even socks. There's not going to be any pepper spray in the back waistband of your underwear, no weapons, no wire, nothing but that flash drive in your left hand or I'll blow you away. I'll be in the doorway. The girls will be in the cabin in handcuffs, hand and foot. I'll have a .454 Casull revolver with a seven-and-a-half-inch barrel aimed at you as you walk toward me. If I see a weapon or anyone but you, you die and those girls get a bullet in the head that would stop a grizzly in its tracks. Try anything at all and I'll put a hole in you big enough to put your fist through. Is all of that clear enough, Sally?"

"Yes." I was starting to really hate that *Sally* shit.

"Want me to repeat any of it?"

"No. But why ten in the morning?"

"Light, dude. I'll have you live on camera, uplinked to satellite, down to my sat phone. I've got several cameras set up on the road in. You'll never see them. If I get a hint of anyone headed my way but you, I will—"

"I get it."

"If you're thinking of coming early, or sending in the troops, say at three in the morning, the girls and I won't be at the cabin and you'll never see them again until you ID them in a morgue. Got that?"

"Yes."

"I found that tracker on my Lexus. Don't try anything funny like that again. And don't expect to see that Lexus up at the cabin. I'm in a different ride now."

"I want to hear Lucy's voice. I want to be sure she's all right."

Fifteen seconds of silence, then Lucy said, "Mort, we—Harper and I—were in the motel room and—"

Then she was gone. Kyle said, "She's fine, Sally. You aren't going to talk with her again so don't ask. Now hold up your right hand and some fingers."

"How many fingers?"

"Your choice. Surprise me."

I held up two, index and little, and slowly rotated my wrist since I didn't know where the camera was.

"Two," Kyle said. "Pointing finger and little finger. I've got you on HD video, friend. As I will tomorrow when all of this is going to go as smooth as silk, won't it?"

I lowered my hand. "Yes."

"Good deal. You and I aren't going to talk again. Got any last-minute questions?"

"Why did Attorney General Leeman have to die?"

"Everyone dies sometime."

"That's not an answer."

Another moment of silence. "Those two idiot girls sent a copy of the video to the lieutenant governor, Sylvia Haas, demanding a million bucks. Half a mil each. One of the girls got cold feet and chickened out. Before Haas had a chance to respond to their demand, the girl sent a copy of the video to the attorney general, probably to get the cops all over Haas's husband. Leeman didn't tell anyone before confronting Sylvia in private. Big mistake. An even bigger mistake was telling Sylvia she'd given a copy of the video to someone for safekeeping. She thought that would keep her safe. She didn't say who she gave it to, but she told Sylvia it was someone she trusted. Sylvia called me while Leeman was still at her house, told me to fix it. I got over there right away, got Leeman out of there. Jake and me went to work on her the next day. We might've gotten more than we did and avoided a whole lot of trouble except she died suddenly when Jake was waterboarding her. It might have been a heart attack. I think he let a session go on too long. Jake wasn't always in control and he liked waterboarding. Leeman died shortly after hinting she'd given a copy of the video to a family member. It shouldn't be hard for you to figure out how things went from there.

"You got two girls counting on you, Sally. Right now they're okay, but that could change. Bring that thumb drive tomorrow or the body count will go up by three—two girls and one dumb shit."

Then he was gone.

CHAPTER TWENTY-FOUR

FOR A MOMENT I stood there. Kyle could see me; see everything I did. Eerie feeling. But he didn't have eyes on all of Nevada, so it was time to get going, try to figure out what I could do about tomorrow.

I got in the Sequoia, backed out and headed north to Tonopah. Kyle thought he would get two million dollars, presumably from Sylvia Haas with whom he'd been having an affair. So much for love. In order to get the money, he had to come up with a video that I didn't have, so Harper, Lucy, and I weren't going to get out of this alive unless I came up with a plan. Even if I had the video and played it his way, I doubted that he would let us live. In fact, I was certain he wouldn't.

Driving to Tonopah, I considered my options, which were limited in the extreme. I had to strip naked as soon as I got out of the SUV at the cabin. I gave that some thought. A Casull .454 was a cannon, bigger than my "Dirty Harry" .44 Magnum. Kyle had placed cameras in a few locations on the way up to the cabin. The police or the FBI were not going to be any part of this nightmare. This would be all on me.

Shit.

I should've stuck it out with the IRS.

* * *

I hauled ass, reached Tonopah at 5:20. By the time I got there, I had
an idea. Not a great idea, not even a good idea, but something, a
glimmer, a shadow of an idea. The chances of it working were somewhere between terrible and zero.

But not quite zero, so I geared up.

My first stop was at a variety store that sold a little of everything,
like a Dollar Store. I looked around in a toy section and bought a
stuffed alligator, green and pink, two feet long, big toothy smile,
perfect cuddly toy for a kid three or four years old. And needles,
thread, an icepick, a pack of pink file cards, red ribbon, a black
marker, a flash drive, a small bottle of isopropyl alcohol.

At a hardware store I purchased copper wire, solder, a soldering
gun, a tube of super glue, a roll of clear packing tape, needle-nose
pliers, wire strippers, black electrical tape, several lengths of chain, a
four-pack of padlocks that used the same key, nylon rope. I didn't
know what I would need so I bought out the store.

I rented a room at the Mizpah Hotel using the David Peterson
credit card and ID.

I got the key for the room but didn't go up. No time. I filled the
SUV's tank at an Exxon station, downed a Red Bull, bought a pre-
packaged sandwich and bottled water, then headed for Ely on
Highway 6, the same road I was on when I'd come across Harper
five days ago.

Five days? It felt more like a month.

I called Ma on a burner when I was eight miles out of Tonopah. I
had to keep her out of this. I told her I'd found Lucy and we were
fine but tired, that we'd be back in Reno sometime tomorrow, if we
didn't decide to hit Vegas and get a suite, visit with Harper for a day
or two. If I'd told her what was really going on, she would've had a

coronary. She would've tried to save us somehow. I lost the signal twelve miles out of Tonopah, which was just as well.

I hustled, hit the straight sections at a hundred ten miles an hour, took the curves as fast as I could. At least the road was dry this time.

The internet gave the distance from Tonopah to Ely as 168 miles, a three-hour, seven-minute drive. I got to Ely in two hours forty-one minutes at 9:02, daylight starting to go. I filled the tank, picked up two sandwiches, another Red Bull, a bottle of NoDoz, and headed north to Wells.

I reached Wells at 10:40, stopped at mile marker 3 on the way in. I filled the tank at the Flying J station in Wells, then raced back to Ely, then on to Tonopah, worried sick about Lucy and Harper. I didn't want to think about what they might be going through.

The night was full of stars. I distracted myself with the thought that in a billion years the night would still be full of stars, but they wouldn't look the same. Stars slowly drift around. Polaris would be somewhere else. Orion would no longer look like Orion. We are specks of transient dust in an extremely slow whirlwind of cosmic debris, but we are important. Lucy is worth more than all the visible stars in the sky. Much more. I would trade every last one of them to save her.

I went over what I had to do, kept looking for ways to better my odds but didn't come up with much.

I arrived in Tonopah at 4:25 a.m., and hiked up to my room in the Mizpah Hotel. I went to work with the needle-nose pliers, wire, soldering gun, electrical tape, a knife, needle and thread. And I wrote a gift card and tied it to the stuffed alligator with red ribbon. When I got done, I could only hope it would work. I was betting our lives on it.

I crashed—after setting the alarm on my cell phone for 8:45 and calling the front desk, requesting a wake-up call for the same time. I had to be at the junction of 95 and 265 at ten. I couldn't afford to oversleep. I gave myself an hour and fifteen minutes to get there.

* * *

The call woke me at 8:44. I felt drugged, eyes grainy. The thought of Lucy in the hands of that maniac snapped my eyes open, catapulted me out of bed.

I took a cold shower to wake up further, dressed, went out to the Sequoia, drove it to a gas station and filled up, grabbed something to eat, bought two more Red Bulls and half a dozen bottles of water, a handful of Cliff bars.

Before leaving, I put my .44 Magnum in the back of the SUV where I could reach it by opening the tailgate. I tried to think about what might happen at the cabin. If Kyle intended to change the game and kill me on the spot I could try to duck and weave, get behind the SUV, open the back and trade bullets with him.

I hoped it wouldn't come to that. If it did, the girls would most likely be dead already.

But he wanted the video. He couldn't do anything to me until he knew I had it. That was my only hope.

I left town at 9:20, gave myself forty minutes to travel thirty-five miles. After thirty miles I slowed to fifty, kept an eye out for the turn. The ice pick was on the passenger seat beside me. The thought about what I was going to do with it made my armpits damp.

Before leaving Tonopah, I'd synchronized the time on my cell phone with the car's clock. I lost cell coverage a few miles before I reached 265. The car's clock showed 9:59 as I slowed for the turn. It read 10:00 as I pulled off 95. I reset the trip odometer to 0.0 then headed south to Silver Peak, taking the SUV up to sixty on a flat, empty paved road through the desert. The temperature on the dash registered 82 degrees.

When the odometer read 14, I started to watch for a dirt track off to the right. It appeared at 15.1 miles. Close enough. I turned and headed west into flat desert devoid of life, rolling hills a short way ahead, low mountains beyond that tinted bluish-green by low scrubby trees.

Four miles in, I came to a fork in the road, took the left fork, and kept going. Kyle might've placed a camera at that fork, so I went six more miles before I stopped and got out of the car.

This was the part I'd been dreading, but it was for Lucy so I turned off my brain and just did it. I removed my shirt, dipped the spike of the ice pick in alcohol, reached around behind my back with my left hand, pinched a roll of skin six inches below my right shoulder blade, took a deep breath, and, with my right hand, quickly shoved the ice pick to the left and slightly down through the fold of skin and out the other side.

I let out a yelp. *Shit,* that hurt! Tears came to my eyes. I blinked them away, felt blood on my fingers.

I took a deep breath, located where the ice pick had come out, then felt down and over about three inches, got hold of another fold of skin, and shoved the pick through that. Which also hurt like a son of a bitch.

I closed my eyes, felt rage at Kyle, happy at what had happened to Jake. The rage helped. Fuck these guys.

The pick was now in a human sheath, hidden behind my back. Kyle had told me I would have to remove all my clothes. When I did, I would be able to reach the handle of the ice pick with my right hand, pull it quickly, use it if he gave me any opportunity at all.

Putting my shirt back on was an exercise in pain. I'd planned for this, worn a shirt that buttoned up the front. The ice pick throbbed like a bad tooth. It hurt to move. I got back in the SUV gingerly and leaned forward to drive, keeping pressure off that sonofabitchin' pick.

I checked the transmitter Jake had taken off his belt at the Monroe Street house. He'd indicated it would fire the shaped charge on my truck's radiator. It had a small toggle switch on top, and a red button beneath a sliding safety cap. The shaped charge also had a switch on it. I'd turned it off to save the battery when I left the charge in the weeds south of Wells. I hoped it would work when I turned it back on, that the explosive would be waiting for a signal. I had no way to test it. I could only hope.

The track wound around the hills, over washboard ruts and axle-breaking trenches, through canyons, gaining elevation. Sagebrush gave way to pinyon pines, juniper, and an occasional bristlecone pine. I passed a handmade sign nailed to a tree that read *7,000 feet*. I kept bumping and thudding up the rocky trail.

Finally, the slope became less steep and I sensed that I was getting close. My heartbeat picked up, making me a little light-headed.

I took deep breaths, drank half a Red Bull, kept going. Then, around a bend I saw the cabin four hundred yards ahead, a low structure of dark wood in the sunlight.

I threw the switch on the shaped charge.

CHAPTER TWENTY-FIVE

I SLOWED TO ten miles an hour, kept going. No one was in sight. The place would have looked deserted but for the black Chevy Silverado parked to one side of the cabin. The place was old and weathered, built of pine logs, windows caked brown with dirt. A sparse pinyon forest surrounded the place on three sides.

Thirty yards from the cabin I stopped where a log had been dragged across the track, turned off the engine.

I waited a moment, unsure what to do, then the cabin door opened and a big guy came out in jeans, boots, a gray Ole Miss sweatshirt with the sleeves cut off, ball cap, dark glasses. He stood on a porch under a deep overhang, two steps up from the dusty yard. He had a huge revolver in a two-handed combat grip, aimed at me.

"Get out," he yelled.

I'd already palmed the transmitter in my left hand. I got the alligator from the passenger seat and climbed out. In Tonopah I'd tied a ribbon in a festive bow around the gator's neck. The ice pick was a wicked throbbing pain in my back. I tried to ignore it and move naturally.

"Strip," Kyle said. "Slow and easy, no sudden moves."

I set the alligator on the hood of the Sequoia, hoping Kyle was far enough away that he couldn't see what it was, wouldn't say anything about it.

He didn't. Yet.

I took off shoes, socks, pants, underwear, then peeled off the shirt without turning my back to him. I piled all the clothing on the hood of the SUV. I'd never before felt so naked and defenseless. He could put a bullet in me at any time. I might not hear it or feel it. I had the queasy feeling I wouldn't be alive in another minute. My lights could go out so fast I wouldn't know I was gone, but this was for Lucy. *And* Harper. Either of them was worth more than fifty of me.

"Where's the video?" Kyle called out. The air was still. His voice carried well.

"Got it with me."

"Then get on over here, Sally." He kept the gun aimed at my chest.

Sally again? One more reason to hate the shithead, as if I needed it.

I picked up the alligator and headed toward him. I slid the protective cover off the transmitter's *go* button.

"What've you got there, dude?"

I held up the gator. "Jake had it in the Suburban."

"Drop it."

I couldn't do that. I kept walking, kept him busy with a story. "It's got a card on it," I said. "He bought it for a kid named Katie, if you know who that is." Which he would; it was his niece in Sioux City.

He grunted.

Ten yards from him I said, "I taped the flash drive to the mouth of this thing." I held it so he could see it through the clear packing tape. "Flash drive has the video on it."

He held the gun on my chest. When I was four yards away, he said, "Stop right there, hoss. Chuck it up here."

Perfect.

I tossed it. He caught it left-handed, gun wavering as I took a half step to one side. I punched the transmit button.

Nothing.

I slid the toggle switch over, hit the button again, and there was a loud bang, like a cherry bomb going off. Kyle's left hand exploded in a spray of blood. Green and pink fluff billowed into the air.

His gun went off. The bullet dug into the dirt inches from my right foot, kicking dirt and gravel into my shin.

I charged him. He was staring at where his left hand used to be. His fingers were mostly intact, but they were dangling from his palm and wrist by bloody tendons. His thumb was lying on the deck at his feet. His forearm was shredded halfway to his elbow, radius and ulna shattered, blood gushing out of torn arteries.

He staggered backward and looked up as I kicked him in the chest, knocked him back against the cabin wall. I grabbed the wrist that held his gun, twisted the Casull out of his grip and yanked him off the porch, into the yard. He landed on his face. His shredded arm dug into the dirt, pumping blood. He rolled onto his back and tried to sit up. I kicked him in the forehead with the heel of my foot. His head slammed back into the dirt. I rapped his head with the barrel of the Casull, trying not to kill him.

He was out.

I couldn't have asked for more. I'd thought about what I would do if the shaped charge worked, if it fired in the right direction, disabled him but didn't kill him and I got him down. I wanted him alive, at least for a while.

I stripped off his belt and wrapped it twice around his left bicep, pulled it tight and found a hole in the belt that cut off the blood pumping from his left arm. He'd already lost a pint, maybe two.

He was still unconscious. I jogged to the Sequoia and got a six-foot length of chain and a padlock. I ran back to him and looped the chain twice around his ankles in a tight figure eight, then padlocked the chain in place. I tried to put the padlock key in a pocket, startled to find I was still naked. I was full of adrenaline, so focused on getting him down and making certain he was going to stay down, that I had tunnel vision. Lucy, however, never left my thoughts. I had to get to her, but I had to deal with Kyle first.

I searched his pockets and came up with a cell phone, a deadly sharp CRKT knife, keys for the Silverado, keys for handcuffs, a wallet. I left him on his back in the dirt and took everything into the cabin, including his revolver.

The interior was dim after the bright sun outside. For a moment I was almost blind, then I saw a wooden table, a few chairs, a doorway right of center in the opposite wall.

"Lucy!"

I heard a muffled yell.

In the back room I found her and Harper handcuffed, gagged, tied to the iron frame of a bed on an old mattress that looked as if it had served as a nest to mice for years.

I took the duct tape off Lucy's and Harper's mouths.

"Are you okay?" I asked Lucy.

"Yes. Is he dead?"

"Not yet. But he's hurting."

"I heard a loud bang and a gunshot, Mort."

"I'm fine. He missed me. He wasn't able to aim with both hands." I was almost sorry I'd said that. Almost.

"If he's not dead, then leave us here. Make sure he's not gonna come after us again."

"I'm sure, Luce. He's not—"

"I mean *really* sure, Mort. We'll be okay for another minute or two."

"Are you sure you don't—?"

"*Go!* Kill him if you have to."

I went. Lucy was still tough, still a fighter. She had her priorities straight.

Outside, Kyle was conscious and trying to sit up, not doing very well with only one operational arm and his feet chained together.

I kept out of his reach and assessed the situation for a moment. Handcuffs wouldn't work on him.

He glared at me through his agony, but even SEALs lose gravitas when they lose an arm. He sank back and lay in the dirt. "Fuck," he groaned. "Shaped charge?"

"Jake put it on the radiator of my truck in Ely. I found it, thought something like that might be useful so I kept it. I would thank him, if he weren't a vegetable."

"A vegetable?"

"He waterboarded Lucy," I said harshly. "She felt like she was dying, so I didn't try to stop it when his air got cut off long enough to turn him into a turnip for the rest of his miserable life. He'll be wearing diapers and having his ass wiped for him until he's gone."

"Aw, fuck." His eyes sought mine. "What about me?"

"What *about* you, *Sally*?"

His eyes blazed for half a second. Guess he didn't like being called Sally any more than I did. But the fire didn't last. He said, "*Whatever you do, don't do to me what you did to Jake. Kill me first.*"

"I'll think about it. Right now, I'll try to keep you from bleeding to death and make *damn* sure you can't cause any more trouble."

His right arm was still free and unhurt. Other than that, he wasn't a threat. I cut a length of parachute cord off a fifty-foot skein, tied the middle of the cord around Kyle's right wrist in a square knot, snugged his wrist tight against his neck and looped the ends of the cord around either side of his neck, tied them off on the far side where he had no hope of reaching the knot with his one good hand.

I stood up and looked down at him. His left hand was splintered bone and hamburger, fingers all but severed and lying in the dirt, still held to his wrist by tendons.

"Stay down," I said. "Try to get up and I'll cut off your air. You and brother Jake can share a minimum-wage nurse named Bennie for the next forty years."

He wasn't going anywhere and I'd spent too long with him. I wanted to get Lucy and Harper off that filthy mattress and out of the cabin.

I got them out of their cuffs, cut the rope holding them to the bed frame, helped them to their feet. They were in shorts and tank tops, what they were wearing when Kyle grabbed them at the Goldfield Inn.

Lucy dragged me to the front door and onto the porch. She wanted to see Kyle, make sure he wasn't about to rise up and come after us again. She stopped dead when she saw him with his ankles chained, one hand tied to his neck, the other hand a bloody stump. He wasn't going anywhere.

She turned and hugged me, broke down into wracking sobs. "He was going to kill you and then us," she wailed. She choked, couldn't say anything more. Then Harper got in on the crying and the hug.

Two gorgeous girls, hugging naked me—a private eye tableau that would make Mike Hammer weep. It lasted a full minute, which would've been perfect except that they hadn't showered in almost two days and they had that *eau de mattress* smell.

But I toughed it out, let them cling.

* * *

Somewhere in mid-hug, Lucy jumped away as if I'd turned into a vampire bat. "What's on your *back*!"

"What? Oh, jeez, I forgot."

She spun me around, then let out a cry of horror and shock. I reached back, pulled the ice pick out of its sheath—me. I'd forgotten it. I had been so awash in adrenaline I hadn't felt it from the time I'd headed toward Kyle while he had that big-ass revolver aimed at my chest.

"Mort! What the *hell*? That's an *ice pick*!"

"I know. He said he'd kill me and both of you if he saw a weapon of any kind. He told me to strip. *All* the way. I had no place to hide anything except behind me. My hands had to be visible. This was a last resort."

"You . . . you stabbed yourself?"

I shrugged. "I couldn't think of any other way to hide it, cupcake. Like I said, last resort. I'm not going to make it a habit with, you know, kitchen utensils in general."

Harper stared at me. "Omigod, Mort."

I shrugged again. "I didn't have to use it. Sort of too bad, really, when you think about it."

By then I had a girl on either side of me, each with an arm around my waist. They appeared to remember Kyle at the same time. Lucy stared at me. "How did you *do* that? I mean, his hand, or arm, or whatever that is, it's all blood and . . . torn up."

"I don't mean to be a prude," I said, "but before we get into that since it'll take a while, how about I put on some clothes?"

"You don't *have* to be a prude," Harper said. She gave Lucy a little grin. "He doesn't, does he?"

Lucy smiled at me. "Don't think so. It's warm out here and you could use a bit of sun, Mort. Vitamin D?"

"Ha ha," I said. "You two are a riot. Stay here, watch this guy. Make sure he doesn't jump up and run." Kyle glared at me. He wanted to say something but held it in. I walked over to the Sequoia. It wasn't easy to affect a jaunty amble with two broads staring at my naked ass. Prude that I am, I got dressed, happy to be back in clothes.

I came back with my cell phone, then went into the cabin and unloaded Kyle's wallet. I found driver's licenses and credit cards for Kyle Anza and a George Crowley. The Crowley ID had Kyle's picture on it. Outside, I crouched in front of him and said, "How's the arm, chief?"

His mouth tightened, but he remained silent.

"Hurts a little, huh?" I said. "I'm not surprised. Pain is nature's way of telling you something isn't right. I've got a first aid kit in the car. I might get you some aspirin, but not yet.

"So here's how it's gonna work. I'm going to video you telling the three of us who hired you to kidnap those high school girls and why, who killed the attorney general and that lawyer, Eystad. You're going to tell us who decided what and why. I'll send the video to a few law enforcement agencies and let them fight over who will claim the credit for breaking the case wide open. You're also going to tell the world how you kidnapped Lucy and Harper and why you took them up here, handcuffed them and tied them to that bed, what you intended to do with them and to me after you got your hands on the video. You are going to ensure that if you survive, you will spend the rest of your pathetic life in prison."

His look turned defiant. "And if I don't? What? I don't get aspirin?"

I smiled. Probably not a very nice smile. "You will end up drooling in diapers like Jake. I'm not in the mood to screw around with you. You'll do it or fifteen minutes from now you won't know your own name."

He sagged, which wasn't easy on his back. It was more like he closed his eyes and deflated.

"Whatever," he breathed. "What the fuck ever, man."

* * *

Lucy cleaned my ice pick wounds and applied liberal gobs of Polysporin to the punctures before covering them with gauze and tape. Kyle got seven aspirins, probably less medical care than he would've received if he'd crawled into an emergency room with a shredded forearm, thumb gone, fingers hanging on by gory threads. I wasn't sure about the aspirin. I think I heard somewhere that it inhibits clotting, which didn't seem optimal in his condition, not that I'm an expert in things like that. But he chucked them down and swallowed them dry, so I guess his arm was bothering him. Therefore, *c'est la vie* about a possible clotting problem.

I propped him against a porch post and untied his one good hand, thinking it would look too much like coercion on video if he had a hand awkwardly bound to his neck. He was still strong, no telling what he could do with one hand, so all of us kept out of reach. I got his confession on my cell phone. Lucy got a backup video on Kyle's phone. Harper acted as a witness.

It took twenty minutes to get most of it down. I didn't know how it might be received by a district attorney who would have to hand down an indictment, and the video would probably still be *he said, she said*, but I didn't think Lieutenant Governor Sylvia Haas would find Kyle's story amusing. This was the kind of lever that would move her universe. Now that the Anzas were out of play, I wanted to get the power-hungry bitch who'd hired them.

It was time to get out of there, time to decide what to do with Kyle. I went through his stuff in the Silverado: food, bottled water, clothes, rope, wire, flex cuffs, chain, padlocks, Taser, knives. He'd brought along a tomahawk, same model as Jake's. A shovel—to bury bodies? A two-gallon can of gasoline—for cremations? Butane lighters, a G20 Glock, a .30-06 rifle, enough ammunition for both the handgun and rifle to fight a war.

Lucy and Harper grabbed bottles of water and lunged at the food, power bars of various kinds.

"He didn't feed us or give us anything to drink," Lucy said. "He said there was no point, so we knew he was going to kill us. *And* you." She looked weepy as she said it. "You still haven't said how you did that to his hand and arm."

"Judo," I replied.

She hit my arm. "Jerk." Then she kissed me.

"Tell you later," I said. "Let's get out of here." I looked at Kyle and hefted the Glock. "Always wanted one of these. Okay if I borrow it?"

Other than giving me a savage yet wary look, he didn't respond.

"Thanks," I said. "Got two of 'em now. I'll also borrow your truck, unless you have some objection."

Still no response, other than a homicidal stare. Then he said, "There's a hand axe in the truck. I need it."

"Not happenin', chief."

"I'll give it back. I need it, dude, half a minute, that's all. With these chains on my feet, I ain't coming after you. Keep a gun on me if you're all a-scared."

I shrugged. I had to see what he was up to. Might be a suicide in the offing, which would solve a problem.

"By hand axe, do you mean the tomahawk?" I asked.

His smile was part grimace. "You got that from Jake, didn't you? That it's called a tomahawk."

"Yup. Turns out he didn't care for the way it was used on him. Nor did your idiot nephew Joe."

I got the weapon, set it on the porch where he could reach it with his good hand. Lucy and Harper stood ten feet away. Lucy had my

.44 aimed at Kyle's chest. I pointed the Glock at his head, put light pressure on the trigger.

He picked up the tomahawk, flopped his ruined arm on the wooden porch, and chopped the tendons holding his ruined fingers to his shattered wrist. It took four hits to get them all. He tossed the tomahawk at my feet, picked up his fingers and flung them at the two girls. They landed in the dirt, bounced and tumbled, came to rest curled as if trying to get a grip on something.

"Oh, *ugh*," Lucy said, stepping to one side.

"Yours if you want 'em," Kyle said. His grin was that of a demonic jack-o'-lantern. "I'm done with 'em."

Lucy and Harper backed away.

I put the tomahawk back in his truck, got in, backed the Silverado in a half circle and left it aimed downhill.

"Think you can drive this thing?" I asked Harper. "It's a hell of a rough trail out of here."

"Three tires and I'd sit on your lap while you drove. But it has all four so I'll manage." A glint of humor was in her eyes. Good for her. She wasn't as tough as Lucy, but she wasn't just another pretty face, either.

"Okey-doke then," I said. "Let's saddle up."

She gave Kyle one last look then climbed up into his pickup. Lucy got in the passenger side of the Sequoia.

Kyle called out to me, "You're not gonna leave me here with my feet chained like this, are you?"

I strode over to him. "What I *want* to do is put a bullet in your head, drag you into the trees and leave you for whatever might have a use for your carcass."

He blinked, then said, "But?"

"But that's too good for you. And I'm not sure it's up to me to decide something like that, so I'm not going to do anything with you. Or *to* you." I glanced at his ruined arm. "Anything more, that is."

Hope flared in his eyes. "Nothing?"

"I'll release your ankles, that's all. Which is more than I *should* do, but I'm a nice guy."

"You're going to leave me up here, twenty miles from anywhere. That's nice?"

"I'm going to leave you in God's hands. Whatever He wants to do with you is entirely up to Him, not me."

"God." He chuckled darkly. "There is no God, man. If there was, I couldn't have done the things I did."

"Huh. Same thing the Schutzstaffel said in Germany in 1941 when they were running the chambers. Bet they're sorry about that now. I imagine you will be too."

I removed the padlock holding the chain around his ankles, but left the chain in place. He could unwind it in a matter of seconds. I left the belt tight around his left bicep. Gangrene would set in soon if it hadn't already. If the belt were removed, he might bleed out quickly. He had several ways to die. Medically speaking, he was in a bad way—not that I felt it was my fault. He'd made his bed; therefore, he could lie in it and good luck.

I set two bottles of water on the porch nearby. "You're a resourceful guy. I'm sure you'll figure out how to open a bottle one-handed."

"Fuck you, dude." He sounded weary. I tend to have that effect on people. It's a knack.

Speaking of weary, he was having that effect on me. I smiled and said, "Years ago one of my uncles had the lead of a horse wrapped around a finger when the horse reared up. The rope snapped off the end of the finger on his left hand. Uncle Charlie was a nice enough guy, but a hell of an independent cuss. He wouldn't let his wife tie his shoes. He did it one-handed, got surprisingly adept at it too, until he got the use of his left hand again."

"Shit, dude. What's the point?"

I reached down and untied his right bootlace. "If my uncle could do it, so can you. It'll give you something to do before you start walking—if you decide to do that. Or you can let the laces flap around. If so, try not to trip and fall on that bad arm. That'd hurt."

He glared at me. "Asshole. You could at least leave me a little food."

"I'll leave you with as much as you gave the girls last night and this morning. I would leave you that much water too, but let's give God a chance."

I headed toward the Sequoia, then turned and looked back. "If I see you again, I'll have to kill you—unless it's in a courtroom. Otherwise, God or the state will take care of you from here on out. Have a nice day."

CHAPTER TWENTY-SIX

KYLE WAS STAGGERING to his feet when I last saw him in the rearview. I had a last-minute thought that I should go back and rid the world of him, like I would a rattlesnake in a kid's playground, but the Silverado blocked my view, the moment passed, and he was gone.

Lucy leaned back and closed her eyes. "You are my all-time hero," she said softly.

"All-time, huh?"

"Now, yeah. When I was in high school it was Justin Timberlake—not sure why, but you're in the lead now."

"Cool beans."

Lucy turned slightly in her seat. "She's sort of in love with you, you know."

"Timberlake? He's a she? Since when?"

"Harper, silly."

I didn't know what to say to that. It felt like the kind of trap I could escape only by gnawing off my foot.

"Just saying," Lucy said, throwing me a life preserver. "It's not a surprise. I was smitten with you the moment I first saw you, so I get it."

"Smitten, huh?"

She smiled. "I'm still quite fond of you. You're sort of a likeable guy. I just wish you weren't into piercing yourself. I've never found that attractive. Also, I've never heard of anyone using an ice pick before. That's pretty extreme."

"I'll keep it in mind."

"Please do." She was quiet for a moment, then, "You didn't kill him back there. Kyle."

"I've had enough of that, Luce."

"You're referring to that woman, what's-her-name? In Paris."

"Julia. She filled my quota for this lifetime."

Lucy bit her upper lip. "What happened with Jake? He makes me nervous. You said he's not dead."

"You really want to know?"

She let out a heavy breath. "Yes and no. But he *is* still alive, isn't he?"

"Technically. He's breathing, but that's about all."

She thought about that, then left it alone. "What about Kyle's arm? How'd you do that?"

I reminded her of the shaped charge I'd found and left at the side of the road. Then I told her about the drive last night to Wells and back, the soldering gun and wire I used to reconnect the wires I'd clipped to deactivate the charge, hoping like hell it would still work, sewing it into the toy alligator, telling Kyle that Jake bought the gator for a girl named Katie, their niece in Sioux City, tossing it to Kyle, blowing off his left hand and part of his arm.

When I was finished, she was quiet for a moment. "He got what he deserved," she said at last. "It would've been better if he'd caught it in his teeth, then I wouldn't still be worried. I think you should've killed him."

"He's not going to be a problem, Luce."

"Even so."

* * *

The trail down was a washboard of ruts and rocks that wanted to flatten tires, break axles. Deep grooves in the track caused the Sequoia to bottom out in places. We took it slow. I kept an eye on Harper in the Silverado. I imagined Kyle hiking downhill behind us, dehydrated and weak from blood loss, hurting. Strong guy, but I gave him no better than a fifty-fifty chance of surviving the trip. He was truly in God's hands. I hoped God wanted him.

Two and a half hours of careful driving got us down to the Silver Peak road. I was beat. Once we were on paved road, I could barely keep my eyes open. Adrenaline only lasts so long and the trip last night to Wells and back had finally caught up to me. Kyle had taken the girls up to the cabin after he called me when I was in Goldfield. Lucy and Harper had slept much of the night in the back room of the cabin. She wasn't tired, so she and I traded places.

She drove the seventy-some miles back to Goldfield where Kyle had left her Mustang and Harper's Corolla. We arrived at the inn at 5:15 that afternoon. Their cars were still there. I told Harper to park the Silverado well off to one side. We unloaded it, put everything in the back of the Sequoia. I decided to keep the tomahawk, maybe mount it on a wall in my den as a souvenir, like the bear trap Dustin Hoffman had on the wall in *Straw Dogs*.

The Silverado was a rental. Papers in the glove box showed it was rented by George Crowley using the fake ID I'd seen in Kyle's wallet. I'd left his wallet in the cabin. If he didn't make it out of the hills, his body—or skeleton—would be easier to identify if he had the wallet with him. It might save a county sheriff's department a day or two of grunt work, trying to run it down, but they would have to figure out which of the two he was: Anza or Crowley. But dead is dead, so that was mostly a matter of dotting i's and crossing t's, notifying next of kin. He still had teeth, and fingerprints on one hand. That should do it.

From Goldfield we caravanned north to Tonopah, I in the Sequoia, Lucy in her Mustang, Harper in her Toyota. Before we left Goldfield, Harper said, "I feel like I'm sort of a fifth wheel now. I should probably go back to Vegas."

"Don't," Lucy said. "We don't know if it's safe yet. We got Jake and Kyle, but Sylvia Haas is still out there and we don't know what that psycho bitch might be up to."

"Sylvia Haas?" Harper asked.

I'd told Lucy about the lieutenant governor on the way down the mountain, but Harper hadn't heard that part of the story yet. I filled her in, which took a few minutes.

"So," Lucy said when I was finished. "Don't go back to Vegas, okay? You should stay with Mort and me. We've got a spare room in our house."

I didn't know if hanging around Lucy and me would be safer, but I didn't say anything. Being the one with the testosterone, I thought I'd better let the gals work out the visiting arrangements and the shower schedule.

Harper looked at me. "What do you think?"

Well, shit. So much for them working it out. "I'm with Lucy," I said. That oughta be safe.

Evidently it was. We arrived in Tonopah at 5:50, and parked our vehicles in the back lot at the Mizpah Hotel, got two rooms on the third floor, and settled in.

I called Ma on a burner, put her on speaker.

"Hola, Ma," I said.

"Hola, yourself. Where the *fuck* are you? I been trying to reach you all fuckin' day after that fuckin' call you made last night. You said you'd be back in Reno today."

"Good work, Ma. You used the f-word three times."

"Damn straight, boyo, now answer the question."

"Been traveling. I couldn't get a signal on my phone. Lucy and Harper are with me. We're fine, except we could use showers, clean clothes, delousing, that sort of thing."

"Well, thank goodness, except for that last item. And why do you need any of that? What've you been up to?"

"We dispatched Jake's brother, Kyle. Sort of."

"Dispatched? Sort of? How? What's that mean? And where the *hell* are you, if it's not a military secret?"

"Tonopah. Mizpah Hotel. Lucy and I have room 301, and Harper's in 303 across the hall."

"And *Kyle*, boyo?"

"Dunno. God's in charge now."

"Shit. Talkin' with you is like talkin' with a teenager on cough medicine."

"Ouch, Ma." I smiled at Lucy. "We're about to upload a video to your special email, not the business one."

"What's on it?"

"Kyle's confession. He names names. It's kinda long so it'll take a while. Lucy will get it going." I nodded to her and she punched buttons to start the upload.

"What'll I do with it?" Ma asked.

"Whatever you think is right after you see it. It might go to RPD or the FBI. Not sure about a TV affiliate yet. You might want to run that past a lawyer. It'd also be amusing to send it to Sylvia Haas—if you can find a way to do that without her knowing who sent it. See if your hacker can route it through Botswana or Muskogee, either one."

"Sylvia Haas. Oh, Lord. From what it sounds like you got, that'll set off fireworks."

"Hope so. Anyway, we're safe, grungy, and hungry. If you need us, call me on this burner."

"Take care, Mort."

She sounded sincere. And worried, which I took to be a crack in her armor. Scary. "Will do, Ma. I'll tell you about Kyle later, but he's no longer a problem."

I ended the call. A minute later I was in a shower and I wasn't alone because water is a valuable resource, not to be wasted, especially in the desert.

The video continued to upload.

CHAPTER TWENTY-SEVEN

AT 9:40, KYLE Anza stumbled out of the hills and onto the Silver Peak road. A half moon was up, illuminating the desert in an eerie bluish-silver glow. Kyle looked north and south at the empty road, then his legs gave out. He landed on his ass in spiky weeds on the verge and toppled onto his back, then stared up at the stars.

"He said, she said," he whispered to the dark. "Be a lot better if *she* doesn't." He chuckled almost silently.

* * *

Twenty-five minutes later, he heard the sound of an engine. Headlights appeared, coming from the north. He staggered to his feet and flagged down an ancient pickup, driven by a guy in his seventies, Arnold Becker. Like most of the folks living in Silver Peak, Becker was half hermit. He'd had his fill of city life, didn't matter which city. They were all the same: traffic and gangs, pollution, noise, fifty kinds of mayhem. He'd escaped from Long Beach sixteen years ago and put his home maintenance skills to good use, eking out a meager but satisfying living in Silver Peak.

Becker slowed, pinning Kyle in his headlights. He rolled down a window and stopped as Kyle came around the far side of the truck, unsteady on his feet.

"Ho-*ly* smoke," Becker said. "You hurt, son? I mean, that looks bad. *Real* bad."

"Rolled my truck up in the hills," Kyle said, having prepared a story in advance. "It pinned my hand against a rock, crushed the palm. I had to cut it off above the wrist with a pocket knife to get myself free."

"Son of a gun. Second time I've heard about someone doing something like that." He leaned over and opened the passenger-side door. "C'mon, get in."

Kyle got into the truck, noting that it was a Dodge, hand-painted a vile pumpkin orange, complete with brushstrokes. He shut the door.

Becker peered at Kyle's arm. "I better get you to a hospital right away. Nearest one's in Tonopah. They got a medical center of some kind there. They might put you on one of them helicopter flights to Vegas."

"How about you take me into Silver Peak instead."

"Got no kind of a medical place there, son."

"Doesn't matter. Right now, I need food and water. I'll pay you for it. I'll get help tomorrow."

Arnold stared at him. "You sure 'bout that? I've seen guys hurt before, but nothin' like that."

"I'm sure."

Arnold shook his head. "Up to you, I reckon. Me, I'd want a doctor real bad." He put the truck in gear and took off south to Silver Peak, nine miles away.

CHAPTER TWENTY-EIGHT

AFTER BREAKFAST THE next morning, Lucy, Harper, and I drove our cars back to Reno. We arrived at the Washington Street house where Lucy and I live at 1:35 p.m. The house used to be Jeri's. Jeri DiFrazzia was my fiancée, my love, and my mentor in the art of investigation two years ago, murdered back then by an evil woman named Julia. Jeri ran her investigation business out of the house. It had two floors, gables, dormer windows, a home gym, covered front entrance two steps up from the front yard, five hundred feet from the Truckee River and a pedestrian and bike path where Lucy and I regularly took ten-mile jogs.

I stashed the stuff I'd removed from Kyle's truck in the detached garage—except for the handguns and the .30-06 rifle. I'd never fired a Casull .454 revolver before. I was looking forward to it. I locked the firearms in a gun safe Lucy's father bought us last year. I didn't need the Sequoia any longer, so Lucy and Harper followed along in Lucy's Mustang as I returned it to Avis.

"Where to?" Lucy asked when we stood outside in the Avis parking lot, temperature in the high nineties.

"Ma's," I said. "Let's see what's going on, make sure she's okay and doesn't need us for anything right away."

Turns out I hadn't thought that through all the way to the endgame, not that it would've mattered in the long run. Ma was at her computer when we went in. Lucy made a beeline to the old Coke ad. She flipped it out of the way to reveal the poster of my nudie picture at the WNBR a year and a half ago.

"Cool," Harper said. "Except for the red body paint, he hasn't changed any that I can see—I mean, that I *saw*."

That got a giggle from Lucy and a bawdy cackle from Ma. I thought about heading out to get a beer somewhere, let the three of them settle down.

Ma still hadn't heard what had happened in the past two days. Lucy told her the story—Kyle capturing her and Harper, taking them into the hills near Silver Peak, that he was going to kill them once he got his hands on a copy of the video the two teenage girls had made. By then, Ma was staring daggers at me. She'd figured out the timing.

"You called me *two nights* ago, boyo, and didn't say one *flippin'* word about these two being kidnapped."

"I didn't want to upset you or make you worry."

"You also called me yesterday evening."

"Uh-huh. I kind of remember that."

She glared at me. "You didn't tell me Lucy and Harper had been kidnapped then *either*."

"Must've slipped my mind. You know how it is with Alzheimer's. Means you only need one novel, one DVD."

"Clean out your desk. You are *so* damn fired, Mort."

"I am . . . *decimated*, Ma."

She glared at me, then faced Lucy. "You and Harper were kidnapped? Then what? I mean, here you are. You're not hurt? Either of you?"

"No. Mort showed up and saved us." She didn't get a chance to elaborate because Ma grabbed her in a hug, then hugged Harper. Then, surprise, I got one too. I usually get left out. "Good job," Ma whispered in my ear.

"That mean I'm not fired?"

"Not necessarily." She backed off and gave me a hard look. "I asked you yesterday if Kyle was dead. Is he?"

"Still don't know, Ma."

"Why the hell *don't* you?"

"It's sort of a long story. How about we catch you up on everything after we shower, change into clean clothes? We only stopped by to say howdy and get hugs. Let's meet up in the Green Room in an hour, maybe a little longer, say three thirty, get all of us caught up on events."

"Booze," she said. "Sounds good. It'll be a mite early for that, but I'll make an exception this time."

Knew she would.

* * *

Back at our house, we got Harper settled into a spare bedroom on the second floor. Freshen-up showers for one and all, clean clothes, a tour of the house, the yard, a walk around the block to stretch our legs and give Harper a feeling for the neighborhood, then we took Lucy's Mustang to the Golden Goose. The girls wore killer sheath dresses, Lucy in black, Harper in emerald green, both of them with lots of leg showing through thigh-high splits. The dresses were Lucy's. She and Harper looked like sisters. I had on black jeans and a white linen Guayabera shirt.

I parked on the fourth floor of the parking garage, and we walked down two flights and across the skyway to the Goose. We rode the escalator to the first floor and strolled through the moronic siren song of a thousand slot machines, the girls turning dozens of heads as they went. We finally got to the Green Room, tucked far enough into a corner of the casino that it was still one of Reno's best kept secrets. We hoped it would stay that way.

By the time Ma arrived, the girls had daiquiris in front of them and were draining them through red straws as thin as hypodermic needles. I had an icy bottle of Pete's Wicked Ale, first one since Harper and I were at the Red Lion in Elko. We were perched on stools at the bar under the eerie green track lighting with a television above the bar running a soap opera designed, apparently, to lower IQs.

Ma was in Reebok jogging shoes, black slacks, and a blue shirt. She was still on a walking kick, averaging four miles a day. She had lost fifteen pounds in the year since she'd started the routine. And she'd given up the Camels, but she was vaping which was weird, especially when she gave off a subtle scent of pineapple.

Traci Ellis was the lone bartender that afternoon. She was twenty-six, gorgeous, slender but curvy, sporting her usual amount of cleavage. Against all odds, she was Patrick O'Roarke's fiancée—O'Roarke being the evening bartender five days a week, forty-seven years old, six-five, Yosemite Sam moustache, and humorless this past year when it came to honoring well-deserved free-drink coupons.

Traci slid a double shot of bourbon in front of Ma, planted her elbows on the bar, stuck her face a foot from mine, and said, "You're lookin' good, kiddo."

"Kiddo is my word, kiddo. Hands off."

"Yeah," Lucy said, "hands off." She said it with a smile, aware that Traci was an unrepentant flirt, but harmless as a golden retriever puppy since flirting was all she ever did. She was an expert at it, however. I thought her tip income would be impressive. I would have to ask O'Roarke if she had eclipsed him as the household's senior breadwinner.

Harper gave me a sidelong look after Traci moved on to a guy farther down the bar. "You've had practice in the art of dealing with a certain kind of woman," she said.

"Yes, I have."

"Explains a lot, actually."

"You mean that night at Olivia's?"

"That's right." She bumped my shoulder with hers, a friendly gesture—and still flirty.

The soap opera ended with someone's nephew coming in French doors and finding a fifty-something vamp in the arms of a twenty-something shirtless stud who was the husband of the nephew's sister. Maybe. I could've been wrong about that because my IQ is well above sixty.

"How about we get a table and talk?" I said.

"'Bout time," Ma replied. She grabbed her drink and stood up. "I want to know what you did about Kyle."

We gathered around a table twenty-five feet from the nearest people in the place, two women wearing skirts and silk blouses, high heels kicked off, laughing raucously and a bit drunkenly about their husbands.

Ma leaned closer to me. "Okay, boyo, where the hell is Elrood Wintergarden? How's that comin' along?"

"Ha ha, Ma. Who's Elrood?"

She smiled. "I probably oughta give that to one of our competitors. I'm thinkin' Yancy Hubbard."

"I would. Those two deserve each other."

She chortled, then got serious. "Early this morning I had Jerry send that video to Sylvia Haas." Jerry Westfall was her most competent hacker, barely nineteen years old, sworn to secrecy with one of Ma's death threats hanging over his head. He was paid enough to keep his mouth shut. So far he had, which was unusual considering his age.

"And?" Lucy said.

"And nothin'. Yet. My guess is she's sweating bullets about now. She can't know exactly where the video of Kyle's confession came from, though she oughta be able to guess in a general way. She might be looking at us. But I ain't heard nothing and it's been eight hours." Ma peered at me. "I still want to know how you got him to say all that. It looked like he was hurting some."

"Worse than you know, Ma," I said. We'd kept his arm out of the videos. I told her about the shaped charge on the radiator, the night trip to Wells, the toy alligator, the whole nine yards. It was the first Harper had heard about it in that much detail, especially the stuffed gator in which I'd hidden the explosive.

"Wow," she said when I was done.

"Yeah, wow," Lucy said. "And he wasn't even wearing his cape and tights."

Harper smiled. "If I remember, he wasn't wearing anything for quite a while after he almost killed Kyle."

"Huh?" Ma grunted. "Did I miss somethin'?"

"Nothing important, Ma," I said.

Lucy stepped up to the plate. "Mort failed to mention that Kyle made him strip when he got to the cabin."

"Thanks, sweetheart," I growled.

She smiled as she sipped her drink. "You're welcome."

"Strip?" Ma said. "What's that mean? How far?"

"*All* the way. Buck naked. He wasn't even wearing flip-flops."

"Really?" Traci said. "Not even flip-flops? How did I miss out on that? Where *was* this? And *why*?"

Aw, jeez. It was dim in the place and she'd snuck up on us on little fairy feet in her dark outfit. Wasn't anyone keeping an eye out for that broad? She needed to drag a chain or wear a string of little flashing lights.

"It was sort of a weird deal," Lucy said, not missing a beat. "I'm still okay with this daiquiri, in case you're here about our drinks."

Everyone else was too, so Traci left. She looked back as she went and gave me a risqué wink.

"*Buck* naked," Ma said, getting things back on track.

"It was so he couldn't hide a weapon," Lucy told her. "Which he did anyway. An ice pick."

"Yeah? Where? Or don't I want to know?"

Aw, jeez.

Lucy described the ice pick holder. My back.

"Christ, Mort," Ma said. She stared at me, then put a motherly hand on my leg. "That musta hurt."

"It did. Still does, sorta. Do I get a bonus for that?"

She patted my leg a few times. "How's that?"

"Much better now, thanks. It's probably a good thing I didn't have to use that ice pick. I didn't get a chance to practice pulling it."

"But he was totally prepared," Lucy said. "He said the Boy Scout oath right after he took care of Kyle."

"Did not."

"So where's this Kyle character now?" Ma asked. I'd ended the story with his confession, didn't tell her how I'd left him.

I shrugged. "No idea." I told her I had unchained his feet, left him with two half-liters of water, no food, twenty miles up in the hills, low on blood, low on fingers.

"I would've turned out his lights," she said.

"That sounds good on paper, Ma. But it would've been one too many."

She thought about that. "Gotcha." She gave that a few more seconds, then shook her head. "I still would've."

"One too many?" Harper asked.

"Those two are always saying goofy things like that," Lucy told her. "How's your daiquiri?"

"Good."

"Mine too. We should have another one, get loose."

Right then, I heard the words "Lieutenant Governor Sylvia Haas." I whipped my head around. Lucy put a hand on my arm. She'd heard it too.

We stared at the TV from across the room. Breaking news. Ginger Haley, talking head for the NBC affiliate, was outdoors holding a microphone, squinting in the sunlight. A sprawling Spanish-style mansion was behind her, police cars with flashing red and blue lights, yellow crime scene tape keeping her from getting too close to the action.

". . . in what appears to be a murder-suicide. Ms. Haas and her husband, Carl Haas, an orthopedic surgeon here in Reno. They were discovered by Ms. Haas's brother and his wife at two fifty this afternoon. Early reports indicate that Ms. Haas and her husband died sometime between noon and 1:00 p.m. today." Ginger looked behind her, then faced the camera and shrugged, at a loss for what more to say about the Haases, which meant she wasn't likely to make it to the big time in Manhattan. Finally, she said, "We'll bring you more news as it comes in."

"Wowie," Lucy said. We all got up and headed for the bar like a school of fish, closer to the television.

Ginger must've been told to keep it going because she said, "Uh, this is the second major, um, upset in Nevada's government in the past couple of weeks. The first was the disappearance of Attorney General Annette Leeman a week or so ago. Leeman's body was discovered in the trunk of a car by Reno private investigator Mortimer Angel in eastern Nevada in the town of Ely, five days ago."

Traci Ellis touched my arm. "Nice goin', spitfire," she said, using O'Roarke's nursery-school name for me when I'd done good. "Your name rolls off Ginger's tongue like, well, like strawberry ice cream."

"Hush, girlie." Though I might have to ask about that strawberry ice cream thing at a later date, find out exactly what she meant and how it worked.

Ginger held an earbud closer to her ear. She nodded slightly, then said, "At this point there doesn't seem to be any connection between

Leeman's murder and the events in the Haases' residence." She listened to the earbud again, then said, "Oh, uh, there is, there might be, some sort of a video that"—she pressed the earbud closer and gazed into the camera lens—"that might pertain to this terrible event? No details right now, but we'll keep you informed as new information is made available." One more look behind her, then, "This is Ginger Haley in Reno for NBC News."

A commercial for Carnival Cruise Lines came on. They didn't show one of their ships ramming another in port, shredding a fantail, so it wasn't enough to keep us glued to the TV. We got up and headed back to our private table.

Quietly, Lucy said, "It sounds like she took that video kinda hard. Sylvia, I mean, not Ginger."

"Kinda," Harper replied. "Both of them, actually, but Sylvia got the worst of it."

"I always thought people in politics were book smart and dumb as turkeys in the rain," Ma said. "Especially U.S. senators if they've been in office more than two terms."

Sounded right to me, although I could think of a few representatives who would drown in a drizzle if they didn't have an aide to keep them from gawping up at the sky.

"Now what?" Lucy said to no one in particular.

"Now nothin'," Ma said. "This mess is cleaning itself up. The hag killed her husband for messing with those two young girls because it meant she's not gonna be vice president, at least not on this planet, *and* she would've had to deny Kyle's video, which she knew wouldn't work for long because more shit is gonna come out once people look harder. Now we sit tight. It's likely this thing will roll over the three of you pretty soon, RPD or the FBI, but it's not a crime to not report a crime when it happens to you and only you. You don't have to put yourself in the public's eye. Shouldn't have to, anyway. It might be a Fifth Amendment issue. Guess we'll find out. If not, I'll post your bail."

She looked at Lucy. "Anza kidnapped you and Harper, but if you don't want to press charges, that's up to you. All Mort did was save you, so they might be forced to pin an attaboy medal on his chest after they get through pissing and moaning—which they always do when they don't get the credit they think they deserve, even though they were sitting around the office eating doughnuts at the time. The state can bring its own charges—if Kyle makes it out of the hills alive and gets caught trying to sneak off to Uruguay or someplace south of El Paso. Which ain't likely if, like you said, he was losing essential fluids."

"Nice, Ma," I said.

She shrugged. "No tellin' what's gonna happen now. Too many ways it can go." She turned to me. "But you're fired, boyo. I'll give a statement to the media to that effect later. I don't want this 'cluster' hurtin' my business."

"Cluster, Ma? It's not like you to pull that punch."

"Huh." She stared at her drink. "That's what I get for hittin' the booze early."

* * *

Historically speaking, I get fired two or three times a year for finding bodies, body parts, and other infractions of the rules, none of which are written down anywhere, which I think is both wrong and prejudicial. This, though, was a banner year for Mort firings.

We headed back to barstools for more drinks and the five o'clock news. Ginger was back in the studio. A video had surfaced implicating Sylvia Haas in some sort of illegal activity, but details were being withheld by the authorities, as was the provenance of the video: yours truly.

Ginger's eyes sharpened as she said, "An unnamed source in the Reno Police Department indicated that the video might be a motive for that alleged murder-suicide at the Haases' residence this afternoon."

"*Might be* and *alleged*," Lucy said. "Good call, Ginger honey. Wait'll you find out the lieutenant governor had her psychotic boyfriend murder a lot of people, including the attorney general. That'll brighten your day."

We abandoned the bar again and went back to the privacy of our table. Ma hadn't heard much of what had taken place earlier that week, so it didn't take long for it to get around to the way Harper and I met, the gun she pulled on me, the iffy drive down the mountain on three tires, one of them squishy. That led to the stabilizing solution that kept the truck upright and steerable, which got more than its rightful share of commentary and girlish laughter. The talk then turned to Olivia Olsen, "Double-O," and clothes so wet they formed puddles, clothes in the dryer, then to my being forced to sleep in a too-small bed with Harper under conditions that might be considered unseemly in one or more Bible Belt soybean states.

"Forced," Ma said. "Right. In one room, one bed, and that old gal had your clothes. You might've come up with a way out of that, which reminds me of the Chickadee."

Oh, no.

"Chickadee?" Harper asked, lifting an eyebrow.

Ma told the story. She loves to tell it, but she doesn't embellish because it's a beaut all by itself. "To avoid having to further grope the left tit of a busty Hispanic girl in a bar in the town of Bend, Oregon—"

"*Further* grope?" Harper interrupted.

"Yep. The size of a cantaloupe was the report. To avoid it, Mort excused himself to the men's room, then squeezed out a back window, which was three sizes too small for a circus midget, and the Chickadee was already there in the back alley watching as he slithered out head-first. I believe she called him a shithead. That right, Mort?"

"Somethin' like that," I mumbled.

"Slithered," Harper said. "What a marvelous image."

"The point of the story," Ma went on, "is that Mort is inventive when it comes to avoiding certain things. Which he obviously didn't at Olivia's place."

"So I got lucky?" Harper said.

Ma smiled. "Not just you. *I* took that picture you saw in my office today. He doesn't always get off scot-free. I'm not convinced he doesn't choose when to run and when to stay put and enjoy himself." She toasted me with her drink. I thought about having Traci cut off her booze.

Then, of course, Harper had to mention the cosmic timing of Olivia returning our dry clothes as I was in mid-stride, crossing the room to retrieve a towel. I was six feet from the door when Olivia popped in.

"You lead a charmed life, boyo," Ma told me.

"Is that what it's called?"

"Olivia complimented me on my man," Harper went on. "One look and she told me I was a lucky little gal."

Lucy choked down a laugh and spilled a bit of her drink.

Aw, jeez. I got up. "Estrogen cloud's gettin' kinda thick here. O'Roarke's on duty now. I could use a buddy fix."

To more girlish laughter, I headed toward the bar.

O'Roarke saw me coming. He opened a Pete's and slid the bottle toward me. "Nice goin', spitfire. You found the attorney general. Beer is on the house for the next three minutes."

"My finding Leeman is old news. You're a day late and a dollar short, but thanks for the adult beverage. I'll take another beer in two minutes, thanks."

"I haven't seen you in a week. I'm catching us up on events and drinks. And good luck with that second beer."

Traci Ellis was still behind the bar. She came around the end and headed toward the women's locker room—the table I'd just left. "Gotta see what all the laughter's about," she said. "You guys stay put."

"Good luck," O'Roarke said to me. "She'll be back."

Which took three minutes.

"The *Chickadee*?" Traci snickered when she returned. "Oh. My. God." She had tears in her eyes.

She popped into a back room and I heard laughter so strangled it sounded almost like crying.

"Told you," O'Roarke said. "You might want to cut and run before she comes back, tell me about this Chickadee thing later."

I marched back to the table and plopped down.

"If we're done discussing my numerous shortcomings under duress," I said, "we can talk about my analysis of how Harper's car was disabled, then my finding the shaped charge Jake put on the radiator of my truck, which was—and it bothers me that *I'm* the one who has to bring this up—sheer freakin' genius, people."

"Granted," Harper said, "but not as interesting as the events in Grange."

I took another hit of Pete's Wicked Ale. "Okay, great, everyone here has seen me in the buff. Let's move on."

"*I* haven't," Traci said. "Uh, how's everyone doing with their drinks? Anyone need a refill?"

Sonofabitch. I was going to have to padlock a cowbell around that dame's pretty, intrusive neck.

* * *

We caught the six o'clock news to see if anything more had been added to the story. Nada, so we left the Green Room and took an elevator to the Golden View, the best restaurant the Goose had to offer, up on the thirty-seventh floor. Before I left the bar, Traci slipped me a packet of free drink coupons held together with a rubber band. I counted them later: fifty. O'Roarke was gonna be pissed.

The Golden View is Reno's only revolving restaurant, whirling around at the dizzying speed of one revolution every forty-eight minutes. I hadn't been in the place since I was there with Holiday when we were following Julia and her lawyer and lover, Leland Bye—both of whom had since shuffled off to their well-deserved rewards.

Reno slowly slid around far below as we ate a leisurely meal. Three of us had been on the move too much. Time to slow down and relax, eat good food, talk about things other than clothing issues. We could mull over Sylvia and Carl's demise later, and how much to tell RPD—*and* the FBI if and when they jumped into the game.

We took our time—the restaurant went around four times while we were there. We finally packed it in at 9:15, dusk, sun below the Sierras, pastel mauve and rose glow in the clouds to the west. The three women grabbed their purses and headed for the elevator. It figured the guy in the cape and the tights would get stuck with the bill, which came to well over two hundred bucks, with tip.

Ma left us on the second floor. She took an escalator down to street level to walk the mile back to her house. Lucy, Harper, and I went across the skyway to the parking garage and up two flights to Lucy's Mustang.

Lucy and Harper went around to the passenger side while I opened the driver's-side door.

"Hold it right the fuck there, Sally," Kyle said. "You two girls stay put. Nobody fuckin' move."

I turned. He was coming around the back of an orange pickup truck, fifteen feet away, shuffling closer. He was a hideous sight, hair in disarray, eyes bloodshot under the security lighting, half his left forearm missing. He had a man's necktie tied around his left bicep, a revolver in his one and only hand, centered on my chest. I caught a stench of decaying flesh.

Lucy and Harper were on the far side of the car. Kyle licked his lips, staggered slightly as he took a step closer to me, then looked past me at the girls.

"You two sluts get over here and stand next to this son of a bitch. Do it now. If you run, he's dead." He aimed the gun at my head.

"Mort!" Lucy yelped. I didn't turn to look at her, but I could tell by her footsteps that she was doing what the murdering bastard told them to do.

"No, Luce!" I cried. I lowered my center of gravity and lunged at Kyle.

His gun went off. A bright light filled my head and I stumbled backward into the side of the Mustang. From an interstellar distance I heard three quick explosive pops as I landed on the concrete floor. My vision went dark. From a million miles away, I heard one last sharp *pop*, then Lucy said, "Ow, ow, ow, *shit*!"

Then the darkness turned black and I was gone.

CHAPTER TWENTY-NINE

LIGHT, PALE AND frosted.

It went away.

* * *

It returned.

Good deal. I expected light. The Pearly Gates would have light, a sign on an alabaster post, maybe a set of rules, and maybe a password or a secret handshake to get in.

I didn't know the password. Well, shit. Who was in charge of handing out the damn passwords?

The light dimmed, faded to black.

* * *

Voices.

"What's the password?"

Hell, I don't know, I thought. No one told me. I wasn't in the loop. Which figured.

"You got a warrant?"

I laughed, maybe. Not out loud. You need a warrant to get past the Pearly Gates? Since when?

"I need a warrant? I'll get one if I have to, but do you really want to play it that way?"

Silence. Then, "It's C-L-i-n-v-#-2-1-3-5-@-L."

Hell. I'm supposed to remember all that? Although it did sound vaguely familiar. Maybe I would get in after all.

"That did it. Let's see what we got here."

I sank back into the depths.

* * *

I opened my eyes. Headache, and the lights were too bright, acoustic tile overhead. An IV bottle was hanging on a stainless-steel stand to my right. Drops of clear liquid fell into a see-through plastic tube. The sight of them made me thirsty.

"You're awake," Lucy said. "Oh, thank God."

So I didn't get in after all.

That probably meant I wasn't dead yet. A moment of disorientation dissipated slowly, then I croaked, "Water," or tried to. It didn't sound right, even to me.

"What, Mort?" Lucy's face floated above mine.

"Wa-a-r-r-t-r."

She held a cup to my lips. I drank a sip, saw a white bandage on her forearm. I lifted a hand, which weighed six hundred pounds, and touched it. "Wazit?"

"That rotten fucker Kyle shot me with his head."

I smiled.

So I wasn't awake yet. I still had a chance at the Pearly Gates, if only I could remember the password. I wished I'd written it down.

I slept.

* * *

Yum. Green Jell-O with shredded carrots in it. Not as good as the steak I'd had at the Golden View.

"When *was* that?" I asked.

Lucy frowned. "When was what, Mort?"

"When all of us were up in the Golden View eating real food."

"That was four days ago."

She was feeding me. Ma and Harper looked on. "That was a pretty good steak," I said. "I could use another one right about now."

"I'm sure it was. And no."

"In fact, it was steak and *lobster*, wasn't it?"

"Yes, it was. Have another bite of Jell-O, dear heart."

"A *bite*, Luce? It doesn't warrant chewing."

"Uh-huh. Eat."

"Yum, Luce. Green slime. Mmmm-mm."

"He's better," Ma said.

"Eat," Lucy commanded, trying to shovel another bite into me. "Open up. It works better than stuffing it up your nose."

So I opened up and ate. Yum.

"Why has it been four days, Luce? That's a long damn time."

"You've been in a medically induced coma."

I stared at her. "My first coma and I missed it?"

"Maybe not," Ma said. "Sometimes we can't tell."

Harper laughed. I had the feeling that the air of black humor in the room was a form of relief.

"Eat," Lucy said.

I pinched my lips together like I did when I was four. "Not until you tell me what you meant when you said Kyle shot you with his head."

She smiled. "You must've hallucinated that."

"Really?"

"Sort of."

"What does *that* mean? And what's *this*?" I touched the bandage on her right forearm. It was smaller than the one I'd seen earlier, but something had happened to her. Being her purported husband, I felt I had a right to know.

She sighed. "When that psycho shot you, I already had my gun out of my purse—that little .22 my dad gave me last year. I wasn't fast enough to stop him from shooting you, but I shot him three times in the chest before he could get off another round at you."

"You shot your dad?"

She bent down and kissed me. "Doofus. He went down but he wasn't dead and he needed to be dead, so I put the gun close to his left eye, pulled the trigger, and the bullet went into his brain, skipped around inside his skull, then came out his right eye and went half an inch into my arm."

"Bet that hurt."

"It did. Fuckin' Kyle."

"I hope you got rabies shots for that."

"Antibiotics, which I'm still on. But they checked for rabies."

Ma smiled. "He's makin' jokes. He's back. He's okay. We oughta sneak a steak in here. And a beer."

My kind of woman.

*　*　*

I wasn't dead after all, but according to more than one doc, it had been close. If the bullet had hit a quarter inch lower, I would've been pushing daisies by now. Kyle's bullet had split my scalp and grooved my skull, half an inch off dead center. For two days the docs had been monitoring my intracranial pressure. I was told I had been put on a ventilator and they'd hyperventilated me for eight hours, something I'd never done before. Lots of cool things had been going on while I was somewhere else.

But all good things must come to an end. By the fifth day, at 11:00 a.m., my intracranial pressure was chugging along nicely at thirteen millimeters, which probably meant something to someone, so my primary doctor permitted the FBI to interview me. As I discovered, when a person is the alleged front-runner to be the running mate of the front-running presidential hopeful for their political party, the FBI wants to be the front-runner when it comes to interviewing the guy who had apparently sunk deepest into the morass of kidnapping and murder bankrolled by that alleged front-runner—kidnapping being the FBI's forte and bailiwick because they're so good at it.

To grab all the credit, they wanted answers.

Their problem, however, was that I had been through several investigative wringers in the past two years: FBI, RPD, county sheriffs, district attorneys. I was tired, so I fell back on something I hadn't done before—I ran them off with the four magic words, "I want a lawyer," which is like yelling "bingo" or turning over a "get out of jail free" card—not that I thought I needed one. But I had blown off a guy's hand and left him miles from the nearest road instead of bringing him out, so I thought it best to hire a shyster to explain it in the kind of convoluted, polysyllabic language the feds would understand and appreciate.

I got them out of there, told them to come back some other time, maybe tomorrow morning, "don't call me, I'll call you." In the meantime, I told them, there was a movie showing at Century 21, something about a couple of rogue FBI agents that they oughta take in, pick up a few pointers. They left grumbling, as they do.

Before involving a lawyer, I wanted to know what the police had found while I'd been in a coma. Ma called Russ who showed up at

1:15 that afternoon, and in a closed-door session with me, Ma, and Lucy—Harper was in Carson City at her mother's funeral at the time—a session that included a chocolate milkshake for the patient, Russell told us everything the police had discovered before the feds waded in to take the credit. That turned out to be pretty much everything of importance since the facts were easy to find and the pieces of the puzzle slid into place as if greased.

We put it together like this:

Kyle Anza made it down to road number 265 alive, flagged down Arnold Becker's pickup and Arnold drove him to the town of Silver Peak. In Becker's house, Kyle stabbed him in the throat with an eight-inch kitchen knife. He then searched Becker's house and came up with a .38 special, not the most powerful handgun, thank God, since that's what he shot me with. The gun was registered to Becker. Early the next morning he drove off in Becker's old orange pickup. In Hawthorne, Nevada, he bought a burner phone at a gas station, filled the tank, and got to Carson City sometime around 10:45 that morning. The phone was found at the scene in the parking garage where Kyle was killed, as was Becker's antiquated orange truck.

Phone records showed that he'd called Sylvia Haas at her government office in Carson City at 10:52. Indications were that he'd followed her the twenty-some miles to her southwest Reno home and they arrived within minutes of each other. More phone records showed that Sylvia called her husband, Carl, at his medical office at 11:38. Witnesses at Carl's office said he left between 11:40 and 11:50.

Then things got sketchy, but clearly Carl went home where he took a 9mm bullet in the forehead in his living room from a CZ SP-01 automatic, a gun registered to him. The gun was found on the floor of Sylvia's office. She had been shot with it in the right temple—a contact wound, hence the early determination of murder-suicide, which was later upgraded to double murder.

The two deaths had taken place so close together in time that it couldn't be determined who died first, not that it mattered since it was likely Kyle killed them both in an effort to clean things up, or in an act of revenge. Or both, since he might've held them responsible, at least in part, for his missing hand, his brain-dead brother, and his lack of prospects for gainful employment in the future.

Kyle had put a GPS tracker on Lucy's Mustang when he kidnapped her and Harper in Goldfield. He'd installed a tracker app on Arnold Becker's cell phone with a code that worked with the tracker on Lucy's car, which is how he'd found us in the parking garage.

Kyle shot me with the gun he'd taken from Becker's place in Silver Peak. He left Carl's automatic in Sylvia's office with her prints on it to make it appear that she had killed Carl and then herself. A neighbor lady remembered seeing an ugly orange pickup truck in their driveway, very much out of place, so that put Kyle at the Haases' house—no surprise there, but it was good to get that nailed down.

At the Haases' residence, the video of Carl with the two girls was found on a computer in Sylvia's office. The so-called missing video that Annette Leeman gave to a family member that had caused all the trouble was still out there, if it existed. So far there was no sign of it. It might have been a lie to put pressure on Sylvia, Annette's last-ditch effort to save herself. If so, it hadn't worked. The video had cost the two teenage girls their lives, and the lives of Chase Eystad, Sylvia and Carl Haas, and the three Anza lads. Roll a boulder downhill and you never know how much damage it'll do before it comes to rest.

Phone records indicated that Kyle and Sylvia had been seeing each other for two years, probably as lovers, long enough for them to have developed a certain level of trust, which might have included a certain level of mistrust and mutually assured destruction, a kind of Mexican standoff that works something like relationship glue.

Russ didn't stay long. It took less than half an hour to give us what he knew that we hadn't heard before and to make sense of it. He took off, our secret agent on the force, sort of like Deep Throat back in the day.

Ma got on the horn and spoke to a criminal defense attorney, Ulysses Morgan Taber. With a name like Ulysses, how can you go wrong?

Taber showed up within the hour. "You're doing the right thing," he said in the first two minutes. "It's only half a joke that a grand jury could indict a ham sandwich—not something I've ever seen, but I won't be surprised when it happens. Not *if*," he said, "but when."

I liked him right away. He was in his fifties, stooped and slightly gaunt, with sharp blue eyes under bushy gray eyebrows, as if he were constantly on the hunt. When you hire a lawyer, you want a killer, so to speak.

"Who's my client?" he asked. "Best if it's just one of you, at least for now."

I raised my hand. "That would be me."

"Thought it might."

Taber laid it out: "I get four hundred bucks an hour out of court, twelve hundred an hour in a courtroom, if it comes to that—but from what I've heard so far on the news, I think a grand jury would be a laughingstock if they indicted you. And if the district attorney put your case before a grand jury, he'd be hard pressed in the next election since you're something of a folk hero. If we go to trial, I'd have the prosecutor's liver for lunch. That's all first-impression stuff. But let's hear your story and I'll tell you what I think then."

He thought it best if he and I were alone as I told him what had happened, but I told him they already knew everything I was going to tell him so even though attorney-client privilege didn't extend to them if I were the client, it didn't matter. He thought about that then shrugged, said something like, "Your funeral," which I think was lawyer humor, and we were off and running.

It took three hours, so telling the story cost us twelve hundred bucks and was worth every nickel.

I told him most of what happened in the basement at the Monroe Street house. I left Russ, Ma, and Officer Day out of it, didn't tell Taber how Jake ended up like he did or that he'd been shuffled around. Maybe it was the bullet he took in the neck, or Lucy's last blow with the hammer. Let the docs figure it out. It wasn't our problem.

"The nutshell version," Taber said, "is that the three of you were taken to that house against your will, threatened, barely escaped with your lives, Joe Anza was killed in the ensuing battle, and Jake Anza got what he deserved."

"That's about it, omitting a few ugly details. Like when Jake waterboarded Lucy."

Taber smiled. "Granted. I would like to see how Lucy got that noose from around her neck." He looked at her.

She stood up, kicked off her shoes, and lifted a foot up to her right ear, then used her toes to rub the back of her head. "Something like that," she said, sitting down again.

Taber's eyes were still wide. "Now *that* would impress a jury. Not that it'll come to that, but good Lord!"

I told him it was my decision not to tell the police after we escaped. We didn't know who the woman was who had hired Jake and Kyle. According to Jake, Kyle was on his way there, but if the police stopped him and held him for questioning, I didn't see anything that pointed enough of a finger at him to hold him—Jake yes, Kyle no. He would be released, he'd be on the loose and dangerous, and we still wouldn't know who the mystery woman was.

"He was out there anyway," Taber said, playing devil's advocate, as lawyers do.

"But he didn't know exactly what had happened in the basement. We knew he'd show up so we could follow him, hoping he'd lead us to the mystery woman." I told him I'd called Maude Clary after we escaped, that she had put the tracker on Kyle's car and we'd followed him to the Grand Sierra Resort. We left Russell and Day out of it. No need to get into any of that, especially Jake's little side trip to Ma's garage. Kyle wasn't in any position to tell anyone Jake was not in the basement when he'd gone in that morning.

Taber thought about what I'd told him. "You didn't notify the police after you escaped because it might have alerted the person you're calling the mystery woman. Which turned out to be Sylvia Haas."

"That's it, because of the timing. If she had a mole in the police department she might've taken off before Kyle had a chance to meet up with her, if that's what they were going to do. If *he* had taken off, disappeared, we wouldn't have known who she was and she would still be a threat."

He smiled at the word *mole*. "You didn't trust that the police or the FBI could—or *would*—tail Kyle Anza and keep it quiet if they held him for questioning."

"Would you?"

"No. The FBI is a 'bird in the hand' organization. Not a lot of self-control. Also, they could get a FISA warrant to surveil a ham sandwich, but that's an entirely different issue."

I really liked this guy.

"It's a bit convoluted," he said. "But considering your state of mind, collectively that is, it makes sense. I'll give it some more thought but I think you're okay."

He turned to Lucy. "Tell me how Kyle Anza kidnapped you and Harper, where he took you and how he held you."

So Lucy put in another two hundred dollars' worth, ending with her and Harper tied and handcuffed on a bed in the back room of the cabin, waiting for me to show up. She told him she heard Kyle call to me after I arrived, then more words and a loud bang, which she thought meant he'd killed me. She had cried. But then there was more talking that she couldn't make out so she thought I was still alive. I showed up soon after that, entirely naked, which, she told Taber, was why I'd had to blow off Kyle's hand the way I did since I couldn't hide a weapon. I let her tell all of that from her point of view.

"Naked," Taber said with a wry smile. "Talk about jury sympathy—not that this is headed that way." He looked at me. "Okay, I get the shaped charge, but where did you get the remote to set it off?"

"Jake had it on his belt. He took it off and put it on a work table in the basement. I took it when we left because I'd left the shaped charge where I could find it again."

"And you thought you might want it? The charge?"

"You never know when you'll want one of those. What if I had a window that got painted shut, wouldn't open?"

He gave me a long look, then tilted his head. "This'll never go to trial, but if it did there's no way I'd put you on the stand without a lot of coaching."

He turned to Lucy. "One question: Did Kyle Anza lift his gun at either you or Mort after you'd shot him in the chest with your .22 in the parking garage? He wasn't dead yet. Were you defending yourself or your husband when you just happened to shoot him in the eye?"

Just happened. I liked that.

"Yes, he lifted his gun at Mort again. I thought he was about to shoot. I was terrified."

Taber gave us each a look. "That's called leading the witness. In a trial, I couldn't do that. Remember what you said, Lucy. Especially about being terrified, which goes to your state of mind."

"Okay."

Taber turned to me again. "After Kyle Anza called you at the Goldfield Inn, you didn't tell the FBI that Lucy and Harper had been kidnapped. Explain why not."

"After everything Kyle told me, I didn't trust the FBI to save them before Kyle could kill them."

Taber smiled. "They'll believe that. A jury would too. Next question: You had your suspicions, but the first time you *actually* heard the name Sylvia Haas in connection with the two teenage girls or Jake or Kyle Anza was when you got the, shall we say, 'upper hand' on Kyle at the cabin, is that right?"

The upper hand. Cool guy, this Taber. I wondered if he would say that during a trial.

"That's right," I said.

"So your decision not to call the police after the events at the Monroe house worked, in a roundabout way."

I nodded. "Well put."

He smiled, then looked into a corner of the room for a few minutes, thinking. Then he stood up. "I'll give all of this more thought, if that's all right, see if I can punch a big enough hole in it to be a problem." He gave me a look. "For four hundred an hour, you understand."

"Cost doesn't matter," Lucy said.

Taber didn't respond to that, other than the corners of his mouth turning up in a little smile. I didn't know if he'd already checked us out and knew Lucy's net worth was in the neighborhood of fourteen million dollars. The interest on that alone could keep him thinking full-time for a year without touching the principal.

He shook my hand, then Lucy's and Ma's, said, "I'll be here tomorrow early, before the FBI rolls in."

Then he left.

* * *

The FBI showed up at 9:05 the next morning. Two agents, sporting short haircuts, cheap suits, darkish circles under their eyes, a professional lack of humor. Lucy, Ma, and Taber were present. Taber kept the FBI at arm's length and frequently interrupted the flow of their questions. His favorite disrupter was, "Already asked and answered, let's move on."

At 10:15 a.m. they threw in the towel.

"Je-*sus* Christ," said the shorter and squatter of the two—which might have been his way of saying *In God We Trust* since he actually said it twice. He glared at me. "You didn't say one thing we didn't already know."

"Shows how smart you guys are," I said. "Good job."

They left.

"Nice," Lucy said. "Nice boys. Their mothers must be *so* proud."

* * *

I left the hospital the next day. The FBI returned for rounds two and three, both of which took place in Taber's office. They didn't learn anything to excite them, so they wrote up their conclusions and that was the last we heard of them. The day they told us they probably wouldn't be back, Lucy, Ma, and I gathered in the Green Room to drink to the boys in the cheap suits. By then, school was back in session and Harper was back in Vegas, teaching English.

* * *

I never did catch up to Elrood Wintergarden. I mean, me, personally. I'd had more important things to do, Ma, too, so she told the will's executor, Stanley Brady, PLLC, that Elrood was still in the wind and that he should find another investigator to continue the hunt.

At Ma's suggestion, Stan hired Yancy Hubbard, who fumbled the ball, not that Elrood had made it easy, and not that Yancy wouldn't have fumbled it in any case. The four-week deadline passed and the money rolled over to those no-kill animal shelters. Yancy kept at it past the deadline, probably because he was being paid two hundred bucks a day, and Stanley Brady also fumbled the ball, failing to take Yancy off the case. As a result, Elrood learned, *five* weeks after the death of Mildred Castle, that he had lost out on six hundred eighty thousand bucks.

A month after that, I heard that he'd been arrested for fraud, pled guilty for a reduced sentence, and was given free room and board at the county jail for six months.

C'est la vie.

CHAPTER THIRTY

DÉJÀ VU.

Seven months after I first met Harper, the WNBR came off in March in San Francisco as planned. My second fresh-air tour of the City by the Bay wearing nothing but a smile, or what was going to have to pass for a smile, was gearing up to be much like the first except that I was told—*told*—that I wasn't going to wear a jock strap of red body paint or any other color.

"I'm not?" I asked. "Since when?" I was standing stark naked on a lawn, ready to get behind a veil of body paint.

"We took a vote," Lucy said. "No paint, not like before, but I'll write *For Jeri* on your back in her honor."

"I like the 'For Jeri,' but who's the 'we' who voted?" As if I didn't know, but I wanted it on the record.

"Harper, my mother, me, and Ma. It was unanimous among those of us who voted, in case you want to know."

"Who didn't vote?" I asked, picking up on a clue.

"My mother abstained, but she made a point of telling us that she wasn't voting no."

Lucy's mother was riding too. A naked side-by-side bicycle ride with the mother-in-law? How much more San Francisco is it possible to get?

"*I* didn't get a vote," I said, looking at Harper, then at Lucy's mother, Valerie, who smiled at me. Neither one had a stitch on. Val had turned fifty-five in June last year but looked thirty-five. Not your basic mother-in-law. She could be my younger sister. I tried not to look, but she was right in front of me, less than three feet away, so I wasn't having much luck with that.

"You would've if it had been a tie," Lucy said, "which it wasn't because, like I said . . . unanimous? Yours would've been a straw vote, so who cares? Turn around, big guy. It's so crowded here I can't get around you."

We were packed in like sardines, "we" being eighteen hundred riders of which about sixty percent were women, so that must've meant something, all of us crammed onto a lawn and a parking lot close to a Starbucks right on the Embarcadero. I turned around and Lucy wrote *For Jeri* on my back in dark blue paint.

The hair where the bullet had creased my scalp had grown in pure white. I had a white streak a third of an inch wide that Lucy said made me look kinda punk. In honor of this day I'd left it white, but otherwise I colored it. With all my scars and discolorations, it was getting more difficult to blend in, making some of my PI work harder.

Lucy was still writing on me when Valerie sidled an inch or two closer. "I haven't had a chance to really say hi, Mort, but it's so very nice to *see* you again." She gave me a wicked smile.

I stared at her. "*Bad* girl. Now I know where Lucy gets it."

She and Lucy both laughed. Harper bumped me with a hip and said, "Ba-boom."

Right then a guy lit off an air horn, announcing the start of the ride. He lifted a bullhorn and told the crowd to keep up, stay together, don't go wandering off unless you get dressed, that strays would be picked up by the police and thrown in a cell in San Quentin until the year 2035.

Funny guy, also naked, but it was hard to tell because he was sporting a uniform of body paint made to look like an SFPD police officer, which I thought was pushing things a bit.

We took off, which took a while. It's not easy to get eighteen hundred people going on bicycles. Lucy, Harper, Valerie, and I ended up about mid-pack.

Half a mile north on the Embarcadero, there was Ma, right where she'd been two years ago. She flagged us down, risking being run over by fifty riders, and made us stand in front of our bikes off to one side while she got pictures.

In *front* of our bikes. *Facing* her.

We were about to leave when she blocked my way and said, "Not you. Hold still while I get a few of you alone."

"Aw, c'mon, Ma."

"C'mon yourself. Stand up straight. Smile, and don't give me that 'I'm-about-to-throw-up' look, either."

Lucy, Harper, and Val grinned, and Harper gave me a bawdy wink.

"Good," Ma said. "Hold that smile. Got that one. Now say cheese and think pizza and beer."

"Aw, fuck. *Cheeeeese.*"

Ma smiled. "I'm gonna retire that old poster and put up one without body paint, boyo. That red jock strap has been buggin' me for two years. You're gonna look like Burt Reynolds in that *Cosmopolitan* centerfold years and years ago—better than, actually."

Well . . . *sonofabitch.*

I was gonna have to kill Ma.

PUBLISHER'S NOTE

Now that you have completed *Gumshoe in the Dark*, we hope that you have become a Mortimer Angel fan, joining *New York Times* best-selling author John Lescroart in his opinion of the *Gumshoe* series: "*Gumshoe* is by a large margin the best and most entertaining mystery I've read in at least the past couple of years. Rob Leininger captures the voice and heart of the classic PI mystery and manages to make it completely original at the same time. No small feat. And Mortimer Angel is my new favorite Private Eye."

The series starts with *Gumshoe*. Mort has just quit his thankless job at the IRS and is now a PI-in-training. Four hours into the job, he discovers Reno's missing mayor's body—make that the mayor's head—in the trunk of Mort's ex-wife's Mercedes. From day one, Mort's career careens out of control.

In *Gumshoe for Two*, as Mort is searching for the missing sister of a beautiful girl, he receives a FedEx package—inside is the severed hand of a U.S. senator. He's starting to build a reputation as the "finder of body parts." This time it has disastrous, heart-rending consequences.

Gumshoe on the Loose is the third in the *Gumshoe* series. Mort is hired by a young girl and as his investigation proceeds, he finds the body of missing rapper Jo-X in her garage. Another body found.

And this time, Mort picks up an alluring young assistant who will change his life.

Gumshoe Rock starts with the startling finding of a skull—stripped clean and white—dropped through the slit roof of his girlfriend's convertible. Grappling with this brings Mort to the most lethal situation of his life—so far. He's suffered incalculable losses in his short PI career, but nothing more horrifying than the trap embedded in *Gumshoe Rock*.

We hope that you will read all four of the "Gumshoes" that preceded *Gumshoe in the Dark*. And if you do, we promise you an enjoyable, humorous read in each, but—and this is a big promise—there will be an explosive ending in one of these novels that you will not forget.

Happy Reading!

Oceanview Publishing